DEADLY ARTS

A Shane Hadley Mystery

Ken Brigham

Secant Publishing
Salisbury, Maryland

This book is a work of fiction. Names, characters, businesses, places, events, and
incidents are products of the author's imagination or are used in a fictitious
manner. Any resemblance to actual persons, living or dead, is purely coincidental.

Secant Publishing, LLC
615 N Pinehurst Ave
Salisbury MD 21801

www.secantpublishing.com

978-1-944962-67-8 (paperback)
978-1-944962-69-2 (e-book)

Library of Congress Control Number: 2020904842

To the remarkable Zeitlins

By Ken Brigham

The Shane Hadley Mysteries

Deadly Science

Deadly Arts

Chapter 1

It was not a new thought, but it had grown more urgent over the years, now requiring, demanding, action. Why this particular night? Hard to say. If the required action was to have any real impact, then the time was short, the window of opportunity rapidly closing. But so what? The end result would be the same regardless of who seized responsibility—Mother Nature or someone else. What difference did it make?

To the intruder, it made all the difference in the world. The aging artist might be dying, but the intruder could not allow him to die with his evil unexposed. Mother Nature was being too kind to the old man, allowing his life to just slip away, peacefully, no punishment for his lifetime of heinous sins. The intruder would see to it that at least some degree of justice was done. Sins, once committed, cannot be undone. There must be consequences.

The intruder approached the Germantown house in the early hours, knowing the back door was never locked. The night was deathly quiet, the intruder thought, walking resolutely around the side of the house and entering the rear door—a person with a purpose. It was a noble deed, the intruder believed, a blow stricken for a right cause.

Like the larger outside night, inside the house was hauntingly still. Some pale rays from the street lights outside leaked into the empty hallway, giving the intruder barely enough illumination to find the door to the old man's bedroom and enter it. He lay in the darkness as quiet as the night, on his back, covered by a thin blanket. The intruder crept to the side of the bed and gently peeled back the blanket and top sheet. The artist did not move. Working quickly, the intruder folded the bedclothes neatly and placed them at the foot of the bed, exposing the naked old man.

The noble deed was easily done. Perhaps Fate shone favorably on one so determined to wrest a modicum of justice from the natural course of things.

The night was deathly quiet as the intruder left the house and returned home, mission accomplished. It had been a restless evening until now. For the rest of the night, the intruder would sleep soundly, the untroubled rest of an innocent.

Chapter 2

By the time Hardy Seltzer arrived at the scene, a modest crowd had gathered in the street in front of the house. Since the gentrification of the area of North Nashville historically known as Germantown, the graciously decaying ancient brick house that had served as both residence and studio for the artist with the unlikely name, Bechman Fitzwallington, for longer than any of the present residents of the area cared to remember, was, like its single resident, a curious anachronism.

Although he would have chosen different words to describe his reaction, the whole area was a curious anachronism to Detective Seltzer. The North Nashville where he grew up, granted a good bit deeper north than Germantown, was nothing like the teeming den of metrosexuals this area had morphed into. Hardy liked it better the way he remembered it.

He ducked under the yellow crime scene tape and climbed the short flight of stairs. The front door was open and some uniformed cops were milling around. Since it wasn't technically a crime scene (after all dying wasn't always a crime; it was more often a perfectly respectable mode of what Hardy's Oxford-educated friend Shane Hadley might have described as *shuffling off this mortal coil*), no murder scene investigation had begun. Even though Hardy was assigned to murder detail, he had not been sent there to formally investigate anything. His immediate superior, Assistant Chief Carl Goetz, had just charged him with rendering an informal opinion about whether there was enough evidence to indicate anything nefarious about the artist's sudden demise, before the powers-that-be decided whether to define this as a crime. Bechman Fitzwallington was well-enough known both locally and in the New York art world that news of his death would be news enough, and any hint of foul play would unleash a veritable media feeding frenzy. That would not please the city fathers. They much preferred to perpetuate the illusion that Nashville was a safe, vibrant, and creative community and that Nashvillians, even those in the north part of the city, were peace-loving folk who did not, unlike earlier denizens of that area, frequently bump each other off.

"Where's the stiff?" Hardy asked the uniformed officer guarding the front door.

"Bedroom," he answered.

"Anything funny about it?"

"Didn't see anything but haven't talked with the neighbors yet. Guy that called 911 lives next door. He's around somewhere. Skinny kid. Hasn't said much."

Seltzer started down the hallway toward the bedrooms. He was struck with how shabby the place was. Paint was peeling from the walls, and watermarks on the ceiling indicated a need for long-overdue maintenance. That seemed odd for an apparently famous artist whose paintings, according to what Hardy had uncovered in his brief search of the Internet, had sometimes sported six-figure price tags. He must have brought in enough dough to live comfortably. But this guy had been subsisting like a refugee. Maybe artists did that sort of thing, deliberately contrasting their lifestyles with those of the people around them. Maybe that was part of their marketing strategy.

Seltzer had no idea if that was the case. How the hell would Detective Hardy Seltzer, who had barely eluded the common fate of his deep North Nashville youth, know anything about how artists behaved? However they lived, it seemed to him that they died pretty much like everybody else.

The naked, cold, blue remains of Bechman Fitzwallington appeared to corroborate Hardy's internal speculation about how artists died. Vocation and pretentious name be damned, it was a corpse not unlike the countless such remnants of humanity that had been the focus of Seltzer's chosen profession for something in excess of twenty-five years. Another stiff.

The body lay uncovered on a brass-framed bedstead. The hands were folded across a generous expanse of stomach, and a hint of a smile tugged at the corners of a mouth that all but disappeared beneath a big bush of ivory-white moustache. Seltzer thought that recently dead people often appeared to be smiling. When he mentioned that once to Doc Jensen, the coroner's response was that as *rigor mortis* set in, there was often a contraction of the face muscles creating a sort of grimace/smile, set in stone once the process completed its task of transforming pliant human tissue into a rock hard stiff. Made sense to Seltzer.

"Anything been touched?" Seltzer addressed the rookie cop who had been assigned to babysit the scene until some decision was made about whether to investigate further.

"Not since we got here."

"So, what do you think, officer?" Seltzer continued. "Do you see any reason to suspect that we are looking at anything other than an old man who died in his bed without assistance from any of his fellow humans?"

"Except he's naked."

"Old guy. Lives alone. Maybe a commando sleeper. I hear artists can have some unusual habits."

Seltzer looked carefully about the room. Everything appeared to be in order. No sign of a struggle. No blood. It looked for all the world like the old guy had just taken off his clothes, lain down on his bed, and died without making much of a fuss about it. Not a bad way to get the job done when the time came.

"Detective Seltzer." Sue Smathers, another junior officer whom Hardy vaguely recognized, appeared at the door to the bedroom and called to him.

"Hi, Sue," Hardy responded. "What's up?"

"We have the fellow who discovered the body and called 911 upfront. And the old guy's daughter has shown up as well. Do you want to talk with them?"

"Sure," he responded, "I'll just be a few minutes here and then I'll come up. Can you put them in separate rooms and have somebody babysit them until I get there?"

"Right," she said and headed back down the hall.

Seltzer stood at the door to the bedroom and surveyed the scene again. "Did this guy just up and die, or did he have some help?" Seltzer asked himself. The scene looked so damned normal, ordinary even. An apparently extraordinary man who lay dead in an ordinary bed in an ordinary room in an ordinary house. Maybe incongruent, but a crime? Hardy Seltzer would need some different information if he was to reach that conclusion.

The skinny kid who hadn't said much wasn't a lot of help. The kid was himself an aspiring artist and often dropped in on Bechman Fitzwallington, hoping to learn something about how to make it in the art world and maybe even to wangle an entrée into the commercial side of the profession. The old artist seemed to have welcomed the visits of the young man from next door, although it wasn't clear exactly why. The old guy had apparently been of little artistic or commercial help to his neighbor.

"Did Mr. Fitzwallington have many visitors?" Seltzer asked.

The young man was probably thirty. A port-wine nevus spread amoeba-like across the center of his forehead, one tentacle extending along the right side of his nose. He was strikingly thin, and except for the deep red birthmark, his skin was pale, tending toward ash gray. He did not look well and fidgeted as the detective interviewed him.

"Oh, yes," the young man answered. "A lot of people were in and out. Some of them I recognized as other artists in the city. Some I didn't know. He was quite famous, you know. A wonderful artist. And a very nice man. His daughter is here. She came to visit him a lot and would know better than I who his other visitors were."

"Yes, I'll talk with her," Seltzer answered. "I'm sure I'll have more questions for you later, so if you'd give the officer here your name and contact information, I'd appreciate that. Also, here's my card." Hardy slipped a business card from his shirt pocket and handed it to the young man. "If you think of anything else that might interest us, please call me."

Seltzer didn't really expect the young man to call, probably hoped he wouldn't. But, hey, you do the drill, right?

The artist's daughter was a piece of work. Hardy guessed she was in her thirties and hopelessly suspended in a cocoon of perpetual adolescence. Too blond hair shaved on one side and streaked with a purplish color that Hardy had never seen associated with any kind of viable biologic organism. Multicolored tattoos with complicated designs but no apparent theme covered her body, most of which was exposed by an ultra-short skirt and halter top. She smoked a lavender cigarette with some determination, flicking the ashes on the floor, and dangled a platform sandaled (and elaborately tattooed) foot, oscillating it through a wide arc in front of her. She was unnaturally thin and probably pale-skinned, although it was hard to tell through the ink. Seltzer just didn't get the ink thing that seemed to mesmerize the youngsters. And then there were the piercings—ears, nose, lip, tongue that he could see and no doubt multiple other sites that were barely hidden from view. Okay. He'd been there before.

Hardy took his small pad from a shirt pocket and clicked the point out on his pen. He pulled up a chair and sat directly in front of the woman. He looked directly at her face, trying to penetrate the translucent glaze covering her olive-green eyes. Probably wearing green contacts. Another element of a façade meant to isolate her from whatever current realities were playing out in whatever space she occupied at any given point in time.

"Your name?" Seltzer asked.

"Salome."

"Salome who?"

"SalomeMe."

"Not Fitzwallington?"

She laughed, a sort of snorted snicker.

"Do I look like a Fitzwallington?"

"Hard to say," Seltzer replied. "You would be the first living one I've seen."

She laughed again. This time with a bit more energy.

"Oh, you mean dear Daddy," she sighed. "Daddy's been dying for a couple of years now, at least. Guess he finally managed to finish the job. About time, I'd say."

She flicked her cigarette butt on the floor and ground it out with the thick cork heel of her sandal.

"I gather the two of you were not close," Seltzer said.

"Close!" she spat. "Dear old Daddy was someone you chose to get close to at your peril, Mister Detective. You can ask anyone who knew him. I kept in touch but from as far away as possible. He was my father, after all, even if I hated him. But then there was quite a long queue of Bechman Fitzwallington haters who kept coming around for whatever reason. He was like that. A morbid attraction. Like his art."

Hardy was pretty sure that what he saw in this tough young woman's green eyes was hate, alright. She wasn't faking that.

"You say your father had been dying for a couple of years. What was wrong with him?"

"Don't know." SalomeMe fished a pack of cigarettes from her purse, shook one out and lit it with a Zippo lighter, the unnecessarily exuberant flame nearly singing a purplish tress that fell over her forehead. "I think he had some high blood pressure, but he was taking medicine for it and it didn't seem to be that serious."

Zippo lighter? Why not one of those little Bics? But then this woman provoked a lot of whys and why nots. A lot of unexplanations.

"Was he seeing a doctor?" Seltzer asked.

"There was a doctor that he'd seen who wrote the scripts for his blood pressure meds, but I don't think dear Daddy saw him very often in person. Dear Daddy wasn't fond of admitting that he needed anybody else's help with anything, including his health."

"Did he have friends, acquaintances? Many visitors?"

"Well, yes, he did," SalomeMe answered. "Mainly other artists. They all hated him but kept up some kind of association. Artists are funny that way, at least the ones I have known."

Hardy asked, "When did you last see your father?"

"I came by yesterday. He didn't look good but not much worse than he'd looked for a while. He was up and around."

Deep drag on the cigarette, the smoke exhaled with some force toward the water-stained ceiling. Eyes rolling. Tired of this shit.

"We about done here?" SalomeMe said.

"I'll need you to give me the name of his doctor and a list of the people that you knew he had regular contact with. I'll most likely need to talk with you again, so I'll need your contact info as well."

"Sure, honey," affecting an incongruous drawl.

"One last question," Seltzer drew his chair closer and looked again directly into her eyes. "Any chance somebody murdered your father?"

SalomeMe looked back directly at him and laughed. A hearty laugh that sounded as authentic as her hate had sounded earlier. For all the orchestrated externals, SalomeMe seemed to have trouble keeping up her façade of inscrutability. Must be hard to ink out feelings.

She swallowed the laugh abruptly and said, "There is every chance of that, if you mean is there a likely killer. A lot of people would have been happy to do him in, given the chance. Including me. But from what I saw of him recently, what would have been the point? Seemed like he and Mother Nature were taking care of the matter without the need of any outside help."

"Your father was dying before your eyes, and you weren't interested in knowing what was the matter?" Hardy shook his head, got up, walked over to a window, and looked out with his back toward SalomeMe.

She lit another lavender cigarette and said, flicking the ashes delicately on the floor before her, "That's correct, Detective." She paused for a moment to relish the warm rush of smoke filling her chest and the gentle nicotine flush, then continued. "You obviously didn't know dear old Daddy."

Hardy was through with this woman.

"You're something, SalomeMe. I'll call the meat wagon to pick up the remains of your 'dear old daddy,' and you can deal with the matter however you choose after that. Lotsa luck."

Okay, Seltzer thought. The old guy probably just died. He'd check with the guy's doc and maybe ask a few more questions of a few more people. And best wait for the obligatory autopsy results before going too far out on the often-deceptive limb of speculation. But he had been around the block enough times to recognize a crime scene when he saw one, and this one, strange as it seemed to be, didn't smell like murder.

As he made his way out of the house down the front steps and ambled toward the post-mature black LTD that, courtesy of the Nashville Metropolitan Police Department, had been his near-constant companion for several years now, he thought, "God protect us from the likes of SalomeMe."

Chapter 3

Shane Hadley could not remember when he first met Richelieu (nee Richard) Jones, the self-styled "Mad Hatter of Music City." Shane's affection for the man certainly dated from a long time ago, well before the name change and the incongruous Francophilia. Jones had been making hats in his Eighth Avenue shop for longer than anyone could remember. He had even presented Shane with a Sherlock Holmes-style deerstalker when Shane first joined the police force. The hat, still unworn, lay quietly on a shelf in the spare bedroom closet in Shane and KiKi's Printers Alley flat.

Now that he was a bit more comfortable manipulating the wheelchair without KiKi's help, on a nice day Shane would occasionally venture from Printers Alley out Broadway to Richelieu's shop. The two of them would chat about nothing specific, and Shane would amuse himself by inspecting the latest collection (*le recueil,* Richelieu affectedly called it) of hats (or *chapeaux* if one was so inclined).

Richelieu Jones was no longer a hat maker in the usual sense of the term. He considered himself an artist, not an artisan. He designed and created the unique chapeaux (there were upwards of thirty thousand reasons why he had both changed his given name and developed an affinity for all things French several years earlier; more about that shortly) favored by the more sartorially adventurous Nashvillians of all genders.

"*Bonjour, mon ami,*" Jones doffed his trademark lavender felt fedora, flashed a toothy smile, shot pinpoint asterisks of light from his deep brown eyes, and greeted his old friend as Shane wheeled himself into the shop. "And how goes the detecting business these days?"

"Cheerio, Richard," Shane responded. "I fear there is precious little detecting for me lately."

Shane remembered the time several years earlier when his own and R. Jones's lives had been coincidentally transformed by two unrelated, sudden, and unanticipated events. The stray bullet that took up residence in Shane's thoracic spinal cord still lived there and, although there was some recent improvement, the persistent paralysis of his legs kept his memory of that event very much alive. The power of a single stray bullet transformed Shane Hadley from the legendary Sherlock Shane of the Metro police into a wheelchair bound unemployed ex-detective.

On the same day of Shane's transformation, Mr. Richard Jones, self-styled *Mad Hatter of Music City*, received the results of the complete analysis of his thirty thousand genes done as part of a study for which he had volunteered at the medical center. It was the genetic revelation that his ancestors were French Canadian fur traders, rather than the Stewart County sharecroppers that he had always believed them to be, that transformed him. That fact actually changed who he was. He Francofied his given name. He bought a pocket French-English dictionary that he frequently consulted. And, determined to be true to his heritage, *Monsieur* Jones researched the old methods for making felt from animal pelts and expanded his hat-making business to include a laboratory at the back of the shop. He made his own felt for his hats, mostly from animal skins that he imported from

Canada. His newly discovered persona also awakened a latent creativity that influenced the design and construction of his line of hats, broadening their appeal. The elaborate Richelieu Jones signature inscribed on the inside hatband of each of his creations was now seen, not only in the Stetsons favored by the faux cowboys down on Lower Broad, but even in some of the elegant chapeaux that hung in the coat rooms at local country clubs. The power of a revealed genome transformed R. Jones from mad hatter to *Chapelier Fou* (At least that is the translation that Jones pieced together from his little French-English dictionary).

Shane thought that there was a particular bond between the two unlikely friends, which he attributed to the simultaneity of the events that changed their lives. Richelieu Jones had liked Shane long before those events and hadn't felt much different since. He didn't really think about things like that.

"How goes the hat business, Richard?" Shane asked, wheeling himself over to the large display case that fronted the shop space. "These specimens suggest 'tis the season for color."

"Indeed, *mon ami*, color indeed," Jones replied. "But do not overlook my glorious new styles. I'm experimenting with the complementarity of color and form. I'm quite pleased with some of these new creations."

Shane did think that the hats on display were striking deviations from Jones's usual collection and not an improvement. The brilliant array of rainbow colors was what caught one's eye at first, but then there were several bizarre shapes that did not conform to any category of hat that Shane had ever encountered. His old friend was braving an entirely new world of hats. Shane supposed that was creativity, although he wondered whether it was more like insanity. He couldn't imagine anyone he knew exchanging legal tender for one of these "creations."

"Well," Shane said, "they're interesting. I'll give you that."

Jones sensed Shane's lack of enthusiasm and frowned but didn't say anything.

There was a long pause in the conversation. Shane hadn't visited the shop in a while, and he looked around. The furniture had been rearranged and some touchup painting of the walls had been done. And Shane noticed an abstract painting hanging over one of the counters that he hadn't seen there before. He wheeled over to get a better look and saw that it was apparently an original oil. And the telltale initials BF were scrawled in the lower right-hand corner.

"Is this a Bechman Fitzwallington painting?" Shane asked.

Shane knew of the painter, had seen his art in various displays, but had never felt attracted to it. The uses of colors and the textures were interesting, but Fitzwallington's paintings to Shane's eye lacked an essential integrity. And there was a lot of repetition that appeared to him more like just copying than elaboration of a theme. But the critics liked the old guy. And not just the locals. The big-time New York critics were, for a time, gaga over B.F.

"Ah, *oui*," Jones replied. "I rediscovered it when I was rearranging things. Old Fitz insisted on using the painting to pay for a hat I made him many years ago. I tried my best to get the skinflint to pay me in dollars, but he claimed that the painting would, in due time, be worth considerably more than the value of the hat. I never forgave him for that, but he never returned anyway. Maybe he didn't like the hat. I discovered the painting stored away for all these years and thought I may as well hang it in the shop as a reminder that I am not in the bartering business. I expect to get paid in real money for my work!"

"I don't know the value of Fitzwallington's paintings for sure, but my guess is that he was right. Due time may have passed, and the painting may be worth a lot in today's market. You should get it appraised."

Shane felt his cell phone vibrate and took it from a shirt pocket, glancing at the screen.

"Sorry, Richard," he said. "I need to take this."

He wheeled himself into a vacant corner of the shop and answered the call.

While Hardy Seltzer had stayed in regular contact with Shane Hadley after the Bonz Bagley murder case several years earlier, they had not worked on another case together in the same way. Seltzer would ask Shane's advice on occasion over lunch or a glass of that special Oxford sherry of which Shane was inordinately fond, relaxing in the afternoon sun on Shane and Katya's Printers Alley deck, but Hardy was reluctant to involve Shane too deeply in his cases. Those were, after all, his responsibility. And he still felt some guilt about taking credit for solving the Bagley case even though Shane had absolutely insisted that the role of the paraplegic ex-detective in the case should be downplayed for the good of both Hardy Seltzer and the Metropolitan Police Department. Hardy still didn't feel right about that.

However, as he sat in his office looking out the window at the midday activity in the city square below, Seltzer wondered how Shane would interpret the death of Bechman Fitzwallington. The doctor who had seen the artist sporadically confirmed that he had prescribed some high blood pressure medication, but the old guy seemed to be deteriorating from an ill-defined condition. He wouldn't permit his doctor to perform the tests that might have pinned down the cause of his declining health. Seltzer had phoned several of the local artists who SalomeMe said frequented Fitzwallington's North Nashville house. Not one of them had much positive to say about the old guy, and one or two were downright hostile toward him. Then there was, of course, SalomeMe herself who had as much as admitted that she would have taken some pleasure in doing in her dear old daddy once and for all.

So, there were several possible candidates for the role of killer, but nothing Hardy could put his finger on that suggested the old guy was murdered. Looked like he just up and died. Still, Detective Seltzer had an uneasy feeling about the situation, and the higher-ups were pressing him for an answer. They would strongly prefer an answer that didn't implicate any of the city's citizens in illegalities, especially any members of the artistic community. The city was anxious to expand its artistic reputation beyond popular (mostly country) music, and nurturing the growing nidus of visual artists was an essential part of that effort. A conclusion that Bechman Fitzwallington had been murdered would trigger a scandal of major proportions that could derail the whole plan of the Nashville Arts Commission, no doubt raining down the ire of the city's most influential citizens on the heads of anyone arriving at such a conclusion. The last thing Detective Seltzer and his department needed was to bear the brunt of the city fathers' anger. No siree. Detective Seltzer was not about to trigger any such scandal if he could possibly avoid it.

But he was very conscientious about doing his job well, and so he was, as always, determined to go where the facts led him. The problem with this situation was that he didn't have many solid facts other than a dead artist who did not seem to be leading him anywhere specific. Dead people aren't an abundant source of information, except for what they don't say or what Doc Jensen divines from mucking about in their earthly remains. I need help, Hardy thought.

His landline phone rang three times before he answered it.

"This is Detective Seltzer."

"Ah, yes," the unmistakably affected Irish accent of Harold Whitsett Jensen, III, the Davidson County Coroner, intoned, "the ever effervescent Detective Seltzer. How are you, Hardy, my lad?"

Hardy usually trusted the pathologist's work but resented the feeble attempts at humor and steadfastly resisted his repeated efforts to engage Hardy in a long, and no doubt inane, conversation. Hardy didn't really like talking with the coroner at all except strictly for business. Hardy thought Jensen should stick to dealing with the dead and forget about trying to connect with the living. Jensen's career choice suggested that was his preference, but he seemed to have trouble recognizing the severe limitations of his communication skills and, as a result, kept trying them out on Hardy and probably the smattering of other living humans he had reason to connect with in the course of doing his job. The effort was wasted.

"What's up, Harry," Hardy answered.

"And how fares the good detective these days? Haven't heard from you in a while. Have our citizens given up their violent efforts to reduce their number? Where have you buried the bodies? My dear Detective Seltzer, I need bodies to ply my craft!"

He had a point. There had been precious few murders in the city of late, since the new chief of police had arrived. Hardy wasn't sure that the new chief had anything to do with it, but he didn't care who got the credit. Whatever the reason that local residents seemed less prone to mortal violence lately, that fact pleased a lot of people. Apparently, the corner didn't share that pleasure. Maybe he was worried about job security.

"Why are you calling, Harry?" Seltzer ignored the coroner's typical efforts at idle conversation.

"Well," Jensen replied. "You see, I finally get a body, but it comes with baggage."

"Baggage?"

"Yes, baggage in the person of one SalomeMe, as she calls herself, a be-inked and be-pierced young woman who claims to be the sole living relative of this body. She insists that neither she nor said body, her dead father, have any need of my services. She says you are handling the situation. Is that so? I mean, do we finally have a murder or not, detective?"

"Does that matter?" Hardy said. "Doesn't there have to be an autopsy regardless?"

"I suppose," the coroner replied, "that is technically true, but if there is nothing at all suspicious about the circumstances and the sole surviving relative feels strongly against the idea. You know, Detective Seltzer, I'm not comfortable with going ahead with it. If you say so, OK. Tell me to do it and I'll gladly whet my knives although I wouldn't look forward to dealing with the be-inked one. Just say the word, detective."

Sure, thought Seltzer, if I knew the word I'd gladly say it. What really bothered him was the word to say was obvious…too obvious. *Nothing so deceptive as the obvious truth.* Hardy remembered a favorite phrase of one of his early mentors in the detecting business. He couldn't remember which one. The phrase had stuck with him, although he wasn't generally enamored of paradoxes. He thought about that. Hardy Seltzer liked his conclusions sculpted cleanly from the bedrock of accumulated facts. He needed help with this one.

"Stall, Doc," Seltzer said. "I don't know what to tell you just yet. Give me a day."

"I shall give you a day, detective, if that is important," the coroner replied. "But I won't be able to fend off the be-inked one much longer than that."

Seltzer ended the call, immediately scrolled to Shane Hadley's mobile number, and rang it.

Seltzer briefly sketched out his dilemma to Hadley. They agreed to meet in the Printers Alley flat in an hour to discuss it.

Shane was genuinely glad to hear from Hardy, especially if it meant an opportunity to use his detecting skills. Those skills were feeling pretty rusty of late.

"Well, Richard," Shane said, wheeling back over to where the hatter was patiently biding his time admiring the collection of his colorful creations, "it may well be that your Bechman Fitzwallington painting has just undergone a major increase in value."

"*Oui?*" Richelieu queried.

"Mr. Fitzwallington has this day departed the land of the living, and there is nothing like the death of an artist to enhance the appreciation, and thus monetary value, of his work. Hang on to your painting for a bit and you may discover that it is a veritable gold mine. You may well be an incredibly lucky man!"

"What irony," the hatter replied, "making a buck off Old Fitz. I would never have expected that."

"I'm off," Shane said. "Always good to see you. Ciao."

"*Au revoir, mon ami,*" Jones called after Shane as the ex-detective wheeled himself out of the shop, headed up Eighth Avenue toward Church Street where he turned right toward the alley and his meeting with Hardy Seltzer. Those meetings had been too rare of late.

Richelieu Jones wondered why his old friend was in such a hurry to go. He walked over to where the painting hung and stared at it for a while. Cheap bastard, he thought. Good riddance! The self-styled Mad Hatter of Music City also thought that he would get the thing appraised. He would be perfectly happy to benefit from the postmortem inflation of the value of Old Fitz's dismal attempt at art. Richelieu had made the old fart a nice hat whether or not it was adequately appreciated. Way past time to get paid for his work.

Chapter 4

Dr. Katya Karpov flicked a stray lock of her long blonde hair from before her eyes. She sat in her office at the medical center, poring over the paper copy of a table of data that lay on the desk in front of her. The data were from a study of the aging brain that was a major research project of several faculty members in the Department of Psychiatry that she chaired. The study planned to follow a number of subjects for twenty years with repeated measures of a lot of health-related variables, including brain function, and they were approaching the halfway mark of the plan.

Dr. Karpov was especially interested in the outliers, a handful of subjects whose brain function pattern wasn't consistent with what was thought to be true about aging. There were some outliers in both directions—some better than predicted and some worse. She pondered that for a bit.

Her interest in the human brain dated back to her Oxford days. That's also where she was first struck with how important exceptions were in medical research. In any study, especially any study of human beings, it was the unexpected results that were the doors to discovery.

So, Dr. Karpov was looking for a pattern. Something the outliers had in common that might be a clue to one of Nature's secrets that, revealed, would unwrap other fundamental facts of human life like a

21

surprise gift at Christmas time. It was a fascination with the human brain that drew Katya to neurology as a profession, and it was the exhilaration of discovery that drew her like a magnet into an academic career. And the enduring expectation of discovery bound her to those choices, a bond almost as strong as the unassailable bond that tethered her to Shane Hadley. Those years in Oxford were where she met and fell in love with the American Rhodes Scholar and where she felt for the first time the exhilaration of discovery that infused her with meaning and excitement. That was the precise point in time and space when her life was transformed.

"Katya?" a gentle knock on her office door, always ajar, half inviting, half discouraging visitors. "Is this a good time?"

Katya looked up, "Of course, of course, Harold. Come in."

Harold Werth's body was very short and his head was very large. The ruddy skin of his face was pockmarked with the residua of a long-lost battle with teenage acne. His large head seemed always to be tilted forward as though he was constantly examining details of the floor before him or admiring the brilliance of his always glistening cordovan penny loafers. Any objective observer would have thought him a strange-looking little man, may even have been distracted by his unusual appearance. But Katya Karpov was not any observer. When she looked at Harold Werth, she saw a brilliant geneticist. She had eventually convinced him to join her faculty after a prolonged academic courtship, not to mention a doubling of his, admittedly modest, salary as a stellar investigator in the Human Genome Project at the National Institutes of Health. Werth was in charge of analyzing the genome data from the subjects in the aging study. There was no one on the planet more qualified for the job and he brought to the task the bonus of a special skill in explaining the data to his non-geneticist colleagues.

Katya motioned Werth to the chair opposite her desk.

"Thanks for coming down on short notice," Karpov said. "I just wanted to get your take on the genome analyses from a few of the subjects in the aging study. There is a handful of outliers from the functional data, and I'm dying to know if there's an explanation; I sent you their study identifiers earlier. Genes are a good place to start looking, don't you think?"

Werth smiled, "Of course I think that. Genes are my life. If they aren't the answer to all of the burning questions in human biology, it's not their fault. It's just that we don't yet understand the whole picture. We'll get there, Katya. We'll get there."

"You know, Harold," Karpov replied, "if there is any person in the world who could convince me of that, it would be you. But while you and your guys are figuring out the genetic details, the nature angle, I'll spend some time and effort pondering the nurture side of the equation."

Although Dr. Karpov was a neurologist and thoroughly grounded in hard science, she was fascinated by the persistent mysteries of human biology and had difficulty toeing the hard science line that understanding humanness was ultimately no different than theoretical mathematics or quantum physics; they were all at root just numbers games. She didn't buy that. There were too many unexplained phenomena. While she was not religious, she was convinced that there was something spiritual about being human that the geneticists would never explain. Even the most brilliant ones.

"So, what about these outliers?" she continued. "Tell me you've discovered the outlier gene, you clever man."

"Well, not exactly," Werth said. "Still need to crunch some more numbers, but so far, I don't see any clear genetic patterns that they have in common. There are some hints, but nothing solid so far. It's pretty simplistic to think that outliers in any direction would have the same cause, even if it is genetic. Don't you think?"

"Probably," Katya said, "but I wouldn't rule out the possibility that whatever the cause for being way outside the norm, it might be a basic tendency. Just a gene for abnormality, greater than normal variability, whether good, bad, or indifferent. Is that imagining a genome that's too creative?"

Werth fidgeted in his chair for a few moments, then said, "That seems a strange concept to me, but then I've seen some pretty strange concepts turn out to be true."

So right, my friend, Katya thought. She trusted Werth's work specifically because he was rarely absolutely certain about almost anything. In human biology, the important answers are never binary—yes/no, black/white. There are a lot of maybes, gray areas to deal with, and the investigator who knows that has much the better chance of discovering something important. Why not a genetic basis for variability, a kind of *uber* gene that injects uncertainty into the sequence of events connecting DNA to flesh and blood reality? Katya didn't see why that possibility should be forbidden territory.

"When will you be finished with the analyses?" Katya asked.

"Shouldn't be long now. We have all the sequencing done, so we just need to get the computer to crunch the numbers."

"Can you put these outliers at the head of the queue?"

"You're the boss. Say the word, and it'll be done."

"The word," Katya smiled.

After Harold Werth left, Katya continued to stare at the table of data. Of course, there were no names and little personal information about the study subjects; participants were promised as much anonymity as possible. That was standard practice as a protection against any use of the health-related information that might hurt the subject. But there was a column on the data sheet with a one-word description of occupation/profession. Katya perused that column for the outliers. There were fifteen outliers, two whose functional data indicated that their brains were aging prematurely and thirteen who were clearly functioning better than the average. The occupation of one of the poor performers was listed as "artist" (that subject had withdrawn from the study a couple of years back) and the other was listed as "artisan." Ten of the thirteen high performers were listed as "artist" and one as "artisan."

Given the low frequency of these occupations in the general population, it seemed more than coincidence that those were the occupations of all of the outliers. So maybe this was a pattern, Katya thought, but not a very distinct one. She wasn't surprised that the brains of artists might function differently than the brains of most folks, but she would have thought that exercising the creative process would preserve function. How about the two poor souls who had done worse? An artist and an artisan. She needed more personal details about these outliers. But that might require compromising the promise of anonymity. She'd have to discuss that possibility with the ethicists and the Institutional Review Board, the panel of experts that kept a close eye on human research. Okay, she would do that. But, maybe wait for the final word from the genetic studies before getting too excited about chasing down the details of a possible role for nurture.

The outliers continued to haunt Dr. Karpov as she left the office and headed for the medical center parking tower. She relished the throaty purr of the Boxster as she cranked it up for the drive downtown. The weather was nice, so she retracted the top, and headed out onto Twenty-First Avenue toward town and the Printers Alley flat. As always in the afternoons, she anticipated some private time with Shane at the end of the workday. She still worried about Shane. She also needed him more than she liked to admit.

Hardy Seltzer and Shane Hadley sat on the deck overlooking Printers Alley, nursing their third glass of Lincoln College sherry. As was his custom, Shane had taken the satin-lined case of crystal Oxford sherry glasses down from the shelf behind the bar and carefully polished two of them before opening a new bottle of the wine, placing the glasses and wine on a bright silver tray and wheeling himself out onto the deck where Hardy waited for him. It had taken some time for Hardy to cultivate a taste for the sherry, but Shane had been a patient teacher and with time, Hardy had become an eager enough student. They now shared in the pleasure afforded by the special wine surreptitiously imported from Shane's old Oxford college as medical supplies by his lovely and attentive wife.

The intensity of the two men's conversation addressing the subject of murder had increased as their blood alcohol levels had crept up into the slightly euphoric range, but the specific question of immediate concern had not been clearly resolved. That question was: "Did the available facts surrounding the death of the moderately famous Nashville artist with the unlikely name, Bechman Fitzwallington, arouse enough suspicion of foul play to warrant a murder investigation?"

Although it might be expected that the answer to such a question arrived at by two slightly inebriated murder investigators would be a foregone conclusion, in this case, that was not true. There was much to consider apart from the facts directly related to the artist's demise. The possibility of some severely unpleasant consequences of such an investigation was real, a fact that had been pounded into Hardy Seltzer's brain by Assistant Chief Goetz, who had phoned the detective twice already in the short time since the artist was discovered dead. Goetz was getting flak from the new chief, and although Seltzer was a full three tiers south of the chief on the org chart, well, you know, stuff rolls downhill. The new chief was extremely sensitive to the importance of city politics to his security in that position. He didn't hesitate to imply that the job security of the rest of the department, especially the people he had inherited, might also be jeopardized by political insensitivity regardless of the length of time they had spent in the department's employ. There was nothing to gain and much to lose by inviting a scandal. Bad idea! A distinctly bad idea!! Shane Hadley understood that. He had been there.

"So, Hardy, my man," Shane said, "let me summarize. You have a dead artist of some note. Although you have no cause of death, there is evidence that the deceased artist was not well, had apparently been dwindling for some time. You saw nothing suspicious about the death scene. But, the deceased was not widely loved, and several people of his acquaintance, including a daughter, flesh of his very own flesh, are sufficiently pleased with his demise that any one of them might have welcomed the opportunity to assist his exit from the land of the living. And, we cannot ignore the fact that to raise the possibility that our artist was murdered would displease your superiors and other influential people in the city. Is that an accurate summary of the situation?"

"That's about it. Shouldn't be too hard a problem for you," Seltzer smiled and sipped his sherry.

"Well, it is, of course, not technically my problem, but I'll do what I can, my friend. Easy for me to advise, since you and your colleagues will own the consequences. In my current situation, I am, to my everlasting good fortune, insulated from consequences. I was never very fond of such things, you know, consequences, intended and otherwise, collateral damage, those sorts of things. Preoccupations with such are distracting and serve no useful purpose."

"Maybe so," Hardy replied, "but you also lose the credit on occasions when you have a right to it."

He was still bothered by the Bonz Bagley case.

"Ah, credit!" Shane said. "A greatly overrated concept. I say Caesar's to Caesar, God's to God, and the detective's to the detective, a title to which, alas, I no longer have a legitimate claim."

"If you say so." Hardy's comment did not sound very convincing.

"But," Shane continued, "what we need here is more information and perhaps a touch more sherry as well." He drained the last few drops from the bottle of wine into their glasses. "When will you have the postmortem results?"

"May be a problem there," Seltzer answered. "Harry Jensen's balking on the autopsy."

"What seems to be the problem? Jensen's job is to do the post. Tell him to do his job."

"Yes, well," Hardy responded, "unless we declare it a possible murder case, Jensen is reluctant to deny the wishes of the person who seems to be the artist's only living relative."

"And that would be?"

"That would be the daughter. Calls herself SalomeMe. Don't ask me why. Also, don't ask me what possessed the woman to pierce and tattoo her not so young body in every available location. In fact, you needn't ask me to explain almost anything about SalomeMe. Waste of time even thinking about explanations for such as her," Seltzer said, wagging his head awkwardly from side to side.

It was not hostility that Hardy Seltzer felt toward the woman. It was just that he was genuinely baffled by behaviors like hers. Hardy liked clear reasons for what people did. Irrationality distracted him.

"Hmmm," Shane rubbed his chin and wheeled himself over to the edge of the balcony, looking down at the people passing below. "While I agree that there doesn't seem to be anything very substantive about this situation that suggests murder, I still detect a faint odor of something amiss. An autopsy might clarify things. Since there is no explanation for the man's death and we have no witnesses to the event, you could probably demand an autopsy if you chose to without committing to the murder thing in advance."

"Yeah," Seltzer replied, "that's probably true. It's just that neither

I nor Harry Jensen is anxious to take on Ms. SalomeMe without being fully armed for what would be, I am certain, an unusual and not very pleasant encounter."

"A charm offensive, my good man. You should marshal your considerable interpersonal skills to convince Ms. SalomeMe that her father's autopsy is in her best interest. It could be, you know."

"I suppose I could give it a try," Hardy answered. "But what if the post is negative? Do we declare it death from natural causes and move on? That would please a lot of people. A different decision would please almost nobody, including me."

"A negative autopsy would certainly diminish the faint odor of something amiss," Shane said. "Would the odor disappear altogether? Hard to say, my man, hard to say."

Katya Karpov was still thinking about her table of data from the outliers, so that she forgot to turn into Printers Alley. She drove right past the big arched sign that marked the alley's entrance. She drove on down Church Street then, realizing what she had done, turned right on Second Avenue to Broadway, around the block, and back up the hill for another try at going home. As she approached their building, she saw that Shane and another man were sitting on their balcony apparently engaged in a serious conversation. Probably Hardy Seltzer, she thought.

Katya thought that Shane's relationship with detective Seltzer was good for him, for the most part. She didn't understand Shane's fascination with crime, but she respected it. It had been a while since Seltzer had come by, and Katya wasn't sure why. Shane hadn't mentioned anything about the detective lately. So, a part of Katya Karpov was pleased to see the two men together again. Another part of her was disappointed that she might have less private time with Shane this evening than she had hoped for.

Chapter 5

The near-skeletal visage of Blythe Fortune confronted an email that appeared unsolicited on her computer screen.

To: bfortune@galleriasalinas.com
From: athenagolden@avantart.com
Subject: Bechman Fitzwallington inventory

Blythe,

You may have heard that BF was discovered dead this morning in his Nashville home. We are making an effort to locate his unsold paintings and determine who has them. His death may obviously affect the value of his works. Is your gallery interested in handling whatever BF works we can locate that are for sale? We at AvantArt have had a few of his later works consigned to us in the past, and we understand that there are other works in possession of either BF's estate or his daughter (those may be the same) and should be available for sale. The circumstances of his death remain unclear, but as you know, this is not an unexpected event. I am contacting you because of your success with selling BF's works in the New York market.

Let me know asap re: your interest.

Best

Athena

Blythe pondered the message. Evening was just starting its stealthy trek up from the dark East River. The FDR traffic was starting to build. Blythe had come home to her Sutton Place penthouse earlier than usual, but as was her habit, she had kept a close eye on her emails. Although this message was not unexpected, it came sooner than she had anticipated. Her communication with the Nashville folks had been pretty infrequent lately. Fitzwallington was the only Nashville artist her Upper East Side gallery had handled, and in the past couple of years, interest in his art had waned as had the quality of the paintings. BF was old and it had certainly crossed Blythe's mind that his health might be deteriorating. She thought that might even prove to be a boon to sales of his art. She had observed that once the quality of their work began to decline, artists were generally more valuable dead than alive.

Blythe needed to discuss this with her partner, Bruce Therault. She was the art expert, but Bruce was the business guy, and she depended on him in situations like this. They had discussed the Fitzwallington issue over the past year or so, and he would have some valuable thoughts about how the gallery should respond to these changing circumstances. She seemed to recall that Bruce had mentioned something about that in the past.

She fired off an email.

To: btherault@galleriasalinas.com
From: bfortune@galleriasalinas.com
Subject: Bechman Fitzwallington

Bruce

I just learned from the AvantArt people in Nashville that BF was found dead in his home there today. They were inquiring whether we would be interested in handling whatever works of his that are available for sale. They haven't done so well for us

lately, but his death could change that. What do you think? Can
we discuss soon?
   Let me know.
   Blythe

Blythe stood up from her computer, walked across the large room to the east windows, and looked out. The expanse of windows on that side of the apartment afforded a broad view of the river and across to Roosevelt Island with a penumbra of Queen's skyline peeking over from behind. A sliver of afternoon sunshine had somehow managed to wend its way from the west side through the darkening maze of the Manhattan glass and concrete forest to dab a gentle smudge of *contra luce* near the far riverbank. The early fall sky was just inviting in the coming night.

Blythe wanted a cigarette. She had quit the habit a couple of years earlier, but the desire for a smoke was as strong as it had ever been, and she occasionally yielded to it. She rationalized that an occasional cigarette was surely harmless, and it could sometimes take the place of food. Food was a major issue for Blythe. When she first quit smoking, she gained weight and hated herself for it. Blythe Fortune had taken the *never too rich or too thin* New York dictum to heart, and while her considerable financial assets did not yet reach the level she aspired to, she dealt with the thin part of the equation with near-religious zeal. She would, by damn, be enviably New York thin no matter what! If the occasional cigarette helped out, all the better. Efficient. She liked efficiency, two birds, single stones kinds of things.

She admired her sharp cheekbones and pencil thin silhouette in the mirror over the small writing desk as she retrieved a cigarette from her stash in the desk drawer. She glanced at her computer screen on her way to the river-view balcony, her usual smoking spot; she never smoked inside the apartment. She sat down in front of the computer and read the new email.

To: bfortune@galleriasalinas.com
From: btherault@galleriasalinas.com
Subject: Bechman Fitzwallington
> *Yes, Blythe*
> *I heard of BF's demise and am pondering what that means for the gallery. Are you free tonight? We could talk over dinner. There is some info you don't have. Could be substantial $$$.*
> *Bruce*

Some info I don't have, wrote the ever-provocative Bruce Therault. Blythe walked to the balcony and lit the cigarette. She leaned on the balcony rail, she inhaled deeply and relished the familiar sensation of warm smoke suffusing her lungs. She pondered her partner's suggestive message. She was used to Bruce's fondness for what she thought of as *mysterious opacity* in his emails, but the practice still frustrated her. She fished her cell phone from a jacket pocket and rang Bruce.

"Blythe, my love, thanks for calling so promptly," Therault answered, noting the caller ID and dealing immediately, as was his custom, with the matter at hand. "An early dinner at the bar at Felidia, okay?"

"Sure, Bruce," Blythe answered. "No hint about your mysterious info?"

"All in due time, my love. All in due time."

He ended the call.

Bastard, Blythe thought. She stubbed out her smoke and went back inside. She was not fond of mind games. She felt a spark of anger. If it reached a flashpoint, the meeting with Bruce was likely to be less than optimal. Her labile temper got in the way occasionally.

It was a nice evening. She would take a leisurely stroll for the few blocks up Sutton Place to Fifty-eighth and across to Third Avenue, where awaited the lovely restaurant, her often exasperating business partner, and very likely an ice-cold, bone-dry martini. That should calm things down.

"What were you and Hardy talking about?" KiKi asked Shane.

They sat on their balcony as the day faded toward black. KiKi drank liberally from her bottle of Voss sparkling water, and Shane, realizing he had overdone the sherry a bit, had made a pot of coffee and nursed a cup, black. He was drifting back into sobriety as the day drifted toward night.

"Well, KiKi, it seems that the artist, Bechman Fitzwallington, was discovered dead in his Germantown home this morning, and Hardy has been assigned the task of determining whether his demise merits investigation as a possible murder. We were exploring that question."

"And did you arrive at an answer?"

"Not exactly," Shane replied. "Something doesn't feel right to me, and I think to Hardy as well, but there are some potentially unpleasant consequences of dealing with it as a murder. And there is no clear yes or no answer or if there is we haven't figured it out yet."

"Aren't there always unpleasant consequences of dealing with murder? If you mean politics, well, since when do you let politics decide what you do?"

Shane thought that KiKi sounded like she was itching for a fight, and that took him by surprise. He was in no mood for a fight. He was never in the mood for a fight with KiKi, because those were fights he was destined to lose, and he studiously avoided engaging in unwinnable battles. His wife did not, as a rule, pick fights. Something was troubling the good Dr. Karpov, and it probably had nothing to do with him.

"KiKi, love of my life," he said, "so tell me what's happening in that magnificent brain of yours."

"Outliers," she said, heaving an uncharacteristic sigh.

"Outliers?" he asked.

"You know," she continued, "observations that aren't what you expected. Why do those things seem more important than the observations that confirm your suspicions?"

"Like the dog that didn't bark, you mean," Shane harkened back to a telling observation by his favorite detective.

"Something like that. Just today, I was reviewing some data from our long-term brain function study and pondering some outliers. Your reference to Bechman Fitzwallington reminded me of that because a lot of the outliers are artists."

"Well," Shane responded, "I guess artists tend to be outliers in more ways than one. Are you saying they are smarter than the rest of us?"

"That's the interesting thing," KiKi said. "Some have way better brain function and some way worse. Outliers in both directions."

"So you have a dog that didn't bark and a dog that barked too much. Hmmm. I guess either one could be a critical clue. Perhaps you're right. Perhaps it's the fact of an outlier, that an aberrant observation exists, that is the clue rather than the direction of the aberration."

"That's what I'm thinking, but it troubles me. I even wondered whether there is something like a variability gene. An enzyme or something that exaggerates normal variability in a few people and so creates these pesky outliers. That sounds pretty strange to my brilliant geneticist colleague. But I still wonder about it."

Shane sighed, "Does everything have to be explained by genes?"

"I don't think so," KiKi answered. "But I may be in the minority among my hard science friends."

"Not a bad place to be," Shane replied. "I find that I identify more easily with the less popular positions on many things. As I say that it sounds undemocratic, but the emotions of the masses can be frightening…and not uncommonly wrong-headed."

"I suppose you're right, but forever swimming against the current can be exhausting."

"Doing anything forever is exhausting, my love. Except, of course, loving my beautiful and brilliant wife."

She smiled.

"To minorities," Shane said, lifting his coffee cup and clinking her water glass.

"Indeed," she said, "to minorities indeed."

Hardy Seltzer was cold. The autopsy room at the city morgue always chilled him to the bone. It chilled him because the actual temperature was kept way below anything even remotely comfortable for living humans and also because just being in that place, the palace of the dead, chilled his soul. In spite of that, Detective Seltzer made a habit of attending the autopsies that were in any way relevant to his cases. The reasons for that were complicated. They included a need to convince himself of some concern for the departed. He needed to believe that there was something humane about what he was doing, even when the humanity of the players involved could be seriously questioned. His part in the big picture, maybe less than noble, was still necessary. And it was more than a job. A calling? Maybe.

That's what Detective Hardy Seltzer was thinking as he stood shivering next to the dead body of Bechman Fitzwallington. The remains of the artist were being unceremoniously carved up into their component parts by Harry Jensen, an annoyingly garrulous faux Irishman whose position as Davidson County coroner granted him license to mutilate the bodies of his fellow humans who were unfortunate enough to turn up dead. Dr. Jensen enjoyed his work. Detective Seltzer did not enjoy observing the spectacle. The coroner was well-aware of that fact, and he sometimes worked more slowly than necessary just to annoy Seltzer.

"So," Seltzer said, "what do you think?"

"Entropy," Jensen said, "the inevitable consequence of human biology's programmed obsolescence."

"You mean like natural causes? You don't see any other explanation?"

"Natural causes," the coroner harrumphed. "Such an inelegant phrase. And so imprecise. But, yes, I'd say natural causes as the term is commonly used is as good an explanation of Mr. Fitzwallington's demise as we dare venture to postulate at this point. It appears to have been a timely death."

"No chance of foul play?" Hardy wanted to be sure he understood exactly what Jensen was saying.

"Not based on what I see here," Jensen replied. "There could be something in the brain, but we won't know for sure until it is sufficiently preserved to slice open and view its interior. The exterior of the brain didn't look particularly suspicious, just looked like an old brain. But there could be some secrets inside. And of course, I'll review the microscopy of some selected tissues. And we'll have the lab run some toxicology screens. But, my dear Detective Seltzer, I will be surprised indeed if we uncover any serious suspicions of malfeasance. Does that frustrate your finely-honed investigative instincts?"

Seltzer ignored the coroner's question.

"Just out of curiosity," Seltzer said, "how did you deal with SalomeMe? How'd you get her to agree to the post?"

"Ah, my good detective," the coroner replied. "As much as I would adore attributing that accomplishment to my native charm and exceptional wit, I cannot take the credit. It was quite strange, in fact. She called from her home to say that she had changed her mind and now agreed to the autopsy. I even asked her to come in to sign the permission form, and she agreed. Just blew in, signed the form, and was off again to wherever the be-inked ones gather to amuse themselves with explorations of the outer boundaries of acceptable behavior."

"Strange, indeed," Hardy thought.

Hardy decided to stop for a beer and to touch base with Marge Bland on his way home to his East Nashville apartment. The seedy bar previously known as the Dew Drop Inn had recently gestured to the city's rampant gentrification by renaming itself TAPS. Otherwise, it hadn't changed much. Marge still worked the afternoon shift at the bar. Hardy maneuvered the government-issue post-mature LTD down the hill toward Broadway and turned left into the small parking lot that was now bathed in neon red radiating from the spanking new giant TAPS sign. He wondered at the all caps, wondered if the name was an acronym for something. He'd try to remember to ask Marge.

Three men sat at the bar. They didn't seem to be together, just guys who happened to wind up sitting next to each other. They were strangers to Hardy, although he thought that one of them looked vaguely familiar, like someone he might have seen in a crowd someplace. They were dressed too well for regulars, but it was harder to identify the regulars lately. The complexion of the Nashville population was changing as all kinds of people wandered into the city looking for something most of them would not find because it wasn't there. Some of these neoNashvillians gravitated to places like TAPS thinking to discover some authenticity that was buried too deep beneath a dense layer of neoNashvilliana to be accessible to strangers. People who came to the city wasted a lot of time and energy searching for the substance of a myth that, if it ever existed, had long since fallen victim to political realities, wrecking balls, and the profit motive.

Hardy took the seat that Marge Bland kept reserved for him at the end of the bar. With a carefully practiced flick of her slim wrist, Marge slid a frosted Pilsner glass of Bud Light down the bar that came to rest directly in front of him. He lifted the glass, tipping it toward Marge, and took a long swallow.

Marge was occupied resupplying the drinks of the three strangers and making small talk with them. The TV above the bar was tuned to the local news, and Hardy looked at it for a few minutes as he waited for Marge to finish shaking it for the paying customers. There was a segment on the discovery of Bechman Fitzwallington's dead body and some footage of the exterior of his home with the yellow crime scene tape. The only statement about the cause of death was a quote from the Chief of Police who said that there was no evidence of foul play but that a preliminary investigation was underway to determine whether that was a possibility. Hardy's name was not mentioned.

I should call Shane, Hardy thought.

Chapter 6

Bechman Warren Fitzwallington, nee Billy Wayne Farmer, was born in 1929 in Clarksville, Tennessee, the only child of a house painter father and a homebody mother who worked occasionally as a housemaid.

Shane Hadley read from the artist's Wikipedia entry. He had awakened early, got out of bed without waking KiKi, and wheeled himself up to the front of the flat. He made a pot of coffee and fired up his laptop, basically biding his early morning alone time by exploring at least superficially the person of Bechman Fitzwallington. He had no real purpose in mind. It was just that since the artist seemed to be a current topic of interest, he decided to see what he could find out about who the man had been.

Shane learned some interesting things about the artist from Wikipedia and from the www.bechmanfitzwallington.com web site. The name change was interesting, especially the strikingly pretentious adopted name vis-à-vis the strikingly ordinary actual one. It wasn't clear when the name change occurred or whether the change had been made legal or was more like a *nom d'artiste*. Shane thought that names often said something important about the persons who owned them and wondered whether Billy Wayne Farmer suffered an identity crisis somewhere along the way to where he wound up.

Could be. He wound up at a very different place than where he started, and it was pretty clear from early on that his life path was not likely to be linear. It was not difficult to imagine a right angle-zig or a left-angle zag in his path, a *Damascus road* kind of epiphany, that suddenly altered his life course and perhaps, as Damascene epiphanies sometimes do, changed his name as well.

Little Billy Wayne was apparently mesmerized by his father's house paints and started messing with them from the time he was mobile enough to navigate the short path from the back door of his house to the paint storage shed. His father would leave cans containing small amounts of unused paint there for Billy Wayne to play with. The kid's life direction appeared to have diverged from any reasonable expectation of him at the time of his first encounter with house paint. He became entranced with the colors, textures, and feel of that particular paint, and he never got over it. The love of house paint changed the course of his life, or so the Internet sources seemed to think.

And that might well be true, Shane thought. Apparently the artist had used a paint formulated much like the house paint of his youth for essentially all of his work. The short period when he experimented with the oil and latex paints used by most artists, produced, according to Wikipedia, his least appealing pieces. After the brief foray into the more commonly used media, he returned to his house paint formula and stuck with it for the rest of his career; it wasn't clear exactly what the formula was or where he got it from.

Shane found all of this particularly interesting, although he had no idea why. After all, the nature of the man had little relevance to the reality of his current state unless one's inclination toward things spiritual was greater than Shane's. Once ended, lives could be interesting as historical artifacts, backstories, but dead was dead. His interest was in how the dead happened to arrive at that state—

especially whether they accomplished the task with or without the aid of one or more of their fellow human beings—but not in what, if anything, happened to them before or after the terminal event. Truth be known, there were precious few living people who interested Shane Hadley and he had no interest at all in the imagined world of human spirits.

The vibrating cell phone in his breast pocket broke the spell of Shane's idle introspection. Caller ID announced Hardy Seltzer as the intruder. Shane had not known Hardy to be an early riser, and he had certainly never called Shane at this hour. Shane sounded surprised and genuinely concerned as he answered the call.

"Hardy, my man," he said, "are you alright? My impression has been that this hour rarely finds you conscious."

"Nothing's wrong that a gallon of strong coffee couldn't cure. I'm working on that. I meant to call you last night but got distracted."

"A pleasant distraction, one would hope," Shane replied.

Seltzer did not answer the implied question. He generally avoided answering questions about his private life from Shane or anyone else. He had his reasons.

"Jensen did the postmortem on the artist last night," Seltzer said.

"And?"

"To quote the coroner," Hardy answered, making a feeble attempt to mimic Jensen's faux Irish accent, "the cause of death was *entropy, human biology's programmed obsolescence.*"

"Natural causes."

"Right. Well, the results from cutting open the brain aren't known yet, and they'll do some microscopy and tox tests, but nothing suspicious so far."

"Hmmm," Hadley mused. "How sure of that was he?"

"Sounded pretty sure to me. Said he'd have a look at the inside of the brain, do some random microscopy and have the lab do a tox screen, but he expected those things would be negative. Jensen thought the artist was just an old guy who had reached the end of his rope."

"So, what will you do with this information, *detective*?"

The hint of sarcasm in Shane's emphasis on his title registered with Hardy, and he winced.

"Look, Shane," he said. "I don't really have a choice. Goetz is getting grief from the higher-ups, including the chief, and God only knows who is breathing down his neck. Absolutely zero evidence of foul play? Cut and dried. As cut and dried as answers ever are."

"Of course, you are correct. But we both know something doesn't smell right. Too many loose ends. Too much unexplained. Just too bloody much weirdness to write it off without further inquiry."

"Maybe so, and I know what you mean. But I can't sell it to my boss. I'm sure of that."

Shane wheeled himself out onto the deck. The sun was just beginning to stripe the alley with the morning lattice of bright white that greeted early risers on clear days. There was a lull in the conversation, each of the detectives thinking to himself. Finally, Shane spoke.

"How long can you stall your people?"

Hardy sighed, "I'm sure Goetz'll be on my case this morning. I don't see how I can delay giving him the obvious answer. What's likely to happen that will change things?"

"Of course, you're right," Shane paused again, still pondering the situation. "Could you come by my place this afternoon, after the dust settles a bit? And bring whatever information you have about this case."

"Case? Not really a case, is it?"

"Please humor me, Hardy, my man. I am accustomed to classifying the things that interest me as cases. Things work better for me that way."

"See you at three."

Hardy rang off.

Shane immediately called a very old number. Although the number had gone unused for several years, since the unfortunate encounter of Shane's thoracic spinal cord with an errant slug from a fleeing perp's handgun, the number was still stored in the list of contacts in Shane's cell phone. It was early, but worth a try.

"Wall Street," the still familiar voice of Pat Harmony answered the call.

"Hello, Pat," Shane replied. "I suspect that your stock of Lincoln College sherry must surely be depleted by now. How about if I drop by after a while with a fresh supply?"

"Son of a bitch," Harmony said. "Son of a bitch. Am I witnessing the resurrection of Sherlock Shane Hadley? Son-of-a-bitch."

"That seems to be a distinct possibility, my long-neglected friend," Shane said. "I'll drop by your place later on, and we can fill in some very long blanks."

"Son of a bitch," Harmony repeated.

When Pat Harmony retired from his long career as a beat cop with the Metro Police Department, he realized a lifelong dream by opening a bar. It was a small place. The entrance was in an alley that ran off Church Street. Because it was sort of near to a financial center and hoping to attract the lawyers, bankers, and their like who haunted that area of town during the daytime and early evening, Harmony named the bar Wall Street. The clientele he actually attracted was mostly cops, ex-cops, and cop wannabees. But Wall Street had done okay, and Pat Harmony was about as happy in his retirement as a cop like him was capable of being.

Before Shane's accident, when he was a high rolling Metro detective, he adopted Pat Harmony's bar as a sort of informal work area, his Wall Street office he called it. Shane made regular deliveries of his favorite sherry to the bar, and Pat kept a stash of it hidden away for the private use of the locally famous detective. The arrangement was good for business and Shane found the ambience of the place favorable for pondering the complexities of whatever challenge he was facing at the moment. Back in the day, most afternoons would find Shane sitting at his regular spot at the end of the bar facing a glass of sherry and either chatting with Pat Harmony, discussing a case with one of his colleagues, or peering intently at the notes in the small leather-bound notebook that he used for keeping information about his currently active cases.

A sudden stroke of abysmal luck ended all of that. Shane's paralysis, his retirement from the force, and his self-imposed isolation severed his connections with the world beyond Printers Alley for a long time. But he felt the strictures relaxing some lately. The renewed friendship with Hardy Seltzer and their collaboration on the Bagley case seemed to crack open some doors that Shane believed his trauma had sealed shut once and for all. And he was a bit more mobile than he had been for a long time. Wall Street was only a couple of blocks from the Alley. He could manage that. And creeping into the margins of his brain was the bare hint of a suspicion that there just might be a plausible excuse for reopening the Wall Street office. He smiled to himself at the possibility.

Shane wheeled himself back inside and over to the bar to check that he had a fresh bottle of sherry to deliver, as promised, to Pat Harmony. As he was retrieving a bottle and setting it on the bar, KiKi wandered into the room, yawning and still in her silk robe. Her hair was disheveled. She looked beautiful to Shane, as always. She went into the kitchen and emerged with a cup of coffee.

"At the sherry a trifle early this morning, aren't we, Shane?" she said.

She curled up in one of the leather chairs that faced the fireplace, tucked her legs beneath her, and cradled the warm coffee cup in both hands.

"Good morning, my love," Shane responded.

KiKi noticed that Shane's laptop was open. She was aware of Shane's reliance on Wikipedia for information and didn't think much of the popular website as a source.

"What are you looking for in the large and largely fabricated world of unexamined mass opinion?" she asked.

"Exploring the artistic temperament," Shane answered. "Maybe perusing an outlier's back story. You raised the outlier issue and I keep thinking about that."

"The Fitzwallington guy. Should have known. I sense a case is afoot. Is that it?"

"Actually, what this very morning will no doubt be declared a non-case is what may be afoot, my love. Perhaps just the thing for a non-detective to take on, don't you think?"

"When it comes to decisions about your choice of activities, my dear," KiKi responded, "I have long since determined to have no opinion. I have never had the slightest idea why you choose to do what you do, so I don't waste time thinking about it."

"You are a wise woman, my love."

"Not sure about wise, but hopelessly practical," KiKi said.

She sipped her coffee and stared off into space, obviously operating on early morning autopilot. She was thinking about those other outliers that were trying so desperately to tell her something, deliver a message that she could not yet decipher.

The morning sun painted a bright magenta stripe across the East River on its way to the broad windows of a Sutton Place apartment and through them to illuminate the fair face of a sleeping Blythe Fortune. She had slept fitfully after a disconcerting evening at the

Felidia bar with her business partner. She had also overdone the martinis in a valiant and ultimately unsuccessful effort to dull the edge of her anger enough to allow the interaction with Bruce to be civil.

It hadn't gone well. She came away from the meeting still essentially ignorant of the "info" he had alluded to earlier. Something to do with a connection with Fitzwallington's daughter in Nashville that he had been working on for a while and which he thought would give Galleria Salinas an inside track with whatever paintings there were that could be sold. Given the intervening events, those paintings should command a premium. Bruce said that there were a good many paintings that should be available to them, although he did not disclose how he knew that or much at all about what these Nashville "arrangements" were and how they had come about.

Blythe often felt uneasy about Bruce's failure to keep her informed about his doings vis-à-vis the gallery. She didn't press him too much because they had enjoyed a financially successful partnership that she didn't want to upset. But he made her uneasy. And sometimes, like last evening, he also made her mad. Bastard!

Hardy Seltzer's prediction of what Assistant Chief Goetz would say that morning was spot on. Hardy's phone rang shortly after he ended the conversation with Shane. Hardy wasn't ready yet to take on his boss mano-a-mano and so he checked the caller ID and did not answer the call. Instead he decided to get dressed and go to work as usual but to go directly to Goetz's office and address the issue.

The Assistant Chief called Hardy's cell phone twice more before Hardy could get to his office. This guy just needs to take some deep breaths and try behaving like a sane person for a change, Hardy thought. Anyone in a managerial role in the metro department who was wound too tight was not likely to survive very long; the job would eat him alive. Goetz was one of only a handful of the department hierarchy who had been brought in from the outside by the new chief. Time would tell whether those guys would be able to figure out how to survive. But Hardy had seen bosses come and seen bosses go and however things turned out, he would still be there, doing his job as best he could. He had never had a boss who made his job easier.

"Answer your goddam phone, Seltzer!" the assistant chief greeted Hardy as he walked, unannounced, into the office.

"Yes sir."

"The Mayor, the director of the arts council, and three councilmen have been on the chief's back this morning. The guy is raising hell and I can't get a detective to answer his goddam phone. That's not acceptable behavior Seltzer. Not acceptable. Do you hear what I'm saying?"

"Yes sir."

"Yessir, yesssir. Is that all you have to say for yourself?"

"Yes sir," Hardy answered again.

He was determined to avoid a shouting match with his boss but couldn't resist delivering a small prick of the verbal needle.

Goetz got up from behind his desk and strode to the window that overlooked the square. His face was a color somewhere between aubergine and fuchsia and he was obviously hyperventilating.

Hardy was in control.

"I assume, Assistant Chief Goetz," Hardy said, his voice firm and steady, "that you are still interested in my opinion about the circumstances of Bechman Fitzwallington's death?"

Goetz wheeled around to face Hardy and started toward him but hesitated and said, "Sarcasm doesn't work with me Seltzer. You're going to learn that, apparently, the hard way."

Hardy ignored the comment.

"Yes sir," Hardy said, then continued. "The Fitzwallington

autopsy, at least the gross part, was completely negative according to the coroner. I don't see any reason to suspect foul play. I recommend against any criminal investigation. I hope that helps to calm the situation for you"

"Of course it will calm the situation, Seltzer. So why couldn't you just tell me that on the phone? Why the melodrama?"

"With all due respect, sir," Hardy answered, "I don't think I created the melodrama. I just thought that a matter that was obviously so important to so many people deserved a face to face resolution. I am sorry you don't agree and apologize for my error in judgment."

"You're a smartass Seltzer. I don't like smartasses."

"Nor do I, sir," Hardy responded.

Chapter 7

Hardy Seltzer was more than an hour late getting to Printers Alley for the promised rendezvous with Shane Hadley. Seltzer had spent much of the afternoon assembling all the relevant information that he had about the death of Bechman Fitzwallington. He had made several phone calls and taken extensive notes. He also dropped by the coroner's office and picked up a copy of the autopsy report. He hadn't looked at it yet.

Although he had been able to get some more specific information about the artist's contacts, what he had just didn't add up to anything resembling a coherent narrative of the events that led up to the old man's death. What he had, Seltzer thought, was a list of facts and observations that bore no clear relationship to each other...no common thread to tug on that would unravel the mystery. If, of course, there was a mystery to be unraveled. If there was, Hardy didn't see it. It would be interesting if Shane saw something Hardy didn't. While that would cause Seltzer to feel some disappointment in himself, he would not be completely surprised. He had no illusions about the relative detecting skills of himself and Shane Hadley. He was okay with that.

"Here's what I have, Shane," Hardy said. "It's not much but I haven't had much time."

Although it was a nice day, the two men had ignored their usual spot outside on the deck and settled in the living room. Seltzer had spread the contents of a manila folder that he had brought with him on the coffee table. Shane had not offered him a glass of sherry as was his custom when they met in the afternoon nor had he offered a reason for not doing so. Hardy thought that Shane was less animated than usual and maybe looked a little pale around the gills.

Shane shuffled the papers about to no apparent purpose.

"Can you give me a summary of the material and how you put it together?" he asked.

"Sure," Seltzer replied, "although I'll have to pass on the putting it together part. I haven't had much luck with that so far."

"Okay, just summarize what you have," Shane sounded a trifle impatient.

"From the daughter I got the names of three local artists of some note who visited Fitzwallington with varying frequency. Daughter wasn't sure the reason, since all of the three frequent visitors were known professional and probably personal enemies of the old guy."

"Hmmm," Shane said, "hmmm. And said daughter has no inkling of reasons for the visits? Wasn't she curious about that? Was she leveling with you?"

"The curiosity of SalomeMe is bounded by the margins of her ego, I suspect," Hardy replied. "Leveling with me? I seriously doubt she ever levels with anybody including herself."

"Yes," the wheels were starting to turn for Shane. "What else?"

"I talked to the doctor he had seen in the past but that was little help. He said the old guy had some high blood pressure and the doc had prescribed medication for that, but that he appeared to be going downhill for reasons that had gone unexplored since the patient refused the necessary tests. As far as this doc knew, Fitzwallington had had no medical attention in a long time."

"I see," said Shane. "Any other information about visitors, activity at his home, other associations?"

"The young man who lives next door and who discovered the body did say that he had seen a couple of new people visit the house recently. Thought one of them must be from out-of-town although he didn't say why he thought that. The other one lives in the neighborhood but was not, to this kid's knowledge, friendly with the artist. Maybe something to follow up there, not sure."

"Tell me more about the regular visitors."

"Well," Hardy answered. "Apparently there were three locally successful artists who came by with some regularity—a painter, a sculptor, and a ceramicist or whatever you call somebody who does ceramics. Not clear what business they had with the old guy but they seem to come around fairly often. SalomeMe gave me some contact information for them but she says they were never her father's friends. Of course, she thinks her father was incapable of friendship with anybody. 'A real shit' was her short description of her father's personality."

"So, we've got some starting places."

"Starting places?" Hardy queried. "I guess I considered this a stopping place. That's sure how my bosses see it."

"That may very well depend on one's vantage point, I suppose."

Hardy was a practical man. He was clearly hands-off anything more to do with Bechman Warren Fitzwallington, nee Billy Wayne Farmer. That much was a definite message from his department. He was troubled by the tone of Shane's comment. What the hell was Shane suggesting? Was he thinking of going at this solo? Surely not. Given his physical limitations, how would he go about that? Those were questions Hardy really didn't want to know the answers to. He had no business knowing anything about any potential solo efforts on Shane's part, much less participating in any off-the-record investigative stuff. So, Hardy didn't ask Shane anything more about whatever he intended to convey by his suggestive comment. No sir! And Shane did not elaborate.

"This stuff is all copies of the originals," Hardy said, gesturing toward the material splayed across the coffee table. "I'll leave it all with you. Of course, you will protect your source if it comes to that. Look, Shane," Hardy walked toward the windows at the front of the apartment and stared out at a flashing neon sign across the alley, "I'm not sure what you're thinking, and I don't want to know. My only request, and I can't be too clear about this. Whatever you have in mind, deal me out. I obviously care a lot about solving murder cases, you know that, but my realities are different than yours. If this is a murder, and I repeat that I see no evidence for that, it will not be solved by me. I want no part of it."

A philosophical response to his friend's declaration formed in Shane's mind. He started to speak, and then caught himself. There was a long pause as the two men looked at each other.

"So be it, my man," Shane said, reaching up and clapping Hardy on the back. "So be it."

The relentless exhortations of the sleek-headed and remarkably buff physical therapist, Mike Borden—push it Shane; harder, harder; of course it hurts, ignore the pain—had significantly improved Shane Hadley's physical strength and thus his ability to navigate in the larger world that surrounded his Printers Alley refuge. Those Monday morning sessions with Borden were pure agony, but Shane could feel results. That and KiKi's insistence on the potential value of the therapy kept him doing it. He did not look forward to the ritual flagellation by Borden, a helluva a way to start the week, he thought. But he was stronger.

Those were Shane's thoughts as he wheeled himself with minimal effort up the Church Street hill toward the alley behind the bank where sat the Wall Street bar. An unopened bottle of Lincoln College Sherry was nestled in his lap. The afternoon was sunny and warm, and Shane was looking forward to renewing his Wall Street connection and getting reacquainted with the bar's proprietor, his old friend, Pat Harmony. If he was honest with himself, Shane would also have to admit he felt some exhilaration at the prospect of investigating the murder of a notable Nashvillian. Of course, Hardy couldn't get involved; he was essentially prohibited from that by his superiors and by the politics. But as his friend had said, the two of them had separate realities. And the more he thought about this case, the more certain he was that something was awry. Too many unexplanations. Something might be, indeed, afoot.

"Sherlock Shane," Pat Harmony boomed as Shane wheeled himself through the doorway that opened directly from the short alleyway into the barroom. "Sunnuvabitch…son-of-a-bitch!"

The old cop grabbed for his cane that he had propped against a liquor cabinet and maneuvered himself out from behind the bar and across the room. He bent over and embraced Shane so vigorously that Shane's wheelchair started to roll backward and Harmony almost fell into the detective's lap.

"Whoa, Nellie," Harmony yelled, Keith Jackson-like, as he regained his footing and rebalanced himself with the cane. "Welcome back to Wall Street, Shane," draping an arm across Shane's shoulder. "Been too long…too damn long, my friend."

Shane had forgotten Pat Harmony's tendency to over-exuberance and was taken aback by the vigor of the old policeman's greeting. He rescued the bottle of sherry from his lap and held it up to Harmony, hoping to distract the ex-cop from his apparent need for physical contact. It was not that Shane was opposed to physical contact where appropriate and consensual, but this situation didn't meet those criteria.

"Thank you, my man," Shane said. "The sherry, here's my special sherry as promised. I trust you will treat it with care."

"That particular spot in the cupboard is still unoccupied. I'll put it there under lock and key and reserve it only for you or whoever you say." Harmony held the bottle up and examined the label. "Is this stuff legal?" he asked.

"I think it would be unwise of you to insist on an answer to that question, my man," Shane smiled broadly. "You can never tell when the gendarmes will come calling with potentially embarrassing questions concerning the wine's provenance."

"I aim to keep on good terms with the law, my friend. But whatever you say," Harmony chuckled. "I'll treat it carefully."

"See that you do," Shane replied. "See that you do."

Shane gently extricated himself from the grasp of the old cop and wheeled over to the bar. He sat for a few minutes remembering his history there. He had mostly tried not to ponder that history, his life before the accident. He wondered as he sat there whether this was such a good idea. Could it be that he was kidding himself and was about to attempt something that was patently futile? Was he hoping that by renewing the trappings of his old life as Sherlock Shane, that long-dormant persona would miraculously emerge, genie-like, from his broken body?

Pat Harmony, leaning heavily on his cane, hobbled back to his post behind the bar. He appeared to sense that Shane was pondering the place, maybe remembering, and so he didn't say anything for a while. He stashed the bottle of sherry in the cupboard that really had been empty since back in the day.

"So, how about it, my friend?" Harmony finally said. "Just say the word and we'll resurrect your Wall Street office. That spot at the end of the bar's never been put to such good use since those days. Don't worry about the wheelchair. I'll take out a stool and put in a platform with a ramp so you can just wheel right up to the bar and do your thing. Anytime you want. Your place. Might even make a plaque or something to mark the spot. Love to have you back, Shane. I'd love that. Old times."

Shane wheeled himself across to the end of the bar and sat there quietly. Mind wheels churning, both inviting and steeling him against a flood of memories of his life when his legs worked right. Old times. Gone for good.

It was early in the afternoon, before Pat Harmony usually opened the place, but he had left the door unlocked and a man came in, walked to the bar, sat down and surveyed the situation without saying anything. Both Shane and Pat Harmony looked at him, wondering.

A stranger to both of them. Probably a stranger to town. He just had that look. Like he was comfortable enough anywhere but this wasn't familiar territory and so he was comfortable enough but still tentative. Casing the joint. Taking his measure of the place and the two people before deciding on a course of action.

"This where the cops hang out?" the stranger said.

"Some do," said Pat Harmony. "Like a drink? A little early but we can handle it."

"So where are they...the cops?" the stranger said. "Out chasing after people who're killing off your local artists? Stupid idea, you know. You southerners," he continued, "just can't help self-inflicting wounds. Just keep doing it. But an artist? Them's unencumbered bucks, my friend. Golden goose. Dead? Not good for this town...any town."

"Uh, mister," Pat said, more than a little annoyed at this guy's tone, "are you looking for an audience or do you want a drink? As you can see there's not much of an audience here, but we do have booze. You a Yankee?"

An antiquated term, even for Pat Harmony, but the visitor's tone sent him dredging in the further reaches of that lingering North-South dichotomy, a territory not often explored but not completely unfamiliar. There when the occasion called for it.

"If you mean do I hail from north of the Mason-Dixon Line, I plead guilty. If, as I suspect, your pejorative term means something more than that, you've probably got the wrong label."

"I presume," Shane had quietly wheeled over toward where the stranger sat and parked, unnoticed, behind him, "you refer to the late Bechman Fitzwallington. Are you an acquaintance?"

Surprised, the unexpected visitor pivoted the barstool around to face Shane. Shane noted the man's receding hairline and the dark ravines sculpted beneath his eyes, bottomless half-moons no doubt etched there by some serious life experiences. His nose was too large for his narrow face and sharp chin. His mouth was small and its default position was slightly open, like a door left slightly ajar, exposing the tips of opposing rows of perfectly spaced and well-aligned but very small yellowish teeth. He wore a nicely pressed but inexpensive dark suit, no pocket square, and a black tie with turquoise stripes tied in a Windsor knot that was loosened over the unbuttoned collar of a white shirt with magenta pinstripes. Shoes. Comfortable shoes of a man who was prepared to walk a lot. Cop shoes. Stylishly brown. Tarted up a bit, but still cop shoes.

"You might consider me an interested party."

The accent. Probably New York.

"I might. Then again I might consider you someone else altogether." Shane looked directly into the man's bland gray eyes. "The coincidence of a suddenly dead artist and the arrival of an 'interested party' from elsewhere must surely tweak one's imagination. Don't you think?"

"Can we stop this dance?" the stranger said reaching to shake Shane's hand. "I'm Mace Ricci, New York."

"Shane Hadley," smiling and clasping the visitor's hand just long enough to get an impression of its strength and texture, an informative but decidedly perfunctory gesture, intended not to convey too much.

Pat Harmony reached over the bar as Ricci turned halfway around to address the bartender. They shook hands.

"Pat Harmony," he said.

"And your interest in the activities of our fair city's police force?" Shane asked.

"Are you a cop?" Ricci asked, in no hurry to explain himself.

Another unexplanation; they seemed to be accumulating.

"You might consider me an interested party," Shane said.

"So, *interested party*," Ricci smirked, "did somebody bump old BF off or did nature do it for us? Any idea?"

"The more interesting question at the moment is why a stranger would venture all the way from the big city to our modest town to pursue such a question," Shane answered. "Any idea?"

"Not an original reason," Ricci said. "Money. You see, my employer has a problem. Bechman Fitzwallington is worth more to him dead than alive, but his value depends heavily on the way he died. Natural causes, good. Murder, not so good. The cops say no murder investigation, but I'm just trying to dig a little deeper. Heard a fella can learn a lot by hanging out at the Wall Street bar. Came early to be sure to get a good seat. Can't always trust what the cops tell the TV and newspaper guys."

"And your employer? Something to do with his art?" Shane asked.

"Is there any other reason to be interested in the old guy?"

"I don't know. Your employer?"

"Are you a cop?"

"Like I said, an interested party," Shane said. "Explain how the manner of Mr. Fitzwallington's demise affects his value to your employer."

"Simple. My employer handles his art in New York. I'm no art expert, but apparently this guy's art hasn't been so hot lately and the fact that he died will bump up the art world's interest for a while. He left some paintings that my employer has reason to believe he can get his hands on, but if there's a drawn-out murder investigation, your cops will no doubt impound the paintings until the case is resolved. By that time, the art world might well have moved on beyond Fitzwallington to something else. My employer says he needs to get the paintings ASAP. Now that the old guy is dead, the longer they are off the market, the lower the prices. That's what I'm told, anyway."

That made sense to Shane. He was pleased to have at least one explanation.

"Who has the paintings now?" Shane asked.

"There's a daughter," Ricci said. "A real piece of work. The only heir, as far as I can tell. She's got a bunch of the old man's paintings stashed away."

"Yes," Shane said, "I know something of the daughter."

Shane pondered the situation for a bit. Finally, he asked, "What makes you think Fitzwallington might have been murdered?"

"I don't necessarily think that. But asking around, there seem to be a lot of people who aren't very disturbed that the old guy cashed it in. Including his daughter and some other artists in town."

"It sounds as though your employer also had much to gain from his death," Shane said.

"That's true," Ricci responded. "But my employer has never, to my knowledge, set foot in this town and bumping the old guy off was not part of my job description. So maybe motive but no opportunity."

"It is not difficult for imaginative people to create opportunities," Shane replied, then gestured toward the bartender. "Pat, perhaps we should sample that bottle of sherry," and to Mace Ricci, whoever he was. "Would you join us for a glass of wine, Mr. Ricci?"

The wine was poured, glasses clinked, and the odd threesome sat for a while quietly sipping their drinks and thinking separate thoughts.

Probably not the last we'll see of Mr. Mace Ricci, Shane thought.

Breaking the long silence, Ricci asked Shane, "Are you a cop?"

"Used to be," Shane replied. "And you?"

"Used to be. Why do you ask?"

"The shoes," Shane said.

Chapter 8

The same North Nashville zip code, Katya Karpov mused... interesting.

She had approval from the appropriate committees to get additional identifying information on the outliers in her department's aging brain study, but the data were arriving in dribs and drabs. The first data to arrive were the zip codes of the subjects' residences. The two downside outliers shared a zip code. Interesting but not that interesting until she had more information. However, they were the only two members of the group of outliers in either direction who shared that zip code. So ... maybe. But needed more data before launching a major effort to identify environmental peculiarities in that part of town. That could open a Pandora's box that Dr. Karpov, for many very practical reasons, preferred to avoid if possible. Keep the possibility in mind but don't get too excited. For starters, need to wait for final word on the genetics. However, it was always risky to underestimate the power of Mother Nature even if, on occasion, she insisted on exposing her dark side.

"Come in," Katya responded to a gentle rap on her partly open door.

Harold Werth entered her office, carefully examining a familiar spot on the floor in front of her desk.

"I have some data that might interest you, Katya," her visitor said, the familiar hesitancy in his voice indicating a completely false lack of confidence in what he was about to say; Dr. Werth did not make statements for which he lacked confidence, but he often found it useful to indicate otherwise.

"What have you got, professor?" Katya responded.

"Well," Werth said, "our analyses are blind, as you know, but…"

"Semi-blind."

"What do you mean?"

"I presume," Katya said, "that you are going to give me information on the outliers. Is that correct?"

"Yes."

"So, you knew they were outliers when you did the analyses. You were semi-blind."

"Semi-blind," Werth mumbled. "Not an easy concept to comprehend. However, I do have some information on a couple of the outliers that might interest you."

"And?" Katya was impatient.

"First, we can find nothing in the genetic sequencing data that indicated any consistent difference between your outliers and the rest of the experimental group. One of the subjects in the outlier group has an XYY trisomy, but none of the others so that doesn't explain anything about the group as a whole."

"But?"

"But," Werth smiled, "we are just finishing the DNA methylation studies and there may be something there."

"Epigenetics!" Karpov exclaimed. "Refuge of the desperate geneticist."

Katya sometimes thought that the gene guys made the basic assumption that genetics explained everything and so were unable to accept contrary evidence, no matter how convincing. Given that attitude, they had no choice but to invent possible vagaries in the genetic machinery that could explain virtually anything. A variation on the *deus ex machina* literary device.

"Well, we do have a tendency to explain what can't be divined from the usual sequencing by looking for other alterations in DNA that could be important. And we know that environmental exposures, toxins and the like, can change how genes function. Methylation is a marker for that."

"Mother Nature's dark side?"

"I'm not sure that Mother Nature distinguishes between dark and light. Maybe she just goes about her business. Until we get in the way, which, of course, we commonly do."

"Whatever," Katya answered, anxious to hear Werth's information. "What have you got?"

"Two of your outliers, including the one with the XYY trisomy, show distinct DNA methylation patterns, different from all of the other subjects. The patterns raise the possibility of toxic exposure. We can't be much more specific than that. A lot of toxins can cause changes like this."

"Which two?"

"I can give you the study numbers."

Katya had the table of study numbers and zip codes in front of her and when Werth gave her the study numbers she saw immediately that they matched up to the two subjects who were outliers on the downside. And who shared residential zip codes. The possible environmental exposure plot might be thickening.

"Nothing on the other outliers?" Katya asked.

"Nothing so far anyway," Werth replied. "We'll keep looking."

Keep looking for sure. Katya most wanted to know what was special about the brains of the artists who were upside performers. She thought they were the interesting ones.

Mace Ricci, following the advice of Bruce Therault, his New York employer, had invested a fair amount of time and energy during his brief stay in Nashville establishing what he believed to be a reliable connection with the odd woman who called herself SalomeMe. That was critical if he was to make certain that Therault's New York gallery got exclusive rights to the remaining Fitzwallington paintings. And that was the job for which he was being paid a moderately obscene sum. He needed to keep that relationship alive and usually either met with SalomeMe or at least talked with her on the phone pretty much every day. He felt okay about how that was going.

However, he had learned, initially from the Fitzwallington daughter and then from some other connections he had made in the art community, that there was a potential complication. It seemed that a local gallery may have some claims on the paintings and his employer was not at all anxious to share what promised to be a considerable pile of dough with another gallery. Therault wanted all of the paintings and exclusive rights to profit from their sale.

That is why Ricci found himself driving slowly out Eighth Avenue on a Tuesday afternoon in a heavy rainstorm, peering intently at the cross-street signs, trying to locate the street where he understood the AvantArt Gallery was to be found and where, presumably, the gallery proprietor, Athena Golden, awaited his arrival. He had talked with her on the phone and was making every possible effort, despite the sudden rainstorm, to arrive at the gallery exactly at the agreed-upon time. He was close.

Athena Golden had never heard of Mace Ricci and was very surprised to get his call. She was especially surprised to hear that he was in the employ of the New York Gallery that Athena associated only with Blythe Fortune, although she knew that Blythe had a business partner. She made the appointment to meet with this Mace Ricci character reluctantly and as soon as she ended the conversation with Ricci, she emailed Blythe, wishing to verify what this stranger had said and hopefully find out what he was up to. When Ricci entered the AvantArt Gallery, Blythe hadn't responded.

"Mace Ricci," the large stranger strode through the door and across the room to where Athena stood, extending his hand.

Athena thought her reluctantly invited guest was a trifle more aggressive than she was used to and it didn't please her. She also thought that his appearance bore little resemblance to her image of a big city art dealer. He was not just large but also seemed less refined than she would have expected, a notch or two beyond rough around the edges. And he appeared distinctly uncomfortable in the gallery. This was clearly not the kind of place that he was familiar with. His large hand was sweaty as she shook it. Athena needed a reply from Blythe Fortune about this character before taking him seriously. She would just have to listen politely and see what this was about.

"Athena Golden, Mr. Ricci," Athena responded, "I own this gallery." Defining the territory.

"So I've been told," Ricci responded. "So I've been told."

He turned and milled about the room, perusing the various art pieces on display. He was drawn to a display case of hats, for some reason. He stood looking at the collection of lady's hats with apparent interest.

"Hats," he said, "are hats art? I didn't know."

"Depends on the hats. Depends on the hatter. The hats you see there are indeed art. They are my creations. My little contribution to the world of art that sustains me."

"Interesting."

"Pardon my asking, but have you a special interest in lady's hats? I must say I would not have predicted that."

"Just didn't expect to find a bunch of them in an art gallery," he responded. "But what I wanted to talk with you about is the recently deceased Bechman Fitzwallington. I believe you and my employer have done some business with his work?"

"Assuming you are employed by the Galleria Salinas, the answer is yes."

"And are some of his unsold works in your possession?"

Cop-talk.

"I will be happy to discuss this matter with Blythe Fortune, my colleague at the New York gallery. I am frankly surprised at your sudden appearance here, Mr. Ricci, and am more than a bit suspicious of your motives. Now, if you will excuse me, I have legitimate business to attend to. You may show yourself out."

"Oh, I'm sorry," Ricci said. "I sense I haven't presented myself very well. Maybe we could start over? The last thing I want is to offend you."

"Goodbye, Mr. Ricci," Athena walked to the door and held it open for a less than gracious exit of Mr. Mace Ricci.

Ms. Golden went immediately to the phone and called the number she had for Fitzwallington's daughter. Better firm up that connection. They had spoken a couple of times since her father's death, but nothing had been accomplished. There was no answer. She left a voice message.

Shane Hadley sat at his newly reconfigured spot at the far end of the bar at Wall Street nursing a glass of Lincoln College sherry and pondering how he had decided to approach the Bechman Fitzwallington problem. He was waiting for the first of the two appointments he had made for the afternoon and enjoying for the moment the nostalgia of the occasion, the first time he had used his Wall Street office in several years. Those years had seen major changes in his life but, excepting the fact that its proprietor had visibly aged, and not that well, Wall Street was pretty much like Shane remembered it.

Strategy. Shane had decided to start by talking with a few

potentially critical players. He had a list of four people that he thought he should probably interview face to face. He wasn't really setting out to solve a murder but rather to determine whether there had been one. He was intrigued by that challenge and thought that it might require a somewhat different approach than when homicide had already been firmly established.

So, Shane Hadley awaited the arrival of one who had adopted the unusual moniker, SalomeMe, not quite sure what to expect. From Hardy Seltzer he had a clue that this was not your usual grieving daughter of the recently deceased, and some hint that she was personally a trifle eccentric, but Shane was anxious to see this young woman for himself and to form his own opinion of her person and of her relationship with her late father.

It was almost half an hour past the agreed-upon time. Not a punctual type, Shane thought. Might not show up at all. She had sounded reluctant on the phone and was less than impressed with Shane's ambiguous professional definition. *Retired metro detective*, an admittedly anemic title, didn't seem to carry a lot of weight with the likes of SalomeMe. In fact, Shane sensed that this woman was not all that fond of the men in blue and their colleagues, even the legitimate ones.

Finally, she showed up. Later, Shane thought that SalomeMe might have played better as a no-show, a role with which she was probably familiar.

"So," she said, striding across the room to the bar where three men sat quietly drinking, "which one of you dudes is the retired cop guy?"

No one responded. The bartender, Pat Harmony, limped over to face the visitor. She leaned toward him over the bar. Major portions of her substantial breasts bulged above a scanty tank top. A red and magenta serpent wound about her neck and headed south wending its way through her cleavage and disappearing toward a southerly destination Harmony was not inclined to speculate about.

"Most likely," Harmony said, "all of us dudes are cops, some retired, some not. But you no doubt are looking for Mr. Shane Hadley. He's at the end of the bar. Can I get you a drink?"

Shane looked at Ms. SalomeMe as she walked over to where he was parked atop the newly constructed platform that brought him to bar height while seated in his wheelchair. She took the stool next to him. She was about what he had expected from Hardy Seltzer's description. And, Shane thought, she was surely old enough to know better than the persona she had chosen to project. The very unreality of it! He was certain that this woman was going to great lengths to hide whoever she really was from others and probably, he imagined, from herself. So, this would be hide and seek with a woman whom Shane decided on the spot to think of as just SM.

"So," says SM, obviously addressing Shane but staring straight ahead at the array of bottled spirits lining the back of the bar, "what business does a *retired* cop have digging into the circumstances of my dear daddy's leave-taking of our fair planet? Doesn't *retired* mean what it says?"

Leave-taking, Shane thought. An unusual choice of words for such an agonizingly hip young woman. He was reminded of conversations from his Oxford days, the Brits' way with language that had so attracted him. Something incongruous here. Better pay attention!

Ignoring her questions, Shane said, "I understand from my colleague, Detective Seltzer, that you were, shall we say, less than fond of dear daddy. Is that correct?"

"Actually, an understatement," she replied, "I hated the old bastard's guts!" Then an aside, "With good reason."

"Really?" Shane did not miss the aside.

"Tell me, Mr. Retired Detective with the fancy accent," she said,

DEADLY ARTS

"exactly what are you trying to find out and what have I got to do with it? What am I doing here anyway?"

Shane didn't answer but swirled his glass of sherry and pondered how to proceed. SM had shown up, at least, but whether their meeting was likely to be worth the effort for either of them remained to be seen.

"Would you like a glass of very good sherry?" Shane asked after a long pause.

"Sherry?" she replied. "How quaint! Bartender," she called over to Pat Harmony who leaned against the back bar trying hard to appear uninterested in the exchange between Shane and the strange young woman. "How about a bourbon and branch water?"

"Coming up," Harmony poured a generous portion of whiskey, added a scant dash of water and handed the drink to her across the bar.

"What I'm interested in determining," Shane now addressed his guest directly, "is whether your father was murdered or left the living world with only the aid of Mother Nature. What do you think?"

SM took a long swallow of her drink and sat the glass on the bar with a decided clunk.

"Afraid I can't answer that for you Mr. Retired Detective. Mother Nature was doing a pretty good number on him for a while now, so she might not have needed much help. But if help was needed there would have been no lack of anxious volunteers. Dear daddy, you see, was a real piece of shit."

"So, you didn't kill him?"

"Not in any obvious way."

"What about an unobvious way?"

"Always a possibility, I guess."

"Do you inherit his paintings?"

"Bet your ass, I do. And I understand they're worth a lot more

69

dough with him dead, too. How about that for good fortune? Rid of the old bastard and making money on the deal."

"Maybe good fortune…or maybe motive?"

"I guess you could think of it that way. But I certainly didn't not kill him for lack of a motive. I've got motives to burn. Been accumulating them for a lifetime."

Shane winced at the excruciating double negative. He was not fond of SalomeMe on this their first meeting, but he thought that if she killed her father by either obvious or unobvious means, she was probably cleverer than an initial impression would suggest. The pre-emptive strike of her paradoxical offense/defense against the possibility would be a complex strategy for such a woman. But it was entirely possible that lurking behind her elaborate façade was someone altogether different. People, like things, Shane mused, are not always what they seem.

Chapter 9

"Sherlock Shane Hadley, my man," exclaimed a tall man as he entered Wall Street and made a beeline directly to the end of the bar where sat the retired detective fondling his glass of wine.

The visitor wore spanking new yellow work boots and gray striped overalls decorated with random splotches of brightly colored paints. His arms were bare. His large hands were also paint-spattered. Shane noticed that as the man's large right hand slapped Shane on the back forcefully enough to make an impression.

Must be Parker Palmer, Shane's second appointment of the afternoon. Shane didn't know Parker Palmer but that was the name of one of the local artists that Hardy Seltzer had suggested that he might want to talk to. So, the appointment was made and conspicuously kept. Shane had been warned that PP was not the shy and retiring sort.

"I am Shane Hadley," Shane responded. "And I gather that you are Parker Palmer. We talked on the phone, but do I know you in some other context?"

The familiarity of the visitor's greeting was perplexing. Shane had done a bit of research on the artist, seen photos of his brightly colored and intriguingly distorted versions of people, famous and not. There was also the impression that Palmer was a garrulous sort, a kind of man-about-town who tended to churn up a hefty wake.

"Of course, I know you," Palmer said. "Hasn't been all that long since the newspapers were full of your exploits, my man. I was a big fan. And then you disappeared."

"I prefer," Shane replied, "to think of myself as having withdrawn rather than disappeared."

"Whatever. Anyway, what do you want from me? Must say, I was surprised by your call."

"Bechman Fitzwallington," Shane intoned, deliberately infusing the words with their conspicuously invited melodrama. "What do you know of the circumstances of his recent demise?"

"Billy Wayne Farmer," Parker Palmer responded, ignoring the pretentious *nom de artiste*, pulling a long serious face, and gesturing with his left hand, "long outlived anything of value that he brought to the society that so handsomely rewarded him. Should have kicked off a long time ago if you ask me."

He sounded serious.

"Not a private sentiment of yours, I gather."

"You gather right, my man," Parker Palmer responded. "You see, Billy Wayne Farmer was a fake, Mr. Hadley, starting with that godawful name he invented. When he first made the Nashville art scene, he seemed okay personally, a yokel from the boonies hoping to make it in the big city. But his art? Totally baffling to most of us what the fuss was about. When the NYC folks got interested, old BWF became intolerably taken with himself. He expected the rest of us struggling artists to idolize him and I guess we sort of did that, primarily because he had figured out how to make money and we were trying to sort out what his secret was … get our hands on the formula for the special sauce. But he just counted his dough and basked in the attention. Never lifted a finger to do anything for the rest of us. Couldn't have cared less."

While Shane had had little direct contact with artists, or perhaps because of that, he admired them for what he thought was their (he might have called it) *aesthetic dedication.* He thought them much less concerned about professional logistics than the beauty and integrity of their work, that they were not salespersons but rather expected the quality of their work to sell itself. Parker Palmer was apparently a moderately successful artist who seemed to belie Shane's imagined stereotype. Parker Palmer was an unapologetic salesman.

"And what did you expect of him?" Shane asked.

"Human decency … and respect for the profession," PP replied.

"And when those were not forthcoming," Shane continued, "why keep up the connection? I understand that you visited with him fairly often."

"Morbid attraction, I guess."

"How morbid?"

"A person needed to nurture a more than a healthy amount of morbidity to keep up any connection with the old guy."

"There seem to be several people who were capable of nurturing such morbidity," Shane said. "Help me out here, Mr. Palmer. This guy up and dies for no apparent reason. He is constantly surrounded by people who appear to have hated him with some vehemence and who had ample opportunity to assist his demise. How about a motive?"

"Clear the decks? Cut out the competition? He distorted the local art scene rather than enhancing it. I don't know a single Nashville artist who wasn't anxious to see him out of the picture, so to speak."

"Will anyone profit directly from his death?"

"I can think of three if he left any significant number of paintings that can be sold. His art had been popular enough for a while that his death will bump the price of his final works for a bit."

"Three?"

"Yes: The lovely daughter known mainly to herself as SalomeMe, who will presumably inherit his remaining works as his sole heir; Athena Golden, proprietor of the Nashville gallery, AvantArt; and Galleria Salinas, the New York gallery that handled some of his work, which is operated and perhaps owned, I'm not sure, by a stereotypical East Sider who goes by the unlikely name of Blythe Fortune. I must add that these people would have only a brief bump in their profits. Although the value of art is, like the value of most things, what someone will pay for it, Billy Wayne's art will not have any staying power in the market, especially his later works. So, one could argue that we other artists might gain more from his death in the long run than the middlemen."

More offensive defense, Shane thought. Too bloody many murderers and no bloody murder! Maybe he was wasting his time. OK. He had time to waste.

"So," Shane, tired of the banter, cut to the chase, "who did it?"

"The smart money would probably be on the daughter," Parker Palmer smiled. "Me? I'd stick with Mother Nature. She is surely the more dependable of those two. And we of the artistic persuasion overvalue ourselves and each other even when we misbehave, as we are prone to do. So, you'd have to do something worse than treat your artistic colleagues like pieces of shit to provoke them to violence."

"Well," Shane replied, "thank you for meeting with me. You've been of marginal help in this little drama, but I appreciate the effort," he proffered his business card. "If you think of anything else that might enlighten the situation for all of us, please call me."

"Yo, my man," PP responded with a hearty clap on Shane's shoulder. "Will do."

He arose from the barstool, strode deliberately to the door, and disappeared.

Shane watched the tall man lope across the room, trailed by the comet-tail flash of his neon-yellow work boots that smeared across Shane's retinae, the most enduring imprint of the odd encounter, as the door banged shut.

The detective then returned his attention to the glass of sherry and for perhaps the first time in his life, thought seriously about the nature of art and artists. He seemed to be testing the waters of a strikingly strange world where illusion, not reality, was the essential element. These were not real people. This was not at all what he had expected.

Well, there was one reality—the old guy was really dead. But who was he? And SalomeMe? Even the gangly Parker Palmer, glad-handing salesman that he seemed to be, had an air of unreality about him, like he was acting a role. Who are these people? And how to navigate a world with no clear coordinates, locate anything close to true events? Answering the essential question here—was there a murder or not—was likely to require something more than the detective's usual bag of tricks. And if the answer to that question turned out to be affirmative, then how the hell would the crime ever be solved?

Verities, thought Shane Hadley, were the essential pieces of any crime's jigsaw puzzle . Without the verities, there were no real puzzle pieces to assemble. And so … no solution. The files of unsolved crimes bulging the dusty archives of every police station in the known world were comfortably ensconced there for lack of verities. "Facts!" exclaimed The Great Detective. "I need facts, Watson. I cannot make bricks without straw!"

Shane took the small leather notebook from his shirt pocket and opened it to some notes he had taken when Hardy Seltzer ceded the material on the Bechman Fitzwallington matter to Shane's custody. Two more artists' names—*Fiona Hayes*, a ceramicist who according to Hardy's information tended to "keep to herself," and *Vernon LaVista III*, a socially well-connected sculptor who worked mainly in bronze but had done some large marble commissions for the city's public art program as well. They were both regular visitors to the deceased and according to the daughter were certainly not there to express their undying devotion to the old guy. Shane would need to talk with these two. And now there were the two gallery owners possibly implicated by Parker Palmer. Shane uncapped his trusty Waterman fountain pen, another relic of a past life, and wrote, *Athena Golden (AvantArt Nashville)* and *Blythe Fortune (Galleria Salinas New York)* near the bottom of the page. The ex-cop, Mace Ricci, might have more to reveal about the New York connection as well. Yes, he definitely needed another encounter with the Ricci character. He wrote *Mace Ricci temporarily Nashville via New York*.

Given his circumstances, Shane was not at all sure how he would deal with the logistics essential to explore whatever these people had to add to his nascent pot of information. He still wasn't all that mobile. He would need to think about that. Hardy Seltzer came to mind.

Shane was starting to miss the help and the companionship of his re-discovered friend and colleague. That had been true since the Bonz Bagley case—that case was a kind of rebirth for Shane. But the feeling was gaining momentum. Shane was starting to doubt whether the solo route would be as interesting as he originally thought it would be. Camaraderie was important to most cops. Even though Shane, in his prime, was considered to be a "private man," that was more a carefully nurtured perception than his personal reality. No matter. At least for now Hardy was strictly off-limits. Sherlock Shane Hadley was going it alone.

Chapter 10

On rare occasions Sally May Farmer extricated herself from the confines of her meticulously constructed and maintained alter ego, abandoned for an evening three of the cardinal principles that had guided her life since adolescence, and went to bed early, sober, and alone.

There was a ritual. She undressed, scrubbed her face free of all traces of her habitually excessive makeup, and stood naked before a full-length mirror. She then removed each of the jeweled rings from their pierced sites—ear lobes, eyebrows, nose, lower lip, tongue, left nipple, an insinuatingly outie umbilicus, and the right labial fold of her vagina. Only the tattoos remained as indelible vestiges of the other woman who could not be erased completely. She heaped the mass of jewelry into a ceramic dish on her dressing table and regarded her largely unadorned body in the mirror for a few minutes. She often wept quietly at these times as she stood alone, naked ... vulnerable. Eventually she sighed deeply and went to bed.

On these rare occasions she was often visited by the ghost. He came in the deep of night and again touched her, often roughly. She felt the long-familiar parchment texture of his dry bony hands on her thighs and breasts and was at once revulsed and aroused. The dream could last the entire night. She often awakened the next morning tangled in the bedclothes from the violent thrashing about—writhings of both agony and ecstasy—and drenched in cold sweat. She invariably awoke with renewed loathing for the ghost and the man. But, oddly, the bond endured. It might even have been strengthened by their secret. Humankind's most powerful and enduring emotions are, after all, love and hate.

Why? Why, even rarely, with full knowledge of the consequences of what she was doing, issue an open invitation to a visitation by the ghost? Sally May Farmer pondered that question as she reassembled her alter ego the next morning. She rationalized that now the invitation would fall on dead ears and she would be finally free of the dread that visited her all those years in the night, free to experience a periodic escape from the pretense without resurrecting the evil that drove her to seek refuge in an invented life. Apparently not.

So, Sally May Farmer carefully reassembled the invented woman who gave her the strength necessary to venture into the real world. She could only view reality from a false face through artificial lenses. Thank you, Daddy.

Chapter 11

Blythe Fortune and Bruce Therault met once in a while for lunch at a little unpretentious French restaurant on First Avenue, just around the corner from Blythe's building. They always ate at the bar. The reason for these meetings was to catch Blythe up on Bruce's business plans for the gallery. The current topic was the art of the recently deceased Bechman Fitzwallington.

"Who in bloody hell is Mace Ricci?" asked Blythe.

Blythe had returned Athena Golden's call and was as baffled as the Nashville woman by the sudden intrusion of this completely unknown ex-cop into the Fitzwallington matter.

"You don't need to worry about him," Bruce responded. "He's my guy. He's sizing up the lay of the land down south."

Blythe had often thought recently that Bruce was becoming less and less forthcoming about what he was doing for the business and she worried about that. The gallery had always dealt with midlevel artists—up-and-comers, solid performers with a following, that sort of thing. Blythe didn't have the chops or the desire to deal in the high rollers, compete with the big galleries. And the model had worked OK for them ... not great, but OK. They had made a few bucks on Fitzwallington's stuff before his obvious decline. The chance to make a few more bucks on his unfortunate demise was certainly appealing.

But Blythe worried that Bruce had an agenda that might put her gallery at risk. She loved that gallery. She loved the art. She recognized that they had to make money or go out of business. But her passion, what drove her, was the art.

"So," Blythe responded, "exactly what is he doing down there?"

"Just firming up connections," Bruce replied. "Determining how many paintings there are, their quality, and establishing our exclusive claim to them."

"And?"

"Well, it appears everything is moving in the right direction," Therault said. "There is one possible complication."

"And?"

"There is a local retired cop who seems intent on determining that old BF was murdered in spite of everything pointing to natural causes for his death. That's a problem for us."

"How so?"

"Well," Therault sighed and gulped a deep slug of his Manhattan, "if it's a murder case, they will confiscate the paintings until God knows when—but certainly until the bump in their value has disintegrated and we are left with no added value from Fitzwallington's death. Pisses me off to think about the possibility."

"Well, not the end of the world."

"Maybe."

Therault drained his drink and ordered another. He was not a man at peace this noon and that was obvious to Blythe Fortune.

"You see," Bruce said, "this is not just about our gallery."

"Really?" Blythe responded. "Then what is it about?"

"Well, Blythe," Therault began hesitantly, "I've tried to spare you the gory details about some things. But perhaps it's time you became acquainted with some activities and interests of our investors."

Blythe was not sure that she liked the sound of this, but she listened.

"Yes, go on."

"You see," Bruce continued, "our investors have interests in other galleries as well, modest shops like ours that deal in mid-level art and have persisting needs for operating capital. There are several of them scattered around the country. So, they have considerable experience with this sort of thing business-wise. That is an asset for us of course."

"I see. And who are these mysterious investors? I should have asked that question earlier I suppose."

"I think, Blythe, that you need not know more about them right now. That's my end of things. However, you probably should know that this Fitzwallington matter fits their business plan."

"Business plan? How so?"

"*Death tax collectors*. That's how I think of them. As you know, the death of a successful artist usually jacks up the prices for his works by twenty percent or so for a few weeks before the market settles down again—the *death tax*. Well, these business guys are speculators and they see that as a financial opportunity. They go looking to invest in galleries that represent aging or ill artists who fit the model. By avoiding the big-name guys, they can operate under the radar, so to speak, and still make a decent profit. That's why they sought us out. So, we owe our capitalization to old BF as well as a substantial amount of our profit over the past couple of years. With more to come if things work out as planned."

"Why operate under the radar, Bruce?" Blythe asked, fearing an answer that she would not find pleasing. "Is this sort of thing legal?"

"As far as I can tell," Therault answered, polishing off his third Manhattan, setting the glass firmly on the bar, and looking directly into Blythe Fortune's questioning eyes. "As far as I can tell."

Chapter 12

MUSIC CITY HATTER GOES MAD

The glaring headline on the front page of the morning *Tennessean* and the accompanying three-column story was read with varying degrees of interest and understanding by several of the people with connections to the Bechman Fitzwallington matter.

The story recounted a bizarre incident in which one Richard (Richelieu) Jones, self-styled *Mad Hatter of Music City*, proprietor of a venerable hat shop on Eighth Avenue, who resided in a nice Germantown apartment, was apprehended after breaking into the vacant former home of a neighbor, the painter Bechman Fitzwallington, and painting graffiti on the walls, messages to the effect that the house's former resident was a skinflint, a cheat, a charlatan, and a fake. When apprehended, Mr. Jones was irrational and somewhat combative and was armed with a handgun although he did not discharge it. He was taken by the police to the university hospital emergency room where he was evaluated and admitted for further observation and tests.

Athena Golden sat at the writing desk nestled into a far corner of her gallery, laid her copy of the morning newspaper aside, and stared at the small painting with BF boldly smeared across the bottom right corner. She pondered the odd story about the hatter. Athena thought of her hat-making as an art form, quite different from the commercial monstrosities produced by the guy with the shop. Of course she knew of the *Mad Hatter of Music City*, had seen examples of his creations online and occasionally on the head of a sartorially adventurous local citizen, but she had not met him until the previous day when he brought the little painting that he claimed was an early work of Fitzwallington to her, requesting an appraisal. He left the painting at the gallery for a few days to give her time to establish its value.

Athena thought that "Richelieu" Jones's behavior the previous day seemed strange at the time but she hadn't thought more about it until reading the story in the *Tennessean*. The small dark man wearing a lavender fedora and carrying an unwrapped oil painting under his left arm like a schoolbook just strode into the AvantArt gallery late in the morning and ambled about for a while, apparently studying the art pieces hanging on the gallery walls. He stood for some time gazing at the display case of hats. He did not speak until Athena approached him.

"How may I help you?" she asked.

"*Bonjour*, madam," he replied, doffing his lavender hat and bowing slightly. "I am Richelieu Jones and I wish to know the value of this painting." He shifted the painting from under his arm and showed it to her, holding it shield-like with both hands in front of his chest. "Are you able to establish that? It is an original painting by Bechman Fitzwallington, given to me by him many years ago."

There was slight tremor in his voice, and he seemed to have trouble holding the painting steady. His gaze darted randomly about the room as though he was expecting an intruder but was unsure when and from what direction the intrusion would come.

"I'm sure I can get you a reliable appraisal," Athena said, looking directly at him and trying without success to engage his eyes. "It may take a few days. Are you aware that the artist recently died? That could affect the painting's value."

"So I am told," he replied.

He handed the painting to her and without saying anything more, turned on his heel and left the gallery.

Reflecting on the encounter, Athena Golden thought the man's behavior strange, very strange indeed. Strange but with no inkling of any potential for violence. There was nothing about her encounter with Richelieu Jones that would have led her to expect anything like the story in the newspaper. Something seemed wrong about him. But not that wrong.

Shane Hadley and Katya Karpov sat, as usual of a morning, at the table in the front room of their Printers Alley home, nibbling on brioches that KiKi had picked up the previous evening from Provence, the elegant little shop that was a convenient stop for her on the way home from work. They were sipping coffee and scanning the morning *Tennessean*. As always, KiKi got first dibs on the front page while Shane absently perused the sports page, a habit from long ago when he had a passing interest in some of the local teams.

Shane was looking at the sports page but he was thinking about the death of Bechman Fitzwallington, still puzzling over the as-yet empty space between his feeling about that and the available facts. When KiKi held the front page toward him and read the headline, he was startled.

"Isn't this your friend with the hat shop?" she asked.

Shane took the paper from her and scanned the story.

"Indeed it is," he answered. "How strange. He had seemed a little spacey lately, and his creations have taken a turn toward the strange, bizarre really. But I didn't see him often enough to know whether something more serious was going on."

He handed the paper back to KiKi and she started to read the story.

Shane watched his wife's emerald green eyes moving back and forth across the newspaper. So many things about her were beautiful. He remembered the first time he had spotted her strolling about a courtyard at Oxford. Dumbstruck was what he felt, and he was dumbstruck all over again every day that they were together since.

KiKi lay the paper aside, sipped at her coffee and said, "What possible connection could your hatter friend have had with that artist?"

"There is, in fact, a connection," Shane replied. "An admittedly tenuous one. Richard Jones apparently made a hat for the artist many years ago, before Fitzwallington was 'discovered'," gesturing the punctuation, "and he paid for the hat with one of his paintings. Richard had only recently rediscovered the painting and displayed it in his shop. He was not happy to have the painting in lieu of cash at the time, but, as I told him, the painting may well be worth a great deal more than the hat, especially since the artist's recent demise."

"Hmmm," KiKi responded. "Did you know he was a neighbor of the artist in Germantown?"

"No clue," Shane said. "I had no idea where Richard lived."

Shane retrieved the newspaper and started reading the article more thoroughly.

Katya poured herself some more coffee, stared toward the long room's big front window, and contemplated outliers.

SalomeMe did not feel well that morning. She often did not feel well in the mornings. That fact was usually explained by her behavior on the previous evening and was often magnified by her frequent insomnia. Despite all that, most mornings she dragged herself from her troubled bed, made a pot of strong coffee, and retrieved the newspaper from her front porch. On that particular morning SalomeMe sat at her kitchen table resting her throbbing head in her hands and staring blankly into the space before her as she waited for the coffee pot—which seemed to be taking an inordinate amount of time—to wheeze its way through the agonal throes of the brewing process and signal that its task was complete. Her hand trembled some as she lifted the pot and poured the dark liquid into a mug. She sipped the hot coffee, relishing the searing pain as it washed over her tongue, scalded her soft palate, and burned a path down her esophagus.

"Aaahh," she said aloud and turned to the newspaper.

Pain was SalomeMe's long-nurtured friend.

So, yet another Bechman Fitzwallington hater, she thought as she scanned the front page story. She recognized the small picture, apparently retrieved from the paper's files, of a thin-faced man with a razor-sharp nose wearing a fedora and smiling for the camera. She had seen him around the neighborhood occasionally and knew that he lived in the area. She also was aware of his identity as the hat maker with the shop in town. She didn't recall ever seeing him at her father's house and was unaware of any connection between the two of them. But dear old daddy had a way of angering even people whom he hardly knew, so she wasn't particularly surprised. Get in line, Mr. Richelieu Jones. When dear daddy chose to depart the land of the living, he left behind a very long queue of folks impatiently waiting their turn to have a go at him. Yes, Mr. Jones, just take a number and get in line.

She lay the paper aside and nursed her cup of coffee for a bit. That New York detective was supposed to come by her place later. She didn't like Mace Ricci, but he seemed to be the best bet for extracting maximum dollars from the final works of Bechman Fitzwallington. Should be a sizeable sum. She smiled. Thank you, Daddy.

Mace Ricci was not an early riser. He figured he had done enough of that when he was full time on the force so that since his retirement, he availed himself of every opportunity he had to sleep in. It was probably close to ten o'clock when he retrieved a local newspaper from a coin box beside the door and entered the diner a block up Union Street from his hotel. He sat at the counter, ordered black coffee and a bacon and eggs breakfast, and unfolded the paper.

The headline about the hatter didn't attract him until the name of Bechman Fitzwallington leapt at him from the text beneath. That caused him to read the entire account with some care. Anything newsworthy that involved the deceased artist interested him. There was always the possibility that such an item would have implications for what happened to those paintings. And he was determined to lay claim to those paintings. That was the job he had taken on and he took his job commitments seriously.

What is it with hats in this town? Ricci thought. He was remembering the showcase of hats at the gallery he had briefly and unsuccessfully visited. He had to figure some way to follow up on that Fitzwallington connection. Could be trouble. And now another hat maker with some apparent beef with the dead artist. And this guy seemed to be totally off his rocker. The crazy ones can be a special problem.

It appeared to Ricci that virtually everybody who encountered Fitzwallington wound up hating him. Something about the old guy seemed to have an organic link to the human dark side. He brought out the worst in people. That troubled Ricci. He feared that the growing list of serious haters of the old guy would feed the notion that the cause of his death might not have been as natural as originally thought. That was an especially troubling idea since that paralyzed ex-cop was digging into the matter. If he didn't suspect foul play, then why was he wasting his time? Ricci could imagine the potentially valuable paintings getting tied up for ages in the legal morass that often complicated dealing with a dead guy's estate in a situation like this. He was meeting with the daughter later and maybe she could be persuaded to speed up things, get the possession and disposal of the paintings resolved before the Hadley guy insisted on muddying the waters. Ricci was especially concerned about how his New York employer might react to any muddying of the waters. Not likely to be a pleasant experience.

If you imagine the artist's life as filled with free-wheeling, unstructured, carefree, impulsive, and irresponsible days and nights spent biding time while awaiting the arrival of the muse, you would find the life of Parker Palmer severely disappointing. PP's life was structured almost to the point of compulsion. At 6:30 AM he sat in a wicker chair on the rear deck of his Edgefield area house cradling a large cup of French press prepared coffee in his right hand, a copy of the day's *Tennessean* resting in his lap. He had arisen at five, gone for his habitual morning run during which he picked up the morning paper, returned home, prepared the coffee and positioned himself in his customary morning spot on the deck. He would spend precisely thirty minutes there and then repair to his upper-level studio and paint for four hours. Happened like that every day. No waiting for the muse. No pondering the meaning of art, his or anyone else's. No elaborate plans for what his next work would be. His chosen job was art but that didn't change the fact that it was a job. PP's Scottish heritage had taught him that when you have a job you best be about it.

"Holy shit!" he said aloud. "What in hell got into Richelieu Jones?"

Parker knew the hatter the same way that almost any long-time resident of the city did—who the man was and something about his shop which had become a local attraction. Occasionally he would stop by the shop during one of his frequent walks through the city to chat a bit with the Francophilic hatter and marvel at his creations. Parker didn't wear hats and didn't admire them particularly, although he had painted hats atop some of his more fanciful portraits of imaginary ladies.

PP had noticed that Jones seemed to be evolving into a caricature in recent months. Parker thought it may have started with the French thing that had come to obsess the old guy. His hat designs had taken a very strange turn and the man himself seemed to have followed them, or led them, not sure which. Anyway, PP thought the hatter seemed more distracted lately and would occasionally talk nonsense. But Parker Palmer was still surprised at the newspaper story. What possible connection could the hatter have had with Billy Wayne Farmer? But then old BF had a way of pissing off people whom he didn't even know. So maybe this was just a consequence of the old man's malignant aura. Ah well. Rest in peace Billy Wayne, my man…rest in peace at last.

The part of the extensive and colorful display that most caught Hardy Seltzer's attention was the stylized tombstone outlined in black with *RIP BF* scrolled across it in brilliant red. The scene covered an entire wall and really was best described as a display. It was, technically anyway, graffiti, but much more carefully done than the spray-painted figures on the walls of abandoned buildings downtown. The Jones guy had spent some time and effort depicting his antipathy toward the artist on the walls of the old guy's house. His message was clear and forcefully done. Hardy was no expert, but he thought the hatter's handiwork might even be, ironically, art. *Live by the sword, die by the sword,* Hardy thought.

He was remembering his visit to the Fitzwallington place to help corral Richard Jones and get him safely ensconced in a place appropriate for his condition. Ordinarily he wouldn't have responded to such a call, but since he had been involved in the investigation, such as it was, of Fitzwallington's death, Hardy volunteered to accompany the guys in blue to the scene. He wasn't sure why he volunteered. Maybe hoped he would discover something relevant to the demise of the old artist. He didn't and hadn't thought much more about it until he opened the morning paper and confronted the story. It was a strange story. Seemed like everything about Bechman Fitzwallington was strange.

Hardy sipped at his third cup of coffee. He wondered whether Shane was as interested in this "case" as he had seemed to be at first. Hardy hadn't talked with Shane since then. Probably should give him a call. Couldn't hurt to at least find out what the ex-detective was up to. When Shane Hadley was up to something detective-wise there was a better than even chance that, sooner or later, it would involve Hardy Seltzer.

Blythe Fortune was not an early riser and generally refused to check her emails until after she had consumed at least two cups of coffee and had sat for half an hour watching the sun rise over the expanse of East River that she viewed from her wall of living room windows. But, for some reason, she awoke earlier than usual this morning and immediately opened the message from Bruce Therault. It was a short, urgent note with a scanned copy of the *Nashville Tennessean* story about the Mad Hatter of Music City's vandalization of Bechman Fitzwallington's home attached. She printed out the document, made coffee and sat at the wrought iron table on her deck rereading the story, absorbing the morning sun, and wondering whether there was any reason to be concerned about what appeared to be a minor incident happening a thousand miles to the south of the most interesting city in the world where she lived and mingled with a stratum of society that was probably not represented in the place where this "Mad Hatter's" caper had occurred, the same place where Bechman Fitzwallington had lived, died, and hopefully left a cache of paintings that stood to make a considerable amount of money for her gallery. She wasn't sure why Bruce's email sounded so concerned and would discuss that with him, but she saw no reason to worry herself about it.

Of course, it was obvious now that Bruce had information that she did not have and was probably better off without. Was there something about these mysterious investors that Bruce had told her a bit about that made this incident more significant than it appeared to Blythe? Not her problem. Up to Bruce to deal with it. Just get her the paintings and she would organize her contacts and get the damn things sold, get this whole Fitzwallington thing finished up and taken to the bank. Her better angels were enthralled with the *art for art's sake* thing, but, as with most everything else in the city, esthetics and money were, like energy and mass, convertible entities. And the conversion process tended strongly in the direction toward money.

The sun was well above the horizon now, silhouetting the Queens skyline and slashing a swath of orange across the river toward the Manhattan shore. Blythe really did love this place. Not so much the perpetual bustle, the complexity, but more the calm, simple, and exquisite beauty that appeared suddenly and without warning in the most unlikely places.

Chapter 13

*A*gnes, Katya Karpov thought, *Agnes something. Starts with a C, maybe, not sure. Yes, that's it, Courtland, Agnes Courtland.* Katya was trying to remember the full name of one of the clinical research coordinators for the aging brain study who appeared in her office at the beginning of the day unannounced, looking nervous, and insisting that she had some potentially important information that Dr. Karpov should know about. Katya knew most of the research coordinators by sight and by at least first name. She paid their salaries, but she didn't work directly with them and so had to resort to deeper recall when the occasion required that she remember more detail about one of them.

"Good morning, Agnes," Katya greeted the young woman. "Please come in and have a seat."

"Thank you, Dr. Karpov," the young woman responded, smoothing her blue scrub skirt as she sat down in the chair beside Katya's desk.

"And to what do I owe the privilege of a visit from Agnes Courtland this morning?" Katya engaged her visitor's eyes and tried to sound pleased with the young woman's unexpected and unarranged visit to her office, but it took some effort.

As was true most days, the Karpov calendar was stuffed to the gills and this unplanned interruption would mean starting the day already behind schedule. But, Katya both knew and felt that paying attention to the real workers, the people who made the entire enterprise function, was at least as important as debating space needs with the dean, quibbling with senior administrators over next year's budget, or holding one-on-one meetings with each of her forty-odd faculty to go over their mostly useless but required annual performance review forms. She'd get all of that stuff done, but first she would listen carefully to whatever Agnes Courtland had on her mind.

"Well," the nervous young woman began, "I'm not sure if I should tell you this. You know, patient confidentiality and so forth. But I think you should know."

"I guess since you felt strongly enough about it to go to the trouble of coming to my office this early in the day," Katya tried to put her visitor at ease, "that you might just as well get it off your chest and trust me to deal with it properly. Don't you think?"

"I suppose," Agnes replied. "But I don't want to put you in a difficult spot."

"My dear," Katya smiled, "I am often in a difficult spot. It's part of the job. I am very familiar with difficult spots and usually do pretty well at extricating myself with minimal damage to all involved. Trust me, my dear. Trust me."

"OK. What I think you should know is that the mad hatter guy that was admitted yesterday—there's a *Tennessean* story about him this morning—well, he's one of the subjects in the brain study. He's one that I've been following, study subject number BS24. Of course, I don't know anything about his test results, but the last few times I saw him in follow up, I thought he was behaving a little strangely. I just thought that if there was some reason that we knew about that might help explain his violent behavior, that someone in charge should at least know about it. So, I came to you. I hope that was OK."

"You've done the right thing, Agnes," Katya said. "Please don't reveal this to anyone else. And trust me to deal with it. You needn't worry about it any longer."

Katya got up from her chair and took the young woman's arm, gently ushering her toward the door. Katya really did need to get on with her duties for the day.

"Thank you again, Agnes. Rest assured that you have done well," Katya said.

Agnes left. Katya Karpov closed her office door, went to her desk and removed the brain study datasheet from her top desk drawer. She ran a finger down the column of subject study numbers until she located BS24. She moved her finger to the right, along the corresponding row, digesting each datum. BS24 was one of the outliers. He was, in fact, one of the two subjects identified as artists (in his case artisan) whose brain function appeared to have worsened over the period of the study. And she now knew from the story in the morning paper that he lived in the same neighborhood as the dead artist. The dead artist, Bechman Fitzwallington, whom she had discovered, after getting permission from the appropriate committee to unblind some of the data, was the other downside outlier.

Were there connections among these apparently disparate facts that could help to explain the biology? And what about the ethical dilemma that had fallen into her lap? She couldn't ignore that. Although her professional and personal lives since marrying Shane had sometimes abutted at the interface between biology and crime, she had tried to maintain the interface, keeping her and Shane's professional passions separate from their personal ones. Now Katya might be forced as a moral imperative to invite exploration of a possible causative link between biology and crime in the unlikely person of the *Mad Hatter of Music City*. Not a pleasant thought. Too likely to distract attention from her real interest. But facts are facts. They must be dealt with.

"Dr. Karpov," her secretary rapped gently on the office door and opened it a crack, "you're late for the appointment with the dean. His office called and I told them that you were on your way."

"Thank you, Lois," Katya answered, forcing a smile. "To avoid impugning the ethics of a less than truthful secretary, I suppose I should do as you promised."

Katya picked up a folder with a tab marked *Dean Stuff* and headed out.

"Off to see the wizard," she remarked as she breezed past her secretary, out the door, down the hall, and up a flight of stairs to confront face-on the person of the dean, a largely useless requirement of her position. Most of her duties were pleasurable, but some were endured rather than enjoyed. Meetings with the dean rarely left her feeling anything remotely akin to pleasure.

The eight finely toned limbs of Fiona Hayes and Vernon LaVista, III were still entangled from their previous evening's bedtime activities when they were awakened by the glare of the late morning sun beaming through the east window of their loft bedroom nestled deep in the priciest section of the epicenter of Nashville renaissance known as The Gulch. They were both artists, but not the starving variety of the species. That fact was thanks to the happy accident of Vernon having been born into a family of old Nashville money to a socially preoccupied mother and a thoroughly self-centered father, both of whom much preferred lavishing him with a limitless supply of legal tender to the necessary inconveniences of any attempts at serious parenting. Their disappointment in their only son's decision to take up sculpting as a vocation rather than a respectable career had not restricted the flow of cash in his direction. His parents might even have opened the cash spigot more generously in order to ensure that, despite his less than completely respectable choice of vocation, he could maintain a lifestyle that would not embarrass them among their friends at The Club.

Unlike her patron and lover, Fiona Hayes was the third daughter of artistically inclined parents (a painter and a cellist) and grew up on the northern fringes of what was now known as Germantown. Her formative years there predated the excessive gentrification of the area, and the Hayes ancestral home was too far north to be trendy anyway. Fiona's painter father, of course, knew (and also of course loathed) Bechman Fitzwallington. However, Fiona, living in the same general neighborhood and sharing the fact that each of their fathers was a painter, befriended Fitzwallington's daughter, Sally May Farmer, aka (currently) SalomeMe. The intensity of their friendship had ebbed in recent years as they took somewhat different routes toward maturity, but they remained friends. Fiona's hatred of Bechman Fitzwallington, while influenced by that of her father, was greatly exaggerated by adolescent confidences shared with the daughter of the hated artist.

Perhaps influenced by the artistic miasma in which she was immersed as a consequence of her parents' professions, Fiona felt compelled to identify for herself an artistic niche. She had no musical talent. She abhorred the technical simplicity and subjective value judgments inherent in painting, but she did consider herself a *visual person*. Fiona's search for an art form that attracted her ended in ceramics, pots at first and then what she called tile paintings. These were big *bas relief* representations of stylized people with backgrounds meant to encapsulate the personal stories of the foreground figures. She enjoyed the physicality of molding the clay, firing and coloring the finished product. Her bold creations had achieved some local popularity, especially among businesses with large wall spaces and a yen for patronizing local artists.

Fiona and Vernon gravitated toward each other more because of

their artistic interests and sexual availability than from personally
directed passion—i.e., they did not fall in love. But they enjoyed each
other and lived a comfortable and, in many ways, satisfying life—
mornings at the gym, afternoons sculpting and making tile paintings
in a studio space they rented just on the south edge of town, and
evenings partying, visiting the growing number of excellent
restaurants and trendy bars scattered about the city, and making love
(or, in their case, more accurately, having sex). Vernon would
occasionally visit Bechman Fitzwallington, paying homage to the
Nashville art community's most successful citizen. Sometimes he
could talk Fiona into joining him for such visits, but her intense
loathing of the old artist was difficult for her to hide, making such
visits often less than pleasurable.

Fiona Hayes and Vernon LaVista, III were on the short list of
people Hardy Seltzer had suggested to Shane Hadley that he might
want to interview, and they had arranged to meet the ex-detective at
Wall Street that afternoon.

Not my usual sort of customer, Pat Harmony thought, sizing up the
couple entering his bar late in the afternoon, *probably here to see
Shane.*

Not our usual kind of place, Fiona whispered in Vernon's ear. They
paused just inside the door to look the joint over.

The only customer at the bar was the guy at the end in the
wheelchair. Vernon recognized him from the old newspaper
photographs from when the name Shane Hadley was a household
word, at least in many area households. Vernon was an adolescent
when Shane took the career-ending bullet, and, as is often true of
adolescent boys, was lured by the violence to follow the stories in the
paper. It was in fact his memory of those stories of Sherlock Shane
that caused him to agree to meet with the ex-detective and to

convince Fiona to join him. That the meeting was to occur in a downtown bar they had never heard of seemed odd to both Vernon and Fiona, but they were intrigued by the adventure of it. Fiona, more than Vernon, was also interested to know what the former detective was up to relative to the death of the old bastard, BF. So here they were.

Incongruous. That was the first word that came to Shane's mind as he observed the handsome couple who stood hesitantly just inside the door to his Wall Street office looking more than a little self-conscious in their designer jeans and tasseled (his) or stiletto-heeled (hers) Italian leather shoes. Their pause at that spot was pregnant with incongruity, that asymmetrical sort of sensation which often leads one to ask *What am I doing here?* No doubt that question was troubling the brains of these two unlikely Wall Street guests.

Good, Shane thought. Asymmetry is an interrogator's friend.

Shane wheeled himself down the ramp from his spot at the bar and over to where the couple stood. He extended his hand which they, each in turn, shook weakly without speaking.

"I'm Shane Hadley," he said. "And I presume that you are Vernon LaVista and Fiona Hayes. Thank you so much for coming here to meet with me for a bit. I realize the nature of the place may surprise you, but I can vouch for its decency, the integrity of its spirits, and the honesty of my fellow ex-policeman and bartender, Pat Harmony." He gestured toward the bar and Harmony offered an anemic finger-wriggling wave in their direction. "Please join me."

Shane turned and headed back to his regular place, followed by the couple who still had not spoken and who continued to explore the ambience with swivel-necked doe-eyed wonder. It just wasn't the kind of place that they imagined still existed in this town. How had this place managed to withstand the onslaught of rampant gentrification and warp-speed development smack in the middle of the financial district? It felt almost like a mock-up scene for a movie set in an earlier epoch, maybe a leftover from the old Robert Altman's *Nashville* movie that was still reaired occasionally late at night on an old movie channel.

Shane motioned for his guests to sit beside him at the bar and ramped himself up to his spot.

"Look," he said, "there is only one question here of interest to anyone, I suspect including you and the dead artist's circle of acquaintances. Was Bechman Fitzwallington murdered? If so, who did it?" looking directly into the eyes of Fiona Hayes. "Was he murdered and did you do it or do you know who did?"

"Really, Mr. Hadley," Vernon finally broke the couple's silence, "we are artists, not assassins. We would hardly have the necessary skills for such a thing even if neither of us was particularly troubled by Bechman's death. He was after all a thoroughly unlikable son-of-a-bitch."

Something less than a ringing denial but spoken convincingly enough on its surface.

Fiona, still a little wide-eyed and swivel-necked, not quite yet assimilating completely the incongruity of the situation said, "Surely, Mr. Hadley, you have learned that Bechman Fitzwallington did not leave behind many admirers. I'd venture that you'd have a lot of trouble finding a single person in the local art community who mourns his loss. He was an evil man. An *evil* man!"

The intensity of Fiona's statement struck Shane.

He queried, "Evil?"

"Evil," Fiona replied with conviction and without elaborating.

"So, is an avenger of evil among his acquaintances?"

"Look," Fiona continued, engaging Shane's eyes directly now, "I think it very likely that someone hastened the old man's death and avenging evil would have been a perfectly defensible motive. But there could have been other motives. I have no idea about that. However, I do know that the art world in this town and the world in general are better off without him. It would seem to me that this dead dog should be permitted to lie without any excessive probing of the matter. What's the point?"

"You mean apart from the fact that murder is a crime? And we, the societal we, tend to frown on condoning transgressions of our laws. Would you agree that such an attitude toward human behavior usually serves us well?"

"Afraid we artists aren't so skilled at philosophical debate," Vernon interjected. "Not very interested in such things either. Art, Mr. Detective, is a different idiom. If looking for something nefarious in the web of events and people surrounding Bechman's death gets your rocks off, then go for it. But I'm afraid we can't help you out. And I've got other rocks to tend to."

Vernon slid down from his stool and took Fiona's arm to assist her dismount. They said nothing more and left Wall Street and Shane Hadley with no farewell, fond or otherwise.

Bloody hell! Shane thought. *I thoroughly blew that.*

Pat Harmony had freshened Shane's glass of sherry unbidden and the two men locked eyes for a second before Pat moved to return the sherry to its private space. Shane sipped at the wine and mused. That woman knows something that could either help to clarify this matter or complicate it further. That much is obvious. But not a chance in hell for me to find out what that is now. If there ever was a chance, I have summarily blown it. I'll need more potent ammunition than suspicion to convince Hardy and his people to open a real investigation. And that may be what it takes if there is to be any hope of getting to the bottom of this. Sherlock Shane indeed!

Bloody hell, Shane, what in heaven's name were you thinking?

Chapter 14

If the value of art is determined by the same demand/supply formula that holds sway in the general marketplace, the death of an artist reduces the value to a single variable.

The denominator is fixed. The value (read selling price) of a given work is completely determined by the demand. There would never be another authentic painting by Bechman Fitzwallington. Zilcho for the supply side. It was whatever it was and if you were interested in establishing the magnitude of the supply, you only needed to locate and inventory whatever paintings the old guy did while he was among the living. That number in hand, you just need to manipulate the demand to control the selling price.

But, if you are working on the business side of the art world, you know that, although the demand is regularly manipulated, that is generally done by people with influence in that world who are not controllable by you and your business guys. You just have to guess where to place your financial bets and hope for the best. You win some, you lose some. It's not an investment strategy for the faint of heart (or light of pocketbook). However, on rare occasions the payoff is, as every venture capitalist anxiously anticipates, unexpectedly extraordinary.

Thus, when Bruce Therault read the belated *New York Times* obituary for Bechman Fitzwallington, he choked on his hot coffee, spitting a large mouthful into his lap, staining his gray silk dressing gown and causing painful stinging sensations in the inner aspects of his thighs.

"Oh shit!" he said.

The Fitzwallington obit was written by the legendary *Times* art critic, Arturo Carbone. Mr. Carbone was generally recognized as the most influential critic of the past three decades. Talk about manipulating the demand side of the market value formula! Old Arturo, at the stroke of his pen, could move the needle either up or down in logarithmic leaps. And he was incorruptible. Numerous attempts had been made over the years to explode that persistent myth without the slightest hint of success.

After reciting the metrics—birth and death dates and locations, parents' names and occupations, name of his sole surviving blood relative, etc.—Carbone's obituary launched into a thoroughly uncharacteristic two paragraphs of praise for Fitzwallington's *distinctive* art. He waxed eloquent about the artist's unique approach, his special choice of medium, his skill at composition, and his extraordinary esthetic. The usually reserved critic concluded that, "*Bechman Fitzwallington's paintings deserve a place among the best of modern works by an American. He is unquestionably the most underrated artist of his generation.*"

"Holy shit," exclaimed Therault aloud, ignoring the burning sensation in his inner thighs. "We could be sitting on the mother lode!"

His cell phone suddenly blared the smoothly syncopated tones of Marvin Gaye belting out his classic, "I Heard it Through the Grapevine".

Therault was fond of the message but thought the tune cliché. He retained the ringtone for its message. He was not opposed to cliché if it served a purpose.

Arturo Carbone's obituary of Fitzwallington triggered a transcontinental avalanche of clichéd ringtones that disturbed the morning quiet time of Blythe Fortune, Athena Golden, SalomeMe, and several other parties with lingering or suddenly rebirthed interests in the dead artist and his work. Amazing how the slightest whiff of a possible windfall can amp up the cliché traffic in the cat's cradle plexus of human connections.

The *Nashville Tennessean* reprinted the slightly belated New York Times obit verbatim. Although he knew precious little about the forces driving the art world, the potential significance of the piece did not escape Hardy Seltzer. This was bound to focus renewed attention on the artist and the circumstances surrounding his demise. Seltzer feared that this was likely to be a pot of trouble that he could not possibly avoid. He needed to get on top of this before it lodged itself in the craws of his perpetually antsy and overreacting superiors, exaggerating their anxiety and precipitating a tirade aimed, no doubt, at Seltzer. Better check in with Shane. That was probably overdue anyway.

When Shane Hadley's cell phone chirped unimaginatively, he had just read the piece in the *Tennessean* and was about to open a related conversation with KiKi. They had finished their light breakfast and were nursing a second cup of coffee. They had chosen that morning to take their coffee and pastry on the deck of their flat that overlooked the alley. It was a lovely morning. Shane contemplated the angular geometry of the sunrise shadows splayed across the Printers Alley floor and pondered the implications of what was likely to be an explosion of interest in Fitzwallington for his floundering investigation into the artist's death.

"Cheerio," he answered after checking caller ID and noting that it was Hardy Seltzer. "To what do I owe such an early morning call, Hardy? Perhaps something to do with the content of our fair city's morning journal?"

"Could be trouble for me," Hardy replied. "Have you discovered anything interesting about the old guy's death? Is there any inkling of murder as a possibility? Please tell me no."

"I fear I can't yet respond to the question so decisively, my man. Still trying to get my mind around the cast of characters. An interesting lot as you suggested."

"If this thing from the NYT causes as big a stir as I'm afraid of," Seltzer sounded more than a little anxious, "any hint of possible foul play will no doubt attract more attention than will benefit anyone, especially the police force."

"Did I not know better," Shane responded, smiling to himself, "I would think you were attempting to influence my investigation. Surely not. Surely not. Tell you what, my friend, why don't you meet me around five this afternoon at Wall Street and we'll compare notes and thoughts."

"Sure, Shane. I'll do that, but this day could bring some surprises that may not be pleasant."

"See you at five," Shane replied. "Ta-ta."

"Goodbye."

Hardy tolerated Shane's affected Anglicisms but was not amused by them. He generally chose to ignore them as much as possible.

KiKi was engrossed in the Op-Ed page of the paper. When she realized that Shane had ended the call, she looked up.

"I gather that was your pal Hardy Seltzer," she said. "A trifle early for him to call. Something to do with your dead artist?"

"Well," Shane replied, still looking absently at the sun-shadowed alley geometry, "it's likely that, at the very least, the *New York Times* has decided to make a very troubled young woman exceedingly rich. It should be interesting to witness the consequences."

"And at most?"

"At most, the promise of wealth may flush out the scoundrels in this saga. There are so many possible scoundrels."

"The young woman…you mean the daughter?"

"Yes. The notorious SalomeMe."

"The obituary says that she is his only blood relative. I presume that means sole heir?"

"Apparently so."

"How certain is his paternity?"

"I have no idea. I don't know that anyone has questioned that. I suppose the stakes may be high enough now to raise the question. Why do you ask?"

Katya had avoided getting involved in this discussion up until now. She had strained to keep the interface between biology and crime distinct, the barrier intact. But her resolve was feeling a little shaky at that moment. After all, professional and personal passions were both part of who they were, each and together. She surely didn't intend to risk the integrity of their relationship. Nothing was more important than that.

And she did know some things about Bechman Fitzwallington's biology that might be important to Shane's criminal investigation. But she wasn't sure about revealing things that maybe should stay confidential. True, the subject was dead now, and the potential relevance to a crime might negate the confidentiality requirement, but still…

"Well," Katya replied, obviously hesitant, "I've avoided telling you that Fitzwallington was a subject in our brain health study. He dropped out a couple of years ago, but we had accumulated a good bit of data before then. He was one of the outliers I've been stewing about."

Shane was surprised that KiKi hadn't told him this before now. Sometime very early in their relationship, they had shared an explicit vow of complete honesty and, at least for Shane, the sin of dishonesty included omission as well as commission.

"A trifle late for you to reveal this little tidbit, don't you think? What else have you been concealing?"

"Shane," Katya replied, "don't get your knickers in a knot."

She had passively absorbed some of Shane's frequent Anglicisms and they slipped into her conversation if she didn't pay close attention. She was aware that Shane was jealous of such phrases as the one that had just now escaped her too inattentive lips. She desperately wished that she could retrieve it.

"My knickers, if I wore such, would be just fine, my dear," Shane said, making no attempt to disguise his displeasure. "And, if you insist on using such quaint English metaphors, you should at least respect their gender specificity."

The word that came to Katya's mind was *insufferable*. Shane was the dearest being on the planet to Katya, but he could be, on occasion, insufferable. This seemed to be such an occasion. She refused to take the bait.

"Shane," she said, summoning her most authoritative voice, "I didn't tell you about this earlier because I am honor-bound to respect patient confidentiality and also because I didn't see how any information we had about his biology would be relevant to your investigation. I may have been wrong about that."

Shane didn't react. He was pouting. Even small lapses in their commitment to complete honesty threatened him. He was sometimes fragile. Especially since the accident.

Neither of them spoke for a few minutes. A delivery truck lumbered noisily down the alley. Shadows shrank as the rising sun's angle with the buildings lining the alley sharpened. Shane wasn't sure exactly what troubled him so—the Fitzwallington thing? Something not quite defined with KiKi? The goddam wheelchair? The accretion of years of constant reminders of his lack of independence—death by a thousand cuts? The aging artist appeared to have enjoyed a peaceful exit, whether natural or not. Shane envied that.

Finally, Shane spoke, picking up on Katya's last statement. "You said you might be wrong about that. What do you mean?"

"It may not mean anything, but from what you say, the daughter seems to be a central character in the saga."

"That's true, even more so if there turns out to be a lot of money involved. She is his only heir as far as I can tell. So?"

"Mr. Fitzwallington carried a genetic trisomy, three sex chromosomes instead of two, XYY. Although men with the XYY syndrome are not uniformly sterile, their incidence of sterility is higher than normal. Any chance Fitzwallington is not this SalomeMe's father after all?"

"Meaning that unless the old guy left a will, she wouldn't inherit the paintings. Now that would be interesting. We could get DNA from the autopsy, I presume. I guess we'd also need the same from the daughter to test for paternity. Is that right?"

"That's correct."

"Such a request might be informative. If she knows he is not her father, she would probably resist providing the material necessary to prove that. Not sure what all this says about a possible murder. I suppose that if she discovered this only recently, she might have felt the need to hurry things along so she could claim her inheritance before this became more general knowledge. That could be a motive. Don't you think?"

"You're the detective, my love," Katya finished her cup of coffee, stood up, and bent down to kiss the top of Shane's head. "I have a job to get to."

Katya retreated to their bedroom at the rear of the flat to complete her morning toilette and don her doctor/scientist persona, ready herself for the day ahead. She desperately hoped that she had not betrayed her profession by revealing the information to Shane. She was not at all comfortable trying to straddle the interface between biology and crime and wasn't sure she was capable of doing it well. Katya was not in the habit of attempting things that she was not confident she could do well. She was troubled.

Pat Harmony unlocked the cabinet that served again as the special abode of Shane Hadley's prized sherry, removed the bottle, and limped slowly over to the end of his bar where Shane sat lost in his thoughts. Harmony filled the freshly polished glass that he had put at Shane's place earlier to about an imagined one-quarter mark, recorked the bottle and headed back across to replace it in the cabinet.

"Just leave it out, Pat," Shane patted a spot on the bar beside his glass. "And burnish another glass, please. Hardy Seltzer is supposed to drop by."

"You got Hardy to drinking sherry?" Harmony asked, grinning broadly. "Never woulda thought it. Son-of-a-bitch."

"I prefer to think that our friend discovered the pleasure of sherry for himself, but perhaps I was an accessory." Shane took a sip from his glass and sighed quietly. He was very fond of the wine, perhaps too fond.

It was a little past five and a few of the regulars started to wander in. Since Shane had reappeared there, always positioned at his specially constructed space at the end of the bar, he was acknowledged by the other patrons, nodded to, but they generally gave him a pretty wide berth. The policemen, of course, knew who he was, were at least familiar with the legend, but in the Wall Street setting, they kept a respectable distance. He was often joined by another person with whom he conversed intently, appearing to be conducting business of some sort. The other patrons sometimes wondered what business, but they didn't inquire. After all, they just came for a drink and some idle chatter. The Shane Hadley legend allowed as how he was not given to idle chatter.

When Hardy Seltzer entered the bar, he strolled deliberately to where Shane sat quietly sipping his wine. Offering only a token nod to the other bar patrons, some of whom he knew quite well, Hardy walked directly to the end of the bar and took a seat next to Shane, ignoring the bubble of respected space that usually insulated the ex-cop from unwanted intrusions. Pat Harmony hurried over to pour Hardy a generous portion of sherry.

"Hello, Hardy," the bartender said, nodding somewhat tentatively.

"Good afternoon, Pat," Seltzer replied. "Thanks for the wine."

"You should thank your meditating friend," Harmony responded.

Shane was still staring into the space before him, oblivious to Hardy Seltzer, Pat Harmony, and probably the entire animate world. He was in his thinking space.

Hardy respected that fact and didn't speak. He sat quietly, sipping his sherry. Harmony returned to his usual neutral spot, leaning against the cabinets behind the bar, polishing a glass with a cup towel, and humming to himself what sounded like a fragment of a Gregorian chant but probably wasn't.

Shane finally broke the silence.

"Hardy, my man," Shane said while still staring blankly into space, "the only way I can see that we have a chance to find out whether the departure of our widely hated and newly admired artist was assisted is to open a formal investigation. I've milked this retired detective ruse about as far as the odd cast of characters involved is

KEN BRIGHAM

going to tolerate." He turned to face Hardy and placed a hand on the detective's shoulder. "The badge, Hardy, my man. We need the power of the badge."

"That's going to be a hard sell, Shane. You sure you've gone as far as you can on your own? Why a formal investigation without some evidence to support it? Understand, Shane, if I try to push this and it fizzles," he raked a forefinger symbolically across his neck, "it'll be curtains for me."

"Two things about the situation have changed, Hardy. You know about the *Times* art review that is likely to send the value of Fitzwallington's paintings through the roof. Depending on how many there are, we're talking real money, and, as you are well aware, there is no more potent motive for misbehavior than money. Second, I have come by some information that may warrant determining the paternity of she who has been assumed to be the artist's sole heir. How about that for a complicating factor?"

"What information?"

"While I must protect my source," Shane said, "I have it on good authority that our deceased friend possessed a genetic oddity, it is called a trisomy, that could very well have rendered him sterile. To answer this question will require DNA samples from both Fitzwallington and the lovely SalomeMe. I fear that the tattooed one will not be anxious to participate in this little project, especially if she has any suspicion of the possible results. After all, she could have a fortune at risk here."

"I see what you're saying, Shane," Hardy sipped at his wine. "And what if she knew that she wasn't a legitimate heir even before dear daddy's demise? Might she have hastened things along in hopes of avoiding such an inconvenient discovery?"

"The power of the badge, Hardy, my man. We need the power of the badge."

Hardy sighed. "*A pot of trouble I can't possibly avoid,*" he thought.

Chapter 15

Bruce Therault read the identity of the caller, Mildred Roth, spokesperson for the group of Galleria Salinas investors, before punching *accept* on his cell phone. Bruce didn't know Ms. Roth well, but she had regularly delivered on the financial commitments of the group she represented so that he didn't feel a compelling need to know much more about her. He judged partnerships more by what they accomplished than the character and motives of the players.

Truth be told, Mildred Roth was a pretty scary lady; at least she could sound that way on the phone. Bruce had never actually met her in person. He imagined her a statuesque brunette with dark eyeshadow, pale gray lipstick, midnight blue nail polish, and penetrating hazel eyes who habitually dressed in a form-fitting ankle-length sheath of deeply intense New York City black. Maybe something like a chimera of Morticia and the Dragon Lady. He knew that he could be wrong about that. He really didn't care. Just keep sending the dinero, Dragon Lady.

"This is Bruce," he said.

"Hello, Bruce," Mildred Roth replied. Then, as usual, she cut directly to the chase. "Given these recent developments, of which I am certain you are aware, we believe there is considerable urgency in sewing up the Fitzwallington matter. Have you completed an inventory of the available works and assured your gallery's exclusive rights to their sale?"

"We are working on that," Therault replied. "Mace Ricci is still in Nashville working full time on the matter. We're close."

Bruce Therault was blowing smoke. He didn't know how close they were to nailing this thing down, but he was certain that the fallout from the *Times* obit would be a complication. How much of one remained to be seen. Bruce hadn't talked to Mace Ricci in several days and had intended to contact him after reading the *Times* piece. Morticia Dragon Lady had beat him to the punch. She had a habit of doing that.

"Close has very little value for us. I talked to Mace just now, and it is not at all clear to me how close you are. And who is this ex-cop who appears to have a more than healthy interest in the situation? Either you don't know what's happening there or you are not dealing straight with us. Don't let this thing fall through, Bruce. Especially not now." The tone of her voice changed, each word stretched taut and fired off staccato, like rounds from an Uzi, same intensity, same intent. "We've gone to considerable trouble and expense to make this happen and our group would not take kindly to anyone who fails to deliver on their promises. I am speaking primarily of you, Bruce."… *rat… tat… tat…* "You. Don't. Want. To. Mess. This. Up. Believe me; you don't want to do that."

Wow! Therault thought. He was not particularly surprised to discover that this group was capable of playing hardball, but the verbal blitzkrieg blindsided him. A side of Morticia Dragon Lady that he had suspected might exist but hadn't had the pleasure of seeing in action before. He thought for a few seconds. True, the support of the investment group had been and continued to be important, but now they could be in a position to reap exorbitant returns on their investment, and they couldn't do that without the gallery's connections. He made an executive decision. He disconnected the call without responding.

After barely a second pause, Marvin Gaye launched into his ode to the grapevine.

Such a cliché.

Therault ignored it.

For any interested party, it was a simple matter to identify what dealers held paintings by Bechman Fitzwallington that were available for sale. Just Google them. Consequently, phone lines at Galleria Salinas on Manhattan's Upper East Side and at the AvantArt Gallery on the southern edge of downtown Nashville had burned white-hot since the appearance of the *NYT* Fitzwallington obituary. Ringtone clichés reverberated across the continent. The cat's cradle plexus of human communication hummed.

So, when Blythe Fortune finally got through to Athena Golden, both of them were aware of the possible implications of the situation, and their conversation was guarded. They had spoken only on rare occasions before and never under such intense circumstances.

"Any fallout from the obit?" Blythe summoned her most blasé NYC attitude.

"A few calls," Athena replied. "And you?"

"Some calls," Blythe answered. "Do we know much about the situation with the paintings?"

"I don't know many details yet. I did have a visit the other day from your investigator, Mr. Ricci. Not a very pleasant sort."

"Mr. Ricci?" Blythe pretended not to recognize the name.

"Yes, Mace Ricci. He said he was working for your gallery."

"I see," Fortune mused. "My business partner, Bruce Therault, probably hired him just to give us some eyes and ears there. Shouldn't be a problem."

Damn it! Blythe thought. I wish to hell that Bruce would clue me in when he does something like this.

"Athena," Blythe continued, "I hope we can cooperate. There should be plenty of profit for both galleries if we play our cards right. Neither of us will maximize our benefit by fighting with each other."

"That's no doubt true."

A tepid response, Blythe thought, to a less than convincing proposal.

"Well," Blythe said. "Let's do stay in touch. Perhaps we can share any information that we get about the inventory and availability."

There was a pause, and then Athena replied, "Yes, that could surely be helpful."

They ended the call on a superficially amiable note. Neither of them believed the substance of their conversation. But then, art is not about substance.

Mace Ricci punched the red *end call* button on his cell phone and headed immediately for his car. It wasn't the first time that he had found himself the target of the ire of Mildred Roth (he couldn't resist thinking of such experiences as *the wrath of Roth*). Mace had done work for that group going back to his days as a New York cop and then continuing after he quit the force. Well, he quit the force in a sense, chose not to wait around for the threatened less-noble means of exit that would have had the same outcome but have been less personally satisfying. The work for the group that Mildred Roth spoke for was lucrative, considerably more so than the police force would ever have been. Although the *wrath of Roth* always annoyed him, the outbursts didn't happen too frequently, and his compensation was sufficient motivation to tolerate them. Mace Ricci, gainfully employed private citizen, was not at all unhappy with the course he had chosen. People who gravitate to careers as policemen are generally pragmatists, if prone to somewhat simplistic interpretations of that philosophy. The same is true of professional assassins.

Ricci was headed as fast as was practical from the parking lot of his hotel downtown to the Germantown abode of SalomeMe. He had tried to call her as soon as he got off the phone with Mildred Roth but didn't get an answer. It was abundantly clear that the daughter was the key to discovering the number, location, condition, and ownership of her father's remaining paintings. Ricci had spent considerable time cultivating a relationship with her that was meant to assure his employers exclusive rights to handling sales of the paintings (and therefore exclusive recipients of the commissions). He thought he had done pretty well, but she had resisted giving him any specific information, and it appeared that the time had come to move ahead with this project. Better to do that in person.

The time was approaching noon, and the lunchtime parade of cars packed with downtown workers heading for lunch at the trendy Germantown restaurants was starting to build. Ricci maneuvered across Eighth Avenue, around by the Capitol building and the park, home of a row of fountains for kids to romp in when the weather was hot, the farmer's market, and a carillon. An odd trio of attractions, Ricci thought.

At last, he turned into the quiet street in the residential heart of the area where SalomeMe's house sat silently, resting on its haunches like an aging widow resigned to her fate. A striking contrast to the persona of its owner. Ricci pulled to the curb in front the house and parked close behind a late-model midsize Chevrolet that he had not seen there before. SalomeMe opened her front door in response to Ricci's several impatient punches at the doorbell. She was in the full uniform of her public self. She appeared to be uncomfortable. Her body language was like she had been caught *en flagrante delecti* with an illicit lover. Ricci was confused by that until he looked past her and saw the woman sitting on the living room sofa. The AvantArt Gallery owner, Athena Golden.

Damn!

The afternoon was warm, and Parker Palmer sat on the deck in back of his house pondering the caprice of his chosen profession. He was still baffled by the obituary of the artist that he steadfastly refused to think of by the pretentious name that the old man had assumed. To Palmer, the guy was Billy Wayne Farmer. Always had been. Always would be.

How could such a knowledgeable and highly respected New York critic suddenly decide to see Farmer's art as deserving of such unbridled praise? The old guy was a son of a bitch. Okay, you could live with that. But also, his art was just not that special. It was without depth and, especially in the last couple of years, it was basically just repeating a lifelong formula. The fact that he was dead didn't change that.

Palmer had managed to create a niche for his own work and had made a decent living at it. He was proud of that accomplishment. While early in his career he had aspired to wider recognition in the art world, he had long ago accepted the reality that he was not a great artist…good enough to make a living at it, but not great. He was comfortable with who he was and satisfied with the life he had made for himself. What galled him about Farmer's posthumously blossoming fame was that Farmer's talent was no greater than his own.

Art is not about reality, Palmer thought, it is entirely about perception. *The eye of the beholder* as they say… caprice. Reality had nothing to do with it. If the beholder happened to be Arturo Carbone who perceived something that wasn't there, then perception became, with the stroke of the revered critic's pen, reality.

Thus mused Parker Palmer in the afternoon sun of a warm day, raptly gazing at his green lawn and the lone elm tree standing tall and proud in its center. He thought of his mother. She was a gifted artist who lived her entire too-short life with very few people aware of her gift. She certainly made very little money at it. So, how come Palmer, his mom, and Billy Wayne Farmer shared the artist gene, if there was such a thing, but not the spotlight? Where was the justice? A silly question. There was no justice in the creative world, Palmer thought. He was feeling a little sorry for himself. That wasn't like him, and he didn't like it. Damn Billy Wayne Farmer.

The haunting twang and drawl of Jimmy Reed's *Bright Lights Big City* called to Palmer from his cell phone. He didn't answer it.

Had he interrupted his musings to answer the call, Palmer would have been greeted by a voice that he had not heard in several years, since the death of his mother. The caller's reason for trying to reconnect after such a long absence had something to do with Billy Wayne Farmer's recent death. The caller had read the *Times* obituary and was struck with the opportunity this turn of events might present. Time to mend fences with the family. You never know. You just never know.

Fiona Hayes, Shane thought. He sat in the center of his invisible insulating bubble at the end of the Wall Street bar, periodically sampling the glass of sherry that sat before him, and pondering the notes he had made in the small leather-bound notebook that was always present in his left shirt pocket. He had opened the notebook and laid it on the bar before him. He was going carefully through his notes from each of the interviews and came to a sudden stop at the name of Fiona Hayes. Of this entire group of Bechman Fitzwallington haters, Fiona Hayes was the most vehement.

Shane's legs hurt. Both of them. A sort of nerve-grating ache; endurable pain but distracting. KiKi said that could be a good sign, that he might still be regenerating some nerves down there. And he was gaining a little strength in the excruciating Monday morning workouts with the physical therapist. But he didn't find any of that particularly consoling at the moment. His legs hurt.

Fiona Hayes. He tried to refocus his thoughts. He had pretty much blown the interview with her and her arrogant sculptor friend. But he had written in his little embossed brown leather book, *she knows something that she is not telling me.* And *evil* she had said of the old artist…*evil.* That sounds a bit more of a character indictment than something like rascal or even son-of-a-bitch. Evil sounds like you're talking big-time misbehavior.

"The money, paternity, and Fiona Hayes," Shane greeted Hardy with the substance of his triptych argument for opening a formal investigation, foregoing any preliminaries.

They hadn't planned to meet, but Hardy Seltzer had been stewing about this thing ever since they last talked, and he knew that Shane was likely to be at Wall Street around five in the afternoon, so he just dropped by.

"Fiona Hayes?" Hardy queried. "Who the hell is Fiona Hayes?"

Setzer had forgotten the name that he had given earlier to Shane as someone to follow up on. He had not thought of her as a major player.

"The lovely Fiona Hayes, local ceramicist, is reason number three for opening this thing up to the full attention of our esteemed law enforcement apparatus. Primarily meaning, of course, getting you involved. The power of the badge, not to mention the skill of an active investigator carrying the city government's imprimatur."

Hardy made a mental note to add the word to his list of words to look up as soon as he had a chance.

"Murder," Hardy moaned. "Has to be something credible to indicate foul play. Like I said, Shane, there's no law against dying, famous or not."

"Don't loose ends count? Unexplained discrepancies in the narrative? Come, now, Hardy, my man. There is a story here begging to be told. It's just that it hasn't come together yet. Still too many blanks that need filling in. You are very skilled at filling in blanks."

"I'm sure there's a story. There is always a story. But I'm also sure that my people would be very quick to tell me that I don't get paid to flesh out stories. I get paid to investigate murders. No murder, no job. Look, Shane," Seltzer looked directly into Shane's eyes, "what do you really think? Does your gut tell you this is a murder case?"

"Oh," Shane replied, smiling, "I am quite sure the artist was murdered, at least in a technical sense. However, some blanks need filling in to confirm that suspicion. And, of course, to identify the killer…or perhaps killers. There seem to be so many possibilities."

Hardy Seltzer was shocked and showed it.

"How in holy hell can you be so sure about that?" he said.

"Gestalt," Shane replied.

Hardy made a mental note to add the word to his list.

"Perhaps, given the circumstances," Shane continued, "an artistic metaphor is more appropriate. You see, my man, there is a picture emerging here but it is not finished yet, *non finito,* the Italians would say."

Another potential entry to Hardy's lookup list.

"However," Shane continued, "the picture is complete enough to allow a perceptive observer to sense the intended message."

Seltzer was thinking hard about exactly how he could present this to his superiors without sounding a complete fool. It was not immediately obvious to him that it would be possible to do that. He really did trust Shane's remarkable powers of perception, even when the logic was not entirely clear. Shane just seemed often to know stuff before it was obvious to anyone else. Even Shane wasn't very good at explaining how he knew nonobvious stuff. He just did. And he was usually right. Usually. In this case, usually might not be good enough for Hardy Seltzer. His career, the principal investment of his entire life, could be on the line. Was Shane Hadley's hunch (gestalt?) enough to justify the risk? Well, was it?

Seltzer's cell phone launched suddenly into a fully orchestrated version of *The Battle Hymn of the Republic*. Hardy answered the call without checking caller ID.

"Seltzer," a long pause. "Mmm, hmm. Got it. I'm downtown. Be there is a few minutes. Tape a perimeter and keep the scene intact." He ended the call.

"And?" Shane queried.

"That hatter guy," Hardy answered. "He somehow escaped from the hospital and holed up in the Fitzwallington house. He had a gun and chose to play shoot out with the guys in blue. He lost the game."

Chapter 16

Solving the enigmatic riddle of Richelieu Jones required the naïveté of a second-year medical resident. The young man had not yet learned to ignore the obvious and so he spent some time on the Internet exploring the origin of the term *Mad Hatter*. He discovered that the term resulted from the effects of mercury poisoning on the brain, but that the use of mercury in the converting of animal pelts to felt had long since been abandoned. Nowadays, hatters went mad at about the same rate as everybody else so that the term no longer had any practical value. Still intrigued by the possibility and refusing to let the facts spoil his brilliant theory, the resident spent more time talking to Mr. Jones. To his delight, the resident discovered that this hatter had, several years ago, reverted to the old mercury-based felt making methods. And, Mr. Jones linked that change in his felt making procedure, and other Francophilic behaviors, to the discovery, resulting from the genome analysis done as part of the university's brain health study, that his ancestors were French Canadian, probably fur traders. Unfortunately, Mr. Jones had flown the coop before specimens for measurements of mercury levels could be collected to nail down the diagnosis.

It was the geneticist, Harold Werth, his large head bobbing slightly back and forth nervously, who told this story to Katya

Karpov. It was immediately obvious that Dr. Karpov was not pleased.

The eventual decision about what genomic information to reveal to the participants in the brain health study was debated broad and long and never reached a consensus. Werth had argued forcefully for total disclosure, not just ancestry, but physical traits, disease proclivities, the whole shebang. Karpov was not at all convinced that total disclosure was such a good idea. So much of the interpretation was more speculation than hard fact, and the possibility of unanticipated consequences was enormous. The Institutional Review Board would not approve feedback of speculative genome interpretations to the participants anyway. However, Katya was convinced that people who volunteered to participate in a study deserved something tangible from it. And revealing ancestry information seemed to give them something of value (a lot of people paid commercial companies for that information) and seemed unlikely to cause harm. So that was the compromise reached in the end, although it didn't please everyone, most notably Harold Werth. Dr. Karpov was now confronted with the very real possibility that their diligent efforts to prevent harm to the study participants resulting from the gene studies had failed miserably.

"Well," Katya stood up from her chair and paced about her office, obviously upset, "we have here an SAE, Harold. A goddam SAE in a study where there wasn't even any intervention. How did we let that happen?"

SAE, serious adverse event, was the dreaded bane of any scientist doing studies in humans. Usually an SAE was a bad reaction to a new drug or something like that. But an unusual reaction to ancestry information that turned out bad? Were investigators responsible for that? Katya was interested in assigning responsibility for Mr. Jones's mercury poisoning but even more concerned about the larger question of assigning responsibility for how genetic information was dealt with. Maybe this was a major flaw in the design of this study. Should she cancel the whole thing?

Dr. Karpov knew that Richelieu Jones had somehow escaped from the hospital. She was more than a little disturbed by the fact that hospital security was that porous. Had she known that Mr. Jones lay at that very moment stone cold dead on the front steps of the former dwelling of Bechman Fitzwallington, not far from the body of a metropolitan policeman whom the *Mad Hatter* had managed to take down with him, God only knows how she would have reacted. Talk about a serious adverse event? Richelieu Jones had suffered the most serious and most adverse event possible. Dr. Karpov would discover that soon enough.

"OK, Harold," Dr. Karpov sat back down behind her desk and tried hard to engage the eyes of the geneticist. He continued to stare at the floor before him and gently nod his large head. "I think we have to cancel the entire brain health study. Throw out the data, shred the records, purge the computers. We're risking doing a lot more harm than good with this, Harold. A lot more harm than good."

"Come now, Katya," Werth responded, his head bobbing back and forth more rapidly, as though searching for a frequency that would sync with the rhythm of his speech, "we both know that you know better than that. Destroying records would probably be a felony, for starters, and I don't think you are looking to commit a crime as a means of atoning for what you surely see as an honest mistake in study design. You are a wise woman, and that would not be wise."

Katya was not sure that wisdom had anything to do with it, but she realized that she was overreacting and needed to gather her wits in order to deal with the situation. She did, however, believe that even honest mistakes could have negative consequences, and negative consequences demand responsibility. Dr. Katya Karpov was painfully aware that she sat behind the desk that was the buck's terminal stop.

Werth continued, "Stuff happens, Katya. Clinical research always carries risks, and sooner or later, any active investigator is going to come up against the probability of having done harm while trying to do good. You can't worry too much about that."

"How about informed consent, Harold? Was Mr. Jones told that providing him with genetic information about his ancestry could result in major changes in his behavior that could result in mercury poisoning that would drive him mad? Of course not. No way could we have anticipated that."

"Unanticipated consequences are a major part of the stuff that happens," Werth replied. "And this study promises to tell us a lot about how the brain functions or fails to. It could lay the groundwork for major advances in early recognition and treatment of cognitive decline. Risks? Sure. We shouldn't kid ourselves about that. We are even asking people to take risks that can't be defined or anticipated. If you think that's unethical or immoral or whatever, then you're in the wrong business, Katya."

"You're preaching to me, Harold," Katya said. "Apparently a talent of yours that I hadn't been aware of. I strongly prefer that you stick with your chosen scientific profession," she smiled, beginning to have some success as recollecting her wits.

Werth also smiled and finally looked directly at Katya. "Steady as she goes, Katya," he said. "Steady as she goes."

After Werth left her office, Katya sat for a while going through in her mind the things she had to do: report the SAE to the review board; convene the scientific advisory group to review the event and make recommendations; report the situation to the funding agency, and collect all of her faculty and staff involved in the study to thoroughly analyze how they were going about the entire project. All of that had to be done before making any big decisions. After all, they were not actively recruiting new participants anymore.

Rationalizations, she thought. They come so easily. Not much help to the *Mad Hatter of Music City*.

Shootouts tend to attract attention. If you want to drum up a crowd and aren't too concerned about the threat of bodily harm, just choose up sides and start shooting at each other. You will draw a crowd.

So, the scene in the vicinity of the Fitzwallington house in Germantown where the *Mad Hatter of Music City* had chosen to engage the Metro Police Department's finest in a gun battle was pretty much chaos. The chaos lasted longer than the shooting of the Mad Hatter and the lone policeman whom he had managed to mortally wound in the brief and very lopsided battle. The chaos lasted plenty long to greet the arrival of Hardy Seltzer. Hardy pushed his way through the crowd and ducked under the yellow crime scene tape.

Anyone who has not experienced the intangible bond that develops among people who routinely risk their lives in the everyday practice of their profession cannot understand the impact of the first sight of the dead body of a policeman on a living colleague. Seltzer just stood still, staring at the body of a young officer whom he had come to know pretty well. A good cop. Young wife. Couple of kids. A common enough story. But the tragedy and the threat were as potent as ever. No matter how many times you'd been forced to play your assigned part in the story, the tragedy of human potential snuffed suddenly out, and the knowledge that you could be next were excruciatingly real. And the love of a brother or sister, a comrade-in-arms, now lost. That, too.

Hardy looked up at the body of Richelieu Jones sprawled lifeless on the front porch steps and spoke to Harvey Schorr, the officer who had come over to stand beside him. Hardy did not look at the officer, his head still mired in a treacly morass of thoughts and feelings.

"What the fuck happened?" Hardy said.

The officer was shocked at the profanity. Hardy Seltzer rarely used serious obscenities and didn't admire profanity in others. Most of the guys respected that.

"Apparently," the officer responded, trying hard to keep his voice steady, "the hatmaker guy, his name is Richard Jones, just showed up here out of the blue with a gun. A guy who lives next door saw him pacing about the front porch and waving a handgun. When Jones discharged a couple of rounds into the air, the guy next door called 911. When we got here, Jones had barricaded himself inside the house. We waited him out for a while, but a crowd was gathering, and we feared collateral damage. We called to him on the bullhorn with no response. Then Officer Henderson started toward the front door intending to attempt to establish direct contact with Jones. But Jones came rushing suddenly out the door firing his gun. We returned fire but Henderson took a fatal round before we could bring Jones down. I dispatched one of the officers to apprehend the guy who called 911 so we could at least question him."

"We'll pull all the stops on this one," Seltzer said. "And we'll need to have another look at the Fitzwallington matter. We've got a dead cop, Harvey. A dead cop. And too many goddam coincidences. I hate coincidences, Harvey. The brass may not like this, but they're just going to have to live with it."

"Almost certainly mercury poisoning," Shane said.

He was responding to Hardy Seltzer's puzzled musing about why Richilieu Jones had behaved so irrationally. Hardy was really troubled by his colleague's death and didn't have a lot of sympathy for the man who had killed him. But Seltzer was also troubled by what seemed to him a situation where two people died for no good reason. Why? He was haunted by the question ever since the Germantown scene at the Fitzwallington house had been burned into his brain. Why?

"In this day and age?" Hardy said. "What I learned from Master Google about the Mad Hatter thing was that it didn't happen anymore because mercury-based felt making had been abandoned long ago in favor of more modern nontoxic methods. Isn't that so?"

"That is apparently quite so, my man," Shane responded. "However, I suspect our Francophilic friend is a special case."

Shane and Hadley were sitting on the Printers Alley deck. It was not a prearranged meeting. Hadley walked from his office on the square down Second Avenue and up the hill to Printers Alley. He was ostensibly on his way home, but decided to wander through the alley on the off chance that he would encounter Shane. Indeed, Shane was sitting on his deck, fondling a glass of sherry and watching the afternoon passersby disinterestedly. He was thinking about the Fitzwallington case, trying to fit some more of the pieces of the puzzle together, when he spotted Hardy Seltzer ambling down the alley and called to him, inviting him up. Maybe the meeting wasn't prearranged. Or maybe it was. Depends on who one deems responsible for the business of making prearrangements. Shane had barely had time to retrieve and fill a glass for his guest before they fell into a conversation about the afternoon tragedy in Germantown.

Their conversation was interrupted by the throaty purr of Katya's Boxter and the dull roar of the ground level garage door opening beneath where they sat.

"Ah," exclaimed Shane, "the lady of the house arrives."

"Perhaps I should go," Hardy said. "We can talk later."

Dr. Karpov had been stewing about the Richelieu Jones thing ever since Harold Werth had told her the up-to-date story. She was even more concerned when she heard on the radio news as she drove home that Jones had been killed by police gunfire as he appeared to be assaulting the house of the dead artist. Damn! she thought.

Katya shoved the French doors open with a bit more force than necessary and strode out onto the deck. She pulled up a chair and sat down opposite Shane and Hardy as Seltzer was making motions toward leaving.

"Please, Hardy," Katya said, "don't leave." She motioned him back to his seat. "I would like to tell both of you what I know of Richelieu Jones with a sincere hope that you can tell me something more that will ease my mind. I fear the wall separating science and crime that I've been trying so hard to maintain may be beginning to crumble. It scares me. That possibility really scares me. I respect what you guys do. Really respect it. But I just don't want to have anything to do with crime if I can avoid it. Until now, I thought I could do that, but maybe not."

She looked at Shane. He looked uncomfortable.

"Mercury poisoning," Shane said. "Is that the topic you wish to discuss?"

"How did you figure it out, Shane?" Katya asked.

"A couple of those damned coincidences that I so loathe," Shane replied. "Did I not know better I would begin to think that the whole of human experience is nothing more than bloody chance."

"Not a very enlightened view," Katya said. "But, what coincidences?"

"Coincidence number one I think of as *the riddle of the bullet and the genome*," Shane said. "My and Richard Jones's life course were each dramatically altered by separate, unrelated, but temporally coincident events. The same day that a stray bullet lodged in my spine, Richard Jones was informed that his genomic analysis from the aging brain study he had volunteered for at the university revealed that his ancestry was largely French Canadian. The biologic consequences of my experience on that day compelled a major change in my life that persists until now. Richard's emotional response to his genomic information resulted in his exaggerated Francophilia."

Shane paused for a few moments, wheeled himself over to the railing and stared down at the few people milling around the alley.

"You said coincidences, plural," Hardy Seltzer said.

"Yes," Shane answered, turning to face Katya and Hardy, "Richard's mental deterioration had been apparent for a while. I really should have made more of it. And I was aware that he was doing something different about processing of the material for his hats. Again, I just didn't realize the significance. I didn't really look into it until Jones was caught effacing Fitzwallington's house. That's when I connected the change in his felt processing methods with the changes in his behavior and looked up the basis of the connection."

"So," Katya said, "you think the genomic information caused Mr. Jones to revert to a mercury-based felt making method with the result that he went mad from mercury poisoning and now is dead."

"Along with one of my colleagues," Seltzer inserted.

"KiKi," Shane said, "if you're trying to work up a heavy case of guilt, you might want to first give the situation a bit more thought. I don't see how anyone could have predicted Jones's reaction to the information."

"Outlier! Of course he was an outlier. But that's not an excuse. Our business is to recognize outliers and deal with them as who they are. We, me and my scientific colleagues, have some responsibility here. No doubt about that."

"Perhaps while you are castigating yourself about that, you might also ponder the fact that your attempt to wall off human science from human crime is futile. People behave in complex ways, my love."

Katya sighed. "You make a poor pedant, Shane," she said. "You really should stick with your detecting thing."

Hardy Seltzer had listened intently to Shane and Katya's conversation, but his mind was still haunted by the fact that a colleague had died because of what appeared to be a random and unpredictable sequence of events. No rational explanation. Seltzer was very much committed to rational explanations. Coincidences bewildered him.

Chapter 17

The Metropolitan Nashville chief of police was a product of the new school of policing. Although he had put in the obligatory minimum amount of time on the streets, he was never really a cop like Hardy Seltzer was a cop. He held a bachelor's degree in psychology from Syracuse and an advanced degree in criminal justice from John Jay College, where his thesis was titled *Organization and Implementation of a Service-Oriented Department of Justice in a Medium Size American City*. The job he landed in Nashville was, he thought, precisely in his intellectual sweet spot. His chance to convert theory to practice. When offered the job by the Nashville mayor, he leapt at the chance.

So, while Chief James Horner was intellectually well prepared for the job he held, it was not a good fit emotionally. Horner was insecure and depended mostly on the opinions of others for his sense of self-worth. The political pressures in the Nashville job were inordinate. No doubt there was something in his history that explained his insecurity, something like a dominant father, unloving mother, who knows what, but Chief Horner was, for whatever reason, constantly pinballed around by the politicians, making him a nearly insufferable micromanager. To complicate the matter, most of the handful of managerial types that he brought with him, people

131

whom he had connected with at John Jay, shared his personality flaws. Assistant Chief Carl Goetz, head of the criminal investigations division and immediate supervisor of Hardy Seltzer, was no exception. Hardy avoided all of his superiors as much as he could.

But, he had to deal with the Bechman Fitzwallington situation, Hardy thought, mano-a-mano. Thus, they sat facing each other across the Assistant Chief's large oak desk. Each man was affecting body language meant to establish a dominant position in the impending conversation.

Hardy leaned forward, his elbows planted firmly on the desk and looked directly into the chief's eyes.

"Assistant Chief Goetz," Seltzer said, "we have to open a wide door on this Fitzwallington thing. Open a serious investigation. We have a dead cop, shot dead in the old artist's front yard in broad daylight. Granted the perp was apparently demented, but why there?"

"Maybe coincidence," Goetz replied, avoiding Seltzer's attempt to engage his eyes. "There are such things, you know."

Goetz leaned back in his chair and folded his arms across his chest. He was not a large man, and his efforts to assume postures that would expand his persona generally didn't work very well. This one didn't.

Hardy leaned in even further toward his boss and said, "Coincidences are lazy excuses for faulty investigations. Give me a week. Let me pull at some threads and see if a story unravels."

"Not sure you understand how sensitive this is, Seltzer," Goetz replied. "Politically, I mean. The arts commission people just don't want us stirring up any trouble. Especially now that it looks like Fitzwallington's work may bring some serious attention to Nashville art. You know, New York attention. Big city stuff. And I don't see why this mad hatter thing has any bearing on whether there was anything fishy about Fitzwallington's death. The old guy just died, it appears to me."

Seltzer leaned back in his chair but locked the steely glare of his dark eyes directly on Goetz's face.

"A week, sir," Seltzer said. "Give me a week."

The phone on his desk rang and Goetz reached for it. "I'm expecting a call that I need to take," he said. "I'll think about this but hold off for now."

Goetz answered the phone and motioned for Seltzer to leave.

"Dead cop," Seltzer said as he was leaving. "We have a dead cop to explain. Dead cops don't go quietly away."

Although the apparent reason for an unusually large gathering at the AvantArt gallery on a warm Thursday evening was a widely advertised showing of the latest works by the Nashville artist, Parker Palmer, a large number of the attendees had no interest in Palmer's work. They were present because of other interests in the gallery and its proprietor, Athena Golden. They were tracing the scent of the recently dead Bechman Fitzwallington.

Fortunately, Athena Golden had anticipated a larger than usual crowd for this event so that she had opened up the expandable area at the back of the gallery. She had spaced the Palmer paintings out so that the affair would feel appropriately busy but not congested. She had also hung the small Fitzwallington painting left with her for appraisal by Richelieu Jones in what she thought was an inconspicuous spot in a corner; she still wasn't sure what to do with that painting. She hated to give it up, but it wasn't hers, and now it wasn't clear who owned it. She was hoping for a number of much more valuable companion pieces in the near future.

Ms. Golden was usually pretty good at staging these gallery affairs, anticipating the size and nature of the crowd and setting the thing up appropriately. However, given recent events, leaving the Fitzwallington painting on display, even inconspicuously so, on this evening was a terrible mistake. Much to her chagrin, that little painting became the main attraction, wreaking havoc with Golden's carefully planned symmetry of the affair. Most of the crowd was jammed into an unwieldy clot in the corner of the gallery where the small painting hung, largely neglecting the sizeable collection of Palmer's works. Parker Palmer was enraged and didn't hesitate to let Athena Golden know that, pulling her aside at every opportunity to make his feelings crystal clear.

A thin man in a wheelchair and his striking blonde companion, avoiding the clump of Fitzwallington admirers in the corner, maneuvered casually about the gallery paying only token attention to Palmer's array of colorful paintings. It was an unusual outing for them. He still resented the cumbersome logistics of loading his folding wheelchair into the modest space in the front boot of her Boxster, and so they ventured beyond walking distance from Printers Alley only once in a while. But he wanted to attend this event and she was fine with that.

Truth be told, neither of them found the paintings particularly interesting or attractive. Instead of paying much attention to the art, the paraplegic man engaged in an intense scrutiny of each of a number of the other guests. He wondered why each of them was there and how each might fit into the narrative slowly developing in his mind. He had spent some time on the web learning what he could about these people. They were interesting in a morbid sort of way. But not the kind of people that Shane would have invited to his celestial dinner party.

Bruce Therault: Newly arrived on the scene but with a traceable history. New Yorker. Co-owner of the NYC gallery that had handled Fitzwallington art. Unscrupulous (or to be generous, semi-scrupulous) dealer in several largely speculative areas. Maybe connections with criminal element, carefully camouflaged as legitimate. Not a man to be trusted. Killer? Probably the kind of work he paid other people to do. No doubt he didn't personally involve himself in the wet work. What was he doing in Nashville at a showing of a local artist whose work had not found an audience in the big city? Had to be something to do with the Fitzwallington thing.

Mace Ricci: Ex-NYC cop trying too hard and unsuccessfully to obscure that historical fact (pressed shirt, blue suit, and the shoes, brown, but still cop shoes). Left the force under something of a cloud. Working for Therault and God knows who else. Like a lot of ex-cops with shady histories in law enforcement, probably capable of exploiting his knowledge of the practicalities of the law and the logistics of the street to get done most anything his financers wanted done if the price was right. Did he kill BF? No doubt would have, given the opportunity and a high enough price. But he was operating outside the territory he knew and didn't look comfortable there. And why was Therault here when his operative had already had some time to settle in? Trust? One should never employ a crook one doesn't trust. On a suspect scale of one to ten, Ricci at the moment might rate, generously, a five.

SalomeMe: Ah yes, the lovely and achingly opaque SalomeMe. In full regalia she sat, extensively inked bare legs crossed, on a strategically chosen love seat near the center of the room. That is, she sat there for brief periods interrupted by longer smoking breaks taken outside. Clearly uninterested in the art and determined to make that fact as conspicuous as possible, she sat looking off into space at apparently nothing in particular. Both Mace Ricci and Athena Golden seemed to be paying special attention to her, looking for opportunities to bend her ear. SalomeMe didn't appear to be impressed with either of them. Murderess? A most obvious possibility. Presumed sole heiress to the now excessively valuable trove of Fitzwallington paintings. A deliberately transparent and passionate hater of her father. Lots of opportunity. Maybe a trifle too obvious. Still…could be.

Fiona Hayes: Hard to read. She was loitering around the edge of the group crowded in front of the small Fitzwallington painting. She didn't appear to be particularly interested in the painting but had just gravitated toward the place where most of the people in the room had collected. Her sculptor friend was not with her. Ms. Hayes was a petite woman, an obvious devotee of strenuous physical exercise; that was particularly obvious in the muscularity of her deeply tanned legs, most of which were visible below the hem of a very short and very snug black leather skirt. She appeared to converse amiably with SalomeMe and went out of her way to engage SalomeMe in conversation a couple of times. From the Internet, she appeared to be a moderately successful producer of uniquely designed and vividly colored large ceramic wall hangings that she called tile paintings. *An evil man*! Her description, repeated with vehemence, of the dead artist. Did that passion drive this petite young woman to violence? And what lay behind such intensity? There was more to learn of Fiona Hayes. Would have to keep the possibilities open for her.

Two people whom Shane didn't recognize attracted his attention. One was a middle-aged paunchy balding man who seemed a little chummy with Parker Palmer. When Palmer wasn't talking to the guy or complaining to Athena Golden about the lack of attention to his paintings, Shane asked him about the stranger. Palmer allowed that the guy was a distant relative of his whom he hadn't seen in ages and had no idea why the guy had turned up at the showing. Palmer suspected that his relative's motives were something less than noble.

"Shane Hadley," the other stranger approached Shane and called his name. Shane was quite sure that he had never met the man. "Damian Saturn. So you've taken a sudden interest in the arts?"

The man was medium height, ruddy complexion, neither fat nor thin, physically unremarkable. A generally nondescript persona except for his probably fictional name. Blue business suit. Red tie. Red pocket square. Brown shoes, cap toe, not wingtip. More Mens Wearhouse than anything recognizably designer. A man trying too hard not to attract attention. Must be a fictional name. There surely was no one on the planet actually named Damian Saturn. If it was not a parental felony to burden a child with such a moniker, it should be.

"Do I know you?" Shane replied.

Their eyes met, but neither man smiled.

"Not yet," Damian Saturn replied. "Not yet."

"Can you give me a valid reason why that situation should change?"

Shane was more than a little annoyed by how presumptuous this guy seemed.

"Oh," Saturn responded, still not smiling and keeping eye contact, "there are some excellent reasons for us to know each other a bit better. They will become obvious when the time is right. You see, we share an interest in the art of Bechman Fitzwallington, although the nature of our interests is quite different. We will need to discuss those differences before long. I will be in touch."

With no further word or gesture, Damian Saturn turned and left the gallery.

"What was that about?" Katya asked.

"Hell if I know," Shane said.

Hardy Seltzer sat at his regular spot at the north end of the bar at TAPS (née The Dew Drop Inn), sipping his second beer and waiting for some attention from the bartender, his friend Marge Bland. He was recalling the conversation he had with his boss and trying to decide what to do. The conversation with Assistant Chief Carl Goetz had disturbed Hardy. His boss, and presumably others up the chain of command, had obviously caved in to the pols. Hands off the Fitzwallington situation was the message. Hardy thought that his superiors were way too unconcerned about a dead cop. And, Hardy didn't buy the argument that the two situations—the Mad Hatter thing and Fitzwallington's death—weren't related. Maybe not, but there needed to be more investigation before he'd buy that. There had to be a lot more investigation. And, by damn, Seltzer would do whatever he could to see to it that this thing was explored a hell of a lot more than had been done so far.

"Hi, handsome," Marge Bland had served the other bar customers and now focused her attention on the detective.

Lost in his thoughts and his beer, Hardy hadn't noticed what she was doing for a few minutes and was startled by Marge's sudden appearance in front of him and her greeting.

"Oh!" he said, jerking around to face Marge and sloshing some of his beer from the glass onto the bar. "You frightened me."

"Frightened the brave detective? I must be a pretty scary woman," she said. "What has you so preoccupied?"

"Death and politics," Hardy answered, sipping disinterestedly at his beer.

"Heavy stuff," Marge said. "Need to talk about it?"

"Need to think about it first," Hardy replied. "Talk about it later."

"Suit yourself," Marge replied.

Marge Band was perfectly happy with Hardy Seltzer suiting himself. But she really didn't have a choice.

As Hardy left the bar, cranked up the aging LTD, and headed down the steep First Avenue hill toward the river that marked the border between downtown and East Nashville, he retrieved his cell phone from his jacket pocket, scrolled to Shane Hadley's number and punched it in.

When his cell phone chirped, Shane was sitting comfortably with his lovely wife on the deck of their Printers Alley flat, relishing a glass of wine and quietly reflecting on the better side of his life fortunes. Times like these made Shane feel fortunate in spite of (or because of) the wrinkles in his story. He reached for KiKi's hand and she smiled.

The Alley was unusually quiet this evening, only a few people milling around. One particularly unremarkable man in a cheap suit stood in the doorway shadow of the blues bar across the way smoking a cigarette. He looked up toward where Shane and Katya sat but they didn't notice him. At his phone's insistence, Shane finally looked at the screen. Seeing that the caller was Hardy Seltzer, he answered the call.

Law enforcement is no less susceptible to the ambiguities of human behavior than politics, religion, or love. The imposed structure that is designed to assure consistency and clear lines of authority has to be there. And that structure needs to be conspicuous enough to convince the citizens it serves that responsible people are in control, that the law enforcement apparatus is operating effectively. That justice is being served. But there are human ambiguities.

Regardless of the dictates of the organizational structure, Hardy Seltzer was determined to see that the Fitzwallington case (he now thought that it was indeed a case just waiting to be defined that way) got the attention that the known facts and the dead cop deserved. And the only way to accomplish that without seriously risking his job security had to involve Shane Hadley. Hardy was OK with that, and when he proposed to Shane that he take the lead in the investigation with Hardy as a very silent partner, Shane agreed. After all, he was already doing the job and Hardy's help, even under the table, should speed things along.

Sometimes justice, like water, seeks its own level, regardless of obstacles in its path. So, contrary to the wishes of the departmental hierarchy and the political and social establishment of the city, Detective Hardy Seltzer and paraplegic ex-detective Shane Hadley agreed to pursue an investigation which they were convinced justice demanded. But they would need to be careful. They would need to be very careful for some reasons they were yet to discover.

Chapter 18

Most of the murders that Shane Hadley had investigated as an active member of the Nashville Metropolitan Police Department were not that difficult to solve. The killer was usually fairly obvious—cuckolded husband, rejected boyfriend, drug deal gone south, bar brawl, etc. The culprit was easy to identify, and the task was to locate and arrest him (almost always a man). Of course, the evidence had to be gathered and the substance of a case that would prove guilt in court had to be developed carefully, but those were primarily technical matters. There wasn't, as a rule, much mystery. Apart from the drama that was sometimes involved in actually apprehending the killer and bringing him in, murder investigations in Nashville were generally not very challenging.

And murderers in the city were not very clever, even when they tried to be. Efforts to disguise the cause of death or to divert suspicion from the perpetrator of the crime, point the cops in the wrong direction, were usually clumsy, not the work of professional killers with the skills and experience necessary to pull the thing off without getting caught. Most Nashville killers, even at their most creative, were rank amateurs. There were exceptions. It was his success at dealing with those exceptions that was the stuff of Shane's reputation as an investigator, the enduring Sherlock Shane myth.

If he had an advantage over his colleagues in solving difficult cases, Shane thought it lay in simply paying attention. He would spend a long time alone at the crime scene before it was disturbed in any way, before the technicians descended to document things and collect samples.

Shane would just stand there focusing his five senses on the scene, registering what he saw, smelled, felt, and maybe on occasion heard or tasted. Not rarely, he would discover something that others overlooked by just paying attention. But that was only part of it. There were the sensed facts, but there was also something he couldn't readily describe, a gestalt, a general sense of the situation. What his younger colleagues might call a *vibe*. The vibe revealed to Shane whether something malicious had happened there, and more often than not, the vibe was right. Shane had come to rely on this feeling, but recognized that it sounded spooky and so did not discuss it with anyone else.

KiKi had left for work, and Shane sat in the living room of their Printers Alley flat with his laptop positioned, appropriately, in his lap. He was thinking about the Fitzwallington case. Hardy Seltzer had given everything he had on the case to Shane, either hard copies or by email, and Shane was sifting through it. There wasn't much. In fact, Shane's Wall Street interviews were as enlightening as most anything Hardy had given him.

Except perhaps the hastily taken unprofessional series of pictures of the death scene that Hardy had taken with his iPhone. It was a far cry from having an actual crime scene to observe, but it was all he had. There was no crime scene investigation because it had been assumed that there was no crime and so no crime scene to investigate. Just the innocent death of a sick old man. But something about the photos displayed on Shane's computer screen troubled him. He sat staring at the screen for a while without being able to put his finger on exactly what the problem was. But even from the pictures of the scene, Shane somehow knew, or felt sure anyway, that the scene was not as innocuous as it seemed at first glance. He wasn't sure whether the *vibe* was electronically transmissible, but he was feeling something akin to it.

It was a Monday morning, approaching ten o'clock, the time when Mike Borden, the physical therapist who came every Monday to inflict as much pain as possible on his paraplegic client, was due to arrive. Shane considered a nice glass of sherry to help prepare him for the weekly ordeal. He wheeled himself over to the bar and was reaching for the case that held his Oxford sherry glasses when he remembered his promise to himself and to KiKi that he would try to curtail his drinking. Starting at ten AM would be hard to define as curtailing. He wheeled back, empty-handed, into the room and sat staring out the large front window and thinking again about solving murders.

As memories of some of his most interesting cases sauntered across his mind, Shane thought, as he had often thought, that the old saw, *dead men tell no tales*, just wasn't true. It was probably coined by a Chicago crime boss in the twenties as a justification for ordering the enforced demise of potential police informers among his minions. But it just wasn't true. Dead men often tell tales if one pays attention. He called up Hardy's pictures of the Fitzwallington death scene on his computer screen. It seemed to be the picture of the dead old man that kept reverberating about in Shane's head. Why? Just a mustachioed old man, quite naked, appearing to rest quietly in his bed. But there was something about the picture that screamed murder to Shane. For the life of him, he couldn't tell what it was.

He was sitting there lost in thought when the speaker buzzed from the street entrance to their building. Shane and KiKi's flat was on the second floor (first floor European), and visitors gained entry by pressing the button opposite the names of the occupants which buzzed an intercom in the appropriate one of the six occupied floors. The occupant then answered and if agreeing that the visitor was to be admitted, released the front door lock by depressing a button located just beside the intercom, went to the elevator, and released the access lock for the specified floor. In Shane and KiKi's case, the elevator opened directly into their living room so that controlling the behavior of the elevator was important to them. Shane did all of those things when he recognized the voice of his physical therapist, Mike Borden, although Shane didn't go about the tasks with much enthusiasm. He liked Borden OK he guessed, but he had trouble separating the person of the slick-headed, muscular, virile man from his role as Shane's clearly sadistic tormentor. Shane was not fond of pain. He was especially disliked the trite *no pain no gain* mantra of which Borden seemed inordinately fond. Shane was much fonder of sherry than of pain. And he probably preferred pain to over-worn mantras related to the subject.

Borden strode from the elevator and flung the gym bag that Shane thought was probably his constant companion onto the living room floor.

"Shane, my man," Borden said, reaching to grasp Shane's hand with his usual vice-like grip. "How the hell are you?"

Although he had never inquired, Shane wondered about the contents of the ever-present gym bag. Granted, Borden would occasionally extract a couple of broad elastic bands from the bag to use during the sessions with Shane. But the bag was big enough to contain the essential workout gear for a modest size gymnastics team. What was in there?

"Apart from having essentially no use of my lower limbs," Shane answered, "I am doing tolerably well."

"Glad to hear it, Shane. Now let's get down to business. And give me some real effort today. Don't concentrate on the pain. It will hurt. You know that. But, *no pain, no gain.*"

Shane cringed.

It was most unlikely that these three men would be together at all, and even more unlikely that they would be getting out of a rental car in the parking lot of an out-of-the-way B-grade First Avenue bar early on a sunny Nashville afternoon. Even in broad daylight, emanations from the huge TAPS sign drenched the men, the car, the entire parking lot, in a color akin to Harvard crimson. The crimson was probably appropriate, at least symbolically, but none of the three was even remotely connected to the venerable Cambridge university. Only one of them had attended college at all, and he graduated at the bottom of his class at CCNY. These men were not intellectually inclined.

Mace Ricci had discovered the bar in his efforts to absorb some local color by visiting establishments on the margins of the city's respectable society. He concluded early on that you were not likely to learn anything authentic about the town by haunting the glitzy places downtown. What you would find there would be cowboy-booted denim-skirted fake blonde Dolly Parton, Patsy Cline, or Loretta Lynn wannabees posed carefully on bar stools, anxiously awaiting discovery by an imagined roving talent agent. Or some serious country music fans who had spent most of a year's earnings from the corn crop on a week in the epicenter of their preferred music genre who were hanging around NeoNashville places—Lower Broad, The Gulch—where they thought they might catch a glimpse of one of their idols. Unlikely, but most people from out-of-town didn't realize that the real stars were probably either reviewing their investment portfolios with a broker at a posh country club bar or resting quietly on the teak deck of their McMansion overlooking Old

Hickory lake, nursing a generously poured glass of Gentleman Jack.

These three men had some business to discuss, and it was business that they did not wish to share accidentally with any significant eavesdroppers. So, they wanted to meet at a place where there were not likely to be any significant eavesdroppers, and Mace Ricci thought TAPS was just the ticket. He doubted that anyone significant was likely to frequent TAPS. He was almost right.

They entered the place and sat at a small round table in the southwest corner of the room that was surrounded by four chairs. Since the only other customer in the place was a solitary man sitting at the bar and staring at an afternoon edition of Headline News playing on an aging TV that hung precariously above where he sat, Mace Ricci did not think it a serious breach of etiquette for the three of them to occupy a table meant for four. Truth was, any serious breach of TAPS etiquette would probably have to involve the use of either firearms or sharp objects; house rules didn't cover seating patterns. It was that kind of a place.

Of course, Bruce Therault and Mace Ricci knew each other, but neither of them knew the third member of their trio. He had just shown up and sought them out. He claimed to have been hired by some of the major investors in Galleria Salinas and sent to Nashville to represent their interests. He also claimed that his name was Damian Saturn, which the other two men thought highly unlikely. Both Therault and Ricci wondered why the investors would send someone else when the interests of the gallery were already well-represented by the two of them. They were anxious to hear Saturn's explanation.

"What chardonnays do you have by the glass?" Bruce Therault was the first to speak to the slightly disheveled fortyish waitress who sauntered over to take their orders, removing a pencil from behind her ear and concentrating on a small avocado green order pad rescued from a pocket somewhere deep in her pleated skirt.

Making no effort to obscure a deep impatient sigh, she replied, "We got Bud and Bud Light, sweetie."

She had, quite pointedly, set the tone for the encounter.

"No hard liquor, either?" Therault continued, undaunted.

"Green Jack and Red Dewars," she said.

"Dewars neat, a double." Therault succumbed to the dictates of availability without pursuing the matter further.

"Same," said Ricci.

"Same," said Saturn.

The waitress didn't write the orders down. She walked over to the bar, spoke briefly with the bartender, and returned shortly to the table where the three men sat, placing the three glasses of blended Scotch whiskey on the table, in the process rattling the several ice cubes in each drink. The men stared at their glasses and then at each other in unison as though their movements had been choreographed but decided not to attempt to define the word *neat* for their charming waitress. It just didn't seem to any of the three men like an interaction worth prolonging. And they had things to talk about.

Shane had developed the habit of wheeling himself up the Church Street hill to Wall Street at five o'clock most afternoons. He liked habits. They were security. But five o'clock on this particular afternoon found him sitting on the deck of his apartment well into a third glass of sherry, trying with all his might to ignore the lingering severe pain in his legs expertly inflicted by the virile Mike Borden and, between surges of activity in the bundles of pain fibers traversing his spinal cord that ferried signals to the conscious parts of his brain, trying to think about the Fitzwallington affair. Fitzwallington *murder,* he was now willing to label it although still not sure why he was so convinced that it was other than a natural and inevitable event given that he was dealing with a human being. We all die one way or another.

Shane had the computer in his lap displaying once more the pictures of the Fitzwallington death scene that Hardy Seltzer had taken on his cell phone. He stared at each of the photos between grimaces of pain and generous swallows of sherry. His cell phone chirped an announcement of a call from Detective Seltzer.

"Hello, Hardy," he said, absent his usual friendly cheer.

"So," Hardy replied, "I've just talked with Doc Jensen, and apparently he has some additional and startling news about or dead artist friend. Some additional analyses of autopsy samples. May not have been murder at all, Shane."

"Lead poisoning? I wondered how long it would take him to figure that out. The information was all there and easily available. Fitzwallington used an old formula house paint for his work. That's on his website and Wikipedia page. Old formula house paints contain large amounts of lead. And, your pictures of his house show peeling paint on ceilings and walls. No doubt old paint. Quite possibly lead-containing paint. I'm not at all surprised that the old guy's tissues contain high amounts of lead. I'm only surprised that Jensen went to the trouble to get the information and have the measurements made. Perhaps I underestimate our voluble doctor of the dead."

"So," Hardy replied, "if you knew all that, why didn't you tell me earlier so that we could wrap this puppy up once and for all."

"Because I am quite certain that Mr. Fitzwallington was murdered, regardless of, or possibly even related to, the amounts of lead that had accumulated in his aging body."

There was a long silence. Seltzer was trying to digest what Shane had just told him and to make sense out of it vis-à-vis the information from the coroner. Hadley was trying to think of some way to justify what he had just said to the detective without knowing exactly the source of his quite firm conviction that the artist was murdered. The answer was right there in the pictures of the death scene. He was certain of that. But he hadn't yet put his finger on exactly what it was. After thinking it over, Shane decided that his only recourse was delay. He would figure out the answer sooner or later, and he had to keep Hardy from ending the investigation until then. He needed more time.

"Would you care to share the reasons for your conviction?" Hardy was starting to think that his friend was losing his edge. In any investigation, you can't just write off the obvious so that you can chase a pet theory. That's basic stuff. Investigation 101. Pay attention! The obvious is sometimes true. Probably true most of the time.

"I'm afraid that I am not yet prepared to do that," Shane replied. "But, all in due time, my man, all in due time."

"Due time is getting pretty close, Shane. I 'm not prepared to carry on this ruse with the department brass for very long."

"Perhaps it won't be long, Hardy. I mean not long before I can convince you that this is a murder. It may well take some time to identify and apprehend the culprit. But first things first."

"If the boss finds out about the lead data, he'll inform the higher-ups and we may be out of business anyway," Hardy said.

"So, don't tell him."

"I won't, but I wouldn't trust Doc Jensen to keep it quiet. I'll ask him to, but you know how much he likes to talk."

There was another pause, longer than the last one, but neither man hung up the phone.

"Another thing," Seltzer finally broke the silence. "I don't think we should meet very often right now. Might give the wrong impression ... well, maybe the right impression with the wrong result. But if you're going to be at Wall Street most afternoons, don't be surprised if I drop by. And Shane, I need to know what you know if I'm to be of any help."

"Right, Hardy, my man. Right," Shane replied. "In due time, my friend. In due time. Cheerio."

The conversation ended.

Shane fired up his laptop and pulled up the pictures of the death scene again. He poured himself another glass of sherry and sat staring at the iPhone picture of a mustachioed old man lying in a bed, dead as a doornail, naked as a jaybird, innocent as a newborn babe. Probably a number of other tired metaphors would fit the scene. But tired metaphors weren't going to answer the question that haunted Shane. He concentrated on the content of the picture, trying very hard to uncover what it was about the photograph that betrayed the criminality of the scene.

It was just as he heard the garage door rumbling open and KiKi's car thrumming into the garage below that it came to him. He wondered why it had taken so long.

Chapter 19

The matters of establishing legal ownership of the Fitzwallington paintings and deciding which of the two galleries was to have the privilege of selling them were heating up. Ownership seemed simple enough since the old guy had only one child who would be his sole heir. However, there was a problem. Her father had left no will that anyone had been able to locate, and SalomeMe had no proof that she was in fact Fitzwallington's child. No birth certificate, no ancient dusty and yellowing family bible with several blank pages separating the Old and New Testaments bearing a diagram of the Farmer family tree. No document of any kind. She had never had any reason to doubt that she was his daughter, although there were times when he did not treat her as would have been appropriate for a father-daughter relationship. For legal reasons, the question had to be resolved. Of course, in the current scientific age, it was easy enough to do that.

On the advice of her childhood friend Fiona Hayes, SalomeMe had hired a lawyer to help work through the situation that seemed to be developing more complexity than she had anticipated. The lawyer, chosen essentially at random from the phone book, was James L. (Jimmy) Holden. He had a single attorney practice with an office on Third Avenue, a block behind Shane Hadley and Katya Karpov's flat in Printers Alley. James L. (Jimmy) Holden was glad for the business. He had plenty of time for the case and also realized that there was likely to be some free advertising associated with it.

It was Holden who first informed SalomeMe of the need to document her parentage in order to claim ownership of the paintings. He had done his homework. He insisted that SalomeMe meet him in his office, and she reluctantly agreed. When she went to light up one of her slender lavender cigarettes, Holden asked her not to smoke in the office. Contrary to her habitually rebellious behavior, she agreed to his request. As a result of being in a strange and unfamiliar place where she was denied the calming effect of cigarette smoke, SalomeMe was agitated and in no mood to deal with anything problematic. Or to deal with anything at all if it took very long.

"What the hell do you mean proof?" exclaimed SalomeMe. "I sure as hell wouldn't have put up with the old bastard all these years if he wasn't my father. Proof? How about time in rank, equity, investment, that sort of thing. Proof my ass!"

Holden was probably about forty, red-faced with a budding paunch about the size of an early second-trimester baby bump, and no doubt would start soon to lose his hair. He was not a jovial sort but was amused by his new client.

"Well," Holden said, "I seriously doubt that a court of law in this day and age would accept your generous investment of time in Mr. Fitzwallington's person as proof of parentage. And, as lovely as your ass is, it is unlikely to play into the legal issues here."

"So what in God's name am I supposed to do?" she asked.

"Well, Miss Me," he said, not quite sure how to extract a surname from the strange moniker and settling on the shortest option, "you are fortunate to live in an age of burgeoning science. Analysis of your and your presumed father's DNA will answer the question once and for all. We should be able to obtain an appropriate sample from your father's postmortem. I'll check with the coroner, and we may need a formal request from you. I will also contact a DNA lab and confirm what kind of a sample they wish from you. This should be easily done although it may take a week or so depending on whether the lab has a backlog. In the meantime, we should seek a court order to assure that the paintings are secure. They are beginning to attract a lot of attention and we should be prepared for some of that attention to be less than well-intended."

"The paintings are secure, Mr. Holden," SalomeMe bristled. "They have been accumulating for the past several years in a carefully climate-controlled storage facility to which I have exclusive access. I long ago determined to reveal their location to no one and see no reason to change that decision. For your information, I would include you among those with no need to have knowledge of the paintings' location."

"I'm perfectly happy to be among the excluded ones," Holden responded. "However, I must warn you that a judge may have a different opinion. To protect the paintings with a court order may require specifying their location, I'm not sure. We'll cross that bridge if we have to."

"Why do I need a court order? They've been resting there perfectly happy for several years now."

"Perhaps," Holden smiled, "but the situation has changed, right? Interest in your father's art seems to have taken a rather dramatic turn for the better ... or at least more lucrative. Your situation is more complicated. The scent of money always brings complications. But for your changing circumstances, I would not have had the pleasure of making your acquaintance. Now would I?"

Having neared the limit of her less than generous attention span, SalomeMe said, "Whatever," fishing a pack of cigarettes from her purse as she rose to leave the office.

"I'll be in touch," said the lawyer, smiling and conjuring up his most lawyerly tone of voice.

The artist Parker Palmer had discussed Billy Wayne Farmer's paintings a couple of times with a friend of his who was a lawyer and a prominent member of the Nashville Arts Commission. Palmer had wondered whether there wasn't some way to divert some of the proceeds from sale of the paintings to support the local art scene, especially talented young artists. He would love to see something of social value to come from the old guy, even if he had to die for that to happen.

Palmer knew from personal experience that it was devilishly difficult for even the most talented young artists to stay committed and focused for long enough to realize their potential. One could only balance the necessary shifts at a MacJob with growing one's artistic gifts for so long before sleep deprivation and other ravages of age and experience led to a divergence of life's available roads, forcing a choice between art and sustenance that universally favored the latter. Biology had its imperatives. At Palmer's insistence, his friend had gone to the trouble to file a lawsuit against the Fitzwallington (Farmer) estate claiming the paintings were not the rightful inheritance of SalomeMe (nee Sallie May Farmer). Although Jay Combs was certain that the suit would be dismissed, SalomeMe was anxious to get the show on the road, and Jimmy Holden advised her that irrefutable evidence that she was the sole heir of her artist father's estate would accomplish that.

Jimmy Holden was doing the best he could to get the show on the road. And so, samples from the young woman and her alleged father wound up in a commercial laboratory housed in a renovated Victorian house nestled among a row of flat-roofed, single-story doctors' offices on Hayes Street. There, white-coated technicians would isolate DNA and subject it to the technical genius of an exorbitantly expensive machine called a DNA sequencer, thus establishing with scientific certainty the nature of the biological relationship between the two people who provided the samples. It had been only a few years since this procedure supplanted blood typing and other much less precise methods for establishing parentage. This use of the technology had nothing to do with the reasons it had been developed. Those reasons were much more grandiose—*exploring the language of God*, one lyrically-inclined prominent scientist had called it. Science marches on with both intended and unanticipated consequences. The Fitzwallington legacy would be among innumerable others to benefit from the halo of discovery.

Hardy Seltzer had given Shane the phone number of the skinny kid with the port wine nevus on his face who lived next door to the Fitzwallington house and had been the first person, except, presumably, the murderer, to have observed the artist dead. Shane had called him and arranged for the two of them to meet that afternoon at his Wall Street office. Shane should probably have talked with the kid earlier, but he had slacked off on the investigation some while waiting for his conviction that the artist was murdered to crystallize. Now that he was convinced, Shane was ready to move more aggressively. He still had the problem of convincing Hardy that this was a murder case with enough credibility that Hardy would have another serious go at persuading his department brass. It had to come to that sooner or later, and sooner would be the considerably better option.

As he maneuvered his wheelchair up the Church Street sidewalk toward Fourth Avenue, Shane was thinking about Richelieu (nee Richard) Jones. It was the Mad Hatter's no-doubt mercury-induced erratic assault on the Fitzwallington house and several members of the Metro police force that had convinced Hardy that the artist's death was not an open-and-shut case after all. But if Jones had any connection to the old guy's demise, Shane could not, for the life of him, see what it was. Maybe the skinny kid would have some information that would help, but Shane doubted that there was anything new to learn about the hatter. Just another Fitzwallington hater who happened to live in the area, Shane thought. The fact that Jones's brain cells had been pickled beyond recognition by breathing in too much mercury was no doubt adequate to explain his erratic terminal spasm of violence. There was no obvious rational explanation for the outburst, but behavior driven by pickled brain cells had no need to make sense. Pickled brains don't play by any ordinary rules. There was not much unexplained in the tragic story of the Mad Hatter of Music City. He lived, he made hats, he found out just enough about his genes to cause him to make a really bad decision, and then he breathed mercury for a while, went mad, and died in a blaze of infamy. Tragic, and more melodrama than was necessary, but explicable. No obvious dangling loose ends to pick at.

Those were the things that occupied Shane's mind as he waited for the light to change and then wheeled himself across Fourth Avenue and turned into the alleyway behind the bank that some city planner with a sense of humor had named Wall Street. The Wall Street bar was half a block down the alley, and Shane was about halfway there when he felt someone behind him take hold of the handles at the back of his chair and so take control of his forward motion.

"Off to the office, are you?" said a voice that Shane had heard only once before.

Shane craned his neck around to confirm that he was being pushed by a somewhat familiar nondescript man in a cheap suit.

"My people think, detective, that you may be spending far too much time at the office. You should seriously consider abandoning your lately discovered interest in the art world and retreating to that cozy nest in The Alley with your lovely doctor wife. Neither you nor the lovely Dr. Karpov is likely to experience any long-term pleasure from your art interest," the man leaned over Shane and spoke directly into his right ear.

Before Shane had a chance to respond, the man laughed quietly, gave the chair a shove toward the bar and disappeared into the modest crowd of people just getting off work and heading home or to wherever people go to amuse themselves for a while on the way there.

If the man who called himself Damian Saturn intended to frighten Shane, he failed. Shane was not frightened. He was curious, but not frightened. In fact, more than curious, he was intrigued. He would need to see what he could find out about the mysterious Damian Saturn, whoever he was. Maybe Hardy could help.

It was just past five o'clock, and the Wall Street bar was much busier than Shane expected. Except for his special place and the adjacent stool, all the seats at the bar were taken, and people were standing two deep around most of the bar as well. Most were regulars who were at least vaguely familiar to Shane, but there were also some strangers. As usual, he wheeled past the other patrons without acknowledging them and hoisted himself up the ramp coming to rest at his reserved spot, the terminal seat at the bar's far end. He set the brake on his chair and thought. Random thoughts for a few minutes: the pointlessness of idle conversation, especially when lubricated by alcohol; how little people in general valued time; left to their own devices, why people congregate into groups. Shane didn't really understand any of those things. He was genuinely puzzled by them. That fact was unrelated to his injury. There was a lot of human behavior that he had never understood, including the tendency of his fellow human beings to kill each other.

The skinny kid with the purplish blotch stopped dead in his tracks upon entering the Wall Street bar. He stood there just inside the door looking anxiously, wide-eyed, around the room. Shane hadn't warned the young man that there were likely to be a lot of people at the bar, and the kid was obviously surprised. Shane often thought that the complexity of most situations was directly related to the number of people present per unit of space and it appeared that this situation was going to support that view; it was more complicated than he thought it would be. Finally, Shane looked over toward the door, spied the young man with the purple blotch and motioned him over toward the far end of the bar, waving his hand vigorously in the air like he was hailing a cab in New York. The kid got the message and joined Shane, taking the stool that the bartender, Pat Harmony, had reserved expecting that Shane had a business appointment scheduled because he usually did when he showed up at this time of day.

The kid was really skinny. Like a hair's breadth short of skeletal. He could easily have been taken for a recent escapee from a war-torn country somewhere in the third world from which he had fled with the aid of an exorbitantly priced pirate who had taken his money, eventually deposited him barely within the borders of the U S of A and wished him well. He was nervous.

"I'm Issy Esser," he said.

"Shane Hadley," Shane replied, rotating toward the young man and extending his hand.

Shane had not told Issy Esser that he was a detective, but he also did not disabuse him of that conclusion. The kid was probably too young to know anything about Shane's previously highly publicized exploits. Except for the wheelchair, Shane probably seemed like any other cop to the kid. That was fine. Maybe preferable to the actual truth about the situation.

"So," Shane said, opening with the basic question that he was determined to answer. Although he seriously doubted that this kid knew the answer, Shane wanted to see how he reacted. "Who killed Bechman Fitzwallington?"

"I didn't know anybody killed him," Esser answered, still a little shaky but maybe less so. "I thought he just died. He certainly didn't seem well lately. I wasn't particularly surprised that he died."

"Let me rephrase the question, Issy," Shane used the young man's given name to inject some familiarity into their conversation and also to savor the sibilance. "Who do you think *might* have killed Mr. Fitzwallington?"

"Well," Issy replied, "if you mean who had the opportunity, the list is a long one. If you mean motive, well, there seemed to be a lot of people who didn't like him. But it was strange. A lot of them continued to drop by his place fairly often. I would see them come and go. Most of them didn't stay very long. Like they were doing a duty of some kind and just wanted to get it over with. Except, of course, his daughter. She often stayed a while."

Shane took the small leather-bound note pad from his shirt pocket along with a pen, opened to a blank page and wrote something down there. He kept the notebook on the bar to his left, away from the side where Issy Esser sat, shielding what he wrote. Issy was making no attempt to see what Shane wrote. Issy just seemed like he wanted to end this conversation as soon as possible. He had ordered a beer when he first arrived and was drinking it rather quickly, Shane thought. Shane didn't offer to share his precious sherry with this guy. Shane did not like to waste his special wine. It would surely be wasted on Issy Esser.

"And what about Ms. SalomeMe, Issy? I found her an interesting specimen."

"Yeah," Esser said, "she is a piece of work, alright. I didn't know her well, but I wouldn't trust her. And she didn't get along with her father. I occasionally went over there and overheard some pretty vehement stuff going on between them."

"What kind of stuff?"

"Mostly her yelling obscenities at him. I did hear her say once that she ought to do away with him."

"You mean like kill him? Or just disown him?"

"I have no idea what she meant, but it sounded pretty serious and potentially violent to me."

"Okay. Sounds like Ms. SalomeMe deserves some additional attention. Who else?"

"Most of his other visitors were local artists. I did see that hatter guy who shot up the place the other day come by occasionally, but not often. And he never stayed long at all. Maybe the painter Parker Palmer, although he seems like such a happy-go-lucky sort of guy. Hard to think of him doing anything violent."

"What about you, Issy? You seem to have had more contact with Fitzwallington than most anyone else."

"I did spend some time with him," Esser responded. "I was trying to get him to help me with my art. He didn't help much, though. He did have me pose for a painting once a while ago. I didn't like the painting, very abstract. Not sure why he needed anyone to pose for it. Whatever he meant it to be, it didn't look like a person."

Shane wrote some more in his little notebook and put it back into his pocket. He finished his glass of sherry. Issy Esser drained the last of his beer.

"I may want to talk with you again," Shane said.

Chapter 20

Harold Werth bought the *language of God* description of the human genome that his former boss had championed (he even wrote a book by that title), but Werth, a committed atheist, didn't think there was anything divine about it. Werth sincerely believed that the human genome was the ultimate explanation of humanness. Once the genome was sequenced, the human codex was in hand. We had the transcript, the complete biologic narrative, and the challenge was to understand what it meant. There was no need to imagine a God to accomplish that. The human intellect, diligently applied, would eventually figure it out. That conviction was what drove Harold Werth during his far too few waking hours.

"You know, Harold," Katya said, "I really worry about this thing with the hatter, Richard Jones. It keeps me up at night. It seems a pretty straight line from giving him the ancestry information through his unfortunate mercury exposure to his death in a paroxysm of violence and mayhem. We lit the fuse. I'm afraid our concern for human beings is in danger of been buried under the avalanche of science and technology. Don't you worry about that?"

Katya had summoned Werth to her office because she really needed to discuss this issue with someone. Although she didn't always agree with Werth's world view, she had a lot of respect for his intellect and the depth of his understanding of science.

Werth's large head bobbed slightly to and fro; his eyes stayed fixed firmly on an imagined spot on the floor before him. "How could we have known how that guy would react to the information? A very unusual reaction, you must admit."

"Well," Dr. Karpov responded, "we knew he was an outlier. Maybe we should have dealt with him differently."

"Maybe," he said. "I don't worry very much about that sort of thing. I guess I think that if we could figure out how to organize the information avalanche into some configuration that made sense, our concern for human beings would take care of itself. Should be an easier problem if we had all the parts and assembled them correctly. I'll grant you that we may have gotten beyond our headlights, the science has moved so fast. But we just have to be patient. It will all come together at some point. Even the outliers. We'll get a handle on them eventually."

"Patience!" Katya hissed. "Patience! Tell that to Richard Jones."

"You'll no doubt think me a callous bastard to say so." Werth's head bobbed slightly faster and with a slightly longer arc; he still stared at the floor. "But there are always casualties of progress. The unfortunate Mr. Jones may be one of those … collateral damage, the warmongers would call it."

"You are a callous bastard, Harold," she said, looking directly at her colleague's bobbing head. She didn't smile.

Shane did not expect the phone call from Fiona Hayes, the ceramicist and childhood friend of the dead artist's daughter. Not after the distinctly unproductive meeting with her and her significant other at Wall Street earlier. No one had ever called him at Wall Street and so he was doubly surprised when Pat Harmony answered the ring of the landline behind the bar, brought the wireless receiver over to him and said "It's for you," as though Shane regularly received calls at the bar like detectives in old TV shows. He certainly wanted to follow up with the Hayes woman, but he was sure that initiating the interaction would fall to him. The vaguely familiar female voice speaking to him through the landline at Wall Street was certainly unanticipated.

Shane was surprised that the well-toned, sharp-tongued, and rather tightly wound young woman wanted to meet with him, and he was also surprised at her suggested meeting place, his Printers Alley apartment. But that suited Shane fine since he was about to leave for home anyway, so they agreed to meet there in half an hour. Neither Shane Hadley nor Fiona Hayes would keep the appointment. Shane's attempt to work his way there from the Wall Street bar where he had just bid adieu to the pleasantly sibilant Issy Esser would be unexpectedly interrupted; the caller who proposed the meeting had never intended to be there.

It was so unexpected and happened so fast that Shane did not get a look at his abductors or anything specific about the unmarked dark green van with windows tinted opaque black. Just as he was preparing to turn into the alley from Church Street, the van stopped at the curb beside him, and someone took control of his chair from behind. A side door on the van opened, a ramp extended to the sidewalk. Shane was whisked into the dark rear compartment of the vehicle and immediately blindfolded, his wrists zip-tied together behind the back of his chair by whoever was behind him and he felt the unmistakable prick of a needle jabbed into the deltoid muscle of his right arm. The ramp was rapidly retracted, the door slid shut with a solid thud, and off they went, the van wending its way ever so carefully through the afternoon traffic, destination unknown and unknowable at least to Shane. As soon as they were moving, his newly acquired attendant reached into Shane's shirt pocket and retrieved the cell phone. He handed it over to someone in the front of the van and shortly thereafter, Shane hear a soft clink as the phone hit the Church Street pavement, fixing his traceable location to a spot just short of Second Avenue, assuming the discarded phone stayed put.

Besides the obvious physical consequences, the bullet that lodged itself in Shane's spinal cord also introduced him to a range of new emotional experiences. He often felt *compromised*. Sometimes he felt *inadequate*. But he rarely felt *vulnerable*. That is exactly what he felt as he sat suddenly blindfolded in the rear of a dark green van *en route* to God knows where unable to move his legs and rapidly losing his ability to think clearly.

Dr. Katya Karpov was not given to panic even in the most dire situations. She was a problem solver—define the problem, enumerate the possible solutions, and proceed with the best option. That rationality had served her well in many difficult professional and personal situations and she relied on it.

However, when she arrived home at almost eight o'clock, still pondering the ethical dilemma that genetic analysis had forced her to confront, looking forward to discussing that problem with Shane, and finding an eerily empty flat with no sign of her husband, she panicked. Not once in the years since Shane's accident had she come home from work at around this time to an empty house. Shane was always there. She could, and did, count on that. She needed her husband's physical presence in the evenings. She honestly believed that she could not, or would not, go on living without that.

Katya's heart throbbed an ominous deafening rhythm, heaving her chest like a bellows. She couldn't concentrate enough to think the situation through. Her right brain was screaming RED ALERT so loudly that the efforts of her left brain to recapture her attention and get on with doing something logical and productive about the situation were lost in the din. She sat down in the living room, held her head in her hands, and sobbed. Wracking sobs like she had never felt before.

After a time, the sobs began to ebb, and she started to gain some control of her thoughts. Maybe there was an explanation less dire than she feared. Maybe. She retrieved her phone and called Shane's number but there was no answer. She wasn't surprised. She left a message. She then called the Wall Street bar and got Pat Harmony on the phone. Harmony was no help. His information suggested to Katya that her fear of something bad might well be justified. Indeed, Shane had been there earlier but a couple of hours ago he got a phone call at the bar, a woman 's voice, and then left rather abruptly. It was odd. Pat Harmony didn't recall Shane ever having gotten a call on the bar phone before. He always used his cell. The cell signal was good there. Harmony didn't recognize the woman's voice. Shane appeared to know who the caller was but he hadn't mentioned that to Pat. Shane just ended the call, bid Pat ta-ta and off he went.

Hardy Seltzer was leaning over the bar at TAPS engaged in a serious conversation with Marge Bland about whether she was going to join him for a late dinner after her shift was done when his cell phone summoned him. He was surprised to see that the screen identified the caller as Katya Karpov. Why would Katya be calling him at this time of evening? In fact, why would Katya be calling him at all? This had to have something to do with Shane, something that wasn't likely to be good news. Hadley interrupted his conversation with Marge at the risk of losing some of the progress that he felt he had made toward convincing her to grant him some of her time and attention away from the intrusive surroundings of TAPS, and answered the call. For some reason, of which he was unaware, Hadley chose not to reveal that he knew the identity of his caller.

"This is Hardy Seltzer," he answered the call is his most professional voice.

"Hardy," Katya said, "this is Katya." The panic in her voice was thinly veiled but she sounded reasonable. "Have you heard from Shane this evening? When I arrived home at the usual time, he wasn't here, and I've had no message from him. That is very unusual. It has never happened before. He doesn't answer his cell."

"Did you try Wall Street? I meant to drop by there and touch base with him this afternoon, but I never made it."

"Pat Harmony says he was there but left a few hours ago after taking a call from an unidentified woman. Pat assumed that he was going home."

It was all Katya could do to suppress the sobs that threatened to resurface from the place where they lurked just barely below the threshold of her control.

"I don't need to tell you, Katya, that this is not good. He's been after this notion that that artist was murdered, and I fear he may have awakened a monster. Those Fitzwallington paintings are attracting a lot of attention. Not all of it good. Has Shane discussed any of what he was up to with you?"

"Nothing specific," Katya replied. "Some generalities. He certainly never mentioned any thought that he might be in danger of any kind. Of course, he might not tell me that. But I thought he was over the risky stuff. I desperately hoped that was the case."

"My impression has been, although you certainly know the man much better than I do, that risk was not a concept that he paid much attention to. Eyes on the prize guy. Whatever it took to get there."

"That's probably true."

"Tell you what, Katya," Hardy said. "The last place he was seen was Wall Street, and he left there presumably to go to Printers Alley. For starters, I'll go retrace that route and see if I can find out anything that will help us locate him. Maybe people who work along that route saw him or saw something unusual. Shane is well known in the area and easily identifiable. Hard to imagine that he could just disappear, and no one would notice. Meantime, you sit tight in case he shows up with an explanation or tries to contact you. Does that sound a reasonable place to start? We shouldn't panic prematurely. If he doesn't show up by tomorrow, I'll talk to the chief and maybe contact a *Tennessean* reporter who I trust as well. Shane has a lot of admirers out there who would be delighted to help out if this turns out to be a full-fledged manhunt."

"I'm pretty frantic, Hardy. I can't imagine sitting alone in this house with no idea where Shane is for very long. Can you get started tonight?"

"Yes ma'am." One could easily imagine the detective saluting. "I am on my way. Call me if you hear anything. I'll do the same. Shane is a very resourceful man, Katya. I have a feeling that this will turn out okay."

In fact, Hardy did not have anything close to a feeling that this would turn out okay. It smelled pretty foul.

"Sorry, Marge," Hardy was truly sorry to miss the possibility of some quality time with Marge Bland, "but I'm going to have to take a rain check on plans for the evening. Don't forget where we were, though. I'd hate to have to start over."

Marge smiled. "You're a piece of work, Hardy Seltzer," she said.

Hardy settled into the familiar driver's seat in his old faithful LTD, maneuvered the boat out of the TAPS parking lot, and lumbered down the First Avenue hill. He was headed directly to *Sam's Sushi*.

Akanari Sato fell in love with American country music when he was twelve years old, living with his parents in Osaka. He somehow got a guitar and taught himself the few essential chords. As he grew older, he went to work in a sushi bar and used virtually his entire salary to purchase country music CDs. He sat for hours playing the records, strumming his guitar and memorizing the words and tunes to what became a sizeable repertoire of the genre. He got pretty good according to his friends, and often performed at parties and even at a few local bars.

When he was nineteen, he made the leap. He liquidated his entire possessions, maxed out his credit cards, changed his name to Sam Sake, packed up his guitar, and bought a ticket to Nashville, hoping to realize his dream of becoming a successful country musician. He had the twangy accent pretty much down pat by imitating the recordings, and he imagined Nashville as the land of milk and honey for an aspiring country music star, even one so culturally remote from the music's roots. He thought there might even be some appeal in the novelty of his situation.

All that was quite a few years ago now. Nashville did not deliver on Sam Sake's dream, as it does not deliver on the vast majority of such dreams. But a recurring fringe benefit of the city's mythical status as the mecca of country music is that the reputation brings some unexpected things to the city. Eventually being forced by the imperatives of human biology to face the fact that he was not going to be able to get himself fed, housed, and set on the road to fame by picking and grinning, Sam fell back on his skill as a sushi chef. With the help of a modest loan from a local bank, he opened Sam's Sushi, a smallish restaurant at the corner of Church Street and Printers Alley that quickly became *the* place for sushi in Nashville. The restaurant's popularity proved durable, and Sam Sake (nee Akanari Sato) continued to make a more than comfortable living. Recently he had been considering opening additional restaurants in the area, but he was still incubating that idea.

When he traced Shane's likely route home from Wall Street in his mind, Hardy Seltzer quickly realized that the only establishment along the route from which the ex-detective might have been observed was Sam's Sushi. The place had a large picture window facing Church Street, and Hardy knew that Sam was a keen observer of the goings-on in the window. Sam binge-watched those goings-on like other people watched Netflix. Hardy had called on Sam for information in cases before, and Sam rarely disappointed him. As a source of visual information along that stretch of Church Street, the sushi master was almost as good as CCTV.

Shane would have had to pass right by Sam's place. Sam knew Shane, knew the whole Shane Hadley story, and besides, Shane in his wheelchair was a readily recognizable figure easily distinguished among the cast of characters acting out the continual human drama in Sam's window on that fraction of the world. Hardy stuck the blue light on the LTD's roof and left the car at the curb on Church Street directly in front of Sam's place.

"Ah, detective Hardy-san," Sam said without looking up from the sushi order he was preparing. The –san honorific was pretty much the only remaining vestige of his native language, most of which was buried deep under multiple strata of Sam's best approximation of Music City English laid down over the years; a cost of doing business. "Whatever is up?"

Seltzer had entered the shop, walked through the small dining area where all of the six tables were fully occupied and entered the kitchen area where he knew Sam would be. Sam still created all of the sushi himself but had hired some young people to serve the tables. Sam created the dishes and placed them in the large pass-through between kitchen and dining room that served the dual purpose of allowing Sam a clear view of the picture window fronting Church Street and provided a conduit for the sushi to be delivered to the orderer by the young servers. Sam also did a lot of takeout business, especially at lunchtime. Sam was a busy man.

"Evenin', Sam," Seltzer returned the greeting. "Looks like a busy night for sushi?"

"Every night busy night, Hardy-san. Good business. Not like country music star, but good business."

"Take what they give you, my friend. Take what they give you," Seltzer concluded the small talk and then continued. "Have you seen Shane Hadley pass by here this evening? Seems he left Wall Street some hours ago on his way home and never got there. He would have had to pass by your place. Did you see him or see anything unusual on the street tonight?"

"No detective Shane-san tonight, Hardy-san. Unusual. Lately, he passes by here most evenings around 6 or 7. No tonight. Not think much about it, but now you bring it up, seems unusual."

Hmm, Hardy thought. Given Shane's Holmesian obsession, he might think of this bit of information as the dog that didn't bark. Hardy didn't share his friend's obsession but he had found sometimes that non-events, unexpected omissions, were important clues.

"Any unusual goings-on in your window on the world this evening?"

"Now you mention. Around 7:30, there was some little ruckus on the street but to the right of my window. Stage right," Sam smiled. "Could not see what trouble was and busy with sushi, so didn't investigate. Now I think, I could see the front part of dark green car just poking into my window for a minute and then gone away. Didn't think much about it. Busy with sushi."

"Keep thinking over the evening, Sam. If anything comes up, even if it doesn't seem important, give me a call. You have my card?"

"Yes, yes, Hardy-san. Always keep card handy."

"Mr. Detective," a wiry man of indeterminate age with unkempt hair and a deeply pockmarked face leaned against the driver's side door of Hardy's car and called to Hardy as he exited Sam's Sushi.

"What's on your mind, professor?" Hardy answered, moving toward the car and reaching for the door handle.

The homeless man regularly haunted the area around The Alley. He was known as the professor for reasons that no one seemed to know anything about. The cops left him pretty much alone, although they all knew who he was. He was harmless as far as anyone knew. Hardy was in a hurry and wasn't inclined to waste time chatting with the frequently garrulous professor.

"I think I know something that may interest you," the man responded.

"And what would that be?"

"It might be something valuable to you," the professor said, an obvious reference to his desire for compensation.

Hardy produced a twenty and said, "OK, what have you got."

"Thank you, sir," the professor said. "You are most generous. It's about your friend in the wheelchair. Earlier tonight, I was just hanging around here and saw him wheeling down Church Street toward The Alley, just like most nights. But it looked like someone behind him grabbed his wheelchair and wheeled him into a big van that had stopped at the curb and put down a ramp from the side door. It all happened fast. They pulled the ramp back inside, the door slammed shut, and the van took off. I couldn't tell if your friend resisted or anything, but it seemed strange to me. It all happened so fast."

Twenty dollars well-spent, Hardy thought.

"Can you describe the van?"

"Big, dark green, dark windows all around."

"Anything else about it?"

"Oh," the professor rummaged through the pocket of his frayed tie-dyed vest, producing a scrap of paper. "I almost forgot. I took down the license number." He handed the scrap of paper to Hardy. "Something seemed wrong about the whole thing, so I wrote down the license number. Will that be of any help to you?"

"Maybe," Hardy replied. "But good work anyway. Thank you, professor. Thank you very much."

Hardy got into the car and made four calls. The first was to check out the license number, which turned out to belong to a rental. No surprise there. The second call was to the private cell phone of *Tennessean* reporter Harvey Green. Hardy usually avoided reporters as much as possible, but Green had proven helpful on occasion. His stories were as accurate as you could hope for in a newspaper and Hardy didn't mind the implicit inside track for possible scoops if Green was willing to do him an occasional favor. Hardy knew this call was terribly premature, but he was willing to take the risk without clearing it with anybody. If there was any chance to locate Shane quickly, Hardy would gladly take the blame for trying anything he could think of even if his efforts failed. It was still early enough that a short piece should make it into the morning edition of the paper. And Hardy was betting that even a hopelessly incomplete piece would alert a lot of people to be on the lookout for anything suspicious that might be relevant and that they would notify the police. The third call was to Assistant Chief Carl Goetz, his immediate supervisor. He reported the possible kidnapping of Shane Hadley, gave the AC the license number and listened to his immediate response. He did not tell his boss that he had planted the newspaper story; that may have been unwise. Call number four was to Katya Karpov. She hadn't heard anything. Hardy related everything he had found out and promised to follow up aggressively in the morning. Katya didn't sound so good.

Shane Hadley sat blindfolded, hands bound, in the back of a van heading somewhere unknown, tended to by an unidentifiable person who refused to speak. He couldn't make any sense of the situation. It was all a dream, he thought, although he had never been a dreamer.

It wasn't a dream, but it didn't feel like reality either. Shane couldn't get the experience organized in his head. Something was wrong with his brain. The circuits weren't firing normally. The unusual feeling of vulnerability was rapidly taking over his consciousness, crowding out the confidence that he depended on, and that generally served him well. He didn't like that.

What Shane did not know, what neither of the two other persons in the dark green van knew, was that they were in the process of acting out a serious miscalculation.

Chapter 21

The New York money guys were extremely anxious to close the deal on the Fitzwallington paintings, get them committed exclusively to Galleria Salinas and then get the actual paintings, the product, stashed in the New York gallery and its overflow storage facility, depending on the volume. The Morticia Dragon Lady, Mildred Roth, made it plain in a conversation with Bruce Therault that the money guys were very unhappy having to deal with the yokels in Nashville and couldn't imagine why it should take so long. That's why they sent Mace Ricci as an advance man to nail down the commitment from the daughter. And maybe he had done that. But things were still moving too slowly and so they insisted that Therault, the presumed brains of the operation, go down there to help sort things out. And, beginning to feel desperate, they summoned some serious muscle from their Chicago connections in the person of Damian Saturn to join the other two in Nashville with the firm and non-negotiable charge of getting the job done. Whatever it took! And soon! None of the three was particularly happy with the thinly veiled threat, but they felt the pressure. And they all knew the kind of pressure the New York money guys were capable of exerting should they choose to. They were too aware of the potential unpleasant consequences of the Wrath of Roth.

When the three of them met on a sunny afternoon at TAPS and managed, not uneventfully, to acquire a less than generous glass of an anemic concoction of too much ice and too little of a second-tier blended Scotch whiskey, here's how they sized up the situation.

Everyone accepted that Mace Ricci had managed to extract a firm commitment from the artist's daughter to assign all of her father's paintings in her possession for sale exclusively by the Galleria Salinas in New York. Granted, SalomeMe was something less than a conspicuously reliable sort, but Ricci was sure of this, and the others, somewhat reluctantly, accepted his judgment.

However, there remained two problems that appeared to be delaying the process: establishing the daughter as Bechman Fitzwallington's sole and legitimate heir, and eliminating any possibility that the old guy's death would be considered a possible murder. Although there was absolutely no reason to question whether SalomeMe was the legitimate heir, the pending lawsuit brought by Parker Palmer and his lawyer friend did just that, so the question had to be answered once and for all. Fine. The daughter had retained a lawyer who was having the DNA from both parties analyzed and should very shortly have incontrovertible evidence of her legitimacy as the heir. They'd just have to wait for that information to get the lawsuit dismissed and move on.

Problem number two should never have existed. All of the evidence and the conclusion of the city police department said that the artist had died of natural causes. There should never have been any other consideration. But there was. Although he was obviously a minor player in the situation, the paralyzed ex-cop just couldn't leave this thing alone, and the legitimate police department didn't seem to be doing much to rein him in. These guys feared that if he looked hard enough, the ex-cop might turn up something that would raise enough questions that an official murder investigation would be launched. The problem there was the delay in transfer of the paintings that would undoubtedly result. The New York money guys would not be happy with anything that delayed the deal, which would mean that these three men would not be happy either. They would be really unhappy if they failed to move this deal forward. The big city money guys would see to that.

Although Bruce Therault was a little hesitant, the group finally agreed that if they could suspend Shane Hadley's interest in this situation just long enough to get the decisions about the paintings finalized, their mission would be accomplished. They could go their merry ways, collect sizeable fees for their services, and put all this behind them.

If Damian Saturn's approach to problem-solving could be expressed in mathematical terms, it would have approximated Newton's Second Law, F=ma: force equals mass times acceleration. He was convinced that most of the kinds of problems he was called on to help solve yielded most readily to force, action. The fact that he was a man of action accounted for Saturn's niche in the criminal underworld. As was his habit, before journeying to Nashville, he had done some due diligence, made some connections with kindred spirits in Music City, of whom there were more than most people knew. Anticipating what he might need to use his talents optimally toward solving this particular situation, he had identified some local sources of materials and services that were likely to be essential. He did not consider this a particularly difficult task. They could nab Hadley, dose him up with Midozalam (easily obtained from the Nashville drug network), hold him somewhere remote and inaccessible for a few days, and then drop him a place that allowed him to be found, unharmed and, thanks to the unique properties of the drug, totally unaware of what had happened to him during his time in physical and pharmacological captivity. Piece of cake. Saturn could make the arrangements. Bruce Therault basically washed his hands of the matter and went back to New York. Mace Ricci and Damian Saturn set about activating the plan. They had both been involved in much riskier jobs. They did not view the Nashville Police Department as deserving of very much respect—bush-league, they thought. And this guy Shane Hadley was a has-been nobody, so that his abduction, if carefully done, shouldn't attract much attention.

An initial hint of the magnitude of their miscalculation came the morning after their abduction of Shane Hadley when Mace Ricci returned from a local MiniMart with the morning newspaper and some provisions. He tossed the paper on the table in the kitchen of the small house with boarded-up windows in the largely abandoned South Nashville ghetto where Damian Saturn sat looking bored and drumming his fingers on the Formica tabletop. Shane Hadley was in an adjacent room, sitting in his wheelchair, his head lolling about aimlessly. He may have been dozing off and on. He looked small. He looked vulnerable. He bore precious little resemblance to the Sherlock Shane of Music City myth.

"Holy shit!" Saturn exclaimed, holding the morning *Tennessean* out in front of him as if he feared it would contaminate him if let it get too close. A headline just below the fold on the front page read SHERLOCK SHANE HADLEY MISSING, POSSIBLY ABDUCTED. He laid the paper on the table and read the short article through. Although it appeared to be based on dubious sources (principally a homeless man who didn't sound like a reliable witness), the story recounted the abduction essentially as it had occurred. The description of the van was not detailed but was accurate as far as it went. And the license plate number was accurate. The reader was encouraged to call the police department if they had any information that might be relevant. The article went on to recount Shane Hadley's illustrious history as a member of the Metropolitan Police

Force, the source of the admiration and affection that the people of the city felt for him. Neither Saturn nor Ricci had done enough due diligence to realize how well-known their victim was. Had they done so, they would have planned a less conspicuous operation. Working in unfamiliar territory, they had badly miscalculated. Some problems are not solved by calculations based solely on Newton's Second Law.

Holy shit! Saturn thought to himself. He feared the possibility that all hell might be about ready to break loose. They better get ahead of this in a hurry. As Saturn was about to fill Ricci in on the newspaper story and initiate a discussion of what their next move should be, Ricci's phone blared a tune that Saturn didn't recognize. Ricci read aloud the name of the caller from the screen. It was Bruce Therault.

Although Hardy Seltzer went to work early, by the time he got in to see Assistant Chief Goetz, the phone lines at the department were already white-hot with calls from a variety of people claiming to have information relevant to the fate of Shane Hadley. He had been seen drinking with rowdy friends at a dive on Lower Broad, wheeling far from downtown along Hillsboro Road near Green Hills Mall, driving a dark green van too fast headed south on I-75, and a long list of other creative and irrelevant snippets of citizens' imaginary visions of the ex-detective's whereabouts. And one caller who gave only an address in a deserted part of South Nashville without leaving a name or any other information.

"What in holy hell have you done, Hardy? The whole department is tied up with the phones. Your buddy Harvey Green's article has done a number on us, and I have absolutely no doubt that you deserve total credit for the fiasco. What were you thinking? Talk to me."

Goetz was in a rage, red-faced, eyes bulging, veins pulsating at his temples. He paced a circle around Seltzer, glaring at the detective from all sides as though setting him up for a physical attack. Hardy thought he had prepared himself to take the heat for what he had done, but this was worse than he had expected.

"I was thinking, sir," Seltzer tried his best to speak with reason and calm, to appear confident and in control, to clearly contrast his demeanor with that of his boss, "that the life of a valued citizen of our community was probably in imminent danger and that extraordinary measures were justified if there was any chance of averting that disaster. That decision and the resulting action were mine alone. I will accept the consequences."

"You bet your sorry ass, you'll accept the consequences," the Assistant Chief shrunk the radius of his paced circle around Seltzer, almost brushing against him, closing in for the kill. "And there will be consequences, Detective. There will be consequences." A less than gentle forefinger jab to the sternum.

The two men's eyes met for a long moment before Goetz turned, walked to his desk, and sat down emphatically, implying that he was finished dealing with Hardy Seltzer for the present and was moving on to other responsibilities. He shuffled some papers on his desk unconvincingly. Hardy stood stock-still exactly where Goetz had left him.

"We're done, Seltzer," Goetz said, not looking up from the sheaf of papers.

"Not quite," Hardy replied. "There remains the matter of the possible murder of Bechman Fitzwallington."

"We've been there, Seltzer, and I don't intend to return to the subject. The old guy died of natural causes, and that's that. Let it be."

"I'm sure that Shane Hadley's abduction had something to do with his interest in Fitzwallington's death. He was convinced it was murder. Someone didn't like that."

"So, find Hadley and let's see what he's got. If he's got some convincing evidence, we can talk."

"We may be too late for Shane Hadley. His abductors, whoever they are, are not nice people."

Hardy genuinely feared for his friend.

"The powers that be are very fond of Shane Hadley, Seltzer. If something bad happens to him, the department will catch hell and I and therefore the chief will blame the entire thing on you. Understand? Find Hadley. Forget about Bechman Fitzwallington. For God's sake, forget about him!"

Hardy skimmed rapidly through the stack of pink phone message slips piled on his desk. The messages were brief notes without attribution and mostly without any value in any effort to locate Shane Hadley. Hardy had made a mistake by convincing Harvey Green to include a request to contact the department in his newspaper story without making some advance preparation to handle the calls and to outline a strategy for dealing with them. Too late now. Hardy should have known better. How many times did he need to relearn the lesson that haste, even driven by a noble motive, was more often than not a mistake?

One of the phone messages caught his eye. An address, nothing more. He called up the address on Google maps. A largely deserted lower-class residential area south of town. When he switched to the street level view, the small bungalow at that address was obviously unoccupied, windows boarded up. Interesting. Hardy picked up his desk phone and called the dispatcher.

"This is Detective Seltzer. I need two blues and a cruiser. I'll be down there in ten minutes. Got it?"

The chain reaction of telephone calls triggered by the *Wrath of Wroth* eventually filtered out to Damian Saturn's connections in the dark side of the city's society. It reached as well, in a way, to Martin Reese, and thence to the operator on call for answering the 911 emergency line, and finally to Hardy Seltzer and his two blues in the police cruiser who were diverted from their intended destination of a seedy area of South Nashville to the idyllic environs of Shelby Bottoms.

Mildred Roth, along with the people whom she represented, was following the happenings in Nashville intently, so that she read the online version of the *Tennessean* each morning. When she saw the article about Shane Hadley's abduction, she was livid and acutely aware of the fact that something had to be done. Now! She immediately called Bruce Therault and read him the riot act. Why didn't he stay there and see this thing through? How could he possibly have agreed to such a hare-brained scheme carried out in broad daylight in the middle of town? Ricci and Saturn, supposedly big-league crooks, had behaved like rank amateurs and were absolutely sure to be caught regardless of the skill level of the local police force. They had, the three of them, failed miserably and there would be hell to pay. THERE WOULD BE HELL TO PAY! Bruce Therault could count on that. So Therault called Ricci, read him the riot act and instructed him to get out of this mess and the sooner the better. Ricci placed the reading of the riot act on speakerphone for the benefit of his partner in crime and as soon as the performance of the riot act was completed, curtain descended, and applause acknowledged, Saturn got in touch with his local contacts and obtained advice about where and how they might rid themselves of their captive without undue risk of being found out. Saturn enlisted the help of those contacts in arranging transportation and dealing with the other necessary details.

Martin Reese was awakened by a bright slat of morning sunlight that struck him square and sudden across the eyes just before the alarm he had set the previous evening sounded its shrill and insistent wakeup call. His wife, Muriel, was already up and no doubt in the process of orienting their two-year-old son to yet another wonder-filled day in his short life. Martin got up, had a quick shower, and dressed. It seemed such a nice morning that he volunteered to take their son for a stroll before they got organized sufficiently to make certain that each of them was deposited in their proper place for the conduct of a normal workday—dentist office, law firm, daycare. Because it was walking distance from their middle-class home and because it was an especially appealing place for a stroll on a nice sunny morning, Martin zipped his only son into a bright blue onesie, nestled him into a stroller, and struck out for Shelby Bottoms.

Shelby Park had been a popular outdoor space for East Nashvillians and the occasional wanderer from some other part of the city or from a more remote place, since the Fourth of July, 1912. It was a pretty much standard-issue city park—playgrounds, softball diamonds, picnic areas. But in 2011, the park was transformed. The city acquired adjacent space that included the Cornelia Fort Airpark (a small general aviation landing strip where Patsy Cline was headed when she wound up in eternity instead) and some additional acreage. They created Shelby Bottoms, a thousand-acre greenspace with paved walking trails, vast displays of indigenous flora, and open and ready access to anyone who was interested. On that sunny morning, Martin Reese could not have imagined a more pleasant place to be wandering with his young son and contemplating the blessings of his life

That is until a wheelchair raced by just grazing the edge of his son's stroller, careening off down the sloping path and crashing off into the weeds, dumping its occupant unceremoniously into a patch of what may have been mountain laurel (although Martin Reese's knowledge of botany was more visceral than intellectual; he would not have known mountain laurel from poison ivy). What he did know was that whoever the occupant of the runaway wheelchair was, he was in need of help, and so he whipped out his cell phone, dialed 911, and described the incident to whoever answered the call.

Whoever answered the call was not your average bear. She had read the morning *Tennessean* story. She knew who Shane Hadley was, the myth. She relayed the message to the ambulance service, but then connected with the police department and told them that she believed they might have located the missing ex-detective. The department dispatcher immediately contacted Hardy Seltzer, who instructed blue #1, his driver, to alter their destination. They headed for Shelby Bottoms. Hardy Seltzer's pulse quickened at the thought of rescuing his friend from what he had resigned himself to accept was likely to be a tragic outcome.

When they screeched, siren blaring, into the normally silent parking lot at Shelby Bottoms, an ambulance was already there and the EMTs were just wheeling a stretcher toward the open rear door of their vehicle. Hardy raced over to them. Shane, looking pale but wide-eyed and obviously breathing, looked up at Hardy from the stretcher. His eyes were blank … nobody home.

"How is he?" Hardy asked.

The obviously alpha EMT—older, more overweight, and less jumpy than his young colleague—replied, "His vitals are OK, but he's really out of it. Has no idea of the who's, what's, where's, and how's. Almost certainly drugs. Do you know anything?"

Hardy, angered by the EMT's implication that this was just another unknown junkie who wound up by some vagary of fate out of his depth, said not too gently, "Do you know who this man is?"

"Why would I know that? Even though I see more than enough of them in my line of work, I don't remember the names of every OD I pick up. Never learn the names of most of them."

"This man is Shane Hadley," Seltzer locked eyes with the EMT.

"He is a distinguished and widely honored former member of our police force who would be familiar to most people in the city who are able and inclined to read. I presume you are not among that group. Your job is to get him to the university hospital ER ASAP and to treat him *en route* with the respect and care that he and other human beings deserve. I will call ahead to the hospital to ensure that you do your job in a timely manner and that he is promptly cared for. If you have a problem with that, you should find yourself a job that doesn't require empathy for your fellow humans."

Hardy grasped Shane's limp hand for a moment and tried to engage his eyes without success. He went back to the cruiser and placed a call on the radio.

"Geez Louise," Alpha EMT wheezed to his partner as they climbed into the ambulance cab and cranked up the siren. "What the hell is that guy's problem?"

Katya Karpov raced the Boxster out Broadway toward the university hospital. She knew she was driving way too fast, but she didn't care. She desperately wanted to be there when Shane arrived at the ER. She knew better than to get in the way of the professionals who would be caring for her husband, but she needed to hold him, touch his body, assure herself that he was breathing, that he had a pulse, that he was alive. Hardy Seltzer had said that Shane was alive but he also said that her husband was disoriented, apparently drugged. Alive is good but there are degrees of aliveness. Katya needed the one hundred percent alive version of the man she loved more than anything else in the world.

Chapter 22

"Exposed?" Hardy Seltzer was genuinely puzzled by Shane's single word explanation for his unshakeable conviction that Bechman Fitzwallington had been murdered. "Are you sure there aren't some lingering effects of the drug, Shane? Some residual influence on your thought processes? I mean, *exposed*? What kind of an explanation is that for a conclusion that flies in the face of all the evidence?"

It had been three days since Shane was extracted from a tangle of an unspecified but no doubt certifiably indigenous species of flora in Shelby Bottoms and eventually delivered to the university hospital. He had spent two of the intervening days recovering from what the tox analyses of his serum defined as a rather high dose (or doses) of the drug Midozalam, a major effect of which was amnesia. Shane had absolutely no recollection of his little misadventure beyond being wheeled into a strange vehicle on Church Street in front of *Sam's Sushi*, blindfolded, and jabbed in the arm with what felt like a needle. Zilcho after that until he awoke in a hospital bed being fawned over by his lovely wife, onlooked by a bevy of what appeared to be health care professionals of various sorts.

Except for the gap in his memory, Shane felt that his brain was working perfectly fine now. His interest had returned to the

Fitzwallington case. Either Seltzer was humoring him in light of this recent episode, which both Seltzer and Katya seem to think was clearly life-threatening, or Hardy's interest in the case was also rekindled. Shane believed that his single word explanation for his conviction that this was a murder case was both adequate and precise.

"Yes, *exposed*!" Shane said.

"Sorry to be dense, Shane," Hardy responded. "But I really don't understand."

The two men sat on the Printers Alley deck facing each other, as usual, and each, also as usual, fondled an expensive glass filled with Shane's private and quite illegally obtained sherry. Shane paused for a moment and then wheeled abruptly about and through the French doors into the flat. A few seconds later, he returned to the deck with his laptop computer, opened it, and booted up.

"Perhaps," Shane said, "you will more easily grasp the visuals."

Shane fiddled with the computer a moment and then turned the screen toward Hardy. Displayed on the screen was a less than technically perfect photograph of an old man with a bushy moustache fading from white to the ivory color that emerges with age. The man was completely nude and lay supine on a bed, uncovered…exposed; the dead artist Bechman Fitzwallington in all his postmortem glory lying there before God and everybody.

"Exposed," Hardy said. "And?"

"Do you recall the weather during those few days?" Shane asked.

"Not specifically," Hardy answered. "We've had nice weather of late."

"Actually, there was a cool spell that lasted a few days around that time. I conclude from this photograph that the deceased did not go to bed on a cool night nude and completely uncovered with his hands carefully folded across his chest. That doesn't fit the circumstances. Not only did the murderer leave this unmistakable evidence of his or her participation in the artist's demise, but there is symbolism here."

"Symbolism?" Hardy was trying to keep up with Shane's reasoning.

"Exposed," Shane said. "Exposed," he repeated. "There is something important about the life of Bechman Fitzwallington that is not general knowledge. The murderer was party to that information; perhaps it was even the motive for the murder. But at the very least, the murder scene was certainly staged with the intention of stimulating the interest of a curious observer in the artist's history."

Hardy was having trouble concentrating on Shane's monologue. Seltzer had to address the larger issue of the safety of the city's streets. The department was getting a lot of negative attention in the press and elsewhere after the audacious daylight downtown abduction of Sherlock Shane Hadley. People were concerned for their safety. So, truth be told, Hardy Seltzer was much more interested in discovering who had abducted Shane, the reasons for it, and bringing the culprits to justice than he was interested in the demise of Bechman Fitzwallington. Although he suspected strongly that the two events were related, he intended to focus on Shane's abduction. That was, to Hardy, his most immediate priority. If in the process of tugging that thread, the whole mystery unraveled, that would be fine. If not, they could worry about whether the old artist was murdered and if so, who did it later, after there was enough assurance that the streets were safe to quiet the attacks on the competence of the police force.

Seltzer had grilled Shane as aggressively as he thought was likely to be useful. But Shane remembered nothing, absolutely nothing, about his abduction. Hardy had followed up the license plate number of the van, which also yielded nothing of use—rented van, paid cash, untraceable fake driver's license. The van had not been found, probably dumped in the river or something. A thorough search of the

South Nashville address pretty much confirmed that Shane had been held there but no clues to his captors. No fingerprints, no neglected scraps of anything that might lead to identification of any specific person. Despite the less than sophisticated method of Shane's abduction, the place where they held him looked like a pretty professional operation. As did the way he was released, which also left no traceable connections to the responsible parties. The crime scene people were still working over the wheelchair, but not much hope of finding anything definitive.

"So," Shane said, "given the evidence, is your department ready to investigate this murder as it is accustomed to investigating such misdeeds?"

"Don't think you can count on it, Shane. I'll relay your notion to the powers that be, but you have to admit that you don't really have anything solid. And, you surely understand that the department's priority has to be solving your abduction, identifying the culprits, and bringing them in. You've seen the papers. The media are all over this, and we, the department, which means me for one, are taking a lot of heat for not keeping the streets of the city safe."

"Surely," Shane replied, "you perceive that we are debating a single problem, not two separate ones. There is no doubt but that my alleged abduction was connected, intimately connected, to my conviction that the artist was murdered and my attempts to prove that was the case and identify the responsible party or parties. As is generally true of criminal activities, there is a puzzle to be solved. I am quite sure, my man, that once we have enough of the pieces of the puzzle identified, we will begin to assemble a single picture that integrates what might appear to be separate events."

"Yeah, maybe," Hardy said. "But I'm up to my ass in casual observers and my efforts have to go toward satisfying them. I'll talk to the boss and get back to you. Meantime, you do what you need to do, but first, be sure your brain is working at a hundred percent. Katya should be able to help you with that."

"My brain is working just fine, my friend," Shane responded. "Fortunately, since there is a murder to solve. That is an activity with which my brain is intimately familiar."

"Solving murders," Hardy mused. "I used to do that back before I became the puppet of city politics. I liked my job better then."

"One chooses one's poison," Shane replied.

Hardy Seltzer did not believe that he had chosen the events and people who caused him the most trouble, his poison. But he didn't say so. What the hell did Shane Hadley know about it?

The problem with maintaining a significant cocaine habit is that you can't do it without getting your hands dirty. The supply chain tends to be short. As a user, you can't avoid contact with the serious crooks who control, among other things, the source of your chosen drug. And, depending on a number of undefinable variables, that means that sooner or later you wind up being one of the things that they control. Of course, one does not like that, but what does one like better, cocaine or what seem like relatively minor concessions necessary to keep your lifeline open and in working order? Most times, that is *nolo contendere*— no contest.

While she was completely aware, both when high and during the diminishing times when she was not, that Lucifer held the mortgage on a large part of her soul, she did not believe that the mortgage covered the entire property. She made the concessions necessary to supply her habit, but she honestly believed that she retained an element of personal integrity. She was bad, okay, but not thoroughly so.

So, she hit the send button without hesitating and also without a thorough consideration of the potential consequences. Since she was guessing at the detective's email address, she would not have been surprised if the message had bounced back—no such address. But it didn't. Her guess was from what little she had been able to learn of the investigation. She had the detective's name and imagined an email address—just hseltzer@mnpd.gov, coupling the detective's first initial and surname with an acronym for Metropolitan Nashville Police Department. She had taken some precautions. She was using a computer in the public library that couldn't be traced to her. And she had worded the note to leave the impression that it came from someone less educated and less sophisticated than herself. She wanted to deliver the message, but she desperately wanted to keep her personal distance from any of this. Granted her central nervous system was not exactly at its drug-free baseline at the time, but she honestly believed when she moved the cursor to *send* and clicked the mouse with a decisive flick of her left forefinger, that she was catering to the better angels of her nature. She felt good about that. Those guys had been sorely neglected of late.

It was never a good idea to discuss anything of substance with Assistant Chief Goetz late in the day. Hardy Seltzer knew that. It seemed as though the daytime hours eroded away any façade of amity that might have developed during whatever his boss's after-hours pursuits were, exposing something raw and primitive that was not fertile ground for a meaningful conversation. However, it was late in the day when Hardy returned to his office from meeting with Shane, and he felt some considerable urgency about revealing Shane's *exposed* theory of Fitzwallington's death. The door to Goetz's office was ajar. So, Seltzer took the chance. It was a bad idea.

"So, let me get this straight," said the Assistant Chief, sarcasm oozing around the edges of the words. "You want me to suggest to the chief that we divert the entire resources of the department to investigating a theoretical murder based on a single photograph of a naked dead man when the coroner and you yourself have concluded that the old man died of natural causes. I wouldn't do that if Sherlock Holmes himself appeared, incarnate, and suggested it. You are too taken with this ex-detective. He's no longer of any use to us. He has, in fact, turned out to be a royal pain in the ass. Shane Hadley should be off-limits for you except in the investigation of the perpetrators of his abduction. That is the crime you are to solve, and I don't really give a tinker's damn whether or not that solution has anything to do with the old artist who, according to every professional opinion that I'm aware of, just up and died when his time came."

"That's about what I expected you would say," Hardy responded.

"Then, why the hell bring it up?"

"Not sure. Maybe just getting all the cards on the table."

"Hmmmph," Goetz puffed, "better get a more careful look at your cards. Pick out the useless ones and discard them. Don't waste my time, Seltzer. Bring me something real."

"Yessir," Hardy sighed as he left the office and returned to his desk.

Hardy booted up his computer and called up his email. There were 150 unread entries. He didn't make a very serious effort to keep up with emails. Most of them were useless and they could take up a lot of time if you got too tied to them. He casually scrolled down the list, still distractedly thinking about his next move in trying to solve Shane's abduction. He probably would not have noticed a particular message except for the strange name of the sender—*Moleskin*, like those cute little notebooks that literary types have allegedly used for generations to record their private thoughts.

Mister Detektiv. It was an outside-inside job. Be lookin for connexions between CROOKS (big letters for big crooks). Good luck, Moleskin.

That was it. Had to be referring to the Hadley thing. What else could it be? And Moleskin was trying too hard to sound stupid. Probably an English professor too thinly and not very cleverly disguised. Like, Detektiv? Give me a break. Anybody who couldn't spell detective wouldn't have called themselves *Moleskin*. Much too sophisticated a moniker for an illiterate.

Hardy printed out the message, folded it, and slid it between the pages of his pocket notebook. Could be something. And he was desperately short of clues to guide his next move. Shane might be able to help with the interpretation. No doubt he would have something interesting to say about the message. Goetz just didn't understand about Shane. Most people didn't.

Athena Golden sat in the living room of her Green Hills condo nursing a glass of red wine and thinking. What was going on with the Fitzwallington paintings? She thought that there should have been some public announcement of their disposal by now and, since she had not been contacted by anyone, including, to her profound disappointment, the artist's daughter. She was more or less resigned to the possibility that the New York gallery had successfully laid claim to them. While she had hoped to land at least some of the stash, it wouldn't surprise anyone if her little gallery on the fringe of downtown Nashville failed to compete with the big city art scene. She wondered if Parker Palmer knew anything. She checked her watch. It wasn't that late. She placed the call. He answered after three and a half rings.

"This is Parker," the familiar casual lilt of his voice made her smile; Parker often affected people that way.

"Good evening, Parker. This is Athena. I hope I didn't disturb you."

"Not a problem, my dear," Palmer answered. "What's up?"

"I was just wondering, given that all has gone quiet on the Fitzwallington front, whether you had any idea what is happening with his paintings."

"'Fraid not," Palmer said. "I, too, am deafened by the sound of silence, but no idea why this hasn't moved faster. I guess the Sherlock Shane episode may have distracted things. Hadley obviously had a bee in his bonnet about Billy Wayne's death. Thought he was murdered was my impression. Also, although I don't think it amounts to much, Jay Combs, the lawyer who sits on the Arts Commission and I filed a lawsuit questioning whether Sally May is the legitimate heir. Pretty much a frivolous suit. Long shot. We did it because there is no written record that anybody can locate that documents their relationship. I understand that Jimmy Holden, her lawyer, is getting DNA analyses that will nail it down. That should be available soon. They'll probably dismiss the suit."

What in God's name possessed Parker Palmer to question the daughter's paternity?

Athena asked, "Is there an inventory of the paintings?"

"Not as far as I know, at least not one for public consumption. But I understand that there's quite a stash, hidden away somewhere in storage. I hope they've been properly cared for. If they've gotten moldy from a leaky roof or some such, that would be a fine kettle of fish, wouldn't it? Have you had any contact with the New York gallery?"

"Not lately. I tried earlier to open up that connection, but, like everything else related to those paintings, the connection went black."

"Any follow-up sales of my stuff from the show?" After all, Parker Palmer was a salesman.

"A couple of the larger pieces went just yesterday. We'll settle up in the next week or so."

"Great."

"Let me know if you hear anything."

"You betcha."

New York's time was an hour ahead of Nashville's and it was getting late, but Athena Golden rang the *Galleria Salinas*, the only number she had for Blythe Fortune. Athena recognized that it was unlikely that the phone would be answered at that hour, but she called anyway. After four rings, a pleasant female voice conveyed the business hours and address of the gallery and invited the caller to leave a voice message.

Blythe, this is Athena Golden in Nashville. I realize it's late there, so not surprised you didn't answer. Just wondering if you've had any news about the Fitzwallington paintings. The subject seems to have gone silent here and I continue to be interested in being involved in their sale if possible. Give me a call when you have a chance. Hope all is well there.

Best. Athena.

Probably a waste of time and effort, Athena thought.

Shane was suddenly wide awake at a very early hour. The broad expanse of windows in their bedroom that overlooked Third Avenue were matte black panels sprinkled with occasional reflections from the streetlights below. There was total silence for a long moment until it was interrupted by the reverberating chirp of a police siren and strobes of blue light flickering in the windows. KiKi slept soundly beside Shane, the soft rhythm of her breathing barely audible. KiKi was a marvelous sleeper.

Shane pushed himself up in the bed and reached for his laptop that he had left on the bedside table before going to sleep the previous evening. He had been suddenly awakened from a deep sleep by a compelling need to look again at the picture of a dead Bechman Fitzwallington. Was there something in the picture that he had missed? He fired up the computer and called up the picture. He stared at the naked and dead man, carefully examining the photograph as a whole, and then in detail, as close as he could get to pixel by pixel, desperately trying to discover something he had overlooked. Or was it something that wasn't there?

Chapter 23

Shane shut down his computer, nestled back down into the bed, and reached across to feel the solid gentle curve of KiKi's lower back. Her presence beside him was his rock, his anchor to reality, and his source of the strength he needed to deal with it. He lay there for a while, staring at the ceiling and listening to the slow rhythm of his wife's breathing. But, try as he might, sleep avoided him. Eventually he maneuvered himself out of bed, wheeled up to the kitchen at the front of their flat and brewed a pot of coffee. By the time KiKi appeared, drowsy, somewhat disheveled, and beautiful, Shane was parked near the front windows caressing a cup of coffee and staring distractedly at the flat space before him. KiKi helped herself to a cup of coffee from the kitchen and then walked up to where Shane sat, stood behind him, and caressed his shoulders. He relished the familiar touch of her strong hands. He had always admired her hands. They brought him much pleasure.

"Is knowledge always for the good?" KiKi said, kneading the wiry muscles of his neck and shoulders.

"Well," Shane responded, "usually better than ignorance, I suppose."

"Always?"

"Do you mean are there unknown truths that are better left that way? But I thought you were in the business of slaying the dragons of ignorance."

"You put it so colorfully, my love. Maybe slaying some dragons of ignorance but inflicting collateral damage in the process. Too many slayings of late, it seems to me. Maybe the power of our weapons has transcended our understanding of what they can do."

"The power of the genome, I sense you mean."

"Well, more the power of the technology to explore it. Afraid we scientists are generally more interested in discovering new knowledge than in the potential consequences."

"You're still fretting about the Mad Hatter thing, right?"

"That, and about outliers in general. Fitzwallington was an outlier too. And there are a few others who have been given some of their genetic information. I'm worried that we haven't seen the last of the fallout from this."

"Outliers," Shane mused. "Most of our social capital is spent dealing with outliers. Murderers, thieves, miscreants of other sorts. Those aren't your average folks; they're outliers. But those people are the very *raison d'etre* of the entire elaborate and expensive law enforcement apparatus. Maybe the same is true in your work. Focus on the few to benefit the many? Something like that."

"But, *sacrifice* the few? You are sounding a bit like my geneticist colleague who seems to brush off things like the Mad Hatter episode as genetic collateral damage, the cost of advancing knowledge. That's cold, Shane. I've not thought you such a cold person."

"That's not exactly what I meant. Law enforcement is not in the business of sacrificing innocent people as a matter of practice. But it does happen. Do the bad guys hide behind that possibility? Sometimes. And sometimes they even get away with it for a while. But the bad guys eventually have to pay for their sins. Otherwise the good guys are stuck with the tab."

"What terrifies me, my love," KiKi responded, "is the possibility that we're wielding tools powerful enough to convert good guys to bad guys if we aren't more careful about how we use them."

"Not a pleasant thought," Shane replied.

"Thank you, my love," KiKi frowned. "I do appreciate your honesty in general, but occasionally couldn't you massage the truth a little bit for the benefit of your loving wife?"

"My lovely wife, seeker of truths, wishes to accept only the convenient ones?"

"I just don't want it to be this hard," she said.

"Nor do I, my love," Shane said, leaning his head back against her chest. "Nor do I."

Hardy Seltzer got the news just as he was about to leave his office for a Printers Alley rendezvous with Shane. Word came from the crime scene investigation people that they had lifted a single complete fingerprint from the handle of Shane's wheelchair. (About time they got around to going over the wheelchair, Hardy thought.) A quick run of the print through the FBI database produced a clean hit. The owner of the print was one Dudley (the Dude) Sysco, a known hoodlum from Chicago who worked as hired muscle for the mob or anyone else willing to meet his price. A freelancer. Sort of middle management type. He had served a couple of stints in federal prison for violent crimes but was not incarcerated at the present time. A photograph, obviously not very recent and a little blurry, was attached to the email message. Hardy printed out the message and the photograph, carefully folded them up, slipped them in between the pages of his pocket notebook alongside the earlier message, and headed for The Alley.

"Called himself Damian Saturn," Shane said. "Same initials. Fits."

Hardy's printout of the earlier mysterious email about Shane's kidnapping being an outside-inside job, and the picture and note resulting from the discovery of the fingerprint were spread out before them on the small patio table, and both men pored over the documents.

"He provided me with quite unsolicited assistance toward Wall Street one afternoon. Just appeared behind me and grabbed the chair and shoved it. No doubt an effort to intimidate me. Maybe that's where the prints came from. Could be this doesn't link this guy to my abduction at all."

"Was that the only time you remember seeing him?" Hardy asked.

"Actually, no. He was at that art showing at Athena Golden's gallery that KiKi and I attended. Went out of his way to introduce himself to me. Said something that I don't remember specifically, but said in a threatening way. I recall that well enough."

"Moleskin?" Shane said, looking at the email message. "Now that's odd. And the faux illiteracy is not very convincing. Do you think that was deliberate? An obscure clue to the identity of the author?"

"Maybe. Not sure. It's likely that the FBI will be called on to figure that out. I'm pretty sure the department brass will insist on turning the abduction thing over to them. They aren't very happy with my approach to it anyway. They think I'm too close to it. The chief will also like the *optics* of bringing in the FBI. He likes that word a lot…optics."

"A perfectly good word when used properly which, alas, it seems rarely to be these days," Shane said. "So, you surmise that this Chicago hood is Mr. Outside? How do you figure that? What possible connection would he have had with our fair city? And me? What interest could he have had in my whereabouts? Must have to do with my interest in the manner of our artist's apparently timely demise. And who, do you suppose, is Mr. Inside?"

"A lot of questions," Hardy mused. "Not many answers yet."

"However, my friend," Shane leaned toward Hardy and barely suppressed the urge to poke him in the chest with a forefinger, "you surely must see the connection. The murder of Bechman Fitzwallington is surely integral to my abduction. It has to be."

"While I can see the logic of that, I have been specifically forbidden from exploring the possibility," Hardy sighed.

Ignoring Hardy's statement, Shane continued. "If my abduction was orchestrated by the big city crime guys, they certainly failed to bring their A team. The caper was a total bust. Surely their intent was to either eliminate me from the picture or at least to keep me out of commission for a while until the Fitzwallington matter was settled and forgotten. I presume that the newspaper story, appearing so quickly on the heels of their ill-conceived plan, is what triggered the premature abortion of the scheme whatever it was. Quick thinking on your part to plant the story. A risky move, I suspect, that may have spared me some serious mischief."

"Didn't win me any friends in high places. That's for sure."

"I've observed over the years that the value of friends in high places tends to be greatly inflated," Shane said. "However, be that as it may, Mr. Inside could be the one who links my abduction to the murder, although I'm not sure exactly how. Who is it? You must know some local bad guys with ties to big crime. Perhaps a cooperative venture, old chits redeemed, something along those lines? And what is the connection to Fitzwallington? Must be one. Probably something to do with money. If there are a lot of paintings, there might be an expectation of a considerable sum, perhaps enough to flush out some greedy bad guys."

"Drugs," Hardy replied. "Any big crooks in this city make their money running drugs pretty much like they always have. Hasn't changed much since you were on the force. Some different drugs. Maybe some personnel shuffling. But basically the same operations."

"What about that Ricci guy, the ex-New York cop who's been hanging around town for a while now? Have you any information on him?"

"Well, some," Hardy replied. "He has a connection to the New York gallery that is making a determined play to land the Fitzwallington pantings. He's spent a lot of time sucking up to the daughter. Not sure what else. I haven't been able to find out much about Ricci personally—ex-cop, some checkered history on the force there. No criminal record that I can locate."

"And Moleskin?"

"Not a clue."

"I sense," Shane said, "that we are far overdue for a sherry. Please amuse yourself for a few moments while I tend to that."

Shane wheeled into the apartment, leaving Hardy sitting on the deck looking uncharacteristically morose. This whole matter depressed him. He still wasn't sure about Shane's conviction that the old artist was murdered. But what Hardy felt about that didn't really matter anyway. The official attitude was clear and unequivocal. About Shane's abduction, the higher-ups would probably be right to ding him for being too close to the victim. The involvement of the Chicago hood would probably put the whole thing in the hands of the feds. Hardy might well be relegated to chasing gang bangers and out-of-control spouse abusers. He could do that, but it was not the part of his job that he particularly enjoyed.

He stood up and walked to the railing overlooking The Alley. A few early afternoon stragglers were wandering around looking for someplace open where they could get a drink. Out-of-towners, no doubt. A lot of them in recent years. Hardy wondered what they were really looking for. Why come all this way from Topeka or wherever and spend the afternoon milling about The Alley? What were their questions? What clever Kansas travel agent cooked up the ruse that lured these rubes to a place that didn't pretend to have answers. Maybe some interesting questions. But answers? You'd need to go somewhere else for those.

Shane emerged through the French doors, a tray with two glasses and a bottle on his lap. He wheeled over to the table, placed each of the glasses there, and poured into each a generous amount of the wine. Hardy returned to his seat opposite Shane. Each of the men raised his glass and gestured before each downed a more than genteel sip. They replaced the glasses on the table and sat quietly for a few moments. Shane tried to engage Hardy's eyes without success. Unable to read his friend's mood, he spoke.

"Hardy, my man," he said, "we need to talk. I mean we seriously need to talk."

"Talk away," Hardy responded. "Talk away."

Blythe Fortune was always wound pretty tight; it was just who she was. But the past few days had her mainspring wound to near the limits of its tensile strength. She was as close as she had ever been to a cataclysmic snap. She was going through two packs of cigarettes a day. And Xanax? Like placebo pills. Not doing the job. Didn't matter how many she downed. Finally, she resorted to the less standard drug that she had found effective when conventional pharmaceuticals failed her—the pristine powder didn't relieve the tension, but tension became pleasure, the more the better. She didn't like the idea of doing the drug, but the current situation was serious, plenty serious enough to warrant the legal risk and the certain guilt. There was always the tide of guilt that washed in as the drug-induced euphoria ebbed. She'd worry about that when the time came. She placed the call and made arrangements.

It was Bruce Therault's fault. Following his return from Nashville, he had decided that he must inform Blythe more completely of the situation. In case this thing got entirely out of hand, which it seemed to threaten, Bruce had absolutely no intention of taking full responsibility. He needed an accomplice who was in on the deal. Blythe was already an unaware accomplice, so fully inform her of the situation and she'd automatically share responsibility for any adverse outcomes, especially if such outcomes involved legal trouble. Thus rationalized, Bruce did it.

But Blythe Fortune wasn't made of criminal stuff. She was not a crook and could not possibly think of herself that way. This situation struck her as grossly unfair. What she cared about was the gallery, and what she knew about was art. Granted, she was responsible for getting Bruce involved, but she was convinced that it was essential to do something to rescue the gallery at the time. Bruce seemed to bring a talent for attracting money that Blythe did not have. He had done that, maybe saved the gallery. Happy with the ends, Blythe had paid too little attention to the means. She was vaguely aware that her partner was capable of bending some rules, but outright criminality? What in God's name was he thinking? And now she was party to it, up to her nether parts in what had become essentially a criminal enterprise. The drugs might help for a bit, but they were no answer. She had to do something. She was not a crook!

She listened to the voice message from Athena Golden in Nashville and stewed about it for a while. Blythe was beginning to regret ever having heard of the town. New York was her place. But maybe Athena would have some additional information that would help Blythe figure out more precisely where this matter was and perhaps where it was headed. It was just not going to be possible for Blythe to extricate herself from the situation now that she was informed and so really involved. She needed to know more than she did at present. She phoned Athena Golden.

Most evenings, there was a period of an hour or so, before the clubs were in full swing and before the blood alcohol levels of the assembled patrons were sufficiently high to abolish inhibitions and so raise the volume to acoustically challenging levels, when Shane thought it especially pleasant to sit on their deck with a glass of sherry, allow the soft murmur of the milling crowd and the muted sounds of bar musicians tuning up for the evening to wash over him, and contemplate. This was such an evening. KiKi had not come home from work yet, and Shane sat in the cresting dark, nursing his drink and contemplating the death of Bechman Fitzwallington.

So many pieces to this puzzle: the odd collection of people who persisted in visiting the artist whom they claimed to hate; the aborted abduction just out of the blue and its apparent connection to the Chicago hood; the completely unexpected and still not very well explained review by the *Times* art critic that catapulted the value of Fitzwallington's paintings into the stratosphere; that ex-New York cop hanging around and insinuating himself into the Fitzwallington matter; the dueling galleries, New York vs. Nashville duking it out for rights to the sale of the paintings; the odd email from "Moleskin." Now what in hell was that about?

There must be a key, Shane thought. There was almost always a key, especially when the situation appeared to be so complex. A person? A fragment of evidence? A factual detail, disguised as trivial but in reality, the critical link that made sense of the information fragments, the key.

Shane wheeled himself back into the apartment, retrieved his laptop from behind the bar, and opened it up. Remembering the name of the New York Gallery, he Googled Galleria Salinas, New

York. The search produced, among a lot of uninteresting propaganda, two names, Blythe Fortune and Bruce Therault. From what he could retrieve from the Internet, Blythe Fortune appeared to be reasonably well-respected among the city's art cognoscenti. Bruce Therault had been involved in business deals in the city, mostly real estate, and had become involved in the gallery only in recent years presumably as the money guy. Hard to tell from the information on the Internet, but his history might be something less than simon-pure, legal-wise. Worth keeping in mind.

Shane closed his computer and sat for a few minutes in the living room, thinking. He heard the throaty purr of KiKi's Boxster enter The Alley and nestle into the garage below. He wheeled to the elevator to greet her arrival.

Moleskin, he thought. *Moleskin.*

Chapter 24

Although not quickly apprehended, Mr. Inside in Shane Hadley's abortive abduction was quickly identified by both Hardy Seltzer and by an FBI agent in the Chicago office of the bureau. Hardy reasoned that if the Nashville based participant was a Crook with a capital C and had connections to organized crime, it would almost certainly be, or at the very least involve, Wilton Argent, kingpin of the city's significant illegal drug business. Hardy would love to see the elusive criminal get his just desserts. It would be interesting if that happened as a result of involving himself in a hapless abduction scheme, doing a favor for his cronies in the larger crime world when Argent didn't have a dog in that particular fight. Irony, Hardy thought that must be what it would be, although he wasn't sure of the exact meaning of the word.

Seltzer sat in his office thinking about the identity of Mr. Inside and staring at the screen of his computer, which attracted him from his reverie by signaling the arrival of an email message. Hardy opened it.

Mr. Detekiv, the message read, *Call off the feds. Don ass too many questuns. Jus go for the big Crooks. Moleskin*

Hardy was again tempted to ignore the message but somehow couldn't bring himself to do that. He printed out the message and put it between the pages of his pocket notebook with its companion. He'd talk to Shane about it, but it sounded as though Moleskin was warning against trying to identify the source of these cryptic notes, which probably meant that whoever Moleskin was, he wasn't directly involved in Shane's abduction. Or more likely, the whole thing was a hoax. It certainly smacked of that.

Agent Farley Marsh was very familiar with the man sitting across the table in front of him. Dudley (The Dude) Sysco was well-known to every FBI agent in the Chicago office. Sysco was not a very accomplished crook but managed to make a living by working both sides of the street—doing low-level jobs for the syndicate and acting as a paid informant of the bureau. When the fingerprint of the Chicago hood showed up on the handle of the wheelchair of a victim of an abduction in Nashville, the police there sought help from the FBI in following through on the clue. Marsh immediately summoned Sysco to the office, installed him in an interrogation room, kept him waiting for an inordinately long period of time per protocol, and set about extracting information. This was not too difficult since the rat was bought and paid for, but the information was still often incomplete and usually more expensive than its quality warranted. The Dude rarely earned his keep in either of his chosen vocations.

However, on this occasion, the Dude acted as though he had the goods and appeared to deliver them promptly.

"Guy's name is Wilton Argent, if you can believe it," Sysco said. "Runs the cocaine concession for the Nashville crowd. He would be the local guy if you wanted to set something like this up. He has the necessary connections to do stuff like that, you know, local gofers to make arrangements. Argent's not really big time, but he likes to keep connections with the big boys. Makes him feel more important than he is, I'm guessing."

"OK, yeah, we know about Mr. Argent, Dudley," agent Marsh responded. "What I want to know is what your fingerprint was doing on the wheelchair of the abductee. What was your role in the caper, and who else was involved?"

"Whoa, now Farley," Sysco said. "You're not busting me on a kidnapping charge. I was in Nashville, OK. But my people sent me there just to intimidate the ex-detective, scare him off the notion that the old artist was murdered. That's what I did. I stalked him for a few days. I approached him on the street one day, grabbed the handles of his chair, and acted tough. That's it. That could be when I left the fingerprint. If I had been involved in the abduction, surely I would have worn gloves or wiped everything down."

"I don't really believe you. We both know that you are often less than meticulous with your dirty work. But assuming you are telling the truth, if not you, who?"

"What can I say?" Dudley sighed. "The less I know about these small tasks I occasionally take on solely for the money, the better. I will tell you what I was told about the Nashville thing, but it may not help you very much."

"I'll be the judge of that. Go ahead."

"Of course, it's about the money, or, as best I could tell, the potential money. My employers seemed to be involved in a scheme to pump up the value of the Nashville artist Bechman Fitzwallington's paintings after he died and get them assigned exclusively to a New York gallery where they had a financial interest and could control things. This paralyzed Nashville ex-detective somehow got a bee in his bonnet about how the old guy died, thought somebody bumped him off, and was slowing the whole process down. My guys were anxious to get the paintings and put them on the market while the iron was hot, so to speak, and the detective guy was in the way. So, they hired me to try to scare him off. I tried, but I guess didn't succeed. They must have hired somebody else to put the detective out of the picture. The problem was that nobody involved in the plot realized that this detective guy was a local hero and so the plan was a loser from the start because of the public reaction, which came as a surprise to everybody. My understanding is that the big guys were, shall we say, less than pleased with that outcome."

"Who, Dudley? That's what I need to know. Who were the oafs who bungled the kidnapping."

"I wasn't in on that part of the scheme," Dudley lied. "Whoever it was, they must have worked through Wilton Argent. He had to be involved in the local arrangements. Grill him. And, you might learn something by chasing anyone with connections to the New York gallery, especially if they happened to show up in Nashville."

"Name of the gallery?"

"Galleria Salinas," Dudley replied. "Upper East Side."

Hardy Seltzer had never put much stock in information from paid informants. The incentives were wrong. And there is something particularly repulsive about a snitch, paid or not. Even when the information is useful, it still feels tainted somehow, like you didn't come by it honestly. And besides, in this particular case, the fed's Chicago snitch hadn't really told them very much he didn't either already know or had figured out on his own. Well, maybe except for exactly what part The Dude played in the situation. He was almost certainly more involved than he said.

It was pretty obvious that the Feds weren't especially interested in this case, so while they agreed to question The Dude, they didn't do it very aggressively and just fed what they found out back to the Nashville department, without indicating further interest on their part. So, by default, Hardy was still in charge of ferreting out the culprits in Shane's abduction, and also still under the imposed prohibition from pursuing the murder possibility. Shane was doing that.

Those were the things Hardy Seltzer was thinking as he sat opposite Marge Bland at a corner table in the rear dining room at Mere Bulle, staring out at the river rather than paying attention to his date. He was not deriving the maximum benefit from his investment in the pricey meal. Not yet, anyway. But it was still early. It was not the first time Marge had seen him in this distracted frame of mind. She usually tried to entice him out of it and sometimes succeeded.

Marge was lost in her own thoughts that evening, ruminating over the last several days. Like most of her days, they had been pretty uneventful. Of course, her job gave her an up-close and personal look at a lot of lives, and that intrigued her—razor-thin slices of those lives. She paid some attention to the patrons of TAPS out of a general interest in people and from boredom. She often remembered names that she overheard or read from a credit card receipt. She had stored away a long list of names (she especially remembered the ones that sounded unusual) with no particular meaning to her. She would sometimes amuse herself by making up stories for them; she thought of the stories as *TAPS Tales*. Occasionally she would tell one of her stories to Hardy. She thought that he enjoyed listening to them at least once in a while.

A sternwheeler chugged lazily along down the river, its gentle wake fanning out behind toward the river banks. On its way to nowhere in particular. Just doing its job, amusing the paying customers. Marge understood that. She thought that was how she spent most of her waking hours, amusing paying customers. Her rediscovered relationship with Hardy had been a special and totally unexpected addition to her life. They liked each other. And they were starting to feel comfortable together. He didn't bore her.

She reached across the table and touched Hardy's hand. He looked at her, a vacant look, blank spaces behind his eyes, or spaces occupied by something other than the two of them having a pleasant evening together. Could be almost anything.

"Sorry, Marge," Hardy said, taking her hand in his. "My mind is wandering. Reel me in. You know how to do that."

Marge knew that sometimes a *TAPS Tale* could wrest him from the clutches of his current dilemma, lure him back to the present reality. Worth a try anyway.

"So," Marge began, "the other day when I came in to work to relieve Marva, around five, there were these three guys who she said had been there for a while drinking Dewars and having what looked like a serious conversation. They stayed for an hour after my shift started, and then one of them sprung for the drinks with his credit card and they left. I had the vague notion that I had seen one of them at TAPS in the past but wasn't sure. It was obvious that they were not locals, accents from probably up north somewhere. You might have thought it was a business meeting of some sort except that business meetings don't happen at TAPS and anyway, they didn't look like businessmen, at least to me. If I didn't know better, I might have thought they were cops, maybe dirty cops. Not sure why. But I imagined they were up to no good."

"Just what no good did you imagine they were up to?"

"Something really serious, maybe murder. Dirty cops plotting an intricate scheme to do in a clean cop who was on to their local protection racket and was threatening to rat them out."

"So why would they meet in a public place to hatch the plot?"

"Well, TAPS isn't exactly the town square, Hardy. I wouldn't be surprised if a lot of shady plots get hatched there. We get a lot of characters who are, no doubt, looking for trouble. Seems to me that trouble often finds characters who are looking for it. Trouble is probably a regular customer at our place."

"Yeah, maybe," Hardy said, slowly resurfacing into the present reality, coming up for air. "So why do you remember these guys?"

"Name," Marge replied, "I remember names, especially ones that sound unusual to me. The guy who paid the bill was dressed a little better than the other two. He seemed to be the head honcho. And, unusual name, sounded kinda French. Therault, Bruce Therault."

Athena Golden didn't remember exactly why she had called Blythe Fortune late at night. Maybe the wine. So, Athena was surprised when Blythe returned the call the next day.

"Hello, Blythe," Athena answered the phone after checking the caller ID and noting that it was from the Galleria Salinas, New York. "How are you?"

"Surviving," Blythe answered. "Surviving. Bruce tells me that there has been some action in your town."

"Bruce?"

"My business partner, Bruce Therault. I thought I had mentioned him to you. He does the financial part of our operation. I do the art. It has worked out pretty well for the most part. Although I'm not always sure exactly how these money guys operate. And not totally comfortable with that sometimes."

Athena knew what she meant. From the time Athena had opened AvantArt, she had held to her initial determination to go it alone. She was confident in her appreciation of emerging art and hopeful that there would be enough popular interest in the works she identified to make her little operation a viable business. That had been true so far, although she was certainly not getting rich. She didn't care about that. She felt good about boosting the careers, at least locally, of some up and coming artists whose work she admired. She had not previously had much contact with or, to be truthful, interest in, the art of Bechman Fitzwallington. Her interest now was primarily monetary. She had been gobsmacked by Arturo Carbone's obit in the *New York Times*. Very unlike his usual hypercritical reviews. But there it was in black and white and that made it impossible to ignore Fitzwallington's works for both esthetic and financial reasons. That obituary also introduced major complications to the process of dealing with the old artist's legacy. This conversation was evidence of that.

"I know what you mean."

"Wasn't there something like a kidnapping there that made a lot of news?" Blythe asked. "Did that have any connection to the Fitzwallington matter?"

"All I know is what's in the papers. The episode sounds fishy. A sort of local hero, a paraplegic ex-policeman, was snatched off the street, held somewhere for a couple of days, and then released for no apparent reason. No ransom demands, no obvious reasons for the abduction. I am not aware of any connection of this ex-cop and the Fitzwallington matter." The ghost of a thought wafted through Athena's mind and she continued. "Are you?"

"I have no idea, but Bruce thinks so. He's been keeping tabs on the progress of the disposition of the available Fitzwallington paintings. He thinks that has gone more slowly than it should have because your local hero has been unofficially meddling in the investigation of the artist's death. I mean, the situation looks so straightforward. The guy died. His death was declared a result of natural causes by the powers that be. He has a single heir. What in God's name is the holdup?"

"Not a clue, Blythe," said Athena Golden. "Not...a...clue."

Shane Hadley's mind was focused on three people when KiKi broke the silence that had parked itself between them.

"You might be interested in this, my love," she said. "My molecular guys have been mining the genomes of our outliers, and one thing they found will interest you."

"Yes?" Shane questioned.

"There is a clear genetic connection between the old dead artist and one of the other outliers in our study."

"And who might that be?"

"Not sure. He's still alive, so hasn't been identified. All I have is a study number. I'll need permission from the IRB to link that to a name. I'll try to get that but this study has suddenly attracted a lot of attention from the regulatory people, so I'm not sure what will happen."

"Sorry," Shane responded, "IRB?"

"Institutional Review Board. They control all clinical investigations, enforce the rules."

"Do you think they might be willing to bend the rules a smidge in the case of a possible murder?"

The sarcasm was obvious in his tone, and KiKi didn't appreciate it.

"I hope not," she said.

They had finished most of the penne Norma that Shane had made, their plates bare but for a few lonely shards of eggplant, and were nearing the bottom of the bottle of Rombauer chardonnay. It seemed obvious to both of them that their dinner and their conversation were essentially finished. Shane took his glass of wine and wheeled himself through the French doors out on to the deck. Katya didn't join him.

Three people had regularly visited Bechman Fitzwallington prior to what Shane considered his mysterious death: SalomeMe, Parker Palmer, and Fiona Hayes. A daughter, easy enough to understand, but the other two? What was the attraction? Both claimed to dislike the old guy, in the Hayes woman's case, intensely. Why did they keep coming back? Shane had the gut feeling that one of them was the murderer but, apart from the daughter who seemed to him too obvious a suspect, what was the motive?

Who was it? The carefree and garrulous Parker Palmer or the tightly wired and intense young ceramicist? Or, maybe the obvious one, the daughter? After all, sometimes a murderer will declare themselves openly either out of guilt or as a defensive counter-ploy. It was also possible that Shane was completely off track. Perhaps either there was no murder, as everyone else seemed to believe, or he had yet to encounter the culprit. It had always been the period of uncertainty in an investigation that most interested him. Once that was resolved, the rest was just going through the motions.

Shane wheeled himself back into the living room over to the bar, poured himself a generous glass of sherry, and drank it.

Chapter 25

"Should we just ignore these Moleskin things?" Hardy asked.

Hardy considered the question rhetorical, but wanted his conclusion corroborated by Shane. A printout of the two emails lay in the center of the table between their glasses of sherry. The relationship between the two men, the Moleskin notes, and the glasses of wine reflected their relative importance to the detectives: their wine was closer.

"Of course not," Shane answered. "Ignore is not a word that has any place in the vocabulary of criminal investigation, my friend. The careful investigator does not have the luxury of ignoring anything. All information must be carefully examined, thoughtfully considered, and placed in the context of all the other available information before concluding whether or not it is useful. Surely you know that, my man."

Shane not infrequently yielded to the temptation to preach to his friend about the investigative process. This was one of his most frequent but not one of his best sermons. Hardy tolerated it with some effort. The wine helped. Hardy sat quietly, relishing the taste and feeling of the sherry, and trying hard to ignore Shane's pontificating.

"Yes," Hardy said, not entirely sure what he was assenting to.

"So," Shane continued, "it is possible, although as your demeanor suggests, perhaps unlikely, that this Moleskin is real and has information relevant to your investigation. It is also possible, given the tenor of the missives, that either there is no such person as Moleskin or that such a person has nothing useful to divulge. It could be either. I suggest filing away the Moleskin notes with whatever other information you have, but not forgetting them. Time has a way of ferreting out relevance despite us."

"OK, done," Hardy replied. "Now, does the name Bruce Therault mean anything to you?"

"Why do you ask? And while we're at it, am I to interpret our meeting this lovely afternoon as an interrogation? I should hope that you would save such efforts for your inquiries of the criminal elements."

"Sure," Hardy answered, "but Bruce Therault?"

"I must repeat myself," Shane mumbled. "Why do you ask?"

"Of course," Hardy replied, ignoring his friend's obvious testiness; something was troubling him. "There was someone by that name at TAPS the other day. Marge waited on him and a couple of other strangers sitting with him. She thought they looked like they were up to no good."

"According to the Internet, Bruce Therault is a partner in the New York gallery with a more than passing interest in the art of Bechman Fitzwallington. There is also a suggestion that he may be a man of less than pristine character. Did Marge recognize his drinking friends, or hear any names?"

"She thought she may have seen one of them in the bar at some point but wasn't sure. No other names that she mentioned. Got the Therault guy's name because he paid for the drinks for the group with a credit card."

"Is there any chance that you showed her the likeness of the man I knew as Damian Saturn and to whom you refer as The Dude?"

"I'll do that," Hardy replied, annoyed that he hadn't already thought of it. "And I need to get in touch with this Therault guy."

"Capital idea, Hardy, my man," Shane replied. "Capital idea. And now that I think about it, maybe dig a little deeper into Moleskin."

Except for the fact that they all smeared paint onto stretched canvas, Parker Palmer had precious little kinship with the great artists of the Italian renaissance. For one thing, Palmer never painted any theme that was remotely religious. Some of his paintings did look a little other-worldly, but not in any religious sense. Palmer was very much a man of his current world, perhaps existentially so. He painted that world as he saw it, a unique perspective, granted, but no less real and present for that. It was the developing strength of his tether to reality that finally led to his rift with Billy Wayne Farmer and to Farmer (aka Fitzwallington)'s bitter and public denunciation of Palmer's art. Fitzwallington believed that he had tried to mentor the younger man, get him headed in the right direction, but that Palmer had betrayed him in the end, taking off on his own to produce copious works of mediocrity and shamelessly hustle them to people who knew nothing of art but sought the cache of owning something that was original.

An essential component of Parker Palmer's shtick was to make himself conspicuous, especially at any art-related public function. Thus, he made a late entrance at a lecture by a noted New York museum curator at Cheekwood. He made his way down a long row of occupied seats, bumping knees and apologizing, to alight, not entirely by accident, beside a particularly attractive young woman. He recognized her as a member of the tribe he thought of as the OMNIs, both because of their ubiquitous presence in the local art world, and because the acronym for Old Moneyed Nashville Ilk was an apt descriptor. These were people whom Palmer sought any opportunity to connect with; these were potential customers.

The lecture was titled "Titian and Tintoretto: Selling Genius." Parker Palmer was fond of Tintoretto, his work, and what little he knew of the historical person. But Palmer attended this lecture more for its social potential than for any burning interest in the two Italian Painters. As it turned out, the substance of the lecture was more relevant than Palmer anticipated.

The story of the Venetian Titian, uncompromising master painter of the grandest Christian myths and his ambitious student Tintoretto, who was not above some artful bending of principles if the price was right, set Palmer to thinking of his relationship with Billy Wayne Farmer. It was complicated, and he regretted some of it. But if you wanted to make a living from art in the time and space where Parker Palmer lived, there were things you just had to do. You wouldn't last long perched on your high horse unless blessed with more luck than anyone could reasonably expect. Billy Wayne was lucky. Parker Palmer had earned what he got. Every last farthing of it. If sometimes that involved doing stuff that he would rather have left undone, well, them's the breaks. You do what you have to do. Nobody's going to do it for you.

Yeah, he liked this Tintoretto guy. Old Tintoretto had it figured out.

"So," Athena Golden said, walking up behind Palmer as they threaded their way through the crowd exiting the hall, "how'd you like the lecture?"

"Which part?" Palmer responded.

Athena thought his response uncharacteristically terse. And, unlike his usual behavior, he wasn't glad-handing the people they passed, even some of whom she was sure that he knew.

They worked their way through the exit from the hall, but Palmer turned abruptly to his right, toward the gardens instead of heading toward the parking lot. Athena continued to walk with him, wondering where he was going, but genuinely curious about his reaction to the lecture and for other more selfish reasons. Once beyond the press of the crowd, Palmer lapsed into his normal gait, a slouching lope; the much shorter Athena had trouble keeping up. For a moment, she thought he might be trying to escape her. But that would be very unlike him. After all, she owned the gallery that was a principal outlet for his work. And if Parker Palmer had any inviolable principles, one must be that one never stopped *shaking it for the paying customers*. How many times had she heard him say that?

Since 1960, the palatial mansion and grounds, earlier home to several generations of Cheeks, had been the Cheekwood Estate and Gardens, a public facility supported primarily by private money. There was an art museum, lecture hall, and some truly extraordinary gardens. The whole thing was created originally by the inventors and aggressive marketers of Maxwell House Coffee, named for Nashville's most posh hotel at the time. The coffee was declared by President Franklin Roosevelt to be *good to the last drop*, and that phrase was adopted by the Cheeks as an enduring and wildly successful marketing slogan.

Some serious art aficionados, for obvious reasons, and a lot of the very rich people who valued art as a means rather than an end, with decidedly less aesthetic motives, bought expensive memberships to Cheekwood and visited the place often, sometimes hanging out for a while, seeing and being seen . But on this particular balmy evening, grandly illuminated by a full moon, the crowd attending the lecture made beelines for their cars after the Q&As petered out. So, Parker Palmer and Athena Golden were the only people strolling through the serpentine polished brown gravel garden paths. It may have been the gravity of the amber light of the full moon bathing this hauntingly beautiful and uncommonly serene place that set their moods. They were only steps from a place where a collection of pretentious people had patiently endured a canned lecture by a pretentious lecturer and then beat it for the wilds of Belle Meade or some equally pretentious area south of the city, but the gardens' ambience was a place apart from the evening's busy affair. Palmer and Golden walked together but separately, each in their singular world.

Athena's thoughts were of the world of Bechman Fitzwallington. Since the old man's death, her appreciation of the potential consequences of capturing the rights to his now exorbitantly valuable paintings had overcome her abiding distaste for his work. After all, she had sold some of his paintings in the past, so this wasn't exactly virgin territory for her. But she was increasingly concerned that the New York gallery had the upper hand, and her recent phone call from Blythe Fortune had certainly done nothing to allay her fears. In fact, an imaginative reading between the lines of Blythe's rather obtuse message could make one suspicious of the whole operation of the Galleria Salinas. Athena didn't care about that. She wasn't interested in getting bogged down in her competitor's business practices. Athena just wanted her gallery to be the place where any existing new Fitzwallington paintings would be sold. Hopefully an exclusive deal, but if that wasn't possible, then she was willing to share the riches with Blythe Fortune.

AvantArt needed a shot in the arm if it was to continue to live and do well. The last year or so had been nip and tuck for the gallery finance-wise. Her hats were beginning to attract some attention, but it would be a long time before they would pay the rent if they ever did. The same was probably true of the emerging group of Nashville artists whose works she attempted to sell. Some were beginning to get noticed, but the trajectory from there to enough fame to pay the bills was likely to be a very long and tortuous slog. Such was the nature of the art business.

Athena felt as though she was out of the loop. She wasn't sure who would decide about those paintings; she assumed the old man's daughter, but she was such a flake and seemed of late to be fading from the picture. Athena had a suspicion, with precious little evidence to support it, that Parker Palmer might know more than he was letting on about this situation. She had attached herself to him after the lecture and followed him into the gardens with the hope that she might extract some relevant information.

They had strolled in the lush evening moonlight for a while, neither of them speaking. Athena broke the silence.

"So, Parker," she said, "what's the situation with the Fitzwallington paintings? Any decisions about their disposal in the offing? I haven't heard anything, and I'm obviously anxious to know if my gallery is still in the running."

"Billy Wayne Farmer," Palmer groused and said nothing more for a while.

Palmer had been thinking about the old artist, thoughts triggered by the Titian-Tintoretto lecture. He had also been remembering his mother.

Palmer thought the prissy lecturer had a very simplistic interpretation of the two Venetian painters. He had depicted them as a good guy/bad guy dichotomy, the principled genius, and the blatant hustler. Maybe like him and Farmer. Although Billy Wayne might have been arrogant enough to compare his and Palmer's relationship with those superstars of the Italian Renaissance, Palmer suffered no illusions about the value and staying power of either his or Billy Wayne's art. But the lecture had stimulated him to think about the world of art, how it worked. Didn't it take all kinds?

And Palmer had also been thinking about his mother. Her startling revelations on her deathbed several years earlier had redefined Palmer's life and his art, even redefined who he perceived himself to be. Why had she waited until then? Until her terminal illness, she had been determinedly silent about herself. She never spoke of her past....family... relationships. Even in response to Palmer's questions. Silence. Until she was dying when she unburdened herself and burdened her son with long-concealed information that caused him to make a serious midcourse correction to the direction of his life. He hated her for that. The mother he had loved for all those years was not the woman he believed her to be. How could he love this stranger?

"The lecture," Parker finally spoke. "I liked the part about Tintoretto, but Titian sounded like a pompous fool. Not at all how the pompous fool who was doing the talking meant to paint him, I'm sure. And Billy Wayne's paintings? I don't know much that you don't, but there may be some twists to that story that will surprise just about everybody. Stay tuned, Athena. Stay tuned."

Shane and KiKi had retired early, but they both lay wide awake staring at the ceiling, just visible in the light drifting through from the Third Avenue street lamps outside their bedroom window.

"I probably shouldn't tell you this, Shane, my love, but the two outliers in our study that are definitely linked genetically are Bechman Fitzwallington and Parker Palmer. Looks like Palmer may be something like a nephew."

Although Shane's pulse rate probably doubled, his response to this surprising information sounded almost nonchalant.

"KiKi, my love, you never cease to amaze me. When did you uncover this little morsel?"

"Just a couple of days ago. Why?"

"You might have let your devoted husband know a trifle sooner, you know."

"I also might have never let my devoted husband know," she said.

"Perhaps if I had paid more heed to the ethics of the matter, that would have been the case."

"And perhaps a consequence of heeding the ethics of the matter too strictly could have abetted a serious crime."

"Solving crimes is your job, not mine," Katya said. "My job is doing everything I can to enhance the health and happiness of my fellow humans."

"Certainly. And a noble undertaking it truly is," Shane responded. "But some of our fellow humans make your job exceedingly difficult by taking it on themselves to thwart your efforts. I want to identify those perpetrators of harm and put them out of business."

"I thought what attracted you to the crime-solving business was the intellectual challenge, like your fictional hero."

"Well," Shane said, "there is that too."

He was no longer paying attention to the conversation. He was contemplating where this new information fit in the jigsaw puzzle that was assembling itself in his mind.

Even though he had gone to bed later than usual, James L. (Jimmy) Holden was having trouble going to sleep. Ordinarily he slept quite soundly for a lawyer. His conscience was generally as pristine as the driven snow. He didn't lie and he didn't cheat. He personified the *honest lawyer* oxymoron. He didn't seek the spotlight. Fame—or even public acclaim—was not one of his life goals. He honestly held the law in great regard and felt it an honor to have the opportunity to translate the sometimes daunting legal process for clients who needed his services. He usually chose his clients carefully.

Ever since he had taken on this dead artist's daughter as a client, he had regretted having done so. For one thing, the case was quite possibly destined to attract a lot of public attention—free advertisement but at a cost. He hadn't appreciated all of the possible implications. For another, the young woman was a truly strange person, and he wasn't sure how strange. But the case had looked so straightforward. The suit by the artist Parker Palmer was obviously frivolous and proving that required only the simple application of modern biomedical technology. Just get the DNA paternity data and case closed. He could collect his fee and bid farewell to the strange young woman as well as any possibility of having to deal with a too high profile case. It looked like a quick and easy job, a few quick bucks which he could certainly use.

That is, until the results of the DNA tests arrived.

The power of information to roil a situation should not have surprised Holden as much as it did. Truth was his friend. He was in love with facts. One of his core beliefs was that any conundrum could be solved, any case settled, if you could get your hands on the facts. Accurate information was the bedrock of the law when practiced with the integrity that it deserved. And he had been led to believe that DNA didn't lie, an apparent fact that he desperately wished not to believe on this troubled evening.

As he spent this sleepless night wrestling with a dilemma that he did not expect and was not at all sure how to handle, he began to wonder if his bosom friend, truth, had betrayed him.

Chapter 26

"'Fraid I don't know a helluva lot," SalomeMe half-mumbled, exhaling a puff of blue smoke from a slim lavender cigarette toward the ceiling.

Sensing her emotional fragility, Holden decided not to enforce his usually inviolable *no smoking* rule.

The call had awakened her from a semi-coma long before she was prepared to engage the conscious world. It had taken a while for the summons to her lawyer's office to register with her and even longer to get herself sufficiently organized to respond. Finally, she tumbled from her bed, assembled her quirky public persona, and called for a taxi to ferry her from Germantown to the Third Avenue office of James L. (Jimmy) Holden, Attorney at Law. She was in less than an optimal state for dealing with the news or responding to her lawyer's questions, and she was a full hour later than agreed to, but she was, at last, there.

Holden had asked her to recall everything she could remember about her early life. His revelation of the indisputable biological fact that the recently deceased artist known as Bechman Fitzwallington was not her biological father had elicited a wry smile, the lighting of a fresh slender pastel smoke, and not much else that was obvious. But it was early in the day for the strange young woman, so perhaps her higher integrative functions had not yet awakened sufficiently to react as they normally would. Judging from her tepid response to his request to recall her early life, maybe that was true of her entire central nervous system.

"What about your mother?" Holden asked.

"Never knew her. The old man said she died when I was born."

"Is it possible that he knew he was not your biological father but that he adopted you? That would still make you his heir."

"He never said anything like that. He raised me, if you can call it that, as a single father and never let on that he had any doubts about it. Not that he behaved like a father ought to, but that's the role he claimed. Single father of an only child. He liked that he could claim that, like he should be admired for it. But we both knew that there was nothing admirable about his approach to parenting. He was a bad man, counselor. A bad man."

A bland observation even repeated; no detectable emotion. She yawned and flicked lavender ashes on the carpet absently. Holden grimaced but didn't say anything.

"Look, Miss SalomeMe," Holden said.

"The title," she responded. "You can drop the title."

"OK," he said, "SalomeMe, there has to be some proof of your relationship to Bechman Fitzwallington to establish you as his heir and therefore for you to claim the paintings. This is serious. From what I understand, you could wind up either disgustingly rich or impoverished. We'll need to get your birth certificate and any other documents—adoption records, family bible—anything that supports your claim."

"Isn't that why you get the big bucks?"

She flicked her wrist, spilling more lavender ashes on to the carpet. She smiled. It was an incongruous smile. In another setting, it might have seemed seductive.

Holden was finding it difficult to conceal his anger. When he took her on as a client, he had no way to suspect where the facts would lead him. But here he was. He was up to his unmentionables in the quagmire where this strange young woman dwelled and, despite the unfairness of it all, he felt obligated to see it through as far as he could. He had tried the quick and easy route, going directly for bedrock truth, the DNA test, expecting a rapid and profitable resolution of the situation. And the truth had proven extremely inconvenient. He had assumed that an appropriate exit strategy and its timing would be made obvious by the facts and hadn't considered any other possibility. At least some of the truth was now known, and his planned route of egress was sealed shut. He still felt obligated to do what he could to benefit his client. Damn integrity!

"My dear young lady," Holden did not try to conceal his contempt for the situation and probably for his client as well, "when the dust settles, it is not at all clear that either of us will see bucks of any denomination. But I can assure you that if you make any money out of this debacle, I'll lay claim to what I consider to be my fair share of it."

"Knock yourself out, counselor," SalomeMe's parting shot as she got up and left her lawyer to seethe alone without another word.

The truth shall make you free. Those biblical words circled the official seal of the Christian college where Holden received his undergraduate degree. He believed those words; they had shaped much of his life. With all due credit to Rev. King, Holden believed that those words had bent the arc of his lifeline toward justice.

But nothing was true about this woman. If there was anything remotely authentic about her, it was hidden somewhere deep beneath the pierced and tattooed façade and its accompanying pseudo-personality. And now he discovered that even her claim to be the dead artist's daughter was a lie. He deeply regretted that he had not paid closer attention to the risk he was taking before getting involved with SalomeMe, or whatever her true name was. Nothing about her was as it seemed. So far, what verifiable truth he knew about this woman did not make him free. It did exactly the opposite.

Holden decided to make a sincere effort to locate any additional information that bore on his client's parentage before informing the court of the DNA results. That would have to happen sooner or later, but if he could buy a little time, maybe he could uncover some new information that would be relevant. Parker Palmer and his society lawyer friend did not seem to be too anxious to press their suit. Well, ok then. He would look for other truths, beyond the basics of human biology, those less quantitative and more tenuous" facts" upon which the resolution of a case often turned. Although disturbed by the unanticipated DNA results, disappointed at the implications of that snippet of unimpeachable information, he wasn't yet willing to relinquish his undying confidence in the power of truth.

Hardy Seltzer sat in his office, looking out his window at the activity in the courthouse square. He was thinking about the information that he had been able to glean from the Internet and from some mildly revealing interviews. He was trying to make sense of it, figure out how the pieces fit together, if they did. He was focused on his assigned job, to clarify the circumstances of Shane's abduction and finger the culprits. It looked like a work of rank amateurs in broad daylight that was obviously aborted before accomplishing whatever the goal was; it should be an easy problem to solve. However, from what he had discovered so far, that didn't appear to be the case. It was complicated. He suspected that down the road, there might well loom an intersection with Shane's efforts to prove a murder and identify the murderer. That was fine with Hardy.

But, for the time being, here's what he knew. Shane had been abducted in broad daylight at the corner of Church Street and Printers Alley, just whisked into a van and away. Amazingly, although it was a busy time of day, no reliable descriptions of his abductors could be elicited. Shane was subsequently released, deposited unceremoniously in Shelby Bottoms, after the public uproar from the *Tennessean* article that Hardy had planted, apparently aborting whatever the original plan of the abductors had been. Shane had been obviously drugged and remembered absolutely nothing from the moment he was taken from Church Street into the van until he was recovered in Shelby Bottoms. Shane had been phoned at Wall Street by someone whom he thought was the ceramics woman, Fiona Hayes, and asked to meet her immediately at his Printers Alley flat which was the reason he was at the spot where he was nabbed. Did the young ceramicist set up the whole thing? Why? Fingerprints of the Chicago hood, Dudley (the Dude) Sysco, were found on Shane's wheelchair and the Dude's explanation for that inconvenient fact was something considerably short of convincing. The Dude was in Nashville at the time, was a known lowlife for hire, and almost certainly had some connection with the crime.

Marge Bland had been a valuable resource. She recognized the picture of Sysco as one of the three men she had seen together at TAPS. She had also spent some time rummaging through old credit card receipts at the bar and had finally concluded that one of the other men was Mace Ricci, who had visited TAPS several times prior to the meeting of the troika. She remembered him—unusual name, didn't sound like a local. And he looked like a cop. Hard to explain that, but it's just one of those things. Cop is more than an occupation; it is a persona that is difficult to hide.

And then there was Bruce Therault. From the Internet, Hardy had learned that Therault was a mid-level real estate developer in New York and was a partner in the Galleria Salinas, the Upper East

Side gallery that was making a serious effort to connect with the Bechman Fitzwallington paintings. Hardy had found an old *NYT* article by an investigative reporter that implied a connection of the real estate developer with organized crime, but there was no follow-up to the story that he could locate. When Hardy mentioned Therault's name to Wilton Argent, Nashville's version of a drug lord and the city's best effort at a connection to big crime, Hardy had the distinct impression that the name was not unfamiliar to Argent but was unable to get anything approaching a specific response.

Hardy decided that his next step should be to talk in person with Fiona Hayes. If she was responsible for making that phone call to Shane at Wall Street, the event that triggered the whole episode, then she must at least have information about who was involved even if she hadn't done anything else. She must know something potentially important. He had also begun to wonder whether she had some connection to the weird Moleskin emails. It hadn't been difficult to trace them to a computer at the Nashville Public Library. One of the librarians vaguely remembered a young woman whom he had not seen before coming in a couple of times, using a computer for a few minutes and then leaving. The librarian could not remember anything more descriptive than that she was a young woman who was not a regular visitor to the library. Why Fiona Hayes would do that, Hardy had not a clue, but then this case from its beginning had been chock-full of unexplanations.

Seltzer also placed a call to the hotel where Mace Ricci had stayed. He was told that Mr. Ricci had checked out a couple of days earlier, paid the bill in cash, and left no trace of his having been there.

Hardy decided to drop by Wall Street in the afternoon, hoping to catch Shane. He would like for them to compare notes.

Shane was, again, staring at the image of a completely exposed and quite lifeless body of Bechman Fitzwallington on his computer screen and thinking. He was sure that the fully exposed body, the bedcovers folded neatly at the foot of the bed, was a statement of some kind almost certainly made by the murderer. What was there about the old artist that needed to be exposed? And how had the deed been done? The most obvious means of killing a frail old man in his bed would be suffocation with a pillow, and one of the pillows from the bed had fallen to the floor on the right side of the bed. Is that what happened here? Possibly, but not all the known facts supported that.

Shane would try to arrange separate meetings with Parker Palmer and Fiona Hayes at Wall Street, hopefully, this afternoon. In the meantime, he was constructing three hypothetical scenarios in his mind, each starring one of the three suspects. The key elements were, as always, motive, opportunity, and mental state. The principal facts he had to work with were: the Hayes woman's vehement hatred for Fitzwallington; the daughter's potential monetary gain coupled with her obvious contempt for her father; and the new information from KiKi's DNA data that the two outliers in her brain study, Palmer and Fitzwallington, were blood relatives. There was also the lawsuit by Palmer challenging the legitimacy of SalomeMe as a Fitzwallington heir and the old man's genetic anomaly that might have made him sterile.

A story was assembling itself in Shane's mind. He would see what he could elicit from meetings with Fiona Hayes and Parker Palmer, and then decide about a time and place for another visit with SalomeMe. He also needed to do some additional background research on the not-so-young woman with the odd pseudonym. Shane had thought in the past that when a case had too many loose ends to make any sense of, a solution could sometimes be found by tying all the loose ends to each other.

Shane reached both Fiona Hayes and Parker Palmer by phone on the first try, and both agreed to meet him at Wall Street later in the afternoon. Shane holed up with his computer and set about finding out anything he could about SalomeMe, nee Sally May Farmer.

The paucity of information on the Internet suggested that the target of his searches had apparently kept a pretty low profile over the years. Most of what was there was connected to her artist father. She had indeed been raised by Billy Wayne Farmer as a single parent after her mother died in childbirth. The two of them had migrated from Clarksville to Nashville when she was only two and had lived there ever since. There was some ill-defined association of Sally Farmer with Fiona Hayes beginning when they were quite young. More recently, Shane discovered from available court records that Bechman Fitzwallington as Billy Wayne Farmer had filed papers to adopt Sally May Farmer, now known by her chosen moniker, SalomeMe. That legal action had been filed only a week before Fitzwallington's demise, and no action had been taken on it.

Now that's interesting, Shane thought. The woman was not actually Fitzwallington's biological daughter, otherwise why the adoption thing? Was the suit filed by Parker Palmer not so frivolous after all? Where to tie up that loose end? Was it possible that Parker Palmer was, in fact, heir to the Fitzwallington paintings? Did Palmer know that? If so, now there's a motive if there ever was one. Oldest motive in the book. Follow the money. The afternoon interview with Palmer should be at least interesting and possibly a breakthrough. Shane was starting to feel the old excitement that always came in the home stretch of wrapping up a case.

"It wasn't me," Fiona Hayes said.

Hardy Seltzer had gone unannounced to her Gulch apartment. She had answered the door and reluctantly invited him in. They sat in her living room on white leather Courvoisier style chairs facing an expanse of glass that opened onto a panoramic mural of the Nashville skyline. Her response to his question about the call to Shane at Wall Street was matter of fact and declarative. Although she was somewhat fidgety, not excessively so. Maybe a normal reaction to an unexpected visit from a police detective. Hardy didn't read a lot into her apparent discomfort.

"Why would anyone who would make such a call to set up Shane Hadley's abduction, pretend to be you?" Hardy asked, genuinely puzzled.

"No idea," she responded. "Not sure why anyone would pretend to be me for any reason."

"The name Moleskin mean anything to you?" Hardy tacked suddenly to port.

"You mean like the notebooks? Sure, I know them, even use one to keep notes for my work sometimes. What of it?"

"I have a witness, employee at the public library, that may be able to identify you as the author of some thinly disguised emails to me related to the death of Bechman Fitzwallington," Hardy shamelessly exaggerated the information from the librarian. "The emails were signed, Moleskin."

"Your witness is mistaken, detective. I don't visit the library for any reason. I have a computer, and if I need a book, I buy it."

Seltzer was sure that the young woman was lying.

"Ms. Hayes," Seltzer looked directly into the woman's eyes and infused his voice with as much gravitas as he could muster, "I can't tell you how important it is for you to come clean with me. It would be wise of you to tell me anything you know that has any possibility of being connected to the abduction of Shane Hadley. My job is to assure that our streets are safe, and they won't be considered safe until we apprehend the culprits who snatched Shane Hadley in broad daylight in the middle of the city. Surely you can see how important this is. Don't you read the newspaper?"

"You're wasting your time with me, Detective. I am an artist. That is what consumes me. I have little use for the problems of our society except for the ones that respond to our aesthetic senses. And I rarely, for your information, read the local rag that calls itself a newspaper. Why would I?"

Seltzer's phone pinged, signaling a text message. Since he was making little progress with the haughty Ms. Hayes, he checked his phone. The text was from Goetz. *Where are you? See me in my office as soon as possible.*

Fiona Hayes, obviously impatient with the shift in Seltzer's attention to his cell phone, said, "Are we done here, Detective?"

Hardy responded, pocketing the phone, "Apparently. But it seems to me very likely that this will not be our last meeting. I must say, Ms. Hayes, that I strongly suspect that you have not been completely honest with me."

Hardy got up and left without waiting for the young woman to show him out. He retrieved the aging sedan from the no parking zone in front of the apartment block, removed the parking ticket from under the driver's side windshield wiper, stuffed it along with several others into the glove box, and headed for the station and what was certain to be another unpleasant encounter with his overwrought boss.

On his way back downtown, Seltzer's phone serenaded him with a full-throated version of The Battle Hymn of the Republic. The caller ID said Issy Esser. Who the hell was Issy Esser? Hardy's immediate inclination was to ignore it, but for some reason that escaped him, he answered the call.

"Seltzer."

"Detective, this is Issy Esser. You said to call you if I thought of anything that might shed light on Mr. Fitzwallington's death."

Hardy dredged up a vision of the skinny kid with the birthmark,

Fitzwallington's next-door neighbor. He was the one who had placed the original call about the artist's death. Seltzer had forgotten the young man's name.

"Yes, Mr. Esser," Seltzer replied. "What information do you have?"

"Well," the man spoke haltingly, "I've been thinking hard about the night before Mr. Fitzwallington's death. I had trouble sleeping and was sitting on my balcony that overlooks the artist's house. I heard voices. Loud voices, as though there was an argument. I'm sure one of the voices was Mr. Fitzwallington's. I thought the other one might have been the artist Parker Palmer, but I'm not sure of that. Is this any help to you?"

Hardy thought it just might be and replied, "Thank you so much, Mr. Esser. This could be some help, but we'll need to meet with you and get a formal statement. Is that OK?"

"Sure," the man replied, "just call me when it is convenient."

Shane needed to know about this. If the information was true, it would be more relevant to the old guy's death than to Shane's abduction. Hardy was forbidden from pursuing anything about the artist's mode of exit; he had ceded that territory to Shane. And it was clear that Shane had taken that bit in his teeth. As soon as Goetz was finished with his predictable rant, Hardy would escape and try to meet up with Shane. They needed to compare notes anyway.

Chapter 27

"Look, Blythe," Bruce Therault wasn't going to pull any punches in this conversation; the time for that was long past, "whether you like it or not doesn't really matter anymore. You are going to have to either get on board with this or get out. Your choice."

They sat together at the posh bar in a five-star midtown hotel. This conversation was post two Manhattans (Therault) and one point five martinis (Blythe Fortune). Therault had laid out the situation for her as he knew it. The investors in Galleria Salinas had a connection with some organized crime outfit, and their investment in the New York gallery was only the first in a much grander scheme, probably at least national and perhaps international in scope. The enormously influential *NYT* art critic, Arturo Carbone, was an integral part of it. With the benefit of the critic's vast knowledge of commerce in the art world as well as his ability to manipulate the value of art through his published critiques, the business plan was to identify struggling galleries that handled works by aging midlevel contemporary artists and inflate the value of their art. That might be especially effective if the artist was cooperative enough to die, an occurrence which would provide the occasion for the critic to review the entire body of their work. Therault suspected, but did not say, that the schemers they were dealing with were not above intervening in the course of human events to maximize the profitability of their enterprise. That may even have been a part of their business plan.

Of course, choices would need to be carefully made, and the ruse used infrequently enough to avoid arousing suspicion. This was venture capital. They expected only a few of their investments to pay off. But property number one, Galleria Salinas, with its connection to the Nashville artist, looked like it could be a real winner. Everybody stood to gain from this. Bruce guessed that some mechanism for laundering ill-gotten gain from other sources was buried in the scheme, but he didn't know for sure and didn't mention that to Blythe. No reason to complicate this for her any more than was necessary. He had avoided learning anything about the details of this wrinkle in the plan since he wished to retain the potential for plausible deniability should the necessity arise.

"Get out! What the hell do you mean get out?" Blythe exclaimed. "This is my gallery we're talking about. I birthed this baby and invested my life in it. You think I'm just going to walk away from it?"

"Blythe, my dear," Bruce said, "you will agree to one of those possibilities for two reasons. The first reason is spelled out in the fine print of our contract with the investors; they have an unconditional option to take control of the gallery whenever they choose. Perhaps you paid too little attention to the fine print earlier. The second reason is that these guys play a brand of hardball with which you are likely unfamiliar and ideally will remain so. The wrong choice on your part could be hazardous to your health. Do you understand? Look, Blythe, your choices are limited to two possibilities. In or out!"

Blythe stood up suddenly, knocking over her glass, spilling the remains of her martini in the process. "Godammit, Bruce," she seethed, "I never agreed to any of this. I poured my soul into that gallery. It has become my life. You are doing your best to fuck that up, and I won't stand for it."

Bruce looked calmly into Blythe's angry eyes and said with implacable resolve, "You will do as you are told, my dear."

Blythe picked up Bruce's glass still half full of his third Manhattan, threw it unceremoniously down his shirtfront, and stormed out of the bar.

Bruce studied his soaked shirt front for a moment…and smiled.

Hardy Seltzer did not actually recognize the beefy middle-aged man staring absently out the window in the chief's office, but he knew the type—ill-fitting black suit, comfortable shoes, bad haircut. No doubt FBI, but not from the local office. Hardy knew most of the local agents by sight. The chief sat at his desk, looking even more nervous than usual. He had invited Hardy and the assistant chief into the office immediately on their arrival.

Upon arrival at the office of the Assistant Chief, Seltzer was informed that he had been summoned along with Goetz to the office of the chief. The two men made their way to the unusual audience with their supreme commander, neither completely sure of the reason for the summons. The presence of an FBI guy was the beginning of an explanation.

"Mr. Marsh," the chief said, speaking to the visitor's back, "this is Detective Hardy Seltzer, who is our man working on the Shane Hadley abduction. Hardy, this is Farley Marsh from the Chicago FBI office."

The chief did not introduce Goetz. Perhaps they had already met.

Marsh turned and walked over to where Seltzer stood in front of the chief's desk. The two men shook hands without speaking. Hardy thought the agent's hand was too small, too wet, and his grip too weak for his size and chosen occupation. Hardy was ever suspicious of incongruities in people. He trusted consistency.

"It seems," the chief continued, "that our federal friends have uncovered some additional information that may bear on this case. Would you be so kind as to bring Detective Seltzer up to date, agent Marsh?"

"Well, Detective Seltzer," the agent began.

"Hardy."

"Pardon?"

"Hardy," Hardy repeated. "Please call me Hardy."

"Very well," Farley Marsh replied. "I was about to say that what originally looked to us like a local problem for you guys, may well turn out to be a much bigger deal. We, the bureau, wouldn't ordinarily get very worked up about a botched kidnapping of a local celebrity in a town like this, especially if nobody got hurt. That's just not the kind of thing we spend a lot of time on. We're totally happy for guys like you to handle such things. Most times, guys like you appreciate that. Simplifies the situation."

"I understand, Agent Marsh."

"Farley."

"Pardon?"

"Farley," Farley repeated. "Call me Farley."

Hardy wasn't pleased with the obvious sarcasm but continued.

"Very well," he said. "Very well."

A chill was settling into the room. The four men felt it.

"You are no doubt working yourself up to a *but*," Hardy continued. "Are you not? Otherwise you wouldn't be here."

Ignoring Hardy's comment, Marsh said, "However, from what we have learned so far, this may turn out to be a case of major proportions with your local abduction problem only a minor fringe activity."

"So?" Seltzer queried, unable to control his building resentment of the federal intrusion despite a blatantly disapproving glares from both the chief and the assistant chief.

"Look, Hardy," Marsh went on, "I'm prepared to be sensitive to the territorial prerogatives here, but this is beginning to look like a national, maybe even international, ring of organized crime figures centered in New York bent on subverting the art market somehow to their own ends. We have some very promising leads to pursue. You have to admit that this sort of thing is FBI territory."

"Why," Hardy responded, "would the brain trust of organized crime be interested in this? I mean, there is money to be made, but nothing on the scale those guys usually care about. This isn't going to pay off like drug smuggling and international prostitution. Surely those guys would consider this small-time mischief."

"Yes," Marsh replied, "but they need to control some legitimate business to clean up their dirty money. Maybe that's what they are thinking. Not sure yet. What have you found out about your guy's abduction?"

"Nothing very concrete to date," Seltzer replied. "But I'm pretty sure that your informant, Dudley Sysco, was more involved than he admitted to you. And this New York guy, Bruce Therault. His name keeps surfacing, although as best I could determine, he was in New York on the day of the abduction. There is a third person that we suspect was involved somehow and also seems to have some connection with the New York gallery."

"Ah, the eely wiles of The Dude," Marsh sighed. "We might put the screws to him a bit more aggressively if you think that would help. He needs to earn his keep."

"I'd appreciate that," Hardy said.

"Well," the chief interjected, "I suggest that Detective Seltzer continue his investigation focused narrowly on the abduction of Shane Hadley and that the FBI takes charge of whatever are the larger implications. How does that sit with the two of you?"

"Exactly what I was about to propose," Marsh said.

"Suits me," Seltzer added. "We should stay in contact, share whatever each of us learns that might be relevant to the other."

"Sure," Farley Marsh added unenthusiastically.

"You happy with this, Carl?" the chief spoke to Goetz almost as an aside.

"If you say so," Goetz replied.

Shane sat at his customized spot at the Wall Street bar nursing his glass of sherry and thinking. Fiona Hayes had not shown up, and it was well past the time she had agreed to be there. Parker Palmer was due in half an hour and Shane wondered whether he would also be a no show. He signaled to Pat Harmony to freshen his glass of wine. Shane's cell phone chirped. He retrieved the device from his shirt pocket and answered.

"Hadley."

"Shane," Hardy Seltzer answered, "I had a phone call that might interest you."

"I am prepared to be interested, Hardy," Shane responded.

"Remember the skinny kid who discovered Fitzwallington's body and called 911?"

"Issy Esser," Shane said

"That's him," Hardy continued. "He now remembers hearing what sounded like an argument between the artist and someone who sounded to him like Parker Palmer during the night before the artist was discovered dead. He couldn't tell what the argument was about, and it didn't last long. But he sounded quite sure of what he heard."

"Why does he remember it now?"

"Says he was just mining his memory for anything that might be important."

"Maybe," Shane said. "Maybe. Thanks for letting me know. And incidentally, can you get me a complete copy of the Fitzwallington autopsy report?"

"Maybe," Hardy replied and ended the call.

Shane took his notebook from his pocket and sat quietly reviewing what he had written there about the Fitzwallington case—some facts, some thoughts. His problem was narrowing the short list of possible murderers to one. He felt that he was close, but something still didn't feel quite right. Could he be reading the tea leaves all wrong? Was he overlooking something that didn't fit the story evolving in his mind? But there were always questions if you were honest with yourself. Sometimes you never had all the answers. It was the big answer that mattered.

Those were the things Shane was thinking as the door to the bar burst suddenly open to admit the gangly persona of Parker Palmer. The artist loped across the room to where Shane sat, hoisted himself onto the adjacent bar stool, and spun around to face Shane, turning his back to the bar.

"So, what's cooking, my man?" Palmer said, clapping Shane on the shoulder. "What can I do you for?"

"Well, Parker," Shane started, "there is some new information that may concern the death of Bechman Fitzwallington, and…"

"Billy Wayne Farmer," Palmer interrupted. "The man's name was Billy Wayne Farmer."

"Be that as it may," Shane resumed. "Would you be so kind as to enlighten me about two particular facts?"

"Glad to help. Shoot."

"Although I will not reveal my source, I have come by indisputable information that you, Parker Palmer, are a blood relative of the deceased artist. Is that true?"

"Oh boy," Palmer responded. "I guess I should have expected to have to deal with this sooner or later."

"Given the circumstances, it would seem to me unavoidable," Shane said.

"There is a short and a long answer to your question, detective," Palmer sighed. "The short answer is yes."

"And the long one?"

Palmer looked directly into Shane's eyes and paused for a long moment, "Well, Mr. Sherlock Shane," he said, "I'm not sure you should be privy to the long answer unless you can give me a good reason why I should be answering your questions at all. You are an *ex*-cop, is that not true? I appreciate your history, like everybody else. But…"

Ignoring the artist's reluctance, Shane forged ahead, "And I understand that you had a rather heated exchange with Mr. Fitzwallington…"

"Mr. Farmer," Palmer interrupted.

"…the night before he was discovered quite dead. What was that about? You may have been the last person to see him alive. As I am assembling the known facts in this case, that would seem to me a circumstance deserving of some serious explanation. Would you not agree?"

"Why are you doing this?" Palmer asked, some uncharacteristic steeliness in the tone of the query.

"Mr. Palmer," Shane assumed some formality intended to lend gravitas to the conversation, "while I am no longer an active member of Nashville's finest, I do work with them sometimes, and I suppose take some liberties in my efforts to assist on occasion. Also, I am by nature a curious citizen, Mr. Palmer."

"Well, *Mr.* Hadley," Palmer replied, sliding off the barstool to stand beside Shane and drawing his lanky frame up to full height. "I suggest that you direct your curiosity elsewhere. You might also do well to consider the fate of generations of curious cats."

With those words of advice, the artist Parker Palmer turned heel and loped out the door of Wall Street, leaving Shane Hadley's urgent questions unanswered.

Bloody hell, Shane thought.

Shane had not believed that Parker Palmer was the murderer whom he sought. Palmer just didn't seem to be that sort of person. However, Shane well knew that desperate people were perfectly capable of uncharacteristic behaviors. And this exchange with the artist surely indicated that he was hiding something. Reviewing the situation in his mind, Shane thought that, until more information came to light, Parker Palmer should probably be elevated to position number one on the short list of suspects.

"Hi, Shane," Hardy Seltzer said.

He had entered the bar unnoticed and slid onto the stool still warm from the brief presence of Parker Palmer. Shane was thinking and nursing his glass of sherry, oblivious to whatever else was happening in Wall Street until Hardy's unexpected arrival.

"Oh, greetings Hardy," Shane replied. "What brings you here this fine evening? Pat," Shane called over the bar to Pat Harmony, who was talking to a uniformed cop across the way, "a glass of sherry for my friend."

"Sure thing," Harmony answered, then. "Afternoon, Hardy."

Harmony retrieved the bottle of Lincoln College Sherry from its special spot in a cabinet beneath the bar and poured Hardy a generous glass.

"Thanks, Pat," Hardy said. Then he turned toward Shane and continued. "Some things are developing. Time we compared notes, don't you think?"

"Indeed, my friend," Shane replied. "Time indeed."

Chapter 28

Mace Ricci did not leave Nashville after the abduction of Shane Hadley. Panicked by the thinly veiled threats from Mildred Roth, spokesperson for the New York gallery investment group, Bruce Therault insisted that Ricci stay put as a source of continuing information about the status of the Fitzwallington paintings. Ricci was to find out everything he could and feed the information to Therault. This was serious. They had screwed up and were obligated to assure the proper outcome of the situation or else. Therault assured Ricci that he did not want to know the consequences of disappointing these investors. Ricci didn't need to be told that. He knew all too well how these kinds of people dealt with disappointment. He had no desire to experience their version of *or else* firsthand.

Ricci reflected on that course of events as he headed for the Germantown home of SalomeMe; he would visit her unannounced. He had gone to ground. He had checked out of his downtown hotel doing his best to leave no tracks, contacted Wilton Argent to arrange use of a car that couldn't be traced to him, returned his rental to the downtown Hertz office, and waited at the curb for Argent's minion to deliver the anonymous dark green Kia sedan. He then drove to the south edge of town, checked himself into a Days Inn using an assumed name, and paid cash for a couple of nights in advance. He now drove the surprisingly comfortable sedan back into town and over to the north side, easing into a spot at the curb in front of SalomeMe's Germantown bungalow. She was the key to control of the paintings, and so Ricci needed to keep the relationship he had cultivated with her alive. His welfare probably depended on it.

The house was quiet. Although the chimes of the doorbell were clearly audible, echoing in the eerie stillness, no one came to the door, and Ricci could not detect any other sounds from inside. He rang the bell several times with the same result. He knocked as loudly as he could on the door. Still no response. He tried the door. The knob turned easily. He pushed the door open and entered the empty living room. He listened intently for sounds from elsewhere in the house. Dead silence.

"SalomeMe," he called out, thinking how silly it sounded to actually say the weird name aloud. "Are you home?"

Nothing.

Through the door to the adjacent room, Ricci saw an upholstered chair facing a window that looked out onto the house's rear garden. The tall back of the chair was toward the room, and he thought he could see just a sprig of purplish hair sticking out above the chair back looking for all the world as though it was growing there. He called her name again. When there was no response, he entered the room. The chair facing the rear window was the only furniture.

"SalomeMe," Ricci spoke the name softly this time.

The chair swiveled slowly around to face him. She was in full costume. Black streaks of running makeup creased her face, but the tears had dried. The pinpoint pupils of her dark eyes were fixed in a vacant stare at a location somewhere in the space before her. Except for turning to face him, she gave no immediate indication that she was aware of her visitor. Ricci figured that she was high on something. God only knew what.

"The bastard never told me," she said to the vacant room.

"What are you talking about?" Ricci asked.

"The bastard never told me," she repeated. "He said that I was his daughter and that he loved me."

The importance of what she seemed to be saying started to dawn on her visitor.

"What are you telling me?" Ricci said. "Do you mean you aren't Bechman Fitzwallington's daughter?"

"I'm told," she stood up and turned to face the window, "that is what is written in the DNA. And I'm told that DNA tells only the God's truth."

"Who says?"

"Mr. James L. (Jimmy) Holden, Esquire, tells me that, and lawyer Jimmy claims to be permanently wedded to the truth."

"Why did he get your DNA analyzed?"

She turned to face Ricci, now looking more directly at him. Tears were again painting vertical strokes of black mascara down her face, dripping from her chin, dotting the exposed swell of her breasts, then coalescing to trickle along the spine of the serpent that plunged southward between them.

"Lawsuit," she replied. "That rat Parker Palmer's lawsuit. The DNA was supposed to settle the thing."

"What in hell does Parker Palmer have to do with any of this?"

"Beats me," she said. "Beats the living hell out of me."

She sat back down in the chair and swiveled around to look out the rear window. She had nothing more to say.

Mace Ricci tried to think through the implications of this new information as he drove from Germantown as directly as he could, given the traffic and his less than perfect recollection of the route, to TAPS. He needed a drink and some more time to decide exactly what he was going to tell Bruce Therault. He obviously couldn't conceal this development, but he wanted to have a more concrete idea of what he thought they should do about it before placing the call.

Although he wanted to stay well under any potentially interested radar, Ricci figured that TAPS was a safe enough place to get a drink. He had only been there a couple of times and didn't see any reason why anyone there would recognize him or give a damn even if they did. By the time he parked the Kia and wandered in to occupy a seat at the nearly vacant bar, it was past five o'clock. He took a seat at the bar and ordered a Scotch neat from the barmaid. She thought he looked vaguely familiar but didn't mention it. He checked for cash in his money clip and realized that he would have to pay for his drink with his credit card. Shouldn't be a problem.

Parker Palmer strode out the door of Wall Street, down the alley, turned right at Church Street for a block or so and then hung left, down the hill to a tall building with a local bank that had recently sold out to some conglomerate with a catchy name invented by expensive consultants as the anchor ground-floor tenant. Nashville businesses must be supporting an entire industry of expensive consultants whose only function was to invent catchy company names, Palmer thought. Those names were rapidly appearing in garish signs that fronted places of business the names of which had been familiar to him his whole life. It was happening all over town, a veritable epidemic that threatened the essential character of the city that he loved. His city was in the process of betraying him.

The echo of his footfalls from the glistening marble floors in the lobby saddened him. The words of a song came to mind…Kristofferson "…Sunday morning coming down…" Sad alright. Nobody did sadness better than old Kris.

Palmer walked directly to the south bank of elevators, entered the shiny gilt car, and pressed 19. The offices of Donnely, Hart and

Combs, Attorneys, occupied the entire nineteenth floor. The attractive young woman at the desk that fronted the elevator recognized Palmer and nodded to him as he mimed a salute and walked past her down the hall to the corner office of J. Hayworth Combs, attorney, art patron, longtime friend, and, when the occasion required it, legal eagle counsel to Parker Palmer. Consistent with his general contempt for arbitrary social structures, Palmer ignored the secretary—strategically positioned in front of the lawyer's office door and charged with protecting her boss from unwanted interruptions—and entered the office without knocking. Combs was reared back with his feet up on his desk talking on the phone, but he smiled and nodded to Palmer to have a seat.

Jay Combs and Parker Palmer were both Nashvillians, but they were children of different planets—Belle Meade blue blood old money with A-list parents vis-à-vis an only child of a single parent constantly struggling just to put food on the table, toughing it out in the meaner part of south Nashville. Despite that, they became fast friends in high school. Combs's socially conscious parents, convinced that their privileged son would benefit from exposure to a more diverse group of peers than he would have at the private academy where he had endured an extremely rigorous if highly contrived elementary education, sent him to a public high school. It was a wise decision. Their precocious son thrived academically and developed a delightful group of friends whom he would have never known otherwise. Parker Palmer was one of them.

Their relationship had not only endured but had grown over the years. Combs had developed a passion for contemporary art and, whether because of his affection for Palmer the man or because he had a nose for potential aesthetic value, was especially fond of his old friend's art. Combs probably owned the world's largest collection of Parker Palmer paintings, to the amusement of his Belle Meade A-list friends, the walls of whose homes were adorned with more traditional and more socially acceptable works. Combs bought his old friend's paintings because he liked them rather than as investments, but it was nonetheless satisfying to watch their value steadily increase. His Palmers turned out to be much better investments than the chiaroscuro landscapes favored by the Belle Meade crowd. Old friends could prove valuable on occasion. A fringe benefit.

"Look, Jay," Parker said as soon as his friend hung up the phone and maneuvered his feet to the floor, "I need to tell you some stuff and get your advice. There's a lot of stuff I haven't told you or anyone else that may be more important than I thought it would be."

"OK, pal," Jay said, leaning forward toward Parker and resting his hands on his knees, "shoot."

"Like, this is lawyer to client, right? Privileged information."

"Does that mean I can bill you?"

"You're funny, Jay."

"Humor is a valuable trait in my business."

"Anyway, privileged, right?"

"Fine with me. What is it that has you in such a state, man. I mean Mr. Cool seems a bit het up. Has the muse deserted you?"

"Could be a helluva lot worse than that," Palmer replied. "A helluva lot worse."

"Sounds like you may need a good lawyer. Fortunately, we've got that covered. But spill it, buddy."

"OK," Palmer took a deep breath and told his old friend and lawyer the whole story as he knew it. He had kept most of the story as his own private history that he intended never to be known to anyone else. Very much like his mother had done until she was dying. Only then did she reveal things about their lives that might have changed the course of things if he had known them earlier. Her death bed revelations altered his understanding of the world and his place

---

in it. And kindled in him an intense hatred of his dying mother that was the source of an abiding sense of guilt since her death.

So, Parker spilled most of the beans to his lawyer friend that afternoon. The lawsuit that Palmer had convinced his friend to file questioning whether Sally Farmer was the rightful heir to Billy Wayne's paintings was not frivolous at all. According to Palmer's mother's deathbed revelation, the woman was not Farmer's daughter. Billy Wayne had taken her in as a small child and raised her as though she was his offspring, but that was not the case. Palmer's mother knew this because she was Billy Wayne's younger sister. They were hopelessly estranged for many years. She began to suspect that her brother was sexually abusing his assumed daughter, and possibly others, and swore never to have any contact with him after that. Why she didn't pursue criminal prosecution went unexplained. Still was.

"So Bechman Fitzwallington, nee Billy Wayne Farmer, was your uncle. And the woman who calls herself SalomeMe is not related to the old guy." Combs mused, rubbing his chin and looking out the window. "Maybe that explains the urgent note I got earlier from the presumed daughter's lawyer. I haven't returned the call, but now I'm guessing that he got the DNA results," Combs laughed. "Bet that got Jimmy Holden's Christian blood heated up a bit. And he probably doesn't even know that you're the heir instead of her."

"Probably not," Palmer replied. "But the ex-cop, Sherlock Shane Hadley, who seems to have an unholy interest in this case knows. Says he has incontrovertible evidence of my relationship to Uncle Billy Wayne."

"Does he know about the non-daughter?"

"If not, I'm sure he soon will. He has a real bee in his bonnet about this thing, turning over a lot of stones that would best be left unturned. Seems determined to prove Uncle Billy Wayne was murdered and appears to suspect that I may have done the deed."

"Why would he suspect that?"

"This is privileged, right?" Palmer's anxiety was obviously increasing.

"Come on, Parker," Combs replied. "You know you can trust me."

"Ok." Palmer got up from his chair and stood in silhouette before the expansive window that formed one side of Combs's office. "The evening before Uncle Billy Wayne was discovered dead by his neighbor, I went to see him. I didn't go for any particular reason. It was just that his health was obviously rapidly deteriorating, so I dropped by a little more frequently than usual. I had never told him that I knew of our relationship. In fact, I never told him any of the things my mother had revealed as she died."

"Really?" Combs interrupted. "But wasn't it about the time your mother died that he started to trash your art?"

"I guess you're right, but that must have been coincidence. He and I never discussed it. Once he abandoned me professionally, we never discussed art at all. Of course, he was getting pretty sick by then."

"Why did you keep visiting him? Was it because you knew you were likely to inherit his

paintings?"

"I can't really give you a reason. It wasn't the paintings. I didn't know there were any, and even had I known, I would not have thought them worth much until after he died, and the New York critic saw fit to inflate their value."

"The whims of the art world," Combs sighed. "But go ahead. You visited your uncle in the dead of night, and he turns up really dead the next morning. Did you kill him?"

"I don't think so, but that could be indirectly true, I suppose."

"Go on," the tone of Combs voice was beginning to take on a lawyerly edge.

"We argued," Palmer said. "He revealed to me that Sally was not his daughter but that he had initiated efforts to legally adopt her. Of course, that would make her his sole heir and cut me out of the picture. It wasn't like a life or death matter. I had no illusions about a great windfall for whoever was Uncle Billy Wayne's heir, but I was just pissed off that whatever there was would go to that totally ditzy woman and that any claim I might have would be neutralized. It just didn't seem right. So, we argued, and I left in a huff. But I left him very much alive if more than a little red in the face and breathing a little hard."

"Were you there alone?" Combs asked.

"I thought so, but our friend Shane Hadley says there was a witness to our argument. Probably that nosy neighbor. I guess we were a bit loud."

"And you were the last person to see your uncle alive as far as you know?"

"As far as I know."

"Did he leave a will?"

"I don't think so. He did say one time recently that he intended to do that but had not gotten around to it."

"Well," Jay Combs said, getting up from his chair, walking over to stand beside his friend and draping an arm across his shoulders, "it looks like this could become more interesting than either of us would like, but you've got the two essentials on your side—a good lawyer and the truth. You are telling me the truth, aren't you?"

"As far as I know it," Palmer replied.

"Hello, handsome," Marge worked her way down to the end of the TAPS bar where Hardy Seltzer sat and greeted him in her usual way, trying to infuse her voice with a maximum of seductive undertones. "What is up?"

Hardy had come in later than usual. Marge's shift would end soon. She wondered if he had timed his visit deliberately to be close to when she finished for the day so that he could whisk her away for a late dinner and whatever else seemed interesting to pursue that evening.

"Not much," Hardy replied. "Still trying to find a crack in the Hadley abduction case. Not much luck recently."

"How much is a little luck worth to you?" Marge's eyes brightened.

"Have you got something?

"Maybe. You know the third member of the suspicious group who were here before Shane was grabbed."

"Of course, I remember—a guy named Bruce Therault from New York, a lowlife hood from Chicago name of Dudley Sysco, and an ex-New York cop named Mace Ricci?"

"Well," Marge replied, "if I am not mistaken, the Mace Ricci guy was in here again today. He looked vaguely familiar, so I checked out the name on his credit card, and that's who it was."

"Funny. I've been trying to locate him but haven't succeeded." Hardy was genuinely surprised. He figured that if Ricci was involved in this, he would be long gone from the city by now.

"He came in this afternoon for a drink. Sat at the bar by himself. After drinking two Scotches neat, he made a brief call on his cell that didn't appear to be answered, paid with his credit card, and left. I wasn't totally sure that he was the third guy, so I double-checked the name on the card."

"You are amazing, Marge Bland. You are a truly amazing woman," Hardy responded, contemplating where to take her for dinner and whether to get his hopes up for how they might occupy the rest of the evening.

"It's just names, Hardy," she answered, "I remember names."

Chapter 29

Bruce Therault hung up the phone. He was frightened. Really frightened.

It was mid-afternoon, and light spilled into his living room through the east-facing window that overlooked the park. He was inordinately fond of his Upper West Side flat. He thought that is suited him perfectly—unpretentiously elegant. He walked over to the small and well-stocked bar opposite where he had been sitting and poured a generous amount of twenty-five-year-old Macallan into a cut crystal tumbler. His hand shook, rattling the decanter, the ring of crystal against crystal. He relished for a moment the heft of the leaded glass. Swirling the deep amber liquid, he walked to the window and looked out, across Central Park West to the variegated canopy of lush green.

Things were not shaping up very positively in Nashville. Mace Ricci had phoned him to break the startling news that the identity of the old artist's heir or heirs had been cast into serious doubt and to let him know that the pesky ex-cop was still prying pretty aggressively into the circumstances of the artist's death. No doubt that was delaying resolution of the situation. And now the uncertainty of the heir. A damn mess is what it was.

What to do? Therault sipped at the whiskey, distracting his

thoughts for a moment with the pleasantly acrid aroma and taste of smoke and peat. He took another larger sip with the hope of prolonging the distraction. It didn't work very well the second time. He would have to wait for the active ingredient of the drink to kick in for the solace he sought.

His thoughts drifted toward the implications of the situation for him personally. He had made some of the longer-range life plans that are essential for people like him whose greed or ambition or whatever got them mixed up with the sort of folks who were not reluctant to do one harm if the occasion called for it. He might need to use those plans sooner than he had intended.

First, what not to do. He would not, for the moment at least, give any hint of this potentially serious complication to Mildred Roth. This was no time to invite the Wrath of Roth, not until he had figured out a concrete plan of action that had a chance of assuring the outcome that the investors expected. He walked back to the sofa where he had sat earlier, took his cell phone from his pocket, and rang Blythe Fortune.

"Galleria Salinas," the soft, confident voice of the gallery's proprietor answered. "This is Blythe."

"Good afternoon, Blythe," Therault responded. "This is Bruce with some quite interesting news."

"Of the good variety, I hope."

"I wouldn't characterize it exactly that way. More like challenging."

"I'm tired of challenges."

"Well, you best rest up because I have a new one for you."

Bruce went on to inform his partner of the developments that were critical to any resolution of the future of the Fitzwallington paintings and to issue his challenge. Therault thought their best chance to get their hands on any of those paintings was to cut a deal with the only other gallery that was in contention, AvantArt in Nashville, and that Blythe was the only person likely to be able to strike such a deal. Mace Ricci had thoroughly blown any chance of establishing a relationship with the gallery's owner, Athena Golden, and Blythe had at least had some seemingly pleasant contact with the Nashville woman. If they could agree among themselves on a proposal to share the sale of the paintings, hopefully with the lion's share winding up in New York, that was probably the best they were likely to do, and the deal might be saleable to whoever wound up with custody of the art.

Blythe listened patiently to Bruce's monologue. It was obvious that he was trying to dump the responsibility for attempting to solve this thing on her. She wondered about his motives. Was it really that he thought she was the one with the better chance of working things out? Or was he looking to make her the scapegoat if things really went south? She was having second thoughts about her earlier decision to stay involved. She had hoped that she could do that while keeping a respectable distance from the shady doings that Bruce was clearly abetting. Well, abetting or enabling in some more direct way. She wasn't sure which. How in God's name had she been convinced to hook up with Bruce Therault? She had no idea who he really was and what drove him. Money, or the lack of it, had made her handle what she valued most too recklessly. Look where that got her.

When Therault finished his little speech, Blythe allowed a more than respectable period of quiet to occupy the space between them before finally saying simply, "I'll call Athena."

Blythe was not prepared to commit beyond that.

Having dealt for the time being with problem number one, Therault proceeded to problem number two. He called Mace Ricci and instructed him to implement a new plan to sidetrack that pesky ex-cop. Therault wasn't sure if it would work, but worth a try anyway. It required no appreciation of nuance. It was just the kind of thing that Mace Ricci knew how to do.

Shane had spent the evening poring over the Fitzwallington autopsy report, staring again at the pictures that Hardy had taken of the death scene, reviewing the few brief phrases he had jotted down in his little leather notebook, and googling Issy Esser. There was a wrinkle in the autopsy report that he needed to follow up on with Hardy, but he wasn't sure if it was significant.

He had learned that Isadore William (Issy) Esser was a pharmacist and worked in the research pharmacy (whatever that was) at the university. But so what? None of his evening efforts had produced any major advances in his consideration of the case. He had called Esser and they had agreed to meet the next day at Wall Street, but otherwise, it felt like he had wasted a lot of time. He checked the clock on the lower part of his computer screen and was surprised at how late it was. He had been so involved in wasting time that he had lost track of it.

It was way past the hour when KiKi should have been home. And she hadn't called. He took his cell from his shirt pocket and speed-dialed her number. Five unanswered rings and then her familiar voice mail greeting. He left a message for her to call him, but he was worried. Once in a while she had been this late, stuck longer than she had anticipated by a needy student or a troubled faculty member. But very rare. And she always called to alert him. He called her number again with the same result. He wheeled himself over to the bar, poured a glass of sherry and rolled out onto the deck. Nighttime action in the alley was just getting into gear, the cacophony of sounds that Shane thought of as the Printers Alley serenade beginning its slow crescendo that by midnight would approach a decibel level exceeding the pain threshold for most normal humans. Shane and

KiKi were always in bed by then, at the other end of their flat, out of earshot of the alley.

Shane's phone buzzed and he answered it without checking the caller ID.

"This is Shane," he said, anxiously anticipating a response from his wife.

"Hi, Shane," Hardy Seltzer said. "How's it going?"

Katya Karpov was not easily frightened. She had seen violence in her youth. Rather than saddling her with an abiding fear that harm might come to her when she least expected it, those early experiences inured her to any fear of violence. She recognized that such things happened but did not expect them to happen to her. They never had. Even as a child, she seemed to be exempt from harm for the most part. She still felt that was true, although she had not made any serious effort to probe too deeply for the reasons.

But when Katya left her office a bit later than usual, made her way to her assigned space in the high rise parking garage, and discovered that all four of the tires on her white Boxter were flat, she was frightened. The garage was essentially empty at that hour. The unsigned note trapped under the windscreen wiper blade—*tell your too curious husband to back off, Dr. Karpov*—unleashed a surge of adrenalin that shook her to the core. She had checked her cell phone on the way to the parking lot, intending to call Shane to let him know that she was running a bit late, but discovered that it was dead. She had neglected to recharge it. She often did that. Recharging her cell phone wasn't high on her list of essential tasks, although at this moment, stuck alone with a disabled car in a dark, deserted garage, she thought that perhaps she should rearrange some of her priorities.

As Katya leaned against the side of the car, pondering what to do, she became aware of a rhythmic tromp of footfalls against the concrete floor, echoing about the big hollow space. The sounds moved closer with each clop of heavy boot on hard cement. She looked around but couldn't see anyone. It was dark. There were lights in the garage, but it seemed to Katya that they mainly served to create deep pockets of pitch-black shadows cast by the supporting pillars. She thought she sensed some movement in a large swath of black just across the way but she couldn't make out any detail.

"Dr. Karpov," a voice called her name from the shadows.

Her heart raced, pounding against her chest. She was paralyzed. She couldn't speak.

"Looks like you've got a problem, Dr. Karpov," a uniformed security guard whom she recognized emerged from the shadows and came over to where she stood. He walked around the car, checking each of the tires, "Looks like somebody doesn't want you driving this chariot," the guard said. "The tires have been slashed. Any idea who'd do such a thing?"

Slowly recollecting her wits, the relief she felt clearly evident in the tone of her voice, Katya said, "I have no idea. But my phone is dead and my husband will be worried. Can you help me out?"

"Of course. Of course," he replied. "Let me call for a cruiser to get you home for the evening, and then you can deal with the car tomorrow. I'll also let your husband's friend Hardy Seltzer know about your problem. I'm sure the detective would want to be informed, especially since it looks like something fishy may be at play here. The detective tends to get interested in fishy looking situations."

"Not going so well this evening, Hardy," Shane responded to his friend's greeting. "I seem to have lost touch with KiKi for a bit and I'm concerned."

"Yes," Hardy said, "That's why I'm calling. She is on her way home, escorted by one of Nashville's finest. She is not in any danger as far as I know. But there is more to the story."

"Thank God for that. What in the world has happened?"

"Katya can fill you in. She should be there shortly. There's certainly something very odd going on that bears looking into. We should talk tomorrow."

"Let's do that, Hardy. Many thanks for calling and whatever else you did to help."

"Not a problem, Shane, my friend. Not a problem."

Shane wheeled over to the bar, refilled his glass of sherry, took a large swallow of his favorite liquid, and exhaled a sigh of relief that came from somewhere deep in his soul. Thank God, or whoever, he thought. He would die without KiKi.

By the time Katya arrived at home, greeted by an especially enthusiastic hug from her husband, she was no longer afraid. What she felt was exhaustion. She was not prepared to handle the barrage of questions from Shane. She understood his need to ask them, but the answers would have to wait until another time, after she had managed to regain some of the energy she had spent on dealing with the intensity of what was to her a strange emotion—fear. That really unpleasant feeling had washed over her, a tsunami of sensations that consumed her for what seemed in retrospect like only a moment and then drifted away into an unknown distance leaving her bereft of that vibrant core of energy that she had always been able to depend on to sustain her. She felt vulnerable in a way that was distinctly unfamiliar. She was exhausted and didn't want to talk about it. With apologies to Shane, she went to bed and promptly fell into a deep and silent sleep.

It was the note that most affected Shane. Katya had not shown the note to the guard and had considered not sharing it with her husband. She didn't want to disturb him too much about this incident. But she showed him the note anyway, and he now sat in their living room staring at it. What was welling up in him was anger. At whoever was behind this obvious threat to his wife. And at himself. He had never considered the possibility that his interest in this case could put KiKi in danger. Why would it? He hated the thought of being intimidated by the note, but he would do anything he could to protect KiKi.

Maybe he should back off the Fitzwallington matter. Maybe the bad guys would win this one in spite of him. Of course, KiKi would oppose that. She was basically fearless and admired that in Shane too. He wouldn't score any points with her by retreating from this investigation even if he thought the motive for doing so a noble one. She would probably think him either cowardly or inept. He didn't want to appear to be either of those to his wife…or to himself. He stared at the note, handwritten in large block letters on a piece of lined yellow paper, no doubt torn from a note pad. He read it over and over, hoping for some insight into the identity of its author. Didn't happen.

It was late, but Shane fished his cell phone from his pocket and speed-dialed Hardy Seltzer's home number. Five rings switching to Hardy's voice mail.

"Hardy, this is Shane. The slashers left a note, a warning meant for me. I am really angry about this, Hardy. Really angry. We have to find out who did this and what his connections are. Call me as soon as you get this. I will not stand for KiKi to be put at risk because of what I'm doing."

Hardy's phone lay on his bedside table, and the ring tone woke him up. Well, sort of woke him up. Not enough to make him answer the call but enough to cause him to check his voice mail after a few minutes. He listened to the entire message and sighed.

"Who was it?" Marge Bland said.

"Shane," Hardy answered. "I'll call him in the morning."

There was no way that Shane would be able to sleep. After noticing his wife's cell phone that she had left on the living room coffee table, and plugging it in for recharging, he managed to wheel back to the bedroom and maneuver himself out of his clothes and into the light blue silk pajamas that KiKi had bought for him a while back. He sat for a few minutes next to the bed and looked at his comatose wife. She lay perfectly still, breathing quietly. How could she be so at peace after what had happened to her this evening?

He turned toward the windows and sat there thinking. Why in God's name had he gotten so involved in this Fitzwallington case? He wasn't a cop anymore. The death of the old artist wasn't of any great significance anyway. It was basically selfishness that had drawn him into it and still drove him. Criminal investigation was what he knew how to do and what he loved. Truth be told, he resented having been made to take disability retirement after he was shot. He recognized that the department had meant that as an honor—he shouldn't have to continue working after such a devastating injury suffered in the line of duty. Full pay for the rest of his life. Full medical and rehab expenses. And no expectations. What a deal!

But for Shane, it was a raw deal, no matter how well-intended. They had taken from him what he most valued, the substance of what allowed him to feel good about himself, feel of use to the world. No surprise that he had responded enthusiastically when his old colleague Hardy Seltzer had reached out to him about the Bonz Bagley case. And no surprise that once again having tasted the pleasure that he had always found in the practice of his chosen profession, that he was drawn to this Fitzwallington thing.

Basically selfishness, he thought. While he did indeed value the experience of doing what he was good at and what he enjoyed, he valued KiKi and their relationship a lot more. Was he going to put the love of his life, the source of the only real happiness that he had ever known, at risk to satisfy his need for self-indulgence? No way was that going to happen. Whatever the hell happened to Bechman Fitzwallington and whoever the hell was involved could just be dealt with by the people who got paid to do that sort of thing. It wasn't his problem, and it was foolhardy of him to take it on in the first place.

Of course he knew that KiKi would object. He imagined how the conversation would go:

S: I'm withdrawing from the Fitzwallington case, KiKi. It's not that important, and I will not put you at risk because of it.

K: You are mistaken, my love. You are not withdrawing from that case until you have it solved. In case you hadn't noticed, Shane, I'm a big girl. I can take care of myself. I need you alright, no doubt about that, but not to take care of me. To love me.

S: You know that I love you, KiKi, more than life. But I'm not a cop anymore. I'm basically just playing around the edges of a system that is designed, trained, and equipped to solve crimes. It's selfish of me anyway, and I cannot bear to forge on with activities that could bring harm to you. Don't you see that?

K: Don't do it, Shane. You are the best detective that this city has ever seen and you have never been afraid to go where the truth leads you. Don't start now. And don't make me feel guilty for preventing you from doing what keeps you alive and enthused about your existence.

S: I'll think about it. We'll need to talk some more. Of course, I don't want to make you feel guilt, but I don't want to feel that either.

K: Well, you think about it. But it's too late anyway. Apparently, whoever you're dealing with already thinks they have something to gain by threatening me. They're wrong, you know. I am not easily threatened, my love."

The conversation would go something like that, and Shane would end up continuing on the case. Their relationship was too strong and their mutual respect too deep to let the bad guys win if they could possibly help it. Shane Hadley and Katya Karpov were good people and each in their own way was committed to that kind of a life. Otherwise, what was the point?

Chapter 30

That was, in fact, about how the conversation went the next morning. KiKi made it clear that Shane was not his wife's caretaker. Fortunate for him since Katya Karpov did not need a caretaker and would not look very favorably on anyone attempting to play that role. Probably including her husband. If Shane was going to back off on anything, it would be wise of him to steer clear of the space KiKi needed to take care of herself. What was the advice she had quoted so many times over the years? He could never remember the source. Something about *spaces in their togetherness*. Give Katya room to be her. Was that too much to ask?

So after a brief conversation along the lines that he had anticipated, Shane accepted the reality of his need to pursue the Fitzwallington thing and the reality of his relationship with KiKi. He resolved to do the best he could to carry on as before, although the fear that he might be putting KiKi in danger was still there...and some of the guilt. He would need time to completely reconcile his competing realities.

Shane sipped at his coffee while KiKi called 1-800-PORSCHE to arrange for her car to be retrieved and taken to the dealer to get the tires replaced. She then called the dealer to inform them of the situation and signaled Uber on her cell phone for a ride to work. She kissed Shane goodbye, a substantial if less than passionate expression of her affection, summoned the elevator, and left for the hospital.

The hum of the descending elevator and the dull thump of the lobby door punctuating KiKi's exit into The Alley had barely faded away when Shane's cell phone chirped. It was Hardy Seltzer. Early for Hardy, but then Shane had left him an urgent request for the call late the previous evening.

"I presume," Shane answered the call without preamble, "that you were occupied with important matters last evening and thus the inordinate delay in responding to my near frantic call."

"It was late, Shane," Hardy said. "I had solid information that Katya was fine and didn't see what I could do last night."

"How about something like, console a troubled friend?"

"I somehow have difficulty picturing you as someone in desperate need of consolation," Hardy responded, more than a little testily.

"Perhaps," Shane answered, his tone matching his friend's irritation, "your powers of perception are in need of some attention, my friend. But," not wishing to continue discussing the nature of his relationship with Hardy at the moment, Shane pivoted to more substantive matters, "have you any idea who threatened my wife and thoughts about how the matter is to be pursued?"

"I'm guessing that Mace Ricci, you know the ex-New York cop who was hanging around the Fitzwallington business until recently, might have had something to do with it."

"Why him?"

"A tidbit of information and a hunch."

"Ah, Hardy," Shane said, feigning surprise, "I've not known you to rely on hunches. I seem to recall you disparaging the value of such in the past. But, never mind, what is the tidbit?"

"I talked with the Chicago FBI agent yesterday. Although he was pretty cagey about his source, he says that their investigation is making progress. He especially mentioned that Mace Ricci might have been involved in your abduction. Ricci had dropped off my radar. He disappeared after your little incident—checked out of his hotel, returned his rental car—just seemed to disappear. I assumed that he had left town until Marge told me that she had recently served him Scotch at TAPS. So, he's still here, in town, I mean. Apparently, his job from the beginning was to nail down acquisition of the Fitzwallington paintings for the New York gallery as quickly as possible. Obviously, he and whoever he works for, the Therault guy and God knows who else, see you as an obstacle to be neutralized so the process can move along. It's a short trip from that assumption to the conclusion that threatening your lovely wife might be another effort to get you off the case. So, we need to locate the New York cop and lean on him. The FBI would probably be happy to do the lion's share of the leaning."

"Pull out all the stops, Hardy," Shane's voice quaked with uncharacteristic intensity. "APB, whatever it takes. Find this Ricci guy and milk him!"

"I'm on it, Shane," Hardy said. "Believe me, I'm on it."

Athena Golden thought it probably coincidence that she received the two related phone calls less than an hour apart. Neither call was anticipated. She was at her desk, poring over her gallery's disappointing financial records. There had been little traffic in the place that afternoon, and she had seriously considered locking up and drowning her sorrows in some good red wine that she remembered having on hand in her condo. Athena was not a serious drinker, but she did enjoy a good red on occasion and that afternoon seemed like it might well serve as such an occasion. She was seriously approaching that decision when the first call came.

The caller was Parker Palmer. It was not the caller that surprised her. She still had a few of his paintings on display, and he would check in occasionally although he well knew that she would inform him of any action that concerned him. What surprised her was the content of the conversation. After briefly inquiring about the status of his paintings, he launched into a rather opaque monologue having to do with the fate of the Fitzwallington works.

Although Palmer did not explain how he came by the information, he informed her that he was probably going to be in control of Billy Wayne Farmer's paintings rather than the spacy daughter. In fact, Palmer speculated that Sally Farmer may not be the old man's heir after all. He did not explain why, but claimed that he, Palmer, was likely to be the next in line. The good news for Athena was that Palmer told her that if he did indeed turn out to control the fate of Billy Wayne's works, he would see that they were assigned exclusively to the AvantArt gallery for their sale. Further, Palmer said that should this be how things turned out, he intended to establish a foundation that would be the repository of all profit from sales of the paintings and would serve to support local artists of all stripes. And, Palmer continued, he would wish Athena Golden to chair the foundation's board. Now, what did she think about that?

Well, what she really thought about that was that Parker must be smoking something really potent or otherwise pharmacologically enhanced in order to come up with such a far-fetched scenario. She had never known him to have a drug problem, and he was no doubt an exceptionally creative man, but this was just not a possible sequence of events that she could imagine having any basis in reality. She probed gently in an effort to find out the actual facts of the situation, what realities, if there were any, had triggered the usually pretty sane Parker Palmer's flight into fantasyland. Although her queries didn't produce anything that was verifiably factual, Palmer continued to sound absolutely sure of his fairy tale. Very well, Athena thought. No sense in queering the deal if there was any possibility that there was some truth in it.

Athena was still pondering the call from Palmer when the second call came—Blythe Fortune from New York. Preoccupied with reflections on the Palmer call, Athena didn't answer the call for a few rings. When she finally glanced at the caller ID and saw the call was from Blythe Fortune, Athena picked up the phone.

"Hi, Blythe," Athena said. "I haven't heard from you in a while. What's on your mind?"

"Oh," Blythe answered, "I was about to leave a voice mail."

"Right. Sorry I was slow in answering. My mind was elsewhere, I'm afraid."

"You can probably guess that I'm calling about the status of the Fitrzwallington paintings."

"Sure. Offhand, I can't think of another reason for your call."

"Yes." It sounded as though Blythe cleared her throat, maybe steeling herself for engaging in a conversion that she did not anticipate would be very pleasant. "Yes. I understand that there have been some developments in that situation that may influence the fate of the paintings, and I thought that we should discuss some possibilities."

Athena wondered what Blythe Fortune knew and where her information came from. Athena also wondered if this had anything to do with Parker Palmer's creative story. She would wait to see where Blythe was going with this before responding.

"Please go on," Athena said.

"Well, I presume that like everyone else, you have been proceeding on the assumption that the Fitzwallington daughter was his sole heir and so would control what happened to his paintings and collect whatever cash their sale earned."

There was a long pause. Athena was determined to wait Blythe out, but her resolve failed her after an inordinately long silence and she said, "That's true."

That had been true until the call from Parker Palmer. Athena was beginning to wonder whether truth in this situation was proving unreliable. It was starting to seem prone to change without notice.

"I have it from a reliable source that such is not the case," Blythe said.

"I don't understand. How can that be?"

"My source says that the woman is not the artist's daughter after all, and so is not his heir."

"So, who is?"

"That, I gather, remains to be seen."

"And your source?"

"Can't tell you that. But he's a reliable source."

Another long silence. This time Athena was determined to leave the next move to Blythe if it took all night. It didn't.

"Since our two galleries seem to be the leading players in the Fitzwallington game, we ought to be able, between us, to capture the rights to sell his remaining work. I am told that there is quite a cache of paintings to be sold. The commission for selling them could amount to a sizeable sum, I would guess."

"Yes, go on."

Athena was running out of patience with the New York woman.

"What I mean is this. If you and I can agree on a fair split of whatever paintings there are to sell between our galleries, we should be able to convince whoever controls their fate to deal with our two galleries as exclusive agents."

"And what do you consider a fair split?" Athena was starting to smell a rat.

"Since my gallery has been the major agent for the sale of Fitzwallingtons for some years now, we surely should get the majority of the works. I can't imagine any other arrangement that would seem fair to any objective observer."

Athena suddenly shuddered with a paroxysm of intense anger. This New York woman with her fancy Upper East Side gallery thought she could just steamroll over the Nashville rube. Well, to hell with that. And, what if Parker Palmer's story held water? What then? Miss Blythe Fortune and her pretentious Galleria Salinas might turn out to be just shit out of luck!

Athena held the phone for a few moments without speaking. She thought she heard sounds of deep breathing emanating from the big city. She hung up the phone with no further comment. Almost immediately, the phone rang. Athena did not answer it. When it switched to voice mail Blythe Fortune spoke. After a short time, Athena checked the message.

"So sorry, Athena. We must have gotten cut off. Can you call me back? We really need to discuss this."

I have nothing more to discuss with that woman, Athena thought. She closed the books on her desk, took her coat from the rack by the door, turned off the open sign in the window, drove home, put on her classic recording of *The Elixir of Love* (the one with Joan Sutherland and a young Pavarotti), poured a generous glass of her favorite Italian red, and sat in her living room staring out the large window at nothing, really…thinking.

Shane knew that Pat Harmony was always at his Wall Street bar long before the official five o'clock opening time. Since Shane wanted as much privacy as possible when he interviewed Issy Esser, the arrangement was made for the two of them to meet at the bar at four-thirty. Shane arrived a little after four and settled in at his regular spot—his Wall Street office. Pat produced the bottle of Lincoln College sherry from its special place in the bar cabinet and set a glass in front of Shane. They greeted each other just barely. Pat was busy getting set up for the nightly onslaught of current and former representatives of *Nashville's finest* and Shane was lost in his thoughts.

Issy Esser stood for a few moments just inside the door, his eyes darting about the largely empty room, as though he was expecting to see something threatening in his peripheral vision. He was essentially as Shane remembered him from the earlier interview. The port-wine birthmark that meandered about most of his face was difficult to ignore. And he was thin, very thin with a grayish tint to his skin that didn't look normal. Shane wondered whether the young man was ill. Shane motioned to Issy and he walked over to the bar and sat down beside Shane.

"Good afternoon, Mr. Esser," Shane said. "Would you like a drink?"

"No sir, thank you."

Both men seemed content to forego any introductions. They each knew who the other was, and they both knew the reasons for their meeting. Contrary to Issy's tentative appearance and his reluctant entry into Wall Street, once seated beside Shane at the bar, the young man seemed confident, self-assured, even. If he was nervous at all, it wasn't obvious.

"I'm sure, Mr. Hadley," Issy broke the brief silence, "that you wish me to relate what I know about the happenings of the evening before I discovered Mr. Fitzwallington dead."

"Yes, that's true. But before we go there, what exactly was your relationship with the artist? I am told that you were a frequent visitor. He seems to have had several frequent visitors, and I'm having trouble understanding why."

"Well, I suppose I may as well come clean about this. We were lovers. Or perhaps more precisely, we had sex together. He was surprisingly virile for a sick old man. I hoped that he would assist my aspirations for a career in art, although he didn't really do that."

"So why continue the relationship?"

"His paintings. I knew that he had been rather prolific in the past year or two, and it seemed likely that he would leave a number of his works when he died. And it did seem as though his death was imminent. He implied that he would leave some of his works to me, although there was no formal agreement. I encouraged him to make a will and he said he would, but I don't think he ever did."

"Hmm," Shane sipped his glass of sherry and digested this information for a few moments and then continued, "I understand from what I could glean from the Internet that you are a pharmacist?"

"That is correct. I work in the research pharmacy at the university."

"What does a research pharmacist do?"

"We prepare agents for clinical investigations. If a drug is going to be studied in people, it has to be done 'double-blind.' That is, neither the patient nor the involved medical professionals can know whether the subject receives the active drug or a placebo until the study is finished. So, we research pharmacists are responsible for managing pills of placebo or active drug that are indistinguishable, either supplied by the drug manufacturer or formulated by us and keeping meticulous records of which subject got what. We play a critical role in all clinical studies of drug safety and effectiveness."

"I'm sure you do," Shane said. "Did you ever have occasion to supply drugs to Mr. Fitzwallington?"

"He wasn't involved in any of the studies that I had anything to do with if that's what you mean. However, he did take a drug for his hypertension, and as a favor, I would get those prescriptions filled for him."

"Was he a compliant patient, drug-wise?" Shane called on the terminology that he had heard KiKi use.

"Oh, very," Issy replied. "Took his blood pressure medication with compulsive regularity."

"So, tell me about the night before you discovered the artist dead and called 911."

"Ok. I had been with Bechman that evening. We had sex, and I was preparing to leave when there was a knock at the door. I headed for the back door to avoid being discovered as Bechman went to answer the front door. When I heard the voice of Parker Palmer, I decided to stay inconspicuously in the back hall, where I could overhear most of their conversation. They were shouting at each other."

"What were they shouting about?"

"Well, I couldn't make out everything, but the gist of their argument seemed to be that Parker had discovered that SalomeMe was not Bechman's daughter and that Bechman had started the process of legally adopting her."

"And why was that such a big deal to Palmer?"

"They both seemed to know that Palmer was somehow in line for inheriting Bechman's paintings although neither said exactly why they thought that. If Bechman legally adopted SalomeMe, she would be his sole heir. This is what I gathered from their shouting match."

"How did you react to that information?"

"I never liked Parker Palmer. I suspected that he and Bechman had been lovers at one time, although I'm not sure of that. And I guess I was more than a little angry at Bechman for not including me in any of his deliberations. Yes, I was angry at Bechman."

"Did you confront him after Palmer left?"

"No. I left out the back door and went home. I didn't sleep well and so got up pretty early the next morning and went to Bechman's house hoping to set things right between us. He was dead."

"But he was alive when you left his house the previous evening?"

"Yes. Or at least I think so. I heard them arguing, and I heard the front door slam as Palmer left. Bechman yelled something just before the door slammed."

"So," Shane said, "you were the last person to see Fitzwallington alive?"

"I suppose. Although technically that would have been Parker Palmer."

"Yes."

Shane was not at all sure that he bought the details of Issy Esser's story. It could well be a cleverly constructed alibi. Well, not that clever; there was no way to corroborate his story. Shane rarely accepted one person's version of the truth if there was no way to verify it.

Chapter 31

E ven though he had taken an early morning flight and had slept little, when Vernon LaVista III felt the tremor of the jet's wheels banging down hard on the BNA tarmac, he was as high as a kite. He was all but certain that he had nailed down a commission for a major public sculpture for the city of Baltimore. It had taken him three days of meetings, pitching the proposal with all of the charm and credibility that he could muster, but he was sure that he had succeeded. He was excited about the project. He really liked the sculpture that he envisioned, and a major public space art piece in an interesting city would be some pretty big-league national visibility.

He burst into the Gulch apartment brimming with enthusiasm and anxious to share his good news with Fiona only to discover that his significant other was in no condition to share his excitement. She lay fully clothed in their bed. There were a couple of empty pill bottles on the bedside table. And she was dead. Vernon called 911 and cursed to himself. Damn Fiona Hayes, he thought. What a goddam selfish thing to do to him.

Hardy Seltzer arrived at the luxe Gulch flat as quickly as he could get there after being informed of the situation by the police dispatcher. He was still in bed when the call came. He dressed quickly and skipped his habitual morning coffee. As a result, when he arrived on the scene, his mental faculties were performing sub-optimally, not quite ready to quickly assimilate the implications of the situation.

The note was written in meticulous script. He read it twice before talking to Vernon LaVista III, the person who had discovered the dead woman and who was, apparently, her companion.

To Whom It May Concern, the note began, then continued, *I killed Bechman Fitzwallington. I went to his house in the middle of the night and smothered him with a pillow as he slept. I uncovered him, leaving his body completely exposed. I meant that to be symbolic. He was a bad man. From the time his daughter and I were not quite teenagers, he started to sexually abuse us and continued to do that until we were old enough, and he was unwell enough that we could end it. That evil had to be exposed, as I exposed his hideous body in death. The world had to know of this evil. His artistic ability must not be allowed to forgive his sins. He was an evil man. Killing him was a just act. It had to be done and even now, I must confess that I feel fortunate to have been the one to do it.*

I was also the person who placed the call to Shane Hadley that resulted in his abduction. I did that as a favor to Wilton Argent, who, you will not be surprised to discover, was my coke connection. I had become rather fond of snow in recent years and, in this city, Wilton is a necessary evil in such matters. And I was Moleskin, a feeble attempt to keep the investigation from heading in my direction. Pretty clumsy in retrospect.

So, there you are! The world is rid of a bad man, and this ought to clear up anything mysterious about it. The only remaining question I can think of is, what took so long? I can't answer that. When whoever you are reads this note, that will not be my problem.

I'm taking the easy way out. I weaved too tangled a web. Given the possibilities, enough sleeping pills to end this sordid tale seems the better choice.

Good-bye, cruel world (I know, trite, but why the hell do I care).

The note was signed Fiona Hayes, written in big curlicued letters with a pretentious flourish followed by a large black exclamation point.

Cold, Hardy thought. There was little passion here, just a straightforward recounting of the facts. Only a truly cold person can take the final plunge without feeling. Maybe the stuff of a killer. He could believe that. He took out his cell phone and photographed the note before handing it to an officer to be preserved as evidence should that be needed.

Vernon LaVista III was sitting with another officer in the living room, staring out of the expanse of glass overlooking downtown. Hardy took a seat in a leather chair immediately opposite the quiet and surprisingly calm sculptor.

"I'll need to ask you some questions, Mr. LaVista," Seltzer said, trying without success to engage the young man's eyes.

"Sure," LaVista answered.

"When did you last see Ms. Hayes?"

"Couple of days ago."

"Where were you during that time?"

"Baltimore."

"Why Baltimore?"

"I was pitching a proposal for a sculpture to the city fathers. I finished last night and took an early flight to Nashville this morning. When I arrived home, I discovered Fiona as your people found her and called 911 immediately."

"How did you react to that?"

"Pissed, mostly. I was pissed. I had just landed a major commission, and Fiona had to ruin the occasion by her grand gesture. She was fond of grand gestures."

"Hardly a gesture, I would say. Had she attempted suicide in the past?"

LaVista got up, walked to the window, and sighed deeply. "Not that I know of," he said. "She would threaten to kill herself every time we had a spat, but the threats weren't very convincing. I didn't think she had the balls for it."

"Had she been depressed?"

"How the hell could you tell? She was either tripping out on her compulsive exercise program, snorting coke, obsessing over those damn tile paintings, or banging my brains out. What else went on in her head is anybody's guess."

"I must say, Mr. LaVista," Seltzer said, "that you do not appear particularly upset about the death of your companion. I find that odd."

"Odd?" the sculptor repeated. "Odd? Oh yes, Fiona was an odd one, alright. And so was our relationship. I didn't really know her, where she was actually coming from. But, you know, officer, I'm an artist. The only essential relationship in my life is with my art. I don't care much for people, certainly not in any intimate way. Fiona didn't need that. That's what I found attractive about her. At least she didn't need that from me. And she was one helluva lay."

"Did Ms. Hayes have any close friends?"

"That ditzy woman who claims to be Fitzwallington's daughter. They had been friends when they were young, but they weren't very close lately, I don't think. That's why Fiona wanted to keep visiting the old guy. Can't think of any other reason."

"Have you read the note she left?"

"I didn't see it until your people arrived. They discovered it. I don't really care what the note says. I'm done with Fiona Hayes."

"I suppose that's possible," Seltzer responded. "However, it is quite likely that we will need additional information from you before this is over with. Here is my card," Hardy slipped a card from his shirt pocket and handed it to the young man. "I, or someone from my office, will be contacting you, but in the meantime, if you remember anything that you think we should know, please call me."

An ominous chill crept up Hardy Seltzer's spine as he sat for a few minutes in the LTD without starting the engine. He was trying to digest the ice-cold lump of human indifference that he had just been fed. He didn't know much about art, but it seemed to him that sensitivity to the human condition should be version one of the artistic temperament. If either Fiona Hayes or Vernon LaVista III possessed an iota of that quality, he had not seen it in a situation that, by all rights, should have laid it bare. Neither of them, dead or alive, gave a tinker's damn about the human condition except as it affected them personally. Hardy had been dealing with dead people and the ones who killed them for a long time, but he couldn't remember encountering the likes of these two. Enough to try your confidence in the integrity of the species. He needed some coffee. And a hot shower might help.

He pulled out his cell phone and forwarded the photograph of the suicide note to Shane along with a message, "An interesting development, you will agree. I guess you were right about the murder, and here's your culprit, confession, and justice done by her own hand. Hope you aren't disappointed. Let's talk later in the day."

"Maybe he mixed up the labels or something," Shane said.

He and Katya were just finishing their morning brioche and coffee, and she was recounting an odd occurrence at the medical center. Someone in the pharmacy had been caught pilfering pills. Not so rare an occurrence given the value of drugs on the street. But these were sugar pills…placebo. Why would anyone risk his job by stealing placebo pills? Didn't make sense.

"I guess," KiKi responded. "But still seems strange to me."

"Since when does strange behavior by human beings baffle you, my love?"

Shane's cell phone signaled an incoming email. He looked at the screen and saw that it was from Hardy. Yet another early morning communication from his usually late-rising friend. How interesting.

"I need to look at this," Shane said, punching the appropriate buttons on his phone.

"No problem," KiKi said. "I should be leaving anyway. Ta-ta." She kissed him on the forehead, retrieved her briefcase from beside the bar, and headed for the elevator.

Shane read the note five times, pausing to reflect on its meaning between readings. He then retrieved his laptop, called up the pictures Hardy had taken of the death scene, opened his tooled leather backpack, and took out the copy of the final autopsy report that Hardy had obtained for him.

The pictures were essentially as Fiona Hayes described them in her suicide note. When he first looked at them, Shane had thought that there was something symbolic about the exposure of the old man. The note seemed to confirm that. The killer wanted the symbolic exposure to trigger revelation of a deep secret sin successfully concealed for years by the old man. Fiona knew his secret sin firsthand. Shane could imagine that a strong enough motive for murder. He had seen many people kill for lesser sins.

The autopsy report was another matter. He read it through again several times—advanced cardiovascular disease, large heart, fatty liver—all attributed to age and dissipation. Elevated tissue lead levels but not enough to be lethal. "Death from natural causes," the coroner had concluded. But the findings in the brain troubled Shane. A small area of infarct in the right cerebral hemisphere was revealed when the pickled brain had been methodically sliced up. It was interpreted as consistent with a stroke, but the pathologist had been unwilling to declare that the cause of the old man's death. Even with that finding, "death from natural causes" was still the conclusion.

Shane was convinced that the old artist had been murdered, but he did not believe that Fiona Hayes was the person who had done it, regardless of her motive and intent. The brief story in the suicide note didn't ring true. He was convinced that the autopsy findings conclusively disproved the Hayes woman's story. But why would she feel guilt powerful enough to cause her to take her own life if she didn't do it? Was she covering for someone else whose life she valued more than her own? She didn't seem to be the kind of person who would do that.

Shane was not a pathologist. He needed expert corroboration. He was also thinking that there might be another source of evidence. He decided to place two phone calls. With great reluctance, recalling their interactions in the past, Shane first called Harry Jensen, MD, the Nashville-Metropolitan area coroner for more years than anyone who had to interact with him cared to remember. There was no official reason why Doc Jensen should feel obligated to provide Shane with any information, but the aging and lonely pathologist would frequently respond to a bit of attention and indulgence of his faux Irish persona by revealing more than was strictly appropriate. Shane had used that approach with success in the past, but it had been a long time.

"Top o' the mornin' to ya," Jensen answered the call on the first ring. "To what do I owe the honor of such an early morning call from the venerable Sherlock Shane Hadley?"

Although Shane liked the fact that caller ID identified incoming callers, he didn't like that it took away the element of surprise in his calls to other people. It didn't really matter in this case, but there had been occasions when Shane thought that he had been robbed of potentially important information by the device. Of course, he could block caller ID, but he feared if he did that too many of his calls would go unanswered. He thought that the effects of technology were a mixed bag.

"Good morning, Harry," Shane responded, adopting as amiable a tone as he could muster. "How have you been?"

"Jolly good, lad," Jensen answered. "As jolly good as a lad who lives among the dead can rightly expect to be. And you? Are you missing your old mates and the thrill-a-minute business of detecting?"

"Actually, I've been rather unofficially aiding Hardy Seltzer's detecting on occasion. The department is still grossly undermanned. And I have the time. As to thrill-a-minute, I'm not so sure about that. The detective business is much less exciting than it looks on TV."

"Ah, yes, I'm sure of that. But I suppose everything is relative. You fellas' investigations are certainly livelier than mine."

"True," Shane responded, "but no more important, my friend. The reason I called…"

Jensen interrupted, "No doubt you seek information about our local celebrity, the former artist known as Bechman Fitzwallington."

"You are a perceptive man, Dr. Jensen."

"I do read the papers on occasion, Shane. Information is a much greater asset than perception. At least I find that to be true in my business."

"Difficult to argue with that, my man. Imagination is a poor and often inaccurate substitute for the truth of a matter."

"So, what information do you wish, laddie?"

"About the Fitzwallington postmortem, Doc." Shane wasn't quite sure how much to reveal about the information he was already party to. He certainly didn't want to get his friend Hardy Seltzer in any trouble for betraying police confidence. "I understand from the autopsy report that you concluded that the old guy died of what you experts sometimes call 'natural causes.' Is that right?"

"Entropy, my lad. The old guy's body was a wreck. End of the line."

"But there was an infarct in his brain that could have meant a stroke. Couldn't that have been the terminal event?"

"That's possible," Jensen adopted a more professional tone. "But without some observation of the manner of his death, it is difficult to make that conclusion. The correlates of vascular events observable after death with the manner of dying are not always obvious without knowledge of exactly how the person died. That was true with this case. I suppose the small brain infarct might have resulted in a stroke. But a stroke is a clinical diagnosis, not a postmortem finding, unless there is extensive hemorrhage or more evidence of tissue damage than we have in this case. And, like I said, his whole body was a train wreck."

"Interesting. Is it possible that he was smothered to death with a pillow held over his face as he slept?"

"I think not. No evidence of that—no mucosal petechiae, no down bits in his mouth and nasal passages. Of course, he was a weak old man and might not have put up much of a struggle. That could minimize that kind of evidence."

Just as Shane had suspected. Fiona Hayes had not suffocated the old guy to death with a pillow, as she claimed. She might very well have killed herself for no good reason. Unless she had other reasons not revealed. That was a possibility.

Shane thanked the pathologist for his help and ended the call. He opened the small notebook where he had accumulated information about the case, found the number of the Hayes Street office of Dr. Frederic delaGuardia, and punched it into his cell. After a brief but informative conversation, Shane made an additional call to a number that the good doctor had suggested.

Hardy Seltzer's cell phone summoned him just as he wound his way around the backside of the state capitol on his way back to police headquarters. It was Marge Bland.

"Hi, Marge, what's up?" Hardy answered the call, wondering why she would call him at this time of day, just a little past noon.

"Just thought you might like to know. I'm working the early shift today, and just as I was organizing the bar for the early drinking lunch crowd, who should drop into our establishment but our friend Mace Ricci? He's here now drinking a double Dewars and appearing to settle in for a spell."

"Thanks, Marge. Listen, we need to bring him in for questioning. Keep him occupied until I can get a couple of boys in blue there to collar him. You're better than an APB any day. Should get you on the payroll."

"A paycheck would be nice," she said. "I like paychecks."

Chapter 32

SalomeMe's wardrobe contained not a single black garment. She didn't like black. She feared black. She avoided black like the plague. But she was determined to attend her old friend Fiona Hayes's funeral and thought that she had to go clothed in black, preferably a lot of it. Maybe even a veil. She mourned her friend's death. A part of her thought that by rights it was she, SalomeMe, who should have been the sacrifice, not Fiona, if there had to be a sacrifice. Of course, there had to be a sacrifice. There was a price for sins of this magnitude. They must be dealt with—exposed and dealt with.

SalomeMe was determined to attend the funeral. And she was determined to go covered head to toe in black. One of her Goth friends came to mind. She phoned the friend and requested a loan of the kind of outfit she had in mind. Her friend did not see that as a problem since every item in her friend's entire wardrobe was midnight black. Not only did she volunteer to supply SalomeMe with the outfit she was looking for, but she would deliver said outfit to her forthwith.

Thus, the gravesite of the deceased Fiona Hayes in Woodlawn Cemetery at the northeast edge of town was ringed about by a motley crew of artists, past and present lovers, some family whom no one recognized, and the spectral presence of SalomeMe draped in a shroud of intense and uncharacteristic midnight black totally obscuring the ink and piercings that usually defined her. She stood by the grave and wept. She did not often weep, although she recalled many occasions when that would have been an appropriate thing to do.

Lurking quietly at the perimeter of the gathering were both Hardy Seltzer and Shane Hadley. It was Shane who had insisted that the two of them attend the memorial. And Hardy managed to collect him from Printers Alley, maneuver him out of his wheelchair and into the aging LTD, stow the chair in the trunk and drive the two of them over to the cemetery. Exactly why Shane thought it so important for them to be there was not clear to Hardy, but OK, he would try to understand that later. Shane allowed as how he was close to solving the riddle of the death of Bechman Fitzwallington and only needed a little more time to be sure of the story. For some odd reason, Fiona Hayes's graveside service seemed important to him.

Maybe the clue was in the identity of the other attendees. Hardy looked around. Parker Palmer was there with someone Hardy didn't recognize. Of course, the Hayes woman's partner, Vernon LaVista the somethingth, Hardy couldn't remember the appropriate Roman numeral. And oddly enough, the local drug kingpin, Wilton Argent. Maybe the old guy had a soul after all. Hardy nodded recognition to Argent who responded in kind. Then there was the skinny kid with the birthmark and the lisp, Issy something. Why was he there?

Shane spent several minutes maneuvering himself around the margin of the little gathering. He appeared to be making an effort to get a face-on look at each of the attendees in turn. There was a rhythm to his movements—wheel a short distance, pause for a few moments, then move a bit further, pause—until he had completely circled the group and had apparently seen what he was looking for.

Hard to tell for sure. He arrived back beside Seltzer, where he sat for a few minutes without speaking. The service seemed to be slow getting started, as though no one was quite sure what to do or expect.

Shane touched Hardy on the arm, leaned up to him and said *sotto voce*, "We can go now."

They rode for a while back toward town without speaking, but eventually, Hardy's curiosity got the better of him.

"What were you looking for, Shane?" Hardy said.

"I think more looking *at* than looking *for*," Shane responded. "I was looking at faces, facial expressions. Faces can sometimes say things that resist translation into words."

"So, what did you learn?"

"Nothing new, my man. Nothing new. I think I have the story pretty much fleshed out. Find me some time, preferably on a sunny afternoon on the Printers Alley deck in the company of a generous glass or two of sherry, and I will be pleased to share my version of this little episode and then leave it to you to do as you see fit."

"How about tomorrow?"

"Jolly good, Hardy, my man. Jolly good indeed."

A couple of days earlier, the guys in blue had nabbed Mace Ricci at TAPS after Marge Bland's call to Hardy, brought the New York cop to the station, and installed him in an interview room to incubate alone for a couple of hours as Seltzer had instructed—stew in his own juices, so to speak. Before talking with Ricci, Seltzer had called the FBI agent in Chicago to find out anything he could about where their investigation was going. Seltzer was told that their snitch, Dudley (The Dude) Sysco, had implicated Ricci in the Hadley abduction and possibly other things, but that was all they had so far. They were also trying, unsuccessfully, to locate Bruce Therault in New York and were intensely interested in finding out what the Galleria Salinas proprietor, Blythe Fortune, knew about any of this. The FBI had a strong suspicion that this was a much bigger deal than it originally appeared.

There was nothing implicating Ricci that was solid enough to hold him. He was certainly not going to divulge anything and would be, he assured Seltzer, very shortly lawyered up. Seltzer sent him on his way with a strong urging to leave some local contact information and to stay in town until further notice. Hardy had little expectation that Ricci would do either of those. It might not matter anyway, depending on what happened in New York.

So, Seltzer's assigned case, the abduction of Shane Hadley, was sort of partially solved, but it seemed very unlikely that it would be completely solved until there was progress with the broader investigation being conducted by the FBI and probably involving organized crime types. Hardy could wait for that. Local media interest in that story had almost disappeared so that the pressure of the earlier public outcry was no longer a major factor. The interest of the department brass in the matter had also cooled.

There remained the problem of explaining Fitzwallington's death. Of course, as soon Seltzer had informed his boss of Fiona Hayes's suicide and showed him her farewell note, Goetz took that information directly to the chief who immediately declared the case closed. There was nothing left to explain. The chief arranged a press conference at which he announced the fact that the Hayes suicide note confessed to killing the old artist and described the murder in sufficient detail to be completely convincing. He did not go into the other details and did not release the actual note to the press. There was a minor clamor of demands to see the note from the more inquisitive reporters, but the chief held his ground. Hardy thought that the note should have been made public. After all, exposing Fitzwallington's sins seemed to have been a major motivating factor for Fiona. In a sense, continuing to conceal that history was perpetuating the old guy's misdeeds, protecting a false reputation, and distorting Fiona Hayes's reasons for killing herself. Someone ought to leak the note, Hardy thought, but it wouldn't be him. Subterfuge was not in his nature. Not to worry. Someone would do it.

Seltzer had deliberately avoided telling his boss anything about Shane's continued interest in this case. Too late now. It would have been extremely awkward to reveal Shane's involvement now, especially if, as Seltzer strongly suspected, Shane was going to come up with a story that was much more complicated than the department's official story that the chief had fed with some enthusiasm to the media. Hardy wasn't sure exactly what Shane's version would be, but all the signs were that it would be complicated. Was it possible that the tables were rotated a hundred eighty degrees from where this case started, the official conclusion now being murder and Shane's Hadley's conclusion being something different? That seemed like a possibility. It was at least obvious at this point that Shane didn't buy Fiona Hayes's farewell note, although Hardy didn't see what else could explain her suicide. Maybe Shane had figured that out. Hardy would find out the next afternoon.

It was the lawyer Jimmy Holden's abiding conviction that truth was an existential good in human affairs that was the proximate cause of the strategy session between Parker Palmer and J. Hayworth Combs, Esq. After what he considered a decent interval following his discovery that the DNA tests excluded his client, SalomeMe, as Fitzwallington's daughter and realizing that it would mean the big fee he had imagined was toast, Holden had phoned Jay Combs and revealed to him that particular truth. Combs thanked him politely but didn't seem all that surprised. Combs wasn't surprised, of course, but did realize that as this became more common knowledge, and that was inevitable, there might well be a need for some lawyerly maneuvering in order to protect his friend and client. Thus, a strategy session seemed in order.

Parker Palmer certainly agreed with that. He was anxious to get Jay Combs seriously involved. Although he desperately hoped that Fiona Hayes's suicide and confession would put the Billy Wayne Farmer matter to rest once and for all, Palmer still feared that Shane Hadley might not give up so easily. If that was true, there was a better than even chance, Palmer feared, that he could wind up being accused of murdering his uncle. Although he never intended to do that, he was not completely sure of his innocence in the matter. Maybe their argument was too much for the frail old guy. But, if so, then why did Fiona make up a different story and do herself in. Palmer certainly would never have considered Fiona capable of killing anybody, including herself. That is the dilemma that Palmer posed to his lawyer friend, hoping there was a lawyerly solution.

"Oh," Combs said, "I thought we were developing a strategy to assure that you got possession of the paintings."

"Sure, we need to do that," Palmer replied. "But if I'm doing life without parole for murder in the state pen, I doubt that I would be particularly interested in who gets the paintings. I suspect I would have other more pressing concerns."

"I suppose that is true," Combs replied, deliberately ignoring the sarcasm. "So, we need a strategy to free you of a criminal charge, and then we can work on the original strategy. Is that how you see it?"

"Yes."

"Ok. So why do you think Hadley will keep at it? From the police chief's press conference, it sounded like the Hayes woman's confession was conclusive. Her solution to her dilemma certainly was. The chief sounded like he was closing the books on this one and that there was every reason to do that. Even if Hadley didn't buy it, who was going to listen to any alternative scenarios now?"

"People will listen to Shane Hadley, Jay," Palmer said. "His voice still rings with moral authority in this city. Maybe it should. And when we talked, he seemed to put a lot of stock in this mysterious witness to my late-night visit to uncle Billy."

"Any idea who the witness was?"

"I don't know," Parker replied. "But I suspect it might be Billy Wayne's next-door neighbor. He was always hanging around. The two of them may have been lovers. I suspect that's the case."

"Name?"

"Issy Esser. Skinny kid with a birthmark on his face. I think he lives next door to uncle Billy but not sure of the address. Shouldn't be hard to find him, though."

Combs opened up a fresh legal pad and wrote the name on the front sheet along with some notes summarizing what Parker had told him.

"Look, Parker, my friend," Combs said. "I don't want to get into the business of doing a field investigation of this thing. That's not what I know best how to do. But I would like to talk to this Issy guy. Maybe I can at least learn something that will help to delineate the problem. Maybe you're over-reacting. Maybe the only real problem you have is figuring out how to capture those paintings."

Palmer sighed deeply and looked out the window.

"I hope to God you are right about that," Palmer said.

"Maybe I should talk with our local hero, Sherlock Shane, as well. What do you think?"

"Probably a good idea. But if you do, be damned careful. He's one clever guy."

"Cleverness is often a fatal character flaw, Parker. We lawyers love burying our talons deep into the soft parts of the clever ones. Fresh meat!"

Neither man smiled.

"We may need some help from our friends in the press," Combs mumbled to himself and wrote something more on the legal pad.

Faces, Shane thought.

He was waiting for Hardy to arrive. He had set the small table on the Printers Alley deck with a fresh bottle of his favorite wine, two of his treasured Oxford crystal sherry glasses, and a small array of cheeses and biscuits that he discovered by rummaging about the fridge and the pantry. He was thinking about faces.

A fact about the human race that had intrigued Shane from his youth was the uniqueness of faces. Every one of the billions of the species inhabiting the planet had a unique face. Granted, some were close to duplicates, like in 'identical' twins. But they were never identical. Each person's face was their sole possession. Shane thought that faces must say something about the nature of individuals, who they were, what drove their behavior. And, perhaps, a specific expression of emotions—love, hate, innocence, guilt. Especially guilt. He also thought that if he studied a person's face intensely enough, he might sense some of that.

Parker Palmer had a rather long, sharp nose, thin lips, close-set eyes, and a small mouth that seemed to expand unrealistically when he smiled. His chin was deeply cleft and his forehead remarkably wrinkle-free without any obvious evidence of chemical injections. At the Hayes woman's funeral, there was nothing detectably different about his face. It was just the face of Parker Palmer. An ordinary kind of face that didn't seem to say anything other than *I am Parker Palmer. Deal with it.*

Vernon LaVista, III, had a meaty face that fit with his overall meaty persona. Broad forehead, heavy, wrinkled simian-like brow, large mouth, thick lips. He had the look of one who enjoyed pounding on large rocks with sharp objects. At the funeral, the emotion Shane sensed was more boredom than anything else. He was going through the motions as best he could, but his heart, if he had one, was not in it.

Then, there were the two masked funeral attendees.

The woman who called herself SalomeMe had covered her face entirely with an impenetrable black veil. Why had she hidden her face? Was it only an expression of mourning for her dead friend? Or did she fear that exposing her face would expose a great deal more, personal things that she did not wish to share?

And Issy Esser was born masked. The large port-wine birthmark that meandered amoeba-like about his face seemed to conceal other facial characteristics that might be revealing. At the funeral, the nevus appeared to have taken on a much darker hue as though reacting to physiologic events beyond the young man's control. Maybe Issy Esser was born a pretender, masked from the reality of his behavior by the big red shroud draped across his face by the gods of biology.

Faces, Shane thought. They each had a story to tell. They did it with widely varying styles and results. But faces were a surface phenomenon. Potentially important, but only one small piece of the puzzle.

Shane had assembled enough of the pieces of the puzzle to see the picture. The fact that he had done that was satisfying. But the picture was not.

Chapter 33

"So," Hardy Seltzer said, unable to contain his curiosity any longer, "was the old guy murdered or not?"

"If you will be so kind as to grant me a liberal definition of the term, I am quite certain Bechman Warren Fitzwallington nee Billy Wayne Farmer was indeed murdered," Shane replied with his characteristic wordy excess, reminiscent of Soleri's *too many notes* criticism of Mozart.

Seltzer sat in a heavy cast iron chair, facing Shane, across a wrought iron table. The two pieces of furniture sat on the Printers Alley deck, carefully positioned at the geographic center of the space, poised and ready at any moment to accommodate the whims of their owner. On a sunny afternoon, those whims predictably included a bottle of sherry, sometimes accompanied by a small snack, and in recent months almost always included his detective friend. This afternoon fit the expectations of anyone paying attention to such things.

"So, like the chief, you buy the Hayes woman's note."

"I buy most of it as technically true, but not like the chief's far too simplistic interpretation."

"Most of it?"

"I believe, Hardy, that the note is entirely accurate except for the first sentence."

"How can that be? The first sentence is the confession, and the only imaginable justification for her suicide. The rest of the note is providing the facts that make the confession credible."

"Need I lecture you yet again on the difference between perception and reality, my man? They are quite different phenomena, you know."

There was silence for a while as the men sipped their wine, and Hardy tried to understand what his friend was telling him. Sometimes Hardy felt frustrated by Shane's deliberately obscure approach to revealing information. Of course, it was deliberate, calculated. Hardy realized that it was probably his friend's way of stimulating him to think things through for himself. And it worked sometimes. Hardy had a good brain, but he had not been taught to use it to capacity. Mostly he had been expected to believe what he was told and to behave accordingly. He had made his way through life by usually doing that. His rekindled friendship with Shane was starting to reveal to Hardy some depths in himself that life so far had not stimulated him to explore.

Why would Fiona Hayes make up such a story if the whole reason for it wasn't true? Hardy thought long and hard about that—and about perceptions and realities.

"She thought she killed him, but she didn't," Hardy said. "That's what you're telling me, isn't it? But he's dead. How do you explain that?"

Shane didn't respond immediately. He fondled his glass of wine and looked out over The Alley, splashed liberally with shards of afternoon sun. He was giving his friend space to consider the question he had asked. Hardy, anxious to hear the whole story, waited for Shane to respond.

At last, Shane turned back to face Hardy, leaned toward him, and set his glass down. He placed both hands flat on the tabletop, spreading his thin fingers, and said, "I fear there are several questions the answers to which we may never know—not only how, but when and perhaps even why the old artist died. However, the available information suggests that Ms. Hayes did indeed steal in the middle of the night to the Fitzwallington house, creep into his dark bedroom and, finding him resting quietly, seized a pillow from his bed and held it forcibly over his face for several minutes. She then created the scene that she wished to be symbolic by exposing the old man's body in all its glory and carefully folding and arranging the removed bed linens in order to make it clear to a careful observer that this was not the appearance of a setting in which an old man died of 'natural causes.'"

Hardy listened intently while rummaging about in his brain, hunting for an explanation. After a long pause, he said, "The old guy was already dead, right? Dead when Fiona Hayes arrived. He appeared to be sleeping, and in the dark night and her hurry to do the deed and get out, she didn't realize that she was trying to kill a dead man."

"Very good, my man," Shane said. "Very good. And I'm sure we would agree that attempting to kill a dead man is a truly futile act. Since futility is a poor motive for suicide, we assume that Ms. Hayes believed she had actually done the deed. Well, that and the autopsy findings or lack thereof."

"What about the autopsy findings?" Hardy asked.

Shane didn't answer but just sat there looking directly as his friend. Hardy contemplated Shane's statement implying that the lack of findings at autopsy was important and searched his memory for what that might mean. After a few moments, he vaguely recalled that death by suffocation resulted in small areas of hemorrhage in the mucous membranes of the lips and mouth. He didn't remember any description of such lesions in Fitzwallington's autopsy report. But he had something less than unlimited confidence in the medical examiner's appreciation of such details. Maybe he overlooked them. What else was missing? He wasn't sure.

"The medical examiner didn't describe the mucosal petechiae usually present in a victim of strangling. Is that what you mean? If so, you may have greater confidence in Doc Jensen than I do. Maybe he overlooked such tiny details."

"I doubt that," Shane responded. "I talked with him, and he convinced me that he had looked and that they were not present. There may be something else missing that belies Ms. Hayes's description of events. Did your people examine the pillows on the artist's bed? One of them lay on the floor in the pictures you took of the scene. Likely that was the non-murder weapon. Did someone examine it carefully?"

"I am told they did and didn't find anything of note. A down pillow with no stains or residual deposits of anything."

"A down pillow," Shane repeated. "When one is suffocated with a down pillow, it is not rare that in the struggle bits of down are dislodged and deposited in the victim's mouth and oral pharynx. The good doctor Jensen informs me that the artist's oral cavities were completely devoid of down."

"Ok, I see how you conclude that Fiona Hayes didn't kill Fitzwallington," Seltzer said, nursing his wine, trying to make it as obvious as was proper that his glass was nearly empty. "But, come now, Shane. Do you really think that your story would fly in court? I mean, you have a confession by a person with a motive, even her own description of how she did it, who killed herself because of what she had done. Do you really believe that some non-findings at autopsy would carry the day instead of the hard evidence? I doubt that. I really do."

"Unless, of course, we identified the real killer," Shane replied.

"Humor me for a bit, my friend. Assume that the Hayes woman didn't do it. Whom would you have next in line?"

Hardy answered immediately, "Have to be Parker Palmer."

"And why are you so certain of that?"

"He was obviously angling for possession of the Fitzwallington paintings with that lawsuit he filed challenging the legitimacy of the old man's alleged daughter. From the story in the paper the other day, it looks like the artist may win, too. Apparently DNA paternity tests establish that the woman calling herself SalomeMe is not the old guy's child. And then there's Issy Esser's sudden recollection of Palmer's late-night visit to Fitzwallington the evening before he was discovered dead. Did you follow up with Esser?"

"Yes, there is a story there. But first, a small revelation about Mr. Palmer. Although of possibly questionable ethical purity, I have it on good authority that the younger artist is in fact—by fact I mean, analysis of the relevant DNAs; such information is, I am told, as close to absolute truth as it is possible for information to be—a blood relative of Fitzwallington, possibly a nephew."

Seltzer stared at the face of his friend, trying to read his thoughts about this factual bombshell. Neither man spoke for a bit. These frequent lulls in the conversation seemed important as the story began to coalesce.

"So," Hardy said, continuing to stare at Shane's face, "Parker Palmer may well be the sole living heir to whatever fortune his uncle left behind. Is that what you think? That could be a pretty convincing motive, it seems to me. Palmer is looking more and more like the killer."

"That does seem to be where the facts we have so far point, doesn't it?"

Shane picked up his glass from the table and wheeled over to the railing. There was some gathering foot traffic in The Alley, the usual early arrivers looking like the lost sheep they might well be, ambling about with no sense of purpose. The Alley was a good spot for lost sheep, going nowhere in particular, to wander. Much too early for the hard partiers.

"But there is the rather sordid saga of the birthmarked one to deal with," Shane said as he rolled back over to face Hardy across the table.

Shane picked up the wine bottle and examined it, noting that they were close to exhausting their supply of his favorite beverage. This was his last bottle. KiKi should be bringing a new shipment of the wine from Oxford, thinly disguised as medical supplies, soon. Her desire to bring Shane pleasure sometimes overcame her characteristic scrupulous honesty; the ruse needed to get the wine was one example. Shane emptied the bottle into the two glasses.

"According to Mr. Esser," Shane began, "he was Fitzwallington's lover. He was at the old artist's house late on the evening in question. When Palmer showed up unexpectedly, Esser hid at some spot in the house where he could eavesdrop on Fitzwallington's conversation with Palmer without being seen. The two men argued volubly for a bit. The topic under discussion was the old artist's claim that he had filed the papers necessary to adopt his alleged daughter, which would restore her as his rightful heir, excluding Palmer. Palmer was very angry, apparently. They yelled at each other for a while and finally, according to Esser, Palmer left with Fitzwallington yelling after him."

"What did Esser do then?"

"He says that he went home and did not return until the next morning when he discovered the lifeless remains of his neighbor and called in your people."

"Do you believe that?"

"Actually, I do, although subsequent information may lead you to conclude that I am more gullible that is optimal for a careful investigator."

"Ok," Hardy said. "Give me the additional information before my simple mind fixates on the obvious conclusion."

"A wise man," Shane said. "Occam's razor, employed prematurely, may not cut so cleanly."

Hardy took his small notebook from his shirt pocket, opened it, and wrote *Occam's razor* at the end of a growing list of Shane's words that he needed to look up.

"It seems," Shane continued, "that Mr. Esser is a pharmacist who until recently was employed in the research pharmacy at the university medical center."

"What's a research pharmacy?"

"I'm told that it is a special dispensary that manages drugs that are being used in human experiments. Those experiments require use of both active drug and placebo, inert sugar pills, which are formulated to look identical so that neither the people administering them nor the subjects receiving them know who is getting what. These are called double-blind, placebo-controlled trials. And I discovered by some judicious prying, that our Mr. Esser was recently discharged from his position at the university, *for cause*, in HR jargon. He did not tell me this when I talked with him. I could not find out what the cause was, and even with additional information, have no direct knowledge of it. However, I have what I believe to be a rather solid inference of some potential importance."

"Would you care to share that with me?"

Hardy was losing patience with Shane's predictably dilatory approach to storytelling. When Hardy had tried earlier to encourage Shane to more briefly condense his presentations of information, Shane had informed him that the solutions to many problems hid themselves in the minutiae (the word was on Hardy's list). And the wine was running out.

"I sense that you are hurrying me along," Shane said. "Very well.

I placed a call to a Dr. Frederic delaGuardia. You may recall that he was the physician whom Fitzwallington had seen some time ago. I discovered that the doctor had last seen the artist about a year ago. At that time, the patient had significantly elevated blood pressure and was prescribed a medication. Since the doctor knew the patient to be careless about following up with him, the doctor prescribed a three months' supply of the medicine and specified three renewals, enough to last for a year at the prescribed dose."

"Are you going somewhere interesting with this?" asked Seltzer, less than intrigued by the mundane history of an old man with high blood pressure. And the wine was nearly gone.

"Indeed," Shane responded. "You see, the doctor gave me the name and number of the pharmacy where he had sent the prescription. A short phone call to the pharmacist there revealed from their meticulous records that the initial prescription was filled, but not the remaining three. What do you make of that?"

"The old guy quit his meds. *Noncompliant*, I think the doctors call that, and from what I read, it is not too rare."

Hardy had struck *noncompliant* from his *Shane's words to look up* list a while back and was pleased with himself to find an occasion to use it properly.

"That is quite true, my friend, quite true. However, in this case, it may well be that the patient did not neglect to take the prescribed treatment. You see, Issy Essert, being a pharmacist and thus conversant with drugs, volunteered to pick up his lover's medicines for him and maintain the supply of pills for the once a day regimen."

"Placebo!" Hardy exclaimed. "The little rat substituted sugar pills for the prescribed drug. Right? But why did he fill the first script with the real thing? And why did he do it?"

"Well," Shane responded, "according to what the 'little rat' told me, he was expecting that his lover would leave him something of value when he died. And, like apparently everyone else, Esser didn't like the old man. Since he worked in the research pharmacy, Esser would have had access to placebo pills. I learned from my lovely wife that an unnamed person had been recently fired from his job in that pharmacy for stealing placebo pills, a truly baffling offense to the powers that be. I infer that Issy Esser was that person, an inference that could be easily confirmed."

"Still," Hardy responded, "why fill the first prescription and not the others?"

"I am surmising now, my friend," Shane said, draining his glass of sherry and casting a longing glance at the empty bottle resting comfortably on the iron table, "but I am confident of the basic accuracy of my surmise. Esser's scheme ran a risk that the old guy would recognize that something was amiss with the medicine—an unconvincing container, a suspicious appearance of the pills themselves. So, Mr. Esser filled the first script, emptied the entirely authentic bottle of the active drug, and substituted the placebo pills. Since this was the first time that Fitzwallington had seen the pills, he had no idea what they were supposed to look like. The renewals of the medication did not need to be filled since Esser could just refill the authentic bottle with placebo each three months and those were the only pills the old artist knew. Were any medications recovered by your people from Fitzwallington's home?"

"Not sure, Shane," Hardy answered, looking off into somewhere unspecified and contemplating Shane's tale.

"If so, you could have the medication analyzed. That would establish whether it was drug or placebo."

"I can see that," Hardy said. "But would switching the meds be enough to kill the old guy? I mean, it's not clear to me that we've identified a murderer even if this story is entirely true."

"That," Shane reacted, "is exactly the problem. Why did the old man die, and who was responsible for his death? It would be difficult to prove that he died of untreated hypertension unless something about the autopsy confirmed that. There was a small brain infarct but not enough for Jensen to attribute his death to a stroke. Possible but not conclusive given the general condition of the old man's body. Jensen is sticking with his 'natural causes' conclusion."

"Dying of natural causes is not a crime," Seltzer mused, relishing the last drops of his wine. "Apparently we have two people who aimed to finish the old guy off, and we may not be able to prove whether either of them succeeded."

"Maybe three," Shane said.

"You mean Parker Palmer."

"Right. If Mr. Esser's story is correct, Parker Palmer may have been the last person to see Fitzwallington alive. But the old guy was yelling at Palmer as he left, so was presumably alive at the time."

Hardy sat thinking for a while and then said, "Is it possible that the old guy's blood pressure was so high that the excitement of the argument with Palmer was too much for him?"

"A definite possibility, my man, but how to prove it? He might have had such a surge of adrenalin in the heat of the argument that he died suddenly from a disturbed heart rhythm. The bad news is that such a mode of death leaves nothing specific to be detected at postmortem. So we are still left with no proof."

"And who was the murderer?" Hardy asked? "Esser, who schemed to prevent treatment of the artist's hypertension, or Palmer who caused the argument that may have killed him? Neither alone may have done the trick. Were Esser and Palmer unwitting collaborators? Is such a thing even possible?"

"I fear, my friend," Shane said, "that we may be forced to find satisfaction in the solution of a murder that our system of justice will be unable or unwilling to punish."

Hardy replied, "I would bet you the price of a fresh case of your Oxford sherry that the chief and his chieflets won't buy this story. They've got themselves a killer and don't need another one."

Shane did not respond aloud but thought, the people in charge of the Nashville Metropolitan Police Department seemed to believe in justice when it was convenient while Shane believed in justice as a matter of principle. Perhaps irreconcilable differences.

For the first time that he could remember, Shane thought that his disability may well have spared him some uncomfortable confrontations. But, then, what's so bad about uncomfortable confrontations for a good cause, dammit!

Shane leaned across the table, put a heavy hand on his friend's shoulder, looked directly into his eyes, and said like he meant it, "Take them on, Hardy, my man. Take. Them. On!"

ABOUT THE AUTHOR

Ken Brigham is emeritus professor of medicine at Emory University. He is widely published in the scientific literature and has authored or coauthored two previous novels and two nonfiction books. He lives with his wife, Arlene Stecenko, in midtown Atlanta. For more information see www.kenbrigham.com.

CPSIA information can be obtained
at www.ICGtesting.com
Printed in the USA
FSHW010018260320
68483FS

9 781944 962678